D0204497

About the Author

JOANNA FITZPATRICK was raised in Hollywood and when not living in a 16th Century hameau in southern France, she and her husband, musician Jim Payne, and their son perch in the St. Lucia mountains above Carmel Valley, California. She has been a screenwriter, artist manager, record company executive, and proofreader; an MFA graduate from Sarah Lawrence College; and, most recently, author of *The Drummer's Widow*. She is currently at work on her next historical fiction novel, *The Sketch Box* (She Writes Press).

KATHERINE MANSFIELD

JOANNA FITZPATRICK

LD

PUBLISHED BY LA DRÔME PRESS

Grateful acknowledgment is made to The Society of Authors as the Literary Representative of the Estate of Katherine Mansfield and to The Society of Authors as the Literary Representative of the Estate of John Middleton Murry for giving permission to reprint previously published materials.

FitzPatrick, Joanna
Katherine Mansfield / Joanna FitzPatrick
1. Mansfield, Katherine, 1888–1923--Fiction. 2. Biographical Historic Fiction. 3. Women writers--Fiction. 4. New Zealand / British writers-- Fiction. I. Title

ISBN: 978-0-9916549-9-4
ISBN: 978-0-9916549-8-7 (eBook)

PRINTED IN THE UNITED STATES OF AMERICA
10 9 8 7 6 5 4 3 2 1
Tenth Anniversary Edition

Cover painting:
northampton clamp scape
Samuel Payne © 2008
acrylic on paper

Cover design by MaxmediaStudios.com and J.F.

ladrômepress.com

à mon chéri

James

I live to write.

—KASS BEAUCHAMP, AGE 9, 1897

'...as you ought not to attempt to cure the eyes without the head, or the head without the body, so neither ought you to attempt to cure the body without the soul'; and this said Zalmoxis is the reason why the cure of many diseases is unknown to the physicians of Hellas, because they are ignorant of the whole, which ought to be studied also; for the part can never be well unless the whole is well.

And Zalmoxis added with emphasis, 'Let no one, however rich, or noble, or fair, persuade you to give him the cure, without the charm.' And therefore if you will allow me to apply the Thracian charm first to your soul, I will afterwards proceed to apply the cure to your head.

—FROM THE DIALOGUES OF SOCRATES, 469–399 BC

I know not how it falls on me,
This summer evening, hushed and lone;
Yet the faint wind comes soothingly
With something of an olden tone.
Forgive me if I've shunned so long
Your gentle greeting, earth and air!
But sorrow withers e'en the strong,
And who can fight against despair.

—EMILY BRONTË, 1818–1848

Introduction

I discovered Katherine Mansfield at les fleurs bleues, a used bookstore in a village in southern France. I was flying home to the States and looking for a book to read on the plane. You know the one. Not too large or bulky but entertaining enough to get you through a dull flight.

On a high, dusty bookshelf stacked with English titles, I pulled out a slim, frayed book entitled *The Garden Party and Other Stories* by Katherine Mansfield.

Katherine Mansfield? Why did I know that name? Then I remembered a mysterious quote in Virginia Woolf's journal: "Katherine Mansfield created the only writing I was ever jealous about."

Perfect timing, I thought, I had a six-hour flight to find out why.

And I did. Ms. Woolf's jealousy was understandable. Every time I stopped to take a breath between stories, I thought, who is this extraordinary writer? Upon my return to New York, I read several Mansfield biographies and her voluminous diaries and letters. The more I learned about her, the more determined I became to bring Katherine Mansfield back to life so that others might find inspiration in her remarkable story.

Katherine Mansfield Beauchamp was born in Wellington, New Zealand on October 14, 1888. Her father, Harold Beauchamp, was the Chairman of the Bank of New Zealand and believed like all upstanding British "colonials," that his children should be educated in England. At age fourteen, Katherine and her two older sisters were sent to Queens College, in London, a renowned progressive school for young women, where they spent three years acquiring a liberal arts education. Katherine thrived on language, philosophy, literature, and music. She studied the cello, attended concerts, and frequented museums and galleries.

When her parents came to fetch her, she had no desire to return to provincial New Zealand, but they wouldn't allow her to stay in London without a chaperone.

On the voyage back to Wellington, she had a shipboard romance with a cricket player and back in New Zealand she gained a reputation as the wild bohemian. She had brief affairs with both men and women, camped out with the Maoris in the jungle, and published scandalous stories under various noms de plume. Her explanation for her transgressions: *Why be given a body if you have to keep it shut up in a case like a rare fiddle?*

Finally she persuaded her father to pay for her passage back to London. He gave her a very small allowance, just enough to cover her room and board. A bastion of upper class conservatism, her father believed poverty would drive Katherine back home. He miscalculated. She was more than willing to live in poverty, if she could fulfilll her dream and become a famous author from the Colonies.

On July 6, 1908, at nineteen, Katherine, without a chaperone, which was unheard of at the time, embarked from Wellington on a ship to England. She never returned to her homeland.

—*Joanna FitzPatrick*

KATHERINE MANSFIELD

Wellington, New Zealand

*Here then is a little summary of what I need—power,
wealth and freedom.*

KATHERINE MANSFIELD BEAUCHAMP,
AGE 19—MAY, 1908

I SHALL KILL MYSELF, Katherine proclaimed, as she stared out her
third-floor bedroom window onto the Wellington harbor. *I've
been back home for eighteen months, fifteen days, and six hours and it's
intolerable. Pa keeps promising to talk about it but he never does. Mother
says, 'talk to your father.' Jeanne, Chaddie, and Vera turn away saying,
'Give it up. Pa will never let you return to London. He's too afraid of the
trouble you'll get in.' And my dear sweet little brother Leslie just smiles
and says, 'Pa will let you go. Be patient.'*

*Why did Grandmother Dyer have to die just when I needed her most?
She's the only one who could convince Pa that I have to live in London or
die. And she'd be the only one who'd miss me. That is except Leslie. He'd
miss our walks in the woods and my bedtime stories.*

*No one understands how much I want to be a famous author like my
cousin, Elizabeth. How can I do that if I stay here? You would think after
all the trouble I've caused Pa, he'd be delighted to get rid of me.*

I've certainly convinced Mother. She giggled. *Especially after I published
that story about my childish romance with Edith. How I adored her. Who
wouldn't? She's beautiful. Talented. And she adored me. But that week we
spent at her cottage was so boring. And then I met Maata! Exotic Maata.
A real Maori princess. I never should have asked Pa's secretary to type
that story for me, but I did warn her that she might find it shocking.* She
giggled again. *So did Pa.*

She posed in the mirror. *And you call yourself an independent woman.
You'll never survive in London if you don't stand up for yourself now, here
in this house.*

She turned to face her posh bedroom. The lace curtains. Doilies on the tables. Pink bedspread. *I'm so sick of this child's room. I'm so sick of this life,* she moaned.

A horn blasted from the harbor and she hurried to the window to watch the travelers wave good-bye to their families on the dock. *Oh why aren't I on that ship? Why did Pa promise me I could go and then say no?*

She turned the knob to go downstairs to confront her father. Abruptly, she returned to the window and glared at the ship slipping away.

Coward. You pretend otherwise but you're really a coward.

Katherine picked up the framed family photo taken five years ago aboard the cargo ship *Niwaru*. It had brought her and her sisters to Queens College in London, where their parents dropped them off.

It's their fault. They're the ones who sent me to England for a proper education. Didn't they realize that after I spent three years in London studying and feeling the rhythm of that exciting city that I could never live in this boring town again?

And what's wrong with Vera and Chaddie? Why don't they want to go back to London with me? Pa would never say "no" to the three of us. I tried to convince him that Leslie should go to school in London and I'd be his chaperone. No, said Mother, he's too young. Has she forgotten that I was only fourteen when she sent me there?

On that voyage to London, Katherine had been daddy's girl, sitting with him on the deck in longue-chaises gazing at the stars. Then, three years later on the return voyage, after her "scandalous behavior" with the charming cricket player, her father told her to stay in her cabin.

I should write to Elizabeth and ask her to convince Pa. She shook her head. *No, I wrote her before and she never answered. She has no time for her peculiar cousin.*

I even suffered through those classes in typing and bookkeeping at that dreary technical school thinking he'd let me return to London if I could make a living on my own. But he said I was too spoiled and could never afford to live on a minimum wage.

He just doesn't understand me. I don't care about all this frill. I'll go through my wardrobe right now and throw out all those silly evening gowns. It's Mother who insists that I never wear the same gown twice.

She swung open her wardrobe closet. But one glance at the silver chiffon she wore recently at the ball given in honor of her nineteenth birthday changed her mind. She returned to pacing her room and complaining to herself.

I have to get out of this house before I suffocate. I'll go visit Julia. No I can't do that. After she heard what people were saying about me being a "wild girl" and my "sinful behavior," she walks on the other side of the street when she sees me.

I could visit the Trowells, if their entire family hadn't moved to London. I so much miss my cello lessons with Mr. Trowell. And his son Arnold, my dearest Caesar. He never answered my last letter telling him that I dreamed of his embraces and yet before he left for London he told me I was irresistible.

She picked up the cello propped in a corner and then put it back down again. She sighed and declared to herself, *From now on I will love only myself.*

In the full-length mirror, she studied her profile. *I'm eating too many desserts. And look how pale I am. Oh, I really will end up killing myself.* She returned to watching the harbor from the large bay window. *Yes, that's it. Jump. Wave to Pa before I hit the ground beneath his window.*

Stop it! she raged. *Stop this moaning and complaining. Go downstairs and talk to him. Now!*

She stomped down the staircase and burst into the library. "Pa!" She stood over him at his desk. "Pa, have you been thinking about what I said last night?"

"You mean about your passage to London?" he mumbled, without looking up from his papers.

"Yes."

"I haven't given it a thought."

She plopped down in a chair and stared at him. *Patience. Patience. Everyone tells me to be patient. All right here I am being patient. I'll just keep drumming my fingers on the desktop until he pays attention.*

At last, he looked up.

"I know I've caused you and Mother a lot of trouble since I returned from London. But don't you see how miserable I am? My life is passing by and, besides the few stories I've published, I'm completely unknown and will remain so unless I publish in London. Why did you say yes, and then change your mind? Why?"

"Your recent behavior has shown your mother and me that you are not responsible enough to be on your own. I have some control over your behavior here, but in London, who knows what trouble you will get yourself into?"

"I only get into trouble here because I'm so completely bored!"

"How can you be bored with all the parties you attend? I just saw the accounts of your dress shop expenses. Those hats you had made to your design? They were very expensive."

"Those bills aren't mine alone. It's true I get many invitations, but so do Vera and Chaddie. They are far more extravagant than I am and spend much more on clothes than me. Let me go to London, Pa, and as soon as I'm a published writer I won't need your help. I'll even pay you back when I am famous."

"Kass, I have no problem giving you money. Have I ever been anything but generous to you?"

She thought it better not to answer that question and turned her gaze upon another ship slipping out of view. *How many more ships must I watch disappear from the harbor before I am a passenger?*

She turned back to him, her eyes teary. "Please let me go."

"Do you think you can manage to keep yourself off the scandal page?"

"Of course, Pa. The only talk of me in the papers will be when my novels are reviewed." The ship slipped out of view. Desperate, she leapt up from the chair and climbed onto his lap.

"Pa. Please let me go. I promise to be good. I'll even report weekly to Mr. Kay at your London bank so you can keep a watch on me."

"Stand up, Kass. You're behaving like a child." She slumped back into her seat. He shuffled his papers until he found what he was looking for and said, "Here it is. A letter from your uncle Henry." He handed it to Katherine. "He has recommended a boarding house in London that lets rooms to young, unmarried women pursuing their artistic endeavors. It appears there is a room available for a well-behaved, serious young lady."

She jumped in his lap again and wrapped her arms around his neck and kissed him. "Thank you, Pa."

Embarrassed by her show of affection, he said, "Now off with you. I have work to do."

She hesitated at the door. "Pa, when will I leave for London?"

He'd returned to his paperwork and didn't answer.

KATHERINE WANTED TO LEAVE immediately but Mrs. Beauchamp didn't want anyone to think they were sending their daughter off because she had gotten into trouble. There were tea parties and a formal dance given by the Prime Minister's daughter, where Katherine performed a few mimes and sang. The *Wellington Courier*'s social column described what the young guests, including Miss Beauchamp, wore and ate.

When her father finally handed her a passenger ticket for departure on July 6, 1908, he said, "I've spoken to the ship's captain and asked him to keep an eye on you as you are traveling without a chaperone."

What could be better than being alone on a ship without a chaperone? thought Katherine, but she said, "Thank you, Pa. I do so dread taking this voyage on my own. Do you think Mother could accompany me?"

Katherine knew her mother would say no. Anything to do with her impetuous daughter was an irritation and an interruption from her busy social calendar.

At the embarkation dock, Mrs. Beauchamp embraced her daughter stiffly. "Please behave, Kass. I don't want to read any reports in the London papers that will embarrass our family and make me come and fetch you home."

Katherine waved to her parents until they disappeared from her view. The sudden shift in the ocean current forced her to grip the railing and brace herself against the gale winds. As she plunged toward the open sea, she tossed back her head and shouted, "I'm free!"

DECEMBER, 1918

The Elephant House—London

Grant me the moment, the lovely moment
That I may lean forth to see
The other buds, the other blooms,
The other leaves on the tree…

A LITTLE GIRL'S PRAYER—KM

KATHERINE SHIVERED and put on her canary yellow bed jacket, tying its white silk ribbons to keep out the winter chill. She pulled the eiderdown up around her parched throat and waited for the sun to follow the early dawn and wake the household.

Across the room, LM breathed steadily, her oversized body, too large for the loveseat, squeezed into a child's pose.

When they first met in school fifteen years ago, LM's real name was Ida Baker, but she had adopted her mother's maiden name, Katherine Moore, when she was studying to be a cellist.

The fourteen-year-old Kathleen Beauchamp had also taken the name Katherine as her *nom de plume* and thought if they were to be good friends it was too confusing for them both to be *Katherines*. Instead, she called her Leslie because of her fondness for her brother Leslie. In time she shortened it to LM. Only in anger or in public did she call her devoted companion, Ida.

Katherine listened to Jack snoring on the other side of the wall. He had recently moved into the spare bedroom. His work was very demanding and he couldn't have his essential sleep interrupted by her hacking cough.

To muffle the mantelpiece clock's dreary ticking, she reached for Shakespeare's *The Winter's Tale* on her bedside table, but a stabbing spasm in her spine jerked her hand and *Tale* and several other books fell onto the floor. She smothered her cry into her pillow and with nothing else to do until the sun rose, she counted sheep until she finally fell asleep.

KATHERINE AWOKE to LM's irritating, chirpy voice. "Good morning, dearie, did you sleep well?" Her round face was hidden behind a breakfast tray weighted down with a full tea set, a stack of buttered toast and marmalade. LM set it down on the bed and Katherine's cat Charlie (named after Charlie Chaplin) stretched out her thick, black and white, furry body and sat up.

"Off!" shouted LM, shooing her off the bed, just before her pink tongue lopped off the cream.

"Don't shout at her. What do you expect a cat to do when you put a pitcher of cream in front of its nose. I don't mind if she has a taste."

"She's fat enough already."

"Come here, Charlie. Don't let LM scare you away." The cat leapt back on the bed and took a lick from the pitcher before settling back down at Katherine's feet. "She might be pregnant, you know. Haven't you noticed her swelling teats?"

LM turned away without answering. An irritating habit among a list of others, thought Katherine, glaring at her caregiver's back.

"What a lovely autumn day," said LM, looking out the window over London's rooftops, not considering that Katherine couldn't see the day from her bed. "What a shame you can't take a walk on the Heath. It would do you good but it's too cold, isn't it, my dear Katie?"

Katherine closed her eyes and argued with herself: You're the one who thought the three of you could live in harmony. You're the one who convinced Jack that no one but LM knew better what you needed, that there was no one more loyal and dedicated.

"Careful, dearie, you almost knocked over the tray," said LM, towering over her, blocking the sun's warmth. "You know you mustn't dally today. Did you forget you have an appointment with Dr. Sorapure this morning?"

"No, I haven't forgotten," she answered, miming LM's birdlike voice, quickly forgetting to be nice.

"Here, dearie, drink your tea while it's still hot."

"Is Jack awake?"

"Awake? It's ten o'clock, Katie. You're the only one who sleeps late in this house. He's down in the basement setting the type to print your short story."

"How do you know he's not printing his book of poetry?"

"No, no. He said it was your story."

"Which story?"

"I think it's the one you wrote in Bandol. The one with the French title I can never pronounce correctly."

"*Je ne parle pas français?*"

"Ah, oui," she chuckled. "That's it, though I could never say it like you. Heavens no, not like you. Now what was I just saying... oh yes, his brother Richard has designed a wonderful cover for Je-nee—"

"What?" She coughed into her hankie before adding, "but I must approve the cover before it goes to print!"

"Please Katie, calm down. You don't want to bring on a fever. We all remember very well how furious you were when the Woolfs published your other story without discussing the cover with you. What was it called? ... you know the one I mean."

"*Prelude,* Ida! *Prelude,*" rasped Katherine. "For someone who constantly tells me how wonderful my stories are you might think you'd remember their titles."

"You're so right, Katherine, I wish I had your brains. I just can't remember anything. But how could you understand? You're made so differently. In fact, I almost forgot to tell you that Jack won't be up to see you before dinner."

"Why? He's too busy to visit his invalid wife?"

"Oh my, aren't we grumpy today? Drink your tea, dearie. And after, shall I brush your hair? That always calms your nerves. And certainly you want to look presentable for that nice Dr. Sorapure. Which dress shall I put out for you to wear today?"

Katherine pushed the tray away and Charlie jumped off the bed and ran out the door. How she wished to escape with her.

LM brought the shawl hanging on the chair in front of Katherine's writing table and wrapped it over her patient's shoulders. "There now, we don't want you to catch cold, do we?" She handed Katherine the half-empty teacup. "Finish your tea and then I'll help you get dressed. What did you say you wanted to wear?"

"I didn't say. Stop fidgeting, Ida. Can't you see I'm too tired to dress. I was up most of the night."

"Why didn't you wake me? I would've brought you warm milk."

"I wanted to give you a break from administering to me."

"Oh, Katie, the way you have with words. I don't *administer* to you, dearie, I take care of you. And may I say it gives me great pleasure every day to do so."

"Well I don't know how you bear it." She took one sip and handed the cup back to LM. "It's cold and weak. After all the times I've shown you, I'd think by now you could make a proper cup of tea."

LM, used to her patient's complaints after a bad night, leaned down to pick up the fallen pillows. "Why, who is this down here? Little Rib. Why are you hiding under the bed? Katie's not angry at you, too, is she?"

She picked up the floppy Russian doll and gave it to Katherine. On the other side of the bedroom she sorted through the medicine bottles, then returned to pick up the books from the floor and return them to the bedside table, dusting them off with her apron.

Feeling a rush of guilt, Katherine softened her tone, and using the affectionate nickname she'd given LM, said, "Jones, please forgive me for being so unpleasant. I don't want to be like this. It's just I've been ill for so long that I've forgotten how to be kind. Please bring me my hairbrush. I'll brush my own hair as I'd rather you go downstairs and greet Doctor Sorapure when he arrives."

Katherine had just put the hairbrush away when she heard Dr. Sorapure's light footsteps, followed by LM's heavy plodding.

Dr. Sorapure was a middle-aged handsome man with a charming bedside manner. Katherine had become quite fond of him over the past months under his care.

He opened his satchel and carefully removed the tools of his trade. He laid them out on her bed: a stethoscope, a percussion hammer, a thermometer, and a small black notebook. How different from my trade, she thought, I only need a pen, ink, and paper.

He looped the stethoscope over his head.

"Is that new?" she asked.

"Brand new. And look at this," he held up a rubber disc. "This fits over the metal plate as an anti-chill device so it isn't cold on your chest."

The first time Katherine had unbuttoned her blouse to have a doctor hear her lungs was when a pulmonary specialist examined her on her thirtieth birthday. After listening to her with his icy stethoscope, he shook his head and said, "You won't reach old bones."

Then came the second opinions. A procession of white jackets with stethoscopes hanging down from double-chins and grim looks like mourners at her funeral. They all shook their heads and threatened her with a few years left in her if she didn't enter a tuberculosis sanatorium.

That was when her night terrors had started.

It still amazed her that a slight infection in her lungs after a cold could become the harbinger of her early death. She'd read in the newspapers about tuberculosis killing a thousand people every week in England, but she never thought one of those people would be her. Not her. She'd only just begun to write stories that pleased her. And what about that novel she wanted to write?

Dr. Sorapure was the first doctor who understood her desperation and he also wore a fashionable tweed suit instead of a starched white jacket. From the beginning, she trusted his scientific knowledge and research. Their intellectual conversations about the immensity and wonder of the universe and the incomprehensibility of space had calmed her fear of death. He suggested a home cure rather than a sanatorium so that she could continue to write.

Dr. Sorapure pulled the chair closer to her bed as if they were old friends and he had come to talk about literature. LM was standing behind him, looking over his shoulder.

"Ida, would you please make us a cup of tea."

"Shouldn't I stay?"

"I'll be fine."

LM left but not before showing her hurt face to Katherine.

"So Mrs. Murry, how are we doing today?"

"Well, let's see. My back screams. My head moans. I have to crawl across the room to get to my writing table only to find my fountain pen is too heavy to lift. And oh yes, my right lung feels like someone is plunging a knife in it every time I breathe. Otherwise, Doctor, I'm just fine."

"Let's have a listen, shall we?" He rubbed his hands together so they wouldn't be cold on her skin. And the anti-chill disc was a miracle. She didn't feel like jumping out of her skin when he pressed it against her chest and said, "Breathe deeply."

He had her turn over and he tapped her back several times with his hammer, listening for sounds only he could interpret.

While she put her bed jacket back on and propped herself up against the pillows, he jotted down a few notes. When he looked up, he said, "You look very tired today. Haven't you been sleeping?"

From her bedside table, he picked up the green Bohemian glass bottle that he had given her when she'd admired its color.

"Why haven't you been taking the laudanum I prescribed?"

"Years ago I became addicted to Veronal. The withdrawal was very difficult. I don't want to ever put myself through that agony again."

"You must trust me when I tell you it's all right to take this tincture of opium to relieve your pain. I assure you, once we find a cure for your rheumatism, you will easily throw out the laudanum and fill this pretty bottle with perfume."

LM returned with a tea tray holding three teacups. Katherine threw her a dark frown and she only poured tea in two cups. The other cup she took with her.

When they were alone again, Dr. Sorapure said, "I've been studying your medical history and I think I know the cause of your rheumatism and why it has gotten progressively worse.

"But first I need to ask you a few questions. Questions you might find unpleasant, even disturbing. But I must ask before I can be certain of my diagnosis."

Unconsciously Katherine reached for her doll Rip and lay him next to her. "Patients have no privacy, Doctor. What do you want to know?"

"When did your joint pain start?"

"Ten years ago. After my surgery."

"Is the scar on the left side of your stomach from that surgery?"

"Yes."

"Will you tell me a bit about your sexual experiences before the surgery?"

Katherine wasn't used being without words but when he opened his notebook with pen in hand, she hesitated. "Please trust me, Mrs. Murry. These are my private notes and I won't share them with anyone."

"Did you ever read Oscar Wilde?"

"Yes, when I was at University."

"I was sixteen when I read *The Picture of Dorian Gray*. The narrator said that *the only thing worth pursuing in life is beauty and the fulfillment of the senses. The only way to get rid of temptation is to yield to it.* I was under Wilde's influence when at the age of nineteen I left my home in Wellington, New Zealand, and moved to London to pursue a life of beauty and the fulfillment of the senses."

He helped her adjust the pillows so she could sit up straighter.

"If you are asking if I was sexually active before my marriage to John Murry, the answer is yes."

If he was offended, he didn't show it. His expression was one of curiosity and concern.

"When I arrived in London, I fell madly in love with a young musician. We were to be married, but his parents broke off our engagement for reasons you needn't know about.

"I was young and foolish and heartbroken so I turned to the first man who was kind to me. He was my elocution instructor, George Bowden. On our wedding night I realized what a stupid mistake I'd made and ran out of our hotel room before consummating our vows."

Embarrassed by her confession, she held her gaze on Rip who looked up at her with sympathetic black button-eyes. "My mother whisked me off to Wörishofen, a spa in Bavaria known for its cold water treatments to cure hysterical women. She left me there to fend for myself.

"Someone took pity on me and gave me the love I so desperately needed. I stayed with this man for several months in Wörishofen until I decided to return to my husband.

"I'd only been living with George for a short time when I became ill with excruciating stomach pains. George rushed me to the hospital. I don't remember much after that except the surgeon was most unpleasant." She smiled. "Not at all like you, Doctor.

"He told me that he'd have to operate immediately. Young and frightened, I didn't think to ask why. When I woke hours later, he told me the surgery was a success."

Dr. Sorapure wrote down a few more notes. "I'm sorry but I have to ask you one more question. Did the surgeon ask you if you'd been sexually active before your marriage to Mr. Bowden?"

Katherine hesitated again. "Yes he did. But how did you know that?"

"It's possible that one of your earlier sexual partners gave you an infection that has made you an invalid. If I'm right, your surgeon tested a sample of tissue taken from your stomach and found gonococcal bacteria that he then removed."

Katherine remembered the itchy discharge, painful urination, stomach cramps that started months before the surgery, but she was too poor and too embarrassed to see a doctor. She opened her eyes and turned to Dr. Sorapure.

"Are you saying I am to blame for my illness, Doctor?"

"No. You are not to blame. Unfortunately, women do not recognize the symptoms of gonorrhea, nor do their doctors. With men it's quickly diagnosed and treated before it infects their bodily organs. Because your infection was not diagnosed it spread. I'm sure the surgeon thought he extracted all the bacteria, but I think during the surgery it leaked into your bloodstream, infecting your joints and other organs. It also weakened your immune system and made you vulnerable to tuberculosis, which is another bacteria.

"If he had known what we know now he would have first treated you with antibacterials and avoided risking surgery."

He reached for her hand and held it. "If you're willing, I'd like to try injections of organic compounds to kill the bacteria still growing in your body. Stop it in its tracks."

"Will these injections also arrest the tuberculosis?"

"Unfortunately not. You have to be patient with us scientists and doctors. We keep learning more about how to cure disease. First, Pasteur discovered bacteria, and now we are discovering how to destroy the bad bacteria without damaging the good bacteria."

"Does that have the same meaning as, there is the sky and the sea and the shape of the lily and then there is illness and death; there are parasites and bacteria that grow strong and kill and then are killed?"

"Yes." He smiled. "But I much prefer your poetic description." He reached for the green bottle and she didn't resist when he poured a spoonful of the amber tincture and held it up to her mouth. She swallowed it.

"You're a determined woman, but you can't will away tuberculosis. If the injections for rheumatism give you relief from your crippling pain, at least you won't be bedridden. Isn't that worth something?"

"Do you think I'm a fool to pursue a cure for tuberculosis?"

"No. I don't think any disease is incurable," he said. "It's more a question of time. The experiments of today will provide the link that will make all plain to a future generation. Each person plays but a small part in the history of the world. What is incurable today will be curable tomorrow and you will have shared in that success," he paused, "even if the cure comes too late for you."

"Then I will live until that cure is found as I expect to recover—one has to, you know—from everything."

LM came in just as Dr. Sorapure said, "Do you want me to arrange for your antibacterial injections at the hospital?"

"What injections?" blurted LM.

Dr. Sorapure turned to her. "We have seen success with injections of organic compounds. If it works, maybe one of Mrs. Murry's illnesses will be cured and she will be able to walk and write again without pain."

"*If* it works?" asked LM. "What if it doesn't? Is this treatment dangerous?"

Katherine held her eyes on the wise doctor and said, "Ida, it's all right. I trust Dr. Sorapure. Besides I am only a cog in the wheel. Right, doctor?" She half smiled. "These injections can't be any worse than those electrical treatments I've been taking."

Dr. Sorapure packed his bag and stood up to leave.

"Ida, after you've seen Dr. Sorapure out, please come back and close the curtains. I'm going to sleep now."

"But Mrs. Woolf is coming to see you. It's too late to send her a note."

"Tell her that I'm sorry but I'm not up to seeing anyone today. If anyone would understand, it'd be Virginia." Katherine heard her own voice fading. "I only want to see Jack."

Dr. Sorapure's tincture was having its effect. She felt herself falling into an amber pool but felt no fear of drowning and let go.

SHE AWOKE TREMBLING. She had been dreaming of white-uniformed soldiers marching toward a precipice where she teetered on its edge. Their hilted swords and medals shone in the sunlight, empty grenade holders banged against their hips. As they drew nearer to her, their hollow eyes beseeched her, enormous rough hands reached out to her as each soldier dropped off the precipice into the churning amber sea below.

The last soldier was her deceased brother, Leslie. As he drew closer she saw he was carrying a newborn infant bundled in sheets of hand-written paper, black ink dripped onto his pure white cadet uniform.

He handed the infant to her before he stepped over the precipice and joined his comrades. She was still holding the newborn over the abyss when she awoke.

She often had this dream and knew it was best to just lie still, breathe deeply, not move until the tremors stopped.

AUTUMN, 1908

The Trowells—London

Oh—let it remain as it is—
Do not suddenly crush out this,
the beautiful flower—
I am afraid even while I am rejoicing...

NOTEBOOKS—KM

WHEN KATHERINE ARRIVED IN LONDON from Wellington, the Trowells gave her a warm welcome. They called her by her childhood name, Kass, and she found it quite natural to think of them as her surrogate parents who unlike her real parents shared her passion for the arts and respected her driving ambition to be an artist.

After several visits to their Hampstead home, she realized Arnold, at age nineteen, decidedly loved her, but as a sister. Resilient, she turned her attention to his twin, Garnet, a tall, slender boy who loved books almost as much as he loved his violin. And of equal importance, he was a Trowell, and she so wanted to be a part of the Trowell family. It took only a few months for them to fall in love and soon they were planning a future together as great, bohemian artists.

The night before Garnet was to leave on a winter road tour with the Moody Manners Opera Company, Kass was invited to a farewell dinner. In the kitchen, she helped Mrs. Trowell and their young daughter Dolly prepare the evening meal. Mrs. Trowell, unable to afford a domestic on her husband's music teacher salary, had been hesitant to ask the Bank of New Zealand's daughter to help in the kitchen. Kass convinced her that she felt like a member of the family when she did her share of the work.

She volunteered to peel potatoes while she listened through the thin wall to Garnet playing the violin accompanied by Arnold on cello and their father on piano in the music room. They were learning a new composition that Arnold had just written. This is how I want to live, she thought, here among artists.

She looked up at Mrs. Trowell wiping her flour-covered hand across her perspiring forehead who didn't seem to share Katherine's romantic version of her family.

"It's too stuffy in here," she complained. "Open a window," she said to Dolly, her youngest child, "and go set the table. Tell the men dinner will be served shortly."

After dinner, Garnet came up and softly said, "Kass, let's go for a walk." She turned to invite Dolly. "No, just the two of us. I have something important to ask you."

He put on his brother's overcoat and put his own coat on Kass before they slipped out the back door. Under a gaslight, Kass looked up at the illuminated trees. "See, Garnet, how they cross their limbs, protecting each other from the powerful cold wind trying to break them apart."

"Like us," he said, wrapping his arms around her. "Marry me, Kass," he whispered in her ear. "Marry me, my darling."

She closed her eyes and felt his warmth like a kindling fire. She leaned in closer, wanting to hold on to this magical moment. Through the window into the Trowell's sitting room, she could see the golden tones of the wood-burning fireplace, the vacant seat on the couch that was now hers.

She nodded her head, yes, and he lifted her face up to his and gently kissed her mouth, then reached for her hand. Their laugh was carried off by the wind as they ran back inside to tell his family the good news.

"For heavens sake!" exclaimed Mrs. Trowell. "What are you two doing outside on this frosty night? Come here my children. Get warm by the fire."

He hugged his mom. "I have great news to share with you. Kass and I are engaged."

Mrs. Trowell was the first to recover. With tears in her eyes, she took both their hands in hers. "to "That's wonderful, my children." Mr. Trowell stood up, but before offering any congratulations he said to Katherine, "Have you told your father?"

"How could I? Garnet just asked me a few minutes ago."

"We don't want to offend them or have them think we are taking advantage of your circumstances. They might not take kindly to you marrying a boy from the lower classes who makes his livelihood as a musician. You must get his permission right away."

Arnold shook Garnet's hand, "Why you ole sneak. So this is what you two have been up to. Congratulations, ole man. I'll dedicate my new composition to you two lovebirds. Let's see what shall I call it. I know... *Clandestine Love*."

Garnet and Katherine blushed and still holding hands plopped down together on the couch.

The next morning Garnet came by Beauchamp Lodge to say good-bye to Katherine. He promised to find her a position in the Moody Manners chorus so she could join him on the road. It was a huge theatrical company with over a hundred artists performing six nights a week. If there was no room in the chorus, he was sure they could use her many talents backstage.

And, she thought, when I'm not working I can write stories about our adventures on the road.

WHILE SHE WAITED FOR news from Garnet, she'd go to the Trowell's house several times a week for a cello lesson with Mr. Trowell and would often stay for dinner. When she was alone in her room at Beauchamp Lodge, she'd write to Garnet sometimes two or three times in one day.

Beloved—though I do not see you, know that I am yours. Every thought, every feeling in me belongs to you—I wake up in the morning and have been dreaming of you—and all through the day, while my outer life goes on steadily, my inner life I live with you, in leaps and bounds.

She was disappointed by the long gaps in-between her heartfelt letters. Garnet explained that he only had time to write to her on Sundays when traveling by train to the next venue. There were rehearsals during the day and two to three performances every night.

October 14th was Katherine's twentieth birthday. She and Garnet had been engaged one month. So imagine her delight to receive a letter from him that morning. Inside was a plain gold band. She proudly put it on her wedding finger and showed it off to the Trowells at dinner.

At Beauchamp Lodge she had made good friends with another girl her age, Margaret Wishart. Margaret's father had taken a liking to Katherine and invited her to join them in Paris for a family wedding.

Garnet wouldn't be home for a few more weeks, she thought, and the time would pass much faster if I was having fun in Paris.

It was a fairy tale wedding with all the trimmings a wealthy family could afford. Katherine was pleased to be so popular with the young men who gathered around her, asking her to dance with them at the reception.

On the train back to London, she started to question her future with Garnet. A poor musician was not apt to be taking her to elegant dances unless he was performing in the orchestra and she was watching the dancers from behind the curtain or singing onstage.

But how can I sing if I'm draggled and poor, she thought. She picked up her spirits by reminding herself that she had a splendid voice and that *fine feathers don't make fine artists.*

By the time the Paris train had pulled into Victoria Station her love for Garnet had conquered any doubts she had about living in squalor as a musician's wife.

When Garnet returned from the opera tour, his parents asked him to take care of Dolly while they visited relatives up North. His brother Arnold had moved to Belgium to join an orchestra.

Garnet and Katherine were delighted to finally have some time alone without having to hide every time they kissed. The moment his parents left, Kass moved into his bedroom.

The next morning when she came out of his bedroom in her nightgown she hadn't expected to run into Dolly, who was as shocked as she was.

If Dolly told her parents, all hell would break loose. She saw only one solution and that was to tell a little lie.

"Dolly, can I share a secret with you?"

The little girl nodded, seeming to enjoy their conspiracy. "Garnet and I are married. We didn't want to say anything to your parents until I told mine. Will you promise not to say anything to them about what you saw this morning."

Dolly said, "Does that mean you are going to live with us and play Cribbage and read to me every night before I go to bed?"

Kass laughed and pulled Dolly close to her. "Yes, my dearest, yes. You will be my little sister."

When Mr. and Mrs. Trowell returned home, Kass had already moved back to Beauchamp Lodge to avoid any suspicions. Garnet had to leave again on tour, promising Kass that he would ask the stage manager again to offer her a job.

Kass began to notice that ever since her engagement to Garnet, Mr. Trowell was indifferent toward her, almost rude. If he said anything, it was to ask her again if she'd heard from her father. She got used to lying to him, saying it took a long time for letters to come from New Zealand.

Kass and her future mother-in-law often had a cup of tea in the kitchen after Dolly went to bed and before she returned to the Lodge. On one of those evenings, she asked if she had done anything to upset Mr. Trowell.

"It's not you, Kass. I didn't want to say anything but you're almost family so I don't think he'd mind me telling you. Mr. Trowell moved us to London with great expectations. He thought he would have many students here because of his sons' reputations as popular musicians, but it hasn't worked out that way. He only has a few students and the money the boys bring home isn't enough to live on. We have to bring in a boarder or go back to Wellington."

"Oh, no. You mustn't leave London. I'd be lost without you here. Why not let me be your boarder? I could pay you the same rent I pay at Beauchamp Lodge. And let me talk to my father's cousin, Uncle Henry. He's a teacher at the London Academy of Music and can get the word out that Mr. Trowell is looking for students."

"Would you do that for us, Kass?"

"I'd do anything I can to keep you near me. I've never been so happy as during the time I've spent here with you, and Dolly is like a little sister to me."

AT FIRST, she was very content living with the Trowells. She finally had a home where she could hang her hat on the back door. When Garnet came back, she'd sneak into his room after his parents retired. When Dolly saw her coming out of his room in the morning, Kass would put her finger to her lips, smile, and tiptoe down the hall to her own room.

The problems started when Kass was late on the rent. She was not used to having to budget her expenses and was extravagant, spending her allowance as soon as she had it. Too embarrassed to say she didn't have the rent money, she stopped having teatime with Mrs. Trowell and would escape to her room after dinner. And when she went out to have fun with her friends, Mr. Trowell would wait up for her, angry if she came in late. He was acting like her stern father and she didn't like that at all.

Equally irritating was having to ask for an advance from her father's accountant, Mr. Kay. At the Bank of New Zealand's branch on Regent Street, she'd have to sit in his office and listen to him lecture her on the value of a pound. Then he would invite her to lunch, an invitation she felt obliged to accept, and try to take her hand under the table or squeeze her leg.

She didn't tell Mr. Kay that she'd moved out of the Lodge and was now a lodger at the Trowells, because he would tell Mr. Beauchamp in his monthly report. Her father would never have approved of her living in her music teacher's home or approve of her engagement to a poor young musician whose musical education he had financially supported when Garnet was a student in Wellington. Mr. Trowell was right to worry about what her father would think.

But that's not why she didn't write to her father. She just didn't think she had to ask his permission to marry Garnet. She was an independent woman now and could marry whoever she wanted to marry.

One morning, in a hurry to meet friends for lunch, Kass handed Mrs. Trowell a wash basket filled with dirty clothes.

"Hold on now, Kass. I'll have to charge you for your wash. And you're still late on rent."

"But you've always offered to do it before."

"That was before you became our lodger. Besides, your fancy things need gallons of hot water and we can't afford it when you don't even pay your share of the rent."

Katherine, instead of being contrite, held her head up proudly and said, "I'll have the rent when I come home and the wash money."

"That's what you said last week and I don't believe you anymore. You're not the same sweet girl we invited into our home. If you can't pay what you owe us, we'll have to get a respectable boarder who pays rent on time."

That morning Katherine had frantically searched her pockets for change and had found only one shilling, which she was now rubbing between her fingers. She could give it to Mrs. Trowell, but she needed it for the omnibus from Hampstead Heath to the tube and from there to Regent Street to meet her friends. She had planned to borrow money to pay for lunch and then see Mr. Kay afterward for an advance on her allowance.

Embarrassed, but too proud to say she was sorry, she tried to squeeze by Mrs. Trowell, but the hefty woman folded her arms over her apron and blocked her passage.

Kass took back her wash and said angrily, though she knew she had no right to be angry, "All right, Mrs. Trowell, I'll do my own wash." She stomped back up the stairs and threw the basket on her bed. In her hurry to get away, she almost knocked Dolly down on the staircase, but didn't stop, slamming the door behind her.

That night she paid Mrs. Trowell the overdue rent and without apologizing for her despicable behavior, went up to her room. Dolly followed her up the stairs hoping for a bedtime story but her mother called her back down.

When Garnet came home a few day later, he was excited to tell her that he had finally got her a job in the Opera chorus. She was so pleased to see him and find out she'd be joining him on the road that she didn't tell him about the disagreement with his mother until they took a walk before dinner.

"It's good you got me a job because your mother doesn't want me living here. I can't do anything right by her. And your father keeps looking in the post for a letter from my father. I don't know what he'll do when I tell him the truth."

Garnet knotted his brow and said crossly, "But why haven't you written your father?" She hadn't expected him to take their side. "My parents have made tremendous sacrifices so that my brother and I could become musicians and I don't like you lying to them. It's deceitful and disrespectful."

"Garnet! I thought you understood. I will not ask my father's permission to marry you because it's not his decision. It's mine. We can tell him after we're married."

"I don't see why you have to be so stubborn about this. Your willfulness is going to get you in trouble one of these days, Kass.

"And need I remind you that I'm dependent on my parents' financial help. When we marry, we'll have to live here so you have to find a way to get along with my parents. A bit of humility wouldn't do any harm."

She knew he was right. Her behavior toward his parents was awful. She promised to set things right.

That evening at dinner she told Mr. Trowell that she would write another letter to her father as the first one must have been lost at sea. She didn't think for a moment that he believed her, but this time she would write the letter, if only to make Garnet happy.

After dinner, the family sat at their usual places in the sitting room, Mr. Trowell at his desk, Mrs. Trowell in the rocking chair, bookends on each side of the blazing logs. Dolly, cross-legged, played with her doll at her mother's feet. Arnold's chair was empty as he was still living in Belgium.

As was their habit, Garnet and Kass shared the couch, both reading, his leg pressed against hers under the blanket. They hoped to make love that evening, but his parents had started to keep their bedroom door open when Garnet was home and they were afraid of being caught.

Dolly had been unusually quiet during dinner and now leaned her head on her mother's knee with a long face. Kass invited her to come sit between her and Garnet so she could read to her. Dolly shook her head.

"What about a game of Cribbage?" They hadn't played in weeks and Katherine assumed that was why Dolly was upset.

Dolly didn't answer, but crossed her arms in front of her chest like her mother often did and said, "Why haven't you told them, Garnet!"

"Told them what?" said Garnet, surprised by her anger.

"Tell them that you and Kass are married."

"What?" said Mrs. Trowell looking first at Garnet's red face, then at Kass and then back to her daughter. "They're not married, Dolly. They're engaged."

"That's not what Kass told me. When you were away on holiday, she told me they were married and I wasn't to tell you that she sleeps in Garnet's bed."

Mr. Trowell looked up from the sheet music he was studying. Normally nothing interrupted him when he was working. "Kass is this true? Are you and Garnet married?"

"Not exactly."

"What do you mean, *not exactly*. Are you married or not?"

"Why don't you ask your son?" She turned to Garnet who had backed away from her on the couch. "Garnet, your father wants to know what I mean when I say we are *not exactly* married."

The sock Mrs. Trowell was darning fell on the floor. The ball of yarn rolled across the room stopping at Kass's feet. She picked it up and brought it over to Mrs. Trowell, waiting for Garnet to say something. He didn't.

"All right then, if you won't tell them, I will. Garnet and I are *not exactly* married, but for several months we have been lovers."

Mrs. Trowell dropped down in her seat at the same moment Mr. Trowell rose from his. He stood over Kass. "You never did send that letter to your father, did you?"

Katherine felt like a trapped animal and feeling threatened she snapped back, "I don't have to ask him. Garnet and I are free spirits, we don't need his permission to get married." She turned to Garnet. "Isn't that true, darling?"

Garnet had become very interested in his feet and said nothing.

"How dare you lie to us," said Mr. Trowell. "We took you into our home and treated you as if you were our own child and in return you treat us like playthings. This isn't one of your dollhouses, Miss Beauchamp.

"You might not think you have to ask your father's permission but you certainly have to ask mine. And the answer is absolutely no. I would never let my son marry you. The engagement is off and if it weren't for your father's kindness toward us in Wellington, I would send you packing tonight."

Dolly started crying.

Katherine wanted to take the child into her arms and tell her she was sorry for lying to her, but Mr. Trowell stood between them, literally growling.

He turned toward Garnet and said, "You are not to have any further contact with Miss Beauchamp." Garnet was still studying his shoes and didn't look up. "Do you hear me, Garnet?"

Katherine couldn't believe Garnet was being such a mouse. This wasn't *all* her fault. But he wouldn't even look at her when she touched his shoulder and only a few hours ago he had been holding her in his arms saying how much he loved her.

"Garnet and Dolly go to your rooms!" he finally shouted.

Katherine watched her fiancé run up the stairs with his sister as if he was a child.

"Garnet!" she cried out. "Garnet! Come back here."

She grabbed her coat and hat and rushed out of the house certain Garnet would come to his senses and follow her. The cozy, warm lights that had once welcomed her went out in the house and she suddenly understood what she had lost by being such a willful, ungrateful girl but even still she couldn't forgive Garnet for not coming after her.

A drizzling rain became a downpour and the wet air pushed her down the street. A bus pulled up and she got aboard.

Her old school friend, Ida, pulled Katherine inside her home.

She was too miserable to tell her friend that because of her pride and stubbornness she had lost the Trowell's affection and worse Garnet had abandoned her.

"My poor dear," Ida said. "Come by the fire." She helped Katherine take off her wet clothes and tucked her under an eiderdown for the night.

Early the next morning, Katherine opened her eyes upon a box tied in a wide red ribbon. She'd forgotten it was Christmas week. Inside the box was a black and silver Egyptian shawl. She thanked Ida, promised her a poem in return and rushed back to Beauchamp Lodge, expecting to find Garnet waiting for her, or at least a message. There was no message but there was a cheaper room available on the ground floor. Not as private or as quiet as her previous room upstairs facing the garden, but she could ill-afford to be uppity without a shilling in her pocket.

FEBRUARY, 1909

Mr. Peacock

"Not at all, dear lady. I am only too charmed."

MR. REGINALD PEACOCK'S DAY—KM

KATHERINE KEPT TO HER NEW ROOM, wanting to be there when Garnet came looking for her.

Filling her fountain pen, she started scribbling down sketches in her notebook and as she wrote, a story emerged. A poor girl named Rosabel worked long hours in an elegant millinery shop and spent her evenings in a shabby unheated boarding house. She waited on wealthy women who came to the shop and bought fashionable hats and soft leather gloves. They were often escorted by fine gentlemen who paid their bills; the nicer ones a coin to Rosabel on their way out with a wink and a smile. One evening, a tired, hungry, and cold Rosabel falls asleep watching the rain stream down her window and dreams of a rich gentleman falling in love with her and soon they are married.

The story formed quickly in Katherine's mind and she filled several pages before she came to the final paragraph:

So she slept and dreamed and smiled and once threw out her arm to feel for something which was not there, dreaming still. And the night passed. Presently the cold fingers of dawn closed over her uncovered hand; grey light flooded the dull room. Rosalind shivered, drew a little gasping breath, sat up. And because her heritage was that tragic optimism, which is all too often the only inheritance of youth, still half asleep she smiled with a little nervous tremor round her mouth.

Katherine also smiled until she looked up at her neglected cello leaning against the wall, a painful reminder of better times spent with Garnet and his family. No more tears, she told herself. Look what I can accomplish without you.

She pointed her pen at the cello. "Someday I'll be as famous an author as my cousin Elizabeth. Then you'll be sorry. What a mouse you are, Garnet!"

And now having completed *The Tiredness of Rosabel* she must celebrate. A hot bun at a teashop? She counted her change, a pence short. She walked over to the cello, plucked its out-of-tune strings and made a decision. There was no reason to keep it if she wasn't going to play it. She carefully put the instrument in its purple velvet case and snapped the lid shut.

In her wardrobe chest, she looked at the frayed skirts, drab jackets and unfashionable hats. This will never do, she thought. An accomplished writer needs to make a good impression. She picked up the cello case by its handle, grabbed her coat, and went out.

Often when needing an extra shilling for Abdulla cigarettes to share with Garnet or a concert ticket at Queen's Hall or a bouquet of fresh flowers or, like now, a hot bun at the teashop, she bartered with the pawnbrokers on Abbey Road over her trinkets until she got a good price.

She walked out of the second pawnshop without the cello. After stopping in the teashop to enjoy a hot bun, she entered a dress shop and bought the black evening gown in the window she'd wanted for a week. Her other purchases were a purple coat, burgundy velvet skirt, pale yellow silk blouse, and shiny patent leather shoes with bright green stockings. Broke again but delighted with her purchases, she returned to her room at the Lodge and arranged a fresh bouquet of flowers in a vase.

Her coin purse now empty and counting the days on her fingers before she could collect her monthly allowance from Mr. Kay, she wrote a letter to Mrs. Gladstone, a social hostess. At one of her parties, Katherine had accompanied another guest playing the piano. She was not at all shy having performed at many society parties in Wellington. But she'd never received an honorarium, which Mrs. Gladstone had discreetly handed to her.

Mrs. Gladstone wrote back saying she remembered Katherine fondly and invited her to a party she was giving Saturday night.

Katherine wore her new velvet skirt and yellow blouse. Her Lodge friend, Margaret, came with her. When Mrs. Gladstone asked her to perform, she did a comedic skit impersonating Charlie Chaplin who was a sensation in the music halls that she frequented. The laughter and applause that followed plus the many shillings slipped into her hand by Mrs. Gladstone made her very happy.

But her happiness was short-lived when she sank down on a sofa next to Margaret and started complaining about her humiliating attempt to submit *Rosabel* to one of the publishing houses on the Strand. Even though she had published several stories in New Zealand journals, the Londoners showed no respect to the little Colonialist. One publisher offered her a secretarial position if she could really write.

"What's the point of writing any stories," said Katherine, "if no one ever gets a chance to read what I've written?" She meditated on the bubbles rising up her champagne glass.

"Margaret!" she said, suddenly sitting up. "I have the most brilliant idea. If I can't get published then why not *perform* my stories, along with a few mimes, and sing a few tunes at a music hall. Why I could be as popular as Charlie Chaplin."

"I've never heard of anyone doing anything like that," said Margaret, "but if it's anything like what you just did now it will be a huge hit. I'll certainly come and so will all the other girls at the lodge."

Katherine glanced over at a well-dressed man in gray trousers with matching gray socks and black tie who had laughed and applauded the loudest after her skit.

"Do you know that gentleman?" she asked Margaret.

"No." She smiled. "But he's been leering at you all evening. Rather an old dandy, don't you think? Certainly too old for you."

Before Katherine could respond, he was standing in front of them, introducing himself. Margaret saw a friend enter the salon and went to join him. Katherine found Mr. George Bowden a very attentive listener and before too long he joined her on the couch and she told him her idea for giving public readings of her own short stories.

"Imagine a softly-lit stage," she said. "Flowers everywhere—a shaded red-tasseled lamp—and there I am seated in a great high-backed oak chair wearing a simple but elegant orange silk gown or perhaps what I'm wearing tonight."

She spread out her velvet burgundy skirt on the yellow brocade sofa, sat up very straight and recited the first few paragraphs of *Rosabel*.

When she stopped, worried he'd lost interest, he said, "What a beautiful voice you have Miss Mansfield. And how sympathetic your story is about poor Rosabel."

Katherine blushed. "You're just being kind."

"No I'm not. You are a talent, my girl."

She leaned toward him. "Do you really think I possess the power to hold an audience in my grip?"

"You certainly hold mine," he said ecstatically. "Why I don't know any other young lady who can sing, recite, and mime like you do."

"I've never had any vocal lessons. Don't you think my voice needs refinement?"

"Well, Miss Mansfield, perhaps I can help you with that."

"Really, Mr. Bowden."

He had a very long neck when he sat up. It reminded Katherine of a peacock showing off its brilliant feathers. "I teach voice and elocution to vocal students at London University and I also have stage credits."

Katherine felt embarrassed. "Oh Mr. Bowden, had I known you were a professional artist I wouldn't have been so bold. How amazing that I should meet you tonight. Tell me, honestly, is it silly of me to think anyone would want to hear me give a reading?"

He smiled down at her. "Not at all my dear lady and if you allow me I would be only too charmed to give you speech lessons, even help you in your new enterprise."

"I would be honored, Mr. Bowden, but I couldn't afford to pay you very much."

He laughed. "Have dinner with me tonight and we can discuss the details of our arrangement. That is if you're available, Miss Mansfield?"

She looked down at her barren finger, having just this morning removed Garnet's gold band. She smiled. "Yes, Mr. Bowden, I am available."

"Then I'd be only too charmed to take you to dinner, my dear lady. But please call me George."

"All right. And you must call me Katherine."

SHE NO LONGER WOKE UP in the morning hungry for a hot bun now that she spent her evenings with George who was only too willing to be at her beck and call. If anything she was putting on too much weight. He took her to fashionable restaurants and let her order whatever she wanted. He also escorted her to London's trendy salons where she never before had been invited. He seemed to know everyone important and was adored by many wealthy ladies who were his students.

Mr. Bowden started with three lessons a week at his home teaching Katherine voice and elocution. He said she needn't pay him anything until after her first public reading.

Each lesson began with exercising her lips, repeatedly singing *moo-e-koo-e-oo-e-a* in front of a mirror. She found it all quite silly.

"Katherine, please, I cannot teach you if you keep laughing. You need to train your lips to have more flexibility. Now stand up straight. You are quite petite and will be lost on the stage if you don't stand tall. Okay now turn and face me as if I am your audience. Use those deep somber eyes to draw me in. Don't be timid. You are a beautiful woman and you must show your beauty to the world."

She did as she was told, still trying not to laugh while singing to her reflection. Sometimes when he was showing her how to pose his arm brushed against hers and she'd pull back, worried his intentions were on the shady side. But he was so patient and understanding that in time he gained her trust.

And they were never completely alone. His ancient butler, Charles, often brought her a glass of water when her throat was dry from the exercises. Often, after her lesson, George would invite her to stay for tea, which Charles served in their most pleasant salon. Katherine would accept, not wanting to go back to her lonely room, and then he would invite her to dinner. When his flatmate, Lamont, a musical performer, came home he joined them. Lamont told her that their flat was a far happier place to come home to when she was there.

George offered her the comforts she had so missed since leaving home. The allowance her father gave her barely covered her room and board, and she had come to realize that he thought she would grow tired of being poor and come back home to the luxury she was accustomed to.

But now there was George sending her a bouquet of flowers each morning with a card: "To my best student. Your faithful teacher." Katherine started to see a way out of her impoverished circumstances.

When he started sending her passionate letters written on elegant hand-woven, pale pink stationery, she read them out loud to her girlfriends at the Lodge and they all made fun of him. But when she was with George, she appreciated his generosity and kindness.

He was far more attentive than Garnet had been and they went to the best of parties. With Garnet there had been no parties and he paid more attention to his violin than her. Also, George encouraged her eccentricities. He liked showing her off when she dressed like a gypsy or a Japanese princess. He said it worked in her favor to draw attention to herself for when she was ready to have her public readings.

When he returned from hospital after having his tonsils removed, Katherine took care of him, spent all day by his bedside, helped him to eat and entertained him with her comical skits and made-up stories.

A week after he recovered, they were having tea in his salon when he suddenly got down on one knee and said, "Dear Katherine, marry me. Together we will enchant the world."

She was taken aback and rather amused at his old-fashion proposal but not wanting to hurt his feelings she tried to take his proposal very seriously. "I don't know what to say, George. We've only known each other a few weeks. Don't you think we should slow things down a bit?"

He took her hand, "Come with me. I want to show you something." He took her down a long hallway that she hadn't seen before and opened a door. "This would be your writing room, Katherine. Charles has taken quite a liking to you and he will supply you with whatever you need to write without any interruptions. Lamont, whose room is the farthest down the hall is in complete agreement with Charles and me that you should join us here.

"Please Katherine, don't say no. Let us take care of you."

There was a single bed in the writing room and she asked George if this would also be her bedroom, as she couldn't possibly share his—at least not until they knew each other better.

"I won't rush you, Katherine. For now, think of yourself as a flatmate coming to live with two old bachelors. Our marriage will just give our arrangement legitimacy until your heart is ready to be my wife. I only want to further your emancipation as a woman, rather than in any way cripple it.

Her cousin Elizabeth would have applauded that idea. The theme of her books was women finding ways to live independent lives even when married. Maybe Katherine too could actually profit from such an arrangement.

It'd be like the three of us camping out, she thought, trying to see the benefits. I'd like to see Garnet's face when he finds out but I'd have to stop seeing him!

Katherine hadn't told anyone but twice she'd left the Lodge to join Garnet on short tours outside London. But being on the road was not the life she had imagined. Squalor accommodations. Cheap wine and food. No time to write. And though she still loved Garnet, after what had happened with his father, she questioned his loyalty.

Yes, marrying George could be the perfect solution and it'll keep me from running back to Garnet again, she thought. And hadn't it become impossible to write in a lodge filled with young female musicians practicing instruments all day and having to find ways to make extra money bled into her time at her writing desk. She looked over at the shaft of sunlight coming from the open window and illuminating the writing desk. A retreat from the harsh realities she'd experienced since her arrival in London. And didn't George say he'd find me a publisher for my short stories? She sat down at the desk and imagined the writing she could do in this quiet room without wondering where her next meal would come from.

She looked up at George who had been waiting patiently for her answer. "How can I say no to all that you offer me." She laughed. "Of course I'll marry you."

"Thank you Katherine. You have made me a very happy man." He gently kissed her two cheeks as if to reassure her that all he was asking for was to be close friends. At least, for now.

She immediately wrote to her guardian Uncle Henry, asking him to meet her fiancé. She also sent a cable to her parents announcing her nuptials. She didn't give the date, seeing no reason for them to come all that way for a simple wedding at the registry. She asked Ida to be her witness.

A few days later at the Beauchamp Lodge breakfast table, Katherine stood up and clicked her spoon against her orange juice glass. Ten girls raised their heads to see what their unusual flatmate had to say. She often amused them with wild stories of her adventures in London though they never knew whether to believe her or not—her stories were so risqué.

She didn't disappointment them when she said, "Tomorrow I'm getting married."

The Lodge's matron said, "Miss Beauchamp, you mustn't make light of such things." Several girls giggled into their napkins.

"But I am serious, Mrs. Tate. This is my last breakfast at Beauchamp Lodge. Tomorrow I will become Mrs. George Bowden." The girls, remembering how they had laughed at George's gushing love letters, blushed and giggled as murmurings spread around the table.

"Quiet, girls!" She turned back to Katherine. "If you leave, Miss Beauchamp, you won't be invited back. I've put up long enough with your shenanigans. Coming and going as you please at all hours. You don't seem to realize that this is a respectable lodge for young ladies."

After breakfast, Margaret came to Katherine's room. "You were just having a go at us, weren't you? You really don't mean to marry that old dandy, do you? Why he's ten years older than you. You can't possibly be in love with him?"

"No. But he told me that doesn't matter."

Margaret frowned. "Really? Doesn't matter! Do you think he's marrying you just out of the goodness of his heart? Oh, Katherine how can you be so naïve? He'll expect you to behave like a wife after you promise to 'love and obey him.' Just give me one good reason why you are doing this?"

"Well, I'll give you a few. He promised to find someone to publish my work and he is going to help me find a venue where I can perform my readings and—" Margaret's frown stopped her from listing any other benefits and she offered, "It'll make good copy, material for my stories."

She laughed. Margaret frowned. "Oh Margaret, don't look so worried. After all, it's just a lark."

"Marriage is not a lark, Katherine."

"All right. It isn't a lark. But I'm bored of being poor and lonely. I've been in London for six months and look at the mess I got myself in with Garnet. Obviously I need someone to take care of me." She smiled. "And George is most entertaining. You must come for dinner very soon, then you'll see. He has a gorgeous flat and a butler named Charles. And Lamont is the sweetest of flatmates. You'll see. You must come to dinner and see how much fun the bachelors and I have. Why it's absolutely charming!"

Katherine married George Bowden the following day with Ida and a Registry clerk as their witnesses. It was March 2nd, 1909, six weeks after they'd met.

Virginia Woolf's Visit

Is there another Life? Shall I awake and find all this a dream?
There must be—we cannot be created for this sort of suffering.

LETTERS—JOHN KEATS

A
FTER COPYING KEATS'S WORDS into her notebook, Katherine put down her fountain pen and observed her bedroom. Everything was in its proper place just like the furniture and ornaments she'd so carefully placed in her dollhouse when she was a child. But, she suddenly thought, this current dollhouse has become my cage and possibly my casket. She got up slowly and limped over to the large window that looked out over the entrance to her home from the second floor.

Dr. Sorapure had just left. He had listened with his stethoscope to her lungs and had delivered an ultimatum. "I warned you last winter that it would be best if you left London during the winter season, but you chose to stay. This year you don't have a choice. If you stay in London, you won't make it through the winter."

The side effects of his weekly streptococci injections had kept her languishing in bed with a high fever. And she didn't know if her chronic joint pain that she called *rheumatiz,* but diagnosed by Doctor Sorapure as venereal disease, had been cured because she still had flare-ups. A cane was often needed to hobble across the room. Worst of all was the chill in her bones and the stiff fingers when she tried to write. And then there was the constant threat of the tuberculosis becoming active in her lungs.

Laudanum brought her temporary relief at night and during the day she distracted herself by reading Keats and Chekhov who were consumptives like herself. They kept writing until their dying day just like she planned to do and she felt encouraged just having their books on her bedside table.

She looked out at the trees and streetlights shrouded in fog as if warning her that the end would come sooner than she wanted it to and she better get back to work.

From the window she looked down at Virginia Woolf inspecting the rusty iron gate in front of the home Katherine and Jack fondly called *The Elephant* because of its tall grey walls. Virginia was more apt to call it a white elephant, too bulky, too tall, and in her opinion, quite ugly.

Katherine had heard that Virginia thought the little Colonialist's *Elephant* was an expression of her lack of good taste, and "After all, one must remember, in fact it's impossible to forget, that Katherine's not English by birth. Her saving virtue is that she attended Queen's College at the impressionable age of fourteen. I'm a little shocked at her commonness at first sight. However, when this diminishes, she is so intelligent and inscrutable that she repays friendship."

There was little anyone said in the Bloomsbury group that didn't reach the little *Colonialist*. Yet in spite of Virginia's cruelty, Katherine liked very much that she was coming to visit her. There was no one else she knew who shared her passion for writing.

Virginia drew in her parasol, adjusted her hat, and straightened her shoulders before opening the squeaky gate. Katherine remembered from her last excursion outdoors with Jack that the gate needed oil, but she'd forgotten to tell LM to oil it. Virginia looked up before Katherine could hide behind the curtain and waved.

Katherine sat down on the sofa, closed her eyes and listened to the front door closing after the bell rang. The sound was like an offstage cue for the entry-hall scene to begin inside her head. She saw LM's oversized body (Ottoline had nicknamed her *The Mountain)* filling the entry hall, dwarfing Virginia, an otherwise imposing woman.

Virginia: (stiffly) "Good afternoon, Miss Baker."

LM: "Good afternoon to you, ma'am." Her timid voice belies her size. She curtsies like a delicate hippopotamus and, without thinking to take Virginia's hat and parasol as one should, leads her upstairs.

LM: "Please don't tire her out. She's having one of her bad days."

Virginia's steps are light and tentative, hesitating at every step to look around, while LM plods ahead.

"You needn't rise," said Virginia, entering stage center. End of scene.

Though she'd been visiting Katherine for several months, her first impression was always one of shock at seeing her friend shrink in size and fade in color. The patient herself looked in the mirror too often to notice her own progression, or should she say regression, but she was certainly unrecognizable from the framed photograph of the younger Katherine practicing her elocution in front of George Bowden's mirror.

Virginia, who seemed to want to look anywhere but at her friend, set her gaze on a bouquet of marigolds.

"How lovely," she said.

"Yes. Aren't they. I picked them from my garden this morning."

"Oh, then you do manage to get outdoors?"

Katherine turned away to cough into her hankie.

"Yes," answered LM, bringing Virginia a chair and placing it in front of the patient but not too close, while Katherine arranged herself amongst the pillows on the sofa.

LM asked, "Shall I bring tea?"

"Virginia?" Katherine asked, disliking the pathetic, raspy sound of her own voice.

"Yes, that would be very pleasant."

LM nodded and backed out of the room.

Katherine gathered her black Spanish shawl around her shoulders, hoping its vivid flowers and birds embroidered in silk would distract Virginia from looking at her with such pity. But at that moment the sun slipped out from behind a cloud and a shaft of light fell harshly on her pallid face, exposing her to further sympathy.

"Forgive me for not dressing for your visit," she said, moving out of the sun's glare.

"I must say that you are looking quite marmoreal, my dear Katherine."

The invalid smiled. "An accurate description of a consumptive," said Katherine, holding her marble-white arms in a Grecian pose. "Actually it surprises me that blood still flows through these veins." She dropped her arms and covered them with her shawl.

"I was hoping to have something to read to you today. Instead, I've been working against deadlines for my weekly novel reviews. All for that damn journal. After that, I'm too exhausted and my head too full of other voices competing with my own."

"How well I understand," said Virginia. "Just yesterday, in the middle of a sentence, I had to put down my pen, close the blinds, and retire before the spits of fire assaulting my brain sparked a headache."

I don't think you do, thought Katherine resentfully, at least your headaches are from writing books.

Virginia brought out a packet of the Belgian cigarettes that Katherine liked so much. She lit one for Katherine and then one for herself.

"I've heard talk that you are considering San Remo for the winter?"

"Ah, our dear friend Ottoline is never one to keep a secret, is she?"

"She didn't know whether Jack was going with you."

"No. He won't trust anyone to carry on with *The Athenaeum* in his absence. You know from having your own printing press the urgency of deadlines. I don't know how it is for your Leonard, but Jack's life *is* his literary magazine. And nearly mine, too, what with the editorial revisions and my weekly book review column." She looked over at her crowded desk. "Look at that stack of books waiting for me to plough through. By the time I've read two or three and written their reviews the week is over and I have to start reading again for next week's edition."

"Your reviews are very popular. Everyone is discussing them, including me."

"That's what keeps me doing it. Unable to write any of my own stories at least someone is reading my reviews. I even had a letter from your colleague Lytton complimenting my work, and in the past, as you well know, he has not been an admirer."

Though Lytton Strachey had encouraged Virginia to introduce Katherine to him because he found her intriguing, she'd heard through the gossipmongers of the Bloomsbury circle that he had also described her as having *an ugly impassive mask of a face—cut in wood, with brown hair and brown eyes very far apart—and a sharp and slightly vulgarly-fanciful intellect sitting behind it.*

Katherine had been hurt by such vicious gossip.

"Have you read Lytton's *Eminent Victorians* yet?" asked Virginia. "It's caused quite a stir among those who wish to keep Florence Nightingale on a pedestal. He has brought her back to life in a way never before accomplished in a biography."

"I haven't read it but I hope Jack will give me a chance to review it. Unfortunately too often he gives the books I want to review to others on his staff, and leaves me with the "women stories," some of which should never have been published. He doesn't seem to realize I am just as capable of reviewing a male writer."

"I would certainly have been disappointed if anyone other than you had reviewed *Kew Gardens*. Male or female. Only you understood exactly what I was trying to do."

"I just wrote the truth, Virginia. *Kew Gardens* is your best work. It was a pleasure to review. So modern. There is nothing out there to compare to it. Your writing came alive—" Katherine muffles her cough with her hankie.

"You know the seeds of that story came from our walks in the garden when you visited us at Asheham and you spoke of the need in our writing to break from the mold. I remember telling you I wasn't up to such boldness." She sighed. "It took those late nights I spent hand-setting *Prelude* onto our printing press to fully understand how modern your work is."

"*Prelude* would never have seen the light of day if you and Leonard hadn't included me in one of your first publications on Hogarth Press along with T.S. Eliot's *Poems*."

"That's true but we should have sold all of the three hundred copies we printed of *Prelude*," said Virginia. "Your ability to create a satisfying reading experience in a small space takes a particular skill, and you have it all: the visual, the conversational and the thing unsaid." She laughed. "Damn it, Katherine. Why aren't I the only woman who knows how to write."

Katherine's marmoreal cheeks flushed. She too was very proud of *Prelude* but to hear Virginia speak of it in such glowing terms was unexpected. Virginia was not known to gush over someone else's writings.

Virginia added, "Hogarth Press just doesn't have the staff or for that matter the desire to promote what we print. But at least books like yours and Eliot's, which would otherwise go unpublished, have a chance to be at least read by a few discriminating readers.

"My first novel would never have been published if it weren't for my half-brother's Duckworth Press. He's also going to publish *Night and Day*, but after that I'm only going to publish on Hogarth Press. It's so much easier when only Leonard has to edit and approve of my books before publication. It's insufferable when anyone else makes those editorial decisions. I'm too close to my work to have it torn to shreds."

Silence filled the room, not uncomfortable, just thoughtful as the two women considered their own hurdles as writers and the friendship it had fostered between them.

"You're not going by yourself to San Remo, are you?" asked Virginia.

"No, though I would if I was well. You never know what adventures you might fall into when you travel on your own. That's when I get my best material."

"Aren't you ever afraid?"

"Not so much. It's fun. Even during the war I traveled by train into the War Zone because I thought I was in love with a Frenchman. It took only four days to realize I made a mistake before I hurried back to Jack, a far more sensitive lover. Later I wrote about those adventures in *The Indiscreet Journey*."

Virginia picked up Katherine's doll Rib off the floor and adjusted his silk kimono. Katherine knew how easily her friend was embarrassed by sexual indiscretions, but she liked to tease her.

Virginia put down Rib and looked up at Katherine. "I have never had the opportunity to travel alone. My parents would have never allowed it and now it's the same with Leonard. Even today he tried to prevent me from coming to London on my own without an argument. It made me late and I wasn't able to pick the bouquet of flowers I'd promised you from our garden. I *am* so sorry."

Katherine smiled. "You needn't ever apologize to me, Virginia. I'm just glad he let you come."

"Leonard hopes you will visit us again soon at Asheham when you are feeling better. No one entertains him as well as you do with your witty mimicries. He is very concerned about you and will be displeased when I tell him Jack is not escorting you to Italy."

"What? No, no. You misunderstood me. Of course Jack is coming, at least for the first week or so. After I'm settled, he'll return to London but Ida will stay with me."

"Well that's a relief. But why can't Jack stay longer?"

"I wouldn't want him to really. He's flourishing at *The Athenaeum*. We'd both be miserable if he stopped because of my illness. Besides, I need solitude to write and I'm hoping to use my time in St. Remy to get back to writing my own stories instead of reviewing other authors."

"How fortunate you are to have Ida to take care of all the details of running a home, like Leonard does for me. Where would we be without their help."

Just at that moment, as if she was listening at the door, LM entered with the tea service. She poured tea in their cups, passed the cream, sugar, and biscuits, and left without a word spoken, but the two writers watched her every gesture.

Katherine looked down at Virginia's satchel on the floor. "Have you brought something to read today?"

"Yes, it's the last chapter of *Night and Day*," said Virginia with a satisfied smile. "I wanted you to hear it before Leonard. Sometimes he doesn't understand what I'm doing. And being my second novel I'm very sensitive—"

"Two novels! How I envy you, Virginia," said Katherine. "My notebooks are filled with outlines and vignettes but I'll never be able to piece them together into a full novel."

"Maybe you will on the Italian countryside. You've told me how well you work when surrounded by nature."

"It's not where I write that stops me, it's just not believing that I will ever have enough time to complete a novel. Short stories can be written between illnesses."

Tears welled in Katherine's eyes and she brushed them away. It pained Virginia to have this brief glimpse into Katherine's heart, and she walked over to the window to let her friend compose herself.

When she sat down again, Katherine's tears were gone and there was a smile on her face.

"I would miss my city walks in London where I get many of my ideas. I'd be there now if Leonard didn't insist on us living in Sussex."

Katherine said, "I haven't been able to write anything since *Prelude*. I was so excited when I finished it but then soon after I felt such a frightening letdown. Did you experience something similar when you finished *Voyage Out*?"

Ottoline had told Katherine about Virginia's mental breakdown after completing *Voyage Out*, but she wanted to hear about it from Virginia. Virginia's silence told her not to prod and instead they turned to more comfortable subjects; the challenges they faced as women writers and what first brought them together, their mutual desire to write stream-of-consciousness narrations.

"My characters don't breathe as deeply as yours do," said Katherine. "Their feelings are briefly stated and sometimes misunderstood by the reader."

"I don't agree with you. You have a special talent for economy of words that cut straight to the truth—as clear as glass—refined... even spiritual. My characters immerse themselves into their dense landscapes, their houses, their benches, before they can speak."

"Not so with *Kew Gardens*. You discovered a new way of writing in that story that is what I try to achieve in my own work. That brief moment when the secret life is half revealed; then a wind blows again and covers it over with leaves and flowers. It's so terribly authentic. So real."

Virginia leaned forward in her chair putting down her teacup. "Then you are going to love the passages I'm going to read today."

"While you read I am going to lay back on the sofa but I'll be listening."

"Are you sure you're not too tired?" Virginia looked so disappointed, Katherine raised herself back up again.

Virginia reached into her satchel for her manuscript and a second packet of Belgian cigarettes and offered one to Katherine. She then picked up her manuscript and read through the last chapter finishing with:

> *Moments, fragments, a second of vision, and then the flying waters, the winds dissipating and dissolving; then, too, the recollection from chaos, the return of security, the earth firm, superb and brilliant in the sun.*

Katherine had been listening, but now hesitated saying anything, not wanting to offend her friend but Virginia kept asking for her opinion.

"If you're speaking of the end of the war as the return of security I don't think it's all that simple. We cannot forget what happened. Too many sacrificed their lives for us. Our world, as we once knew it, will never be the same. I personally will never forget the loss of my brother Leslie. The war has changed all of us in ways we don't yet realize."

"You don't like that final passage. Is that what you're saying?"

"My review will have to wait until I've read your book from beginning to end. Certainly the words spoken flow beautifully, as always, you are a master of your craft, Virginia. Just be careful of being too old-fashioned."

"Old-fashioned? I've never thought of my writing as old-fashioned. It's true that this novel is a tribute to all my favorite writers who came before me, but I don't think of them as old-fashioned."

"Our lives were changed forever by the war. What was written before the war is from another time. That's what I mean by old-fashion."

LM came in to take the tea tray and seeing the full ashtray, held it at arm's length, and shaking her head dumped it in the waste basket.

"It's time for your medicine," she said to Katherine, holding a spoonful of Dr. Sorapure's cough syrup in front of her face.

The invalid opened her mouth and swallowed, grateful for Ida's thoughtfulness, as if she knew it would soothe her parched throat after talking at length with Virginia.

"Mrs. Woolf, I asked you not to tire out my patient too much. The two of you haven't stopped talking since you got here. I can hear your laughter downstairs," said Ida. She placed the bottle back on the bureau and backed out of the room.

"Why does she leave the room backward?" asked Virginia.

"I don't actually know," said Katherine. "Ida is a most intriguing character. That's why I like having her around. Many of her gestures are unexplainable and I often use them in my stories though she doesn't recognize herself unless I point it out. Shall we say, she is yet to know her own true identity." Her lips turned up. "Perhaps because she spends too much time with me."

"How interesting that you mention identity. That's my concern with the main character in *Night and Day*," said Virginia. "I feel Katharine's true character is blocked by a shadow and I can't get a clear view of her."

"Katharine?"

"Not you, of course. There's no connection. I just like the name and I spelled it with an 'a'. If anyone, she's like my sister Vanessa."

"That's too bad! I would very much like you to write me into one of your stories. As to your problem with Kath-a-rine, I suggest you merge her true character with her shadow rather than be blocked by it."

Virginia took a long draw from her cigarette. "Why yes, of course. Why didn't I think of that? Though six years behind me in age, you understand the art of writing so well. It distresses me that there will be no one I can talk to with such ease until you return from Italy."

"Let's not talk about me leaving if it distresses you."

Virginia lit another cigarette for Katherine.

"Murry and I have lately discussed having a baby," said Katherine abruptly. "And if so, perhaps we'll lease a cottage in Sussex, perhaps near Asheham. Then you and I can walk together in the park with our children and later our grandchildren."

Virginia got up and opened the window to air the room of their cigarette smoke and impulsively threw her own cigarette out the window.

"Can't you see us taking walks in the park with our children skipping by our sides? What do you want first, a boy or a girl?"

"I don't think I want either," said Virginia. "A child? Is that wise in your condition?"

Katherine felt a flash of anger. "Why? Don't you believe I will be cured? Please, Virginia. I need you to believe that I will have all that I want, that I will again jump in the air, dance and run through the woods—" Katherine's cough prevented her from continuing.

Virginia handed her a glass of water. "I'm sorry. I shouldn't have said that. It's just I'm unaccustomed to anyone speaking so transparently about very intimate subjects that I don't even talk about with Leonard. But believe me when I tell you that we will rival each other for years to come. You must find a cure or who will be my competition? And I must have competition."

Katherine reached for Virginia's hand and they held each other's gaze until Virginia looked down at her watch. "Oh dear, look how late it is. I must go. Leonard is meeting me at Waterloo Station so we can take the train home together."

"You are a very fortunate woman to have Leonard."

"Yes. He is a good man." Virginia stood up. "But so is Jack, isn't he." Without expecting an answer, she said, "You needn't show me out. Next week as usual?"

"Yes, do come. It does me good to talk to you. We have the same job, Virginia, you and I, and it's really very curious and thrilling that we should both, quite apart from each other, be after so very nearly the same thing. We are, you know; there's no denying it."

After Virginia left, Katherine managed to limp with her cane over to the window. Virginia's visit had exhausted her. She gripped the heavy, plush curtain for support as she watched her friend depart.

Her eyes became Virginia's as she stepped onto the street. She felt her standing up very straight and reaching out her arm to hail a taxi. Katherine's mind flowed into the taxi and watched Virginia remove her hat, pin back loose strands of hair, and reach into her purse for a handkerchief to wipe away a few stray tears. Katherine hadn't expected her character to do that.

She felt Virginia's need to reach the train station and find Leonard and have him encircle her in his arms, make her feel safe and take her home.

Katherine felt her own tears fall down her cheek as she whispered Keats's words: *we cannot be created for this sort of suffering.*

LONDON — 1912

John "Jack" Middleton Murry

There was a child once.
He came to play in my garden;
He was quite pale and silent.
Only when he smiled I knew everything about him,
I knew what he had in his pockets,
And I knew the feel of his hands in my hands
And the most intimate tones of his voice.
I led him down each secret path,
Showing him the hiding-place of all my treasures.
I let him play with them, every one,
I put my singing thoughts in a little silver cage
And gave them to him to keep...

THERE WAS A CHILD ONCE—KM

S HE CHOSE A dove-grey evening gown, pinned a single Christmas rose to its bodice, wrapped a red silk turban over her short-cut bob and spit on her bangs to hold them down. Pleased with the results, she admired her reflection. Quite suitable, she thought, for a twenty-three-year-old author who has just published, *In a German Pension*, her first collection of short stories that are now the talk of London Town.

As if she was practicing a Bowden lesson in elocution, she repeated with accentuated lips what the top reviewer had said: *acute insight— unquenchable humor—realistic skill.* Yes, that's me, she thought, and painted her lips bright red.

How odd to now think of Mr. Bowden who she hadn't seen for three years though they were still legally married. He had believed in her writing and would be proud to know how well she was doing and that he hadn't been wrong to encourage her writing career.

It was a chilly night and it wouldn't do to catch another cold so she put on her only coat though it was frayed at the collar and had a few moth holes.

Arriving at the party late, she left her coat with the maid and stepped into the dimly lit salon as if she was an actress making her entrance onto the stage.

Walter Lionel George, her host and writer for *Harper's Magazine*, was the first to pull her over. He pointed across the room at a young man, who could be just a boy if he wasn't so smartly dressed in a waistcoat tweed suit. He was casually leaning against the fireplace mantel as if he was alone in his own parlor tamping down tobacco into his pipe to have a smoke.

W.L. whispered in her ear, "That's John Middleton Murry."

Her heart skipped. He had accepted her short story for his new journal *Rhythm*, but they hadn't met, and she hadn't known how good looking he was.

"Don't get too ruffled," whispered W.L., "but he came tonight just to meet you."

W.L. made the introductions and hurried off to his other guests.

Many men towered over Katherine and she hated having to look up at them when she felt she was their equal. That wasn't a problem with Mr. Murry. He wasn't much taller than her.

How handsome! she thought again, gazing into eyes that were like two pale green pools shaded under thick black lashes and heavy brows. Unconsciously, he raked his hand through thick, wavy black hair, pushing back a few renegade strands that had fallen onto his wide forehead.

"Miss Mansfield, what a pleasure. I was hoping to see you tonight so I could tell you in person how impressed I was by *The Woman at the Store*. I don't know of any other short story that so honestly exposes the revulsion of common life as you have. I do hope you'll submit more stories like it to *Rhythm*."

"Thank you, Mr. Murry. It's always encouraging when someone recognizes what I'm trying to accomplish with my stories."

He was just answering her question as to why his magazine's name was *Rhythm* when a few other guests joined them and their conversation turned to Anton Chekhov. Katherine was an expert on the Russian writer and they wanted to ask her opinion of George Calderon's translation of *The Cherry Orchard* playing at the Aldwych Theatre.

Katherine said she had not had the time to see it, when the truth was she couldn't afford the expensive ticket, but she went on to explain the social significance of the play and Chekhov's brilliance as a writer. Murry's eyes stayed on her as he listened attentively. Known for his intellectual expertise she was surprised he didn't contribute to the discussion. Hadn't he read Chekhov? she wondered. How could anyone not have read Chekhov?

At the end of the evening, he approached her as she was waiting for her coat in the entry hall. "I'm sorry we were interrupted by your friends before I could tell you how much your original style matches my editorial mission to seek out the strong things of life—both in its purity and brutality as you portrayed in *The Woman at the Store*."

She was flattered but wanting to appear as if she had compliments like his every day, she said, "Then you must come to tea someday so that we can talk further about our mutual interests."

"I would like that very much. How do I contact you?"

The maid approached with Katherine's frayed coat, and without answering him, she draped it over her arm and hurried out the door. There was no way she would ruin his admiration by putting on a pauper's coat.

A week later, realizing she hadn't given him her address, she asked W.L. But before she could send Murry an invitation to tea, she caught a cold that worsened into a severe lung inflammation. It made it painful to breathe and she kept to her bed. It was her second case of pleurisy and her pulmonary doctor insisted she leave London immediately for a warmer climate. Not one to take a doctor's advice, she took the train to Brussels to stay with her girlfriend rather than stay alone in a foreign hotel room in the South.

In early February, her lungs had healed and she returned to London's literary salons where she was warmly welcomed back. One evening, John Murry's name came up in a heated discussion centered on the radical content of his new journal *Rhythm*. The Modern writers like D.H. Lawrence, and the Fauve painters, like Matissse, were being published by the young renegade editor and his magazine had created quite a stir in literary circles.

Katherine sent him a note asking him to tea at 69 Clovelly Mansions, her London flat on Gray's Inn Road.

SHE FORGAVE HIM for being late, noticing that, like herself, he didn't wear a watch though she was usually on time without one. When she brought him into her sitting room he looked around awkwardly, "Where shall I sit, Miss Mansfield?"

"As you like."

There was a small wooden chair by her writing table, a round rattan basket chair, and many large floor cushions she had arranged around the straw matted floor like a Fauve painting, a scene as brilliant and abstract as she saw herself in it.

She went into the kitchen and returned with a tray laden with a teapot, bowls, brown bread, butter and honey. Recently influenced by Orientalism, the rage in Paris after Sergei Diaghilev's production with the Ballets Russes, she used bowls for teacups and dressed like an Oriental where before she had worn dark gypsy costumes. Tonight she had chosen a purple kimono that complemented the glazed bowls and cushions.

As she imagined herself a geisha girl, she folded her legs under her and sat up very straight. Placing a cigarette between her lips, she leaned toward her guest for a light, which was a stretch because he had chosen to sit in her sunken basket chair and had trouble sitting upright. He lit her cigarette and then his pipe.

She noticed that his pale green eyes, which were even more attractive in the daylight, were avoiding her. A disappointment seeing the amount of time she'd spent getting ready for his visit.

The tea brewed. The rush of London traffic outside her window seemed louder than usual or was it just so quiet in her flat.

He is decidedly a very serious, quiet man, she thought, I will have to take the lead or we won't talk at all.

"I'm told you graduated from Oxford," she said out loud.

"That's not exactly true," he said, clearing his throat and moving forward on to the edge of the awkward chair. "You see, I haven't taken my final exams."

"Why not?"

"It's rather complicated."

"Good. I like to listen to people tell their complicated stories."

"All right, but don't hesitate to stop me if you get bored."

"I doubt anything you say is boring, Jack," she said flirtatiously.

His pale cheeks turned pink.

"Oh, sorry," said Katherine. "Isn't it all right if I call you by your nickname like your friends do?"

"Certainly," he pressed out his trouser legs, "I'm just not used to a woman being so direct."

"Don't worry," she half smiled, "I don't bite. Please continue.

"I took a leave from Oxford to live in Paris. Since my return, I've been unable to study the works of Aristotle and Plato with any enthusiasm. They've lost their importance—at least from my point of view. And now with *Rhythm* requiring my constant attention I have neither the time nor the inclination to work toward my degree. I know this sounds quite foolish but I've quite the mind to pack it in."

"To the contrary, I think it sounds quite necessary."

"You do?" he said, surprised. "Why do you say that, Miss—Katherine?"

"You simply have more important things to do than spend your days in a stuffy library. How could Oxford compare with a vibrant life in Paris or even here in London? And how much more fulfilling to create your own literary magazine than to read Plato who died a long time ago."

"I wish my father understood as well as you seem to," said Jack. "He made, shall we say, sacrifices, and now demands a return for his investment. He planned on me following him into civil service and strongly objects to my career as an editor. In his view, *Rhythm* is a waste of my time and his money."

"Your father sounds like a tyrant," said Katherine, thinking of her own father who didn't want her to be a writer. She handed him a black lacquered ashtray just before he dropped the amber ashes from his pipe on his pant leg or worse her silk pillows.

She poured the tea and passed him a bowl. "But c'mon. Tell me the truth. Besides reading Plato you must enjoy the scandalous Oxford drinking societies and have acquired medals by playing cricket, etc. Isn't that what you all do at Oxford?"

"That's not the kind of life I've had there. You see," he hesitated, shifting in the chair, "I'm a déclassé student."

"Déclassé? Good god, what does that mean?"

"I'm on scholarship. The other students have always snubbed me. Never invited me to their parties. Even in sports, I've been left out."

"How little-minded they are. That's even more reason to not go back. Why don't you move to London?"

"London! I can't afford to live here. My scholarship barely pays for my room and board at Oxford and I have no other source of income other than what my father doles out at Christmas."

"I see. So this is where it gets complicated. You're worried about money. But I'm as déclassé as you are but somehow I manage to get by in London. Why can't you?"

"You? Hardly. You're too formidable to be déclassé." When he smiled it was a lopsided smile that she found charming.

She explained that as a colonialist from New Zealand she too was excluded from the British upper classes and only was accepted at the literary salons because of her entertaining personality and intellectual wit. She thought to also tell him that she too received a meager allowance from her father but she preferred his impression of her as a successful independent woman.

"The only way I can possibly succeed is to go back, finish my degree and make my father proud. But I don't expect you to understand. I'm sure you didn't feel any pressure from your parents to be educated at Oxford."

Katherine laughed. "Need I remind you that women aren't allowed to study at Oxford? There are only a few universities that will accept us."

"Yes, but my point is that you haven't had to waste valuable time getting a degree just to please your parents. Instead you worked on your own to become a writer and are now published by A. R. Orage who publishes only the best of modern writers. My 'little' magazine will never come close to *The New Age*'s distinguished readership. In fact, I was wondering why you submitted *Woman in the Store* to me instead of Orage."

"He didn't like it." She said simply. "He prefers my more satirical and less sympathetic stories."

"Well then, he's losing his touch and it's his loss and my gain."

She felt very flattered by this young man with the tempting mouth that she so wanted to kiss. As if he was reading her thoughts he leaned toward her, but how disappointing that he only asked for more tea as she had so much more to offer.

She poured and then sliced brown bread from the local bakery and covered it with butter and honey before handing it to him on a plate.

She got up to wash her sticky fingers in the kitchen sink and stopping by the mirror colored her lips and pinched her cheeks.

When she returned, he was leaning against the mantelpiece cupping her grinning brass Buddha in his hand. The light from the two small windows lit his finely chiseled face, a face as thin as the Buddha's was round. She imagined him cupping her face rather than the Buddha's and sensed a slight thrill run up her spine that she found pleasurable.

They both sat down again but now he joined her on the cushions. "I see you've taken a liking to my Buddha," she said.

He hadn't realized he was still holding it. "It's quite unique. Where is it from?"

"I brought it with me when I left New Zealand. I could only bring in my trunk a few special things and he is one of them."

Jack propped up a few cushions behind him, leaned back and crossed his legs, swinging the right leg. Something her brother Leslie might do.

He also had the same turned-down pout of Leslie's when he would sit at the family dining table and listen to his father tell him he couldn't have a piece of cake until he finished eating all his vegetables.

"Shall I tell you what I think you should do?" she asked, wanting to give this man-child the cake.

"Why yes. Please do," he said, sitting up on his elbows.

"Risk! Risk anything! Don't give a damn for the opinions of others, even your father. Act for yourself, even if at that moment it's the hardest thing you've ever done. Don't remain another day at Oxford. Come to London. *Rhythm* has earned respect on Fleet Street. You'll get work, I'm certain of it."

She hadn't meant to get up on her pulpit but it really angered her when people didn't do what they wanted to do, didn't do what they were capable of doing.

"I bloody hell wish I had your confidence. Do you really think *Rhythm* could be successful?"

"I don't see why not. You already have a stellar reputation as its editor. Don't let anyone stop you from doing what you want to do, especially yourself."

She stood up. "Which reminds me. I have work to do." She looked over at the writing table neatly stacked with her notebooks and handed him the last piece of honeyed bread while showing him to the door. "Shall we meet again next week?"

"Sure," he said, stumbling while trying to put on his shoes. With her hand on the doorknob, she hoped for a kiss good night. When he didn't respond, she shooed him out of the house like a badly behaved cat.

MURRY RANG UP a few days later. His Oxford friend, Frederick Goodyear had read and admired her *New Age* stories and wanted to meet her. How would it be if the three of them had dinner? They could dine cheaply at the Dieppe for one shilling, fifteen pence each.

She said yes, but wanted to have tea with him before they joined Goodyear. She hadn't been sure that she would hear from him again, but something had been brewing in her mind if she did, and she keenly wanted to share her idea with him.

When she opened the door, she expected him to notice how smashing she looked in a dark blue serge suit that she'd chosen for their first date. Instead, the first thing he said was, "I'm employed!" He pulled a check out of his pocket to show her. "A five pound advance! I'm buying dinner tonight."

"That's wonderful, Jack. Come inside while I put on my hat and coat."

She led him into the entryway and, while she pinned a tiny bouquet of gay flowers onto her straw hat he told her about his new job as a reviewer for the *Westminster Gazette*, a small weekly paper that published intellectual and literary reviews, sketches and short stories.

Good, she thought. Now I can put forward my plan and show him the flat.

He followed her down the hall into the kitchen, which had a gas-stove, a table, two chairs, and a wide window that opened out from the fourth floor onto chimney-potted rooftops.

After admiring the view, he followed her to the next room.

Like the sitting room, its wallpapered walls were a soft brown. It was sparsely furnished with a grand piano and a divan. Earlier, she had placed fresh lavender on the fireplace grate, its sweet fragrance filled the room.

A giant seashell lay on a straw mat, next to a green-bronze lizard bathing in a flat oval bowl, its long, tapered tail shimmering underwater. When he asked about it, she said, "It's a Pawa shell. Another special remembrance I brought with me from New Zealand." She turned the shell on its side to show him its iridescent colors.

In a short narrow hallway where they could barely fit without touching, she pointed to the bathroom. Across from it was a tiny bedroom—almost a cubicle—just large enough for a camp bed and cupboard. "This is my room," she said.

Back at the entryway, Jack said, "Isn't this flat awfully expensive with so many rooms?"

"Yes, fifty-two pounds a year. But isn't it better to spend money on your home and go short on other things? Better be hungry than miserable. No?"

"Well I don't know if I'd agree with you. I think I'd rather have food and live in a one-room flat.

AT THE ISOLA BELLA TEAROOM, Katherine and Jack sat with their backs to the street window, alone except for one female server.

"Now," Katherine said, after they ordered, "tell me how you got a job in London so quickly."

"When my Oxford mentor realized how determined I was to forego my exams, he gave me an introduction to *Westminster Gazette*'s editor J.A. Spender. Spender offered me freelance work as a reviewer of English and German writings. Of course it's only temporary until *Rhythm* has enough subscribers and I can work on it exclusively."

"Let me look at that check again." She turned it every which way and handed it back. "It's real." She could do with a check of that amount. Ever since Orage dropped her, no one was buying any of her stories and she dreaded asking LM for another loan.

"I think in some way you are responsible," he said.

"Me?"

"Yes. If you hadn't told me to take risks and not give a damn what people think—why I'd still be stuck at the crossroads not knowing which road to take. That's why I'm buying you dinner tonight."

"I was glad to help," she said, brushing her gloved hand over his.

"Listen, Katherine, I know this is rather forward, but I wanted to know if you would like to help me with *Rhythm*?

"Right now it's only a quarterly paper so there wouldn't be much for you to do." The more he talked about the mission behind his magazine the more animated he became. She was beginning to wonder if it was the only thing that excited him as he certainly didn't seem interested in her except as a writer for his magazine.

Finally he finished by saying, "I can't pay you very much but I thought you might start by reviewing Victor Neuburg's *The Triumph of Pan*. It's quite controversial and I'd like to have a review for our summer issue." He sneered. "That's if Orage won't mind me hiring out his best author. He has a reputation for being rather proprietary."

Katherine removed her gloves, reached into her bag for cigarettes and handed him one. They sat back in their chairs blowing rings of smoke into the air. "I don't answer to Orage," she said.

As she took draws from her cigarette she considered his offer. She believed in his mission *to seek out the strong things of life*. It was a noble, modern vision. One that she could wholeheartedly contribute to and if Orage didn't want to publish her, then she had a home with *Rhythm*.

And if she was able to see through her earlier plan, Jack would have a home too and she could worry less about her own money problems.

"When do I start?" she said, snuffing out her cigarette next to his in the ashtray.

"I was hoping you'd say that," he said with his lopsided smile.

FREDERICK GOODYEAR was a robust man with thick curly hair like Jack, but a darker complexion, a foot taller and three years Jack's senior. He was also sophisticated, light-hearted and confident and Katherine took a liking toward him when his first words to Jack were, "Where did you meet this ravishing woman?"

After a most animated dinner, with their literary discussions heard above the other customers in the crowded Dieppe restaurant, they stood around outside. It was a lovely spring evening and nobody wanted to go home.

Katherine suggested walking to Piccadilly Circus. Freddie thought it an excellent idea, and taking Katherine's arm in his, off they went with Jack following behind.

After chasing each other around the fountain, they collapsed on a bench to enjoy the mild air.

"It's going to be difficult finding a room in London for ten shillings a week," said Jack, "but that's all I can afford on my new salary."

Katherine saw her opportunity and leaped up. "I have a marvelous idea."

"Yes, go on," said Jack and Freddie together.

"You can rent a room from me. I'll have to exchange the piano for a bed but I hardly ever play it anymore. We can share the kitchen and the bathroom. And I won't charge you ten shillings. Would eight be acceptable? It's nicer than anything you'll find in London for ten."

Jack stared at her in disbelief, which was becoming a habit of his, but Freddie spoke up at once and said, "Don't just sit there like a fool, Jack. Say yes or at least nod your head so Katherine knows you accept her generous offer." Jack continued to stare at her.

"Well I'll leave you two to sort this out," said Freddie. "May I say, Katherine, it has been a most wonderful evening and I hope to see you again quite soon." He kissed her on the cheek, shook Jack's hand, and called out good night as he strolled away.

When he was gone, Jack said, "Are you really serious—about the room?"

"Of course I am."

"Then I should like it very much."

"Go—ood!" she said, trying to imitate a flute. "When?"

"Well I don't know. What do you think?"

"I think next Monday—at teatime. Do you like eggs?"

Before he could answer, she said, "Auf wiedersehen," and happily ran off across the Circus waving back to him with her straw hat. Her plan to rent a room to Jack had gone off splendidly and now with the sale of the piano and his rent she could chip away at her mounting debts.

ON THE AGREED UPON DATE—April 11—Jack arrived at her doorstep with two battered suitcases. Katherine was dressed to go out and quickly showed him his room that was much larger without the piano. LM had helped her move in the bed and an empty cupboard for his books and clothes. By the window, Katherine had covered a found table with a bright blue tablecloth.

She handed Jack a ring with two keys and said, "I have an appointment. The cupboard is stocked with provisions so you'll find everything there you need. I like to cook but never seem to have the time. Good-bye for now."

The following morning Katherine set the table with a plate of brown bread, butter and honey, and an egg in an eggcup. She scribbled a note on a half-sheet of notepaper: "This is your egg. You must boil it. KM." She set the note between the egg and the eggcup. Counting out the coins she'd borrowed from dependable LM, she dropped a few shillings in an empty sugar bowl and covered it with a second note that read: "Use for supplies when needed."

On her way out to her appointment with Orage, she called out, "The flat is yours for the day. You'll find breakfast in the kitchen."

It didn't take long for the two flatmates to establish a routine. They went out separately during the day or worked in their rooms. Jack was writing reviews for *Westminster Gazette* and Katherine was writing short stories and poems to be published in Rhythm's next quarterly issue in June. Late at night, their work for the day finished, Katherine would put on her kimono, Jack his lounging robe, and they would sip bowls of tea on her sitting room cushions. They would discuss their plans for *Rhythm*, deciding on the contents for its summer issue and their hopes to turn it into a monthly magazine.

To their amusement, before retiring, they'd shake hands and say:

"Good night, Mansfield!"

"Good night, Murry!"

THE PLEURISY SHE'D HAD earlier in the year came back. But this time she stayed home.

Jack tried to be useful, but he wasn't much help. He had a terrible fear of consumption, so anyone, even with a chest cold, made him cringe and she couldn't convince him that pleurisy wasn't contagious.

LM came to make hot broths, cool Katherine's brow with damp wash-cloths, and kept vigil through the nights Katherine was feverish and suffering from stabbing chest pains. But in a few weeks, she was on the mend again and LM stopped her nurse Florence Nightingale visits.

In spite of the hard work Jack put into writing reviews for the *West-minster Gazette*, they were seldom accepted. He barely made a pound in the first two weeks and Katherine had to be prudent with the hundred-pound annual allowance from her father or she'd go deeper into debt. To make ends meet, they lived frugally on homemade soup or shared a greasy meat-pie from the corner shop. They'd kill the oily taste in their mouths at the local pub, where the owner had taken a liking to them. After they paid for two beers, she always insisted to stand them another round.

On one of those evenings at the pub, Jack said, "I never told you this but my job at *Westminster Gazette* was offered on one condition. I had to promise to take my finals at Oxford. I've been putting it off because you were sick and we've been so busy with *Rhythm*'s next issue but now I think I should take those exams. I'll only be gone a few months."

"Why didn't you tell me this before?"

"I didn't think it was important."

"Well it is important that we are honest, not only in print, but between ourselves." They smoked their cigarettes in silence until Katherine put hers out and said, "I'll go with you."

"Really? You'd go with me to Oxford and stay until I finished?"

"Why not?" She smiled. "It's not that far away and I've never been to Oxford. We can save expenses by sharing a room."

"Share a room." He laughed. "I don't know what planet you live on, my dear Katherine, but we won't be allowed to share a room. Not at Oxford or anywhere else. I'll have to stay on campus and we'll get you a room in the village."

Women were not allowed in the Oxford library so Jack studied for his exams in her boarding house parlor. He didn't graduate at the top of his class but he made Seconds and that qualified him to graduate and keep his job at the Gazette.

On their way back to London, they stopped at his parents' house to give them the good news. Katherine had looked forward to meeting them. Since her breakup with the Trowell family, she had never found another family where she could hang her hat on the back door, and was sorely disappointed when they were offish toward her.

Jack explained that his parents didn't think it was proper to be traveling with a single woman and they'd have to leave. In their hurry, he forgot to give his diploma to his father. Later, he posted it from London, hoping his father wouldn't be too upset when he saw the less than average marks.

Upon their return, he and Katherine celebrated his graduation at their local pub. After several drinks, they returned to their flat. Jack propped his head up against a pillow and watched her light several candles around the room while he puffed on his pipe. She was reminded of the first day he came to her flat and took the same position on the floor with his legs crossed over.

It also reminded her that they'd been together for several months and he hadn't made any attempt to kiss her or even take her hand when they went walking. She was used to men desiring her and had started to wonder if he might be homosexual. She'd prefer that to him finding her undesirable.

She shouted out her next thought, "Why not make me your mistress?"

He was offended. "Katherine, that's not funny. My high regard for you would never allow me to do such a thing. Aren't you happy with the way things are, us being the best of friends? I certainly am."

"No, I'm certainly not. Actually, I'm miserable." She sat across from him. "Is it because I'm still married to George Bowden? Is that what stops you? Or are you afraid I'll become another Marguerite?"

Marguerite was a prostitute Jack had met in Paris. They became lovers and, misunderstanding his intentions, she asked him to marry her. Afraid to tell her that he didn't love her, he packed his bags when she wasn't home and returned to London. He'd felt terribly guilty about abandoning her but had made no attempt to contact her.

He cupped Katherine's face with his hands. "You mean much more to me than Marguerite ever did. I just think we should leave things the way they are. Why rock the boat?"

Without a word, she went to her bedroom and closed the door.

The next morning she wouldn't talk to him and, for several nights, she stayed at LM's house. Jack must've missed her because when she came home for a change of clothes, he reached for her before she had taken off her hat and pressed her against the wall, kissing her.

They laughed as they fell down onto the pillows, rolling over each other across the floor. Every time they stopped rolling they kissed and then they would roll again, until their childish game turned into desire and their childish laughter became cries of pleasure.

Later Katherine wrote in her notebook:

> *And there we kissed and passionately*
> *We clung together—all the past*
> *Blotted from out my memory*
> *I knew I had found love at last.*

A FEW EVENINGS LATER they were at the kitchen table having their evening soup and bread when Katherine said, "Jack! Let's go to Paris."

"Paris?"

"Yes, let's go to Paris?"

"How can we possibly afford to do that?"

She told him about her annual allowance, seeing no reason to hide it from him now that they were officially a couple. "And surely there will be money coming in now that Rhythm is a monthly magazine. Oh Jack I'm so tired of being frugal."

"All right, if you think we can afford it, let's go." He kissed her. "We'll pretend it's our honeymoon."

San Remo, Italy

Love! Love! You pity me so!
Chide me, scold me—cry,
"Submit—submit! You must not fight!"
What may I do, then? Die?
But, oh my horror of quiet beds!
How can I longer stay!
"One to be ready,
Two to be steady,
Three to be off and away!"

COVERING WINGS—KM

KATHERINE STUDIED THE CONTENTS of the well-worn traveling trunk to be sure LM hadn't forgotten anything on the packing list for the long "rest cure" in San Remo, Italy. She smiled as she imagined LM's anxious conversation with herself as she fastidiously handled Katherine's possessions as if they were her own and tried not to break anything though she often did.

I must be kinder to Jones, she thought. My dutiful, loyal companion who has never stopped believing in my full recovery. And Jack? I don't know what he really believes other than that I have to go away. It is much easier for him to dream of our future when he doesn't have to hear me coughing.

She saw her Japanese doll, Ribni, peeking out from between the folds of her black Spanish shawl in the trunk and picked him up. "No, Rib, you're not coming." She propped him up on the writing table. "I want you to be here to greet Jack when he returns in a few weeks. He'll be pleased to see I let you stay behind to keep him company while I'm away."

Hearing Jack's hurried footsteps on the stairs, she walked over to the window and pretended to look for something in her writing case. She didn't want to show her impatience at his tardiness, too soon she wouldn't hear his footsteps at all.

"Why, you've packed," he said, glancing at the trunk. "You're way ahead of me. I haven't started." From behind, he wrapped his arms around her waist.

"You don't need much," she said, unable to keep the bitterness out of her voice. "You're only dropping me off. Remember?"

"Katherine, don't say it like that." He turned her around and put his hands on her shoulders. "I'm hardly abandoning you. I would stay longer if I could, but you know as well as I do that I can't leave the paper for longer than a few weeks. I'm as unhappy about this as you are. But there's nothing we can do about it."

"Then there is no justice in this world if I have to leave you or die and you have to stay to make money."

She felt the warmth of his arms enfolding her, pulling her close. She laid her head against his tweed jacket and listened to his heart that for one second beat only for her; a cherished moment that she'd recall when she was lonely and far, far away.

She looked up at him and smiled, "Let's take our last walk, shall we?"

"I don't know if you should," he said, kissing her forehead. "There's a gusty wind stirring up on the Heath. Soon the trees will be bare."

"Dr. Sorapure insists that I take a walk every day regardless of the weather, even if only for a few minutes." Glancing in the mirror, she pulled her dark blue cloche down over her bangs and pinched her cheeks. "Did you know that women powder their faces to look as pale as I am? What kind of world is this, Jack, when to look like you're dying of consumption is fashionable?" She hobbled across the room to the wardrobe looking back at Jack's frown. "Don't worry, my dear, I'll wear my fur coat."

"Ah, yes your marvelous old coat," he said, helping her put it on. "Someday I must buy you a new one."

"But I like this one," she said. Ten years ago LM had surprised her with the coat, telling her that she wanted to protect her from England's raw winters. Had I a presentiment then, Katherine wondered, of how I'd come to dread the winter season even before the autumn leaves were stripped from their branches by the headwinds?

THE RAMBLING, WILD HAMPSTEAD HEATH welcomed their footsteps on its deserted paths and rolling hills. When she and Jack had moved to the Elephant she had expected to race up these hills. But today, only a year later, she had to stop several times, careful to cough into the handkerchief kept under her sleeve cuff.

"Eight months, Jack!" she said desperately. "I don't know if I can bear to be away from you that long."

"But you said yourself that you wanted the time to work without any distractions."

"I know, but eight months is too long without any distractions."

Jack chose a bench in front of an ancient, wide oak trunk that he thought would be a barrier against the blistery wind. He did not notice that its hollowed-out spine was like a wind tunnel. Katherine hugged her arms around the fur coat and was about to tell him she was too cold, but his eyes had turned inward, and he never heard her when he was deep in his thoughts.

Katherine recited out loud her poem *Covering Wings* published in *The Athenaeum* just the week before:

Two bleached roads lie under the moon at the parting of the ways. But the tiny, tree-thatched, narrow lane, isn't it yours and mine?

Jack reemerged from his pool of thoughts and looked toward the setting sun. "Let's get back. I have a bit more work to finish before we leave tomorrow."

"Before we go, I need to ask you something."

"Can't it wait until we're sitting by the fire in our parlor?" He locked his eyes on hers and smiled in his usual lopsided way.

"No it can't. Do you really believe we will actually live in our dream home, the Heron? We've spent so much time furnishing it in our imaginations and talking about it but will it ever be real?"

"I have said it before and I will say it again now. I absolutely believe that after you are cured, we will find the Heron in Sussex and move there.

Italy is the key to your recovery and to our future together. We must hold on to that belief. It's not like you to doubt our future. Why now?"

"I've lost my faith and I don't know how to recover it," she said sadly. "So long the sport of circumstances, my dice are tired of being rattled and thrown."

"You're just tired. You must use your time in Italy to heal yourself, so that we can be together again come May. Promise me you won't work so hard—"

"But don't you want me to do *The Athenaeum* reviews?"

"It's not the reviews I'm worried about. You should of course work on them as they're a very popular supplement to the paper. But that's not what's wearing you down. It's the story writing that must stop."

Katherine thumped her cane near Jack's foot. "You, of all people, should understand that the writing is what I must do above all else. That is why, thank God, I'm not in a sanatorium. It's the writing that keeps me alive and there won't be time for *later*." She coughed and reached for her handkerchief.

Jack got up from the bench and helped her up.

"I love you terribly, Bogey" she said, throwing her arms around him. "I'm too frightened to leave you."

"Katherine, please, I need you to be strong so come May we'll come home together and never have to be separated again because of your health. But we'll only succeed if we remain firm with this plan."

She put her arm in his and together they walked back to the Elephant.

The following morning Katherine placed the notebook she had scribbled in through the night on top of a stack of other notebooks, the layered chronicle of her life, and snapped her smaller trunk shut. When first arriving at the Elephant, she had removed these same notebooks and placed them on her freshly painted yellow writing table in front of the window overlooking the Heath.

What expectations! In the first weeks, every morning, she sat at her table only to write a few sentences and return to bed exhausted. In the weeks that followed she was too weak to get up and instead arranged her writing materials around her bed. But she only stared at them.

And now, after sequestering herself in this house for a year, a cab would arrive shortly and take her, LM, and Jack to Victoria Station where they would embark on a noon train for San Remo.

She sat down and lifted her pen, dipping it in the ink holder, she wrote:

> *My darling boy,*
>
> *I am leaving this letter with Mr. Kay just in case I should pop off suddenly and not have the opportunity or the chance of talking things over.*
>
> *If I were you I'd sell off all the furniture and go off on a long sea voyage on a cargo boat, say. Don't stay in London. Cut right away to some lovely place.*
>
> *Any money I have is yours, of course. I expect there will be enough to bury me. I don't want to be cremated and I don't want a tombstone or anything like that. If it's possible choose a quiet place, please do. You know how I hate noise.*
>
> *All my manuscripts I simply leave to you.*
>
> *That's all, but don't let anybody mourn me. It can't be helped.*

As she stopped to refill her pen, the sunlight streaming through her window caught the glint of the blue-stone setting in the center of a circle of iridescent pearls. Jack had slipped the pearl ring on her finger on their "honeymoon" in Paris, promising to marry her once her divorce from George was finalized.

And when she finally married him on May 3, 1918, instead of admiring a blushing bride, he stood next to a gaunt, pale stranger with dark circles around feverish eyes, unrecognizable as the girl he had first made love to at Clovelly Mansions.

She remembered her coughing spasm just as Jack leaned over to kiss her after they said their vows. He quickly pulled away but not before she saw the fear in his pale green eyes.

She finished her letter:

> *I think you ought to marry again and have children. If you do, give your little girl my pearl ring.*

She folded the letter into an envelope and addressed it to Mr. Kay at the London branch of the Bank of New Zealand, who was still working there after all these years. She enclosed instructions to give the letter to Jack upon her death.

She jumped at the loud knock. LM ushered in a young taxi driver who lifted his cap to Katherine, grinned, and carried out her trunk on his back as if it weighed nothing. She handed LM the sealed envelope and asked her to post it.

Katherine gave the bedroom one last glance and silently whispered 'good-bye.' She'd grown quite attached to her bright, cheerful dollhouse before it became her cage. She gripped the banister and carefully walked down the stairs with the help of her cane.

At the bottom of the landing, she saw the taxi through the opened front door and felt that familiar surge of exhilaration when she was about to leave on a trip. A new adventure meant new possibilities and perhaps this time she would be cured. Her faith suddenly renewed, she asked LM for Jack's letter, but LM had given it to the maid to drop in the post. It was all right. Jack would never receive her letter as it was only to be opened if she died and she wasn't going to do that, at least, not yet.

Jack stood waiting for her. His soft black felt hat shadowed his eyes but she needn't see them. It was that precious lopsided smile of his that drew her across the entry. Together they walked out to the waiting taxi.

KATHERINE WAS RELIEVED at how comfortably the time passed on the train to San Remo compared to the trips she'd taken during the war. Now that the Armistice had been set in place and peace achieved, passing through borders was easier, though the wreckage from the Great War was apparent in the blurred bombed-out buildings they sped past.

At the San Remo hotel, LM registered while Jack and Katherine stood aside with the baggage. Italians feared contagious diseases more than any other Europeans, particularly consumption. Any ill foreigners, particularly those with hacking coughs, were immediately under suspicion. For that reason Katherine had avoided using her cane walking into the hotel lobby, leaning on Jack instead. She kept her head down until they were in their rooms; a suite for her and Jack, a single adjoining room for LM.

Katherine told Jack she would eat her meals in their room. She worried that the other guests would recognize her symptoms as consumption and think she was a threat to their survival. Jack told her she was being unreasonable and why should she care what they thought anyway? He never understood how she felt pinned like a specimen under the public eye that microscopically diagnosed her, judged her, and unfairly feared her. Her stage of tuberculosis was not contagious but who would believe that by looking at her.

"My god, Jack," she said, "I just don't want anyone seeing me hobbling around like an old woman or glaring at me when I cough."

But he insisted. He wanted to show-off his famous wife, the celebrated writer.

She put on her best dress, covered the dark rings around her eyes with white powder that blended with her skin, painted her hollow cheeks with rouge, and drew ruby red lipstick across her chapped lips. She thought she looked like a freak show.

At first, the other diners only glanced at her when she walked into the restaurant and resumed eating their meals. That is until she coughed. Then all eyes were on her, pinning her under the glaring chandelier. She barely touched her dinner. After that she only came down from her room to accompany Jack to the tourist sites in San Remo. Out in the open air, they could share their holiday away from London, away from the heavy responsibilities of running *The Athenaeum*.

Their happiness was fleeting. A few nights before Jack's scheduled return to London, they were summoned to the office of the British hotel manager, Mr. Vince. He told them politely but firmly that the guests were complaining about Katherine.

"I'm sorry but you'll have to leave," he said. "We can't take the risk of you infecting our guests."

"What if my doctor sends you a letter reassuring you that my consumption is at a stage where I am not contagious."

He shook his head. "That won't make them less afraid of you. If you don't leave, my other guests will. Please try and understand my position. You must leave."

"Leave?" said Katherine, enraged. "You are throwing us out? And where, Mr. Vince, do you suggest we go? Our booking at your hotel was for many months."

"I realize that and I think I have a solution. There is a small vacant casa near the village of Ospedaletti, just three miles from here; it has a beautiful view and the accommodations and amenities are pleasant."

Katherine didn't know if she was more furious at Jack for not taking a strong position against Mr. Vince or at least complain about the added charges to their bill for fumigating their room as if she were vermin. She wanted to argue down the price but Jack was against it. "Why embarrass yourself?" he said. "Isn't it better to walk away with our pride and just a small hole in our pocketbook?"

"Whose pride, Jack? You must be talking about yours because I don't have any left. And as far as the 'small hole in the pocketbook,' it's my pocketbook and it's not a small hole. And why didn't you defend me? You know I am not contagious or you wouldn't be with me."

"Now Katherine. Calm down. There was nothing I could do. The guests had made up their minds. You know how ignorant people are about tuberculosis. Their fear is because of that ignorance. That's not something you can fight."

"The point is that by not defending me it was as if you agreed with them and that's what hurts. You too look at me as if I'm vermin and that's why I no longer have any pride left."

Casetta Deerholm—Ospedaletti

*It is on a wild hill slope, covered with olive and fig trees
and long grasses and tall yellow flowers. Down below is the
sea—the entire ocean—a huge expanse. It thunders all day
against the rocks. At the back there are mountains. Many
lizards lie on the garden wall; in the evening the cicada
shakes his tiny tambourine.*

LETTERS—KM

K ATHERINE'S ANGER AT JACK was short-lived. It really would be good to get out of this horrible hotel where she was imprisoned in her room. The idea of moving to a private home that had seemed so vile now seemed to be the best solution.

The next morning, a horse-drawn wagon brought Katherine, John and Ida to Ospedaletti, a small, quaint fishing village on the rocky Italian coastline. The wagon turned inward and climbed up a steep hill.

"Look, Jack!" Katherine shouted as they came to a sign that read Casetta Deerholm. "I love it already!"

She wanted to run down the steps into the wild, flowering garden, the brilliant colors of a Fauve painting, but Jack took her arm and they slowly descended a pebbled path under the shade of ancient olive and fig trees.

LM directed the driver burdened with their baggage to a small pink villa hanging on a precipice over the ocean.

"What a stunning view," said Katherine, standing on the villa's veranda and looking down at the white frothy waves churning against the rocks. A gentle wind touched her face and the azure sky opened up to her smile. She squeezed Jack's hand. "My faith is returning, Bogey. I know I will get better here. And just think of all the stories I will write sitting on this veranda."

"Work, Katherine? Please remember you are on a rest-cure. Let's not talk about work—at least not yet."

She breathed in the soft, sweet Mediterranean air without feeling any pain in her lungs, and silently thanked Dr. Sorapure for keeping her outside the walls of a sanatorium. Only three weeks on the Riviera and she was much healthier.

She smiled at Jack. "Do you remember in Bandol when I read you Emily Brontë's poem: *'Forgive me if I've shunned so long/Your gentle greeting, earth and air!/But sorrow withers e'en the strong/And who can fight against despair.'"*

"Of course. I remember every blissful moment in Bandol we shared, from the chamomile tea sipped in the garden, to sitting by the fire at night reading, writing, and talking, to the wanderings by the sea and into the hills picking wildflowers."

"Here I will fight against my sorrow and despair and win. I only wish you could share in my recovery like you did in Bandol, instead of the Faithful One who you can be sure will take full credit for curing me."

Jack looked to see if Ida was nearby and then said, "I would wish nothing better than to send the Faithful One back to London and be your caregiver instead. Just the two of us here on our own, like in Bandol. I'd have the time to write that second novel I keep putting off and finish my book of poetry. But *The Athenaeum* won't go to print without me there. You know I must go back. Come the—"

She laughed. "I know Jack. Come the month of May—"

A loud clatter from within was followed by cursing.

"Oh God, what has she broken now?" They followed the noise into the kitchen to find a shattered teapot and a distressed LM down on the floor picking up the pieces.

"I was holding it over the tap waiting for water to come out. I banged the tap and the pot slipped out of my other hand. How am I going to make tea if there isn't any water?"

"It's my fault, Ida. I forgot to tell you that Mr. Vince said it would take a few days before we had running water. Until then we have to walk down to the village fountain. I was going to ask Jack to do it."

"But he leaves tomorrow! And look at this stove, if it is a stove. How do you light it?"

Katherine looked over at the ancient contraption. "Look Jack," she said, not letting LM's dark mood disturb her new happiness, "it's just like the one in Bandol." She found a matchbox on the kitchen counter and opened the stove's hatch to light it.

Jack picked up a pail by the sink and went to fill it.

"Ida, don't be so down in the mouth. Don't you think this is a wonderful house and what a spectacular view. Let's have that tea you promised out on the veranda before the sun sets." She reached for the teacups on the pantry shelf.

"But how can we? There isn't a teapot."

"Be imaginative. There must be something in this kitchen you can use as a pot. Look in the cupboards, you'll find something. If not, we'll skip tea and take a walk into the village to buy a new teapot. But please try to be happy," she took Ida's hand, "for me."

THE DAY AFTER they had settled into Casetta Deerholm, Jack hung his floppy, velvet Felti on the hat rack and promised to come back for it in May. He kissed his wife good-bye and with baggage in hand walked out the door and down the street to a local bus stop. The local bus would take him to the train station in San Remo where he'd board a train to London.

Katherine pulled herself up the stairs to their bedroom. She waved a white chemise out the window, hoping he would see her, but the bus arrived and he boarded without looking back. Exhausted from pretending to be happy and well, she collapsed onto the bed and buried her sobs in a pillow.

She woke to the midday sun crossing over her bed and she made herself get up. In the garden she sat down in a comfortable wicker chair under an olive tree. Her dear friend, K.K. Koteliansky, had sent her his translation of Chekhov's letters. Kot was a Russian immigrant introduced to her and Jack by the D.H. Lawrences who were close neighbors in Chesham where they waited out the end of the end of the war. Later they were flatmates with a few other artists in London, all housing together to save money.

Through correspondence and shared pleasure in Russian literature, Kot and Katherine had developed an intimate friendship. He eked out a living by translating Russian literature and had recently asked her to work with him on the English translation of Chekhov's letters. Kot trusted her to smooth out his rough English grammar and fix any awkwardness in meaning.

Today sitting under the olive tree she was moved to tears by Chekhov's anguish. He knew his tuberculosis would prevent him from completing his literary work and he believed as Katherine did that it was his passion for writing that kept him alive. Without it, why live?

She picked up her pen and write to Kot about the Casetta that hung on *a wild hill slope, covered with olive and fig trees and long grasses and tall yellow flowers.*

Warm enough to stay outside, she finished her letter and opened up the well-worn pages of her book of Shakespeare sonnets. LM came out while she was reading and asked ridiculous questions like "shouldn't you come inside" or "do you want company, dearie" and then tucked her in a blanket. Irritated and then feeling guilty at being irritated by her good friend who meant her no harm, she opened her letter to Kot and added a postscript:

It is not being ill that matters it is having to let people serve you and fighting every moment against their desire to share.

Her thoughts turned to Jack returning to London on the train; tired and hungry, longing to sleep, wrapped in his overcoat, too cheap to reserve a sleeping berth. She closed her eyes and imagined their Heron, a small thatched cottage, with two… no, three children playing in its garden, the one boy having Jack's pale green eyes.

The sun slipped behind the Mediterranean while she wrote *twenty-eight weeks* in her notebook, marking the time until she and Jack would reunite and celebrate the success of her rest-cure.

Over dinner, Katherine mapped out a routine for LM to follow. She was to be awakened promptly at ten with a breakfast tray. She was not to be disturbed earlier as she would be writing. Afternoons no talking. She'd fix herself something for lunch, if she were hungry. She'd read or write on the veranda, or, if too tired, recline in bed upstairs as there weren't any sofas downstairs. The sitting room adjacent to the kitchen and the only room in the house other than the two upstairs bedrooms, she designated as her writing room. The door when closed would be a code to LM that she was not to be disturbed for any reason. She then made up menus for LM to cook using her own recipes.

LM was to avoid asking any questions that she could answer herself when it came to running the Casetta, including what to buy at the market, and how to budget the little money they had and not be extravagant.

"Don't be offended by my rules, Jones, it's only because I am under much pressure with *Atheanaeum* deadlines and can't be bothered with domestic chores. If you can follow my orders and leave me alone, I can make enough income for us to remain here." she said.

"I understand, Katie. I will try my best not to bother you. But I thought you were to rest while we were here and not write any stories. Isn't that what Jack said?"

"And what does Jack think we are going to live on? Need I remind you that the only income I receive from my husband is when I deliver the novel-reviews for his weekly magazine and it hardly pays for our groceries let alone the rent. We will be short of funds until I receive the publishing advance for my next short story collection of which I won't get until I have chosen which stories to include and those will have to be reviewed carefully."

Her anger made her cough and could say no more.

LM cleared the table and brought her a cup of tea. "I'm sorry, Jones, you are the last one I should be yelling at. I just hate being so poor and the burden of selecting the stories for my new collection makes me even more anxious as it is so important to choose the right stories and not rush through it because I need the money."

"I do understand, my dearest. May I suggest that you include *Bliss*. It's my favorite and if I recall correctly you were paid very well for it."

"Yes I was." Katherine said proudly. "It is on my list and actually I am considering it for the collection title."

She'd heard that Virginia Woolf thought she had "ruined her literary reputation" with *Bliss* even though it had sold far more copies than anything Virginia had published.

Virginia would never understand that there were some writers who have to earn a living at their craft and not publish their more serious work, not if they needed an income. Besides, she thought, I like writing about the common people and they like reading about themselves. No, *Bliss* wasn't my best work but my readers liked it well enough.

IN THE FIRST MAIL FROM JACK, Katherine received a packet of four novels that he needed her to review immediately to make *Athenaeum*'s deadline. She did as he asked but enclosed with the reviews a letter complaining that these novelists seemed to be unaware that we had just fought a bloody war and the cost of lives from that war could not be ignored. She was insulted that Jack wasted her time with these silly novels, when she knew there was a new printing of George Eliot's *Middlemarch* that he gave to one of his assistants to review.

LM struggled in the primitive kitchen trying to make meals, but even the simplest recipe seemed to frustrate her. Katherine would hear her curses through the wall and with the crashing of yet another plate or glass felt obliged to stop her work to find out what had happened.

Katherine wondered why she had brought her. She was an inept housekeeper who still struggled with lighting the stove and was too embarrassed to ask for help, and she couldn't cook a tasty meal, let alone serve it on time, and was even tardy bringing Katherine the tea tray. Her main asset seemed to be her health as she did manage to carry heavy pails of water up from the village fountain.

But the woman was eating too much. It seemed everyday she was asking for more money to shop in the village or in San Remo. She said she was dieting and hardly touched her plate at their shared meals but then where did all the money budgeted for groceries go? She was known to feed any bird or squirrel that crossed her vision but she only fed them breadcrumbs.

These were Katherine's thoughts as from her bedroom window she watched LM struggle up the hill carrying two full buckets of sloshing water. She didn't remember her being so clumsy when they were students at Queens College in London.

IDA HAD BEEN the first student Katherine met when she and her two much older sisters arrived from Wellington dressed in plumed hats and floor length skirts in what was then the fashion in New Zealand.

She had rushed ahead of her sisters and claimed the corner bed below a bay window.

"Why do you get that bed?" her sister Chaddie asked.

"Because I will value the view more than you and you don't appreciate watching the rain fall. Nor do you watch flowers bloom or stars fall from the sky."

She then left to explore the dorm's bathroom that unexpectedly contained a grand piano. Until she learned otherwise, she had thought all houses in London had grand pianos in their bathrooms.

"Kathleen!" yelled her eldest sister Vera calling her back. "Ida carried your trunk up three flights of stairs and is waiting for you to tell her where you want her to put it down."

She had been immediately curious about this oversized young girl plainly dressed in a dark gray blouse and skirt. Her long, fair hair separated by a severe part down the middle and pulled back tightly, cascading down to her waist. If not so large, she could have been Brontë's Jane Eyre.

Ida stared back and then shyly looked away but not before Katherine saw into her sad and lonely eyes. But she wasn't feeling particularly sympathetic toward others at age fifteen and only thought to describe this tragic figure in her journal.

"Here. Bring it here!" she had ordered, pointing to the side of her bed. Even back then, Ida did as she demanded and then waited as if not knowing what to do next without instructions.

"Kass!" shouted her other sister, Chaddie, using Katherine's childhood name. "Ida isn't your maid, she's the school's monitor and was asked to show us our rooms. Don't you think you should apologize and thank her for bringing up your trunk."

Kass didn't like being told by her sisters how to behave but she managed to mumble a "Thank you." Ida in return gave her a delicate curtsy, which was surprisingly graceful.

She put out her hand. Ida shook it and said, "Hello, Kass—"

"Please don't call me Kass. Or Kathleen for that matter. Only my sisters do that and my friends back in Wellington. Here in London, I will be known as Katie to my new friends."

"Hello, Katie."

"And what did you say your name was?"

"I'm Ida Baker." It didn't seem the right name for this large girl with a tiny bird-like voice.

"Well, Miss Baker, I don't think your name suits you at all. Would you mind if I gave you a new name? I'm very good at it. I do it all the time as a storyteller."

"You're a writer?" exclaimed Ida, showing the first signs of life in her round face.

"Yes, but it's just for fun. I am studying to be a professional musician. And you? What is your ambition?"

Ida blushed. "Ambition? I don't know if I have one though I do study the violin and my teacher says I show great promise. Said I could be a member of the London Symphony Orchestra if I keep up my practice."

"Excellent. I play the violoncello. We can play duets."

"I don't know. I'm not very good," Ida said, turning to leave.

"Wait. I just thought of your new name. It could also be your *nom de plume*. Don't you want to hear what it is?"

"I guess so."

"Leslie. It's also my brother's name and I am quite fond of him. What do you think?"

"I already have a *nom de plume*. My mother's maiden name, Katherine Moore."

"Well that will never do. My *nom de plume* is Katherine. Katherine Mansfield. If we are going to be good friends, it would be confusing for both of us to have the same first name and initials, don't you think?"

Ida had shrugged and said, "Perhaps." At the door she had stopped and turned back to say, "If you like, I'll come back when you've unpacked and show you the school."

"Why wait?" said Katherine, "I want to see everything now."

KATHERINE RECLINED BACK on the bed, after watching LM climb up the steep hill to the Casetta, and returned to the letter she was writing. She and Jack had promised to write each other every day. She started off saying that she wished he was carrying the pails instead of LM and was bringing her a deep red geranium. Outside the open window the waves seemed to whisper "Boge" each time they rolled over the rocks.

She wrote:

My dearest Boge, you are more loved than anyone in the world.

OCTOBER, 1919

I Shot the ALBATROSS

And a good south wind sprung up behind;
The Albatross did follow,
And every day, for food or play,
Came to the mariners' hollo!
In mist or cloud, on mast or shroud,
It perch'd for vespers nine;
Whiles all the night, through fog-smoke white,
Glimmer'd the white Moon-shine.
"God save thee, ancient Mariner,
From the fiends, that plague thee thus! —
Why look'st thou so?"—With my cross-bow
I shot the ALBATROSS.

THE RIME OF THE ANCIENT MARINER
SAMUEL TAYLOR COLERIDGE

HER THIRTY-FIRST BIRTHDAY arrived without fanfare. Jack sent a delicate silver spoon for when they moved into the Heron, without any mention of finding their dream home. The letter from her father didn't mention her birthday at all. Katherine knew he gave money to her sisters on their birthdays, but not her. Was he still hoping if he continued doling out a meager allowance she would return to New Zealand? You'd think after eleven years he'd know better and be more generous.

Propped up in bed, seething at LM who hadn't brought her morning tray, she marked in her journal *199 days*, which was way too long. *Stay firm*, as Jack would say.

Her beaming companion burst into the room singing "Happy Birthday Katie!" She proudly brought over a tray with a steamy pot of coffee, a mug, and a pretty bouquet she picked in the Casetta garden.

"I thought you couldn't find any coffee beans in the village?" was Katherine's grumpy response, ignoring the birthday wishes. If she wasn't having fun on her birthday no one else should, particularly LM.

"I didn't say I couldn't find any, I said there were none to be had on your budget. But just this morning I found a quaint little shop selling small bags at a bargain price."

"How much?"

"Oh, not so much, considering how tightly the beans are packed in the bag."

"How much, Ida?"

"Ten lira."

"Why that's almost as much as a doctor's visit. You know we can't afford it. Not only do you break the dishes I am collecting for the Heron, but you frivolously use my money for your own pleasures. I'm deducting these coffee beans from your pay. Now take it away."

Unfazed, LM continued to grin from ear to ear like a pumpkin. "My aren't we the happy birthday girl. Deduct it from my pay, if you like, though I haven't seen any pay for quite a while and have no idea how much it is. But now that I am paying for the coffee, I freely give it to you as a birthday present. Enjoy!"

Before Katherine could reply she was gone.

The fragrance steaming from the pot of fresh coffee could not be ignored and she poured a cup. A small bottle of Genet Fleuri perfume, her favorite, had been hidden behind the flower vase.

She dabbed her wrist with the perfume and said to herself, what a detestable person I am. Why does she stay? If not for me, she'd be married and starting a family. Why sacrifice all that for me? And worse, why do I let her?

A book that she kept putting down from boredom, but must be read, was sitting on her bedside table waiting for her to review and send out before *Athenaeum*'s deadline. A fine way to spend my birthday, she thought, picking it up.

She was just starting to read when she was startled by a loud crash in the kitchen. "I will never get any work done as long as *she* is in my house," she said out loud, quickly forgetting the gifts of perfume and coffee. She hurriedly dressed and went downstairs.

In the kitchen, LM was sweeping up shattered glass.

"What have you broken now?"

"Just a silly brandy glass. Way too fragile for the likes of me. Oh, Katie, don't look so angry. I know that's a terrible excuse, but it's true. I don't do well with delicate things, but I am trying. You must give me more time. I've never been a housekeeper."

"That's what you said in London. Well at least we don't have any more *delicate* items for you to practice on. In one week you've broken the thermometer—"

"That's unfair. It fell off the bed table when I accidentally set your milk glass on it."

Katherine continued. "A plate and a saucer."

"They were delicate, too. And isn't it rather nice and homey when you occasionally smash a thing or two?"

Katherine wished the young, cheerful village maid, Augusta, hadn't left without giving notice.

She'd just sat down at her writing table in the sitting room when LM entered without knocking, another cardinal rule broken. "Have you no scruples," she shouted. "Can't you see I'm working!"

"Oh sorry Katie, I just wanted to tell you I'm going shopping. I thought I'd purchase those muttonchops for a nice birthday dinner. And we need eggs. And wouldn't you like some figs, dearie, for your birthday?"

Katherine set down her pen. "You seem to think I just write in this notebook and money magically appears. You just bought groceries. Where did that food go to, certainly not into *my* stomach?"

"Nor mine," said LM, offended. "Haven't you noticed how little I eat?"

You certainly can't tell from your wholesome figure, thought Katherine. She didn't want LM to know she'd been spying on her and just the other day had seen her eating an entire Italian baguette when she thought Katherine was napping.

THE AFTERNOON WAS SPENT reading on the veranda. When LM came out to check on her, she exclaimed, "Katie, what's happened?"

"What do you mean *what's happened*?"

"Look at your legs."

"Oh my god, what is it?" She was so focused on her reading that she hadn't noticed her legs turning red and growing twice their normal size.

LM ran to the neighbor for help.

The neighbor took one look at Katherine and said, "Pa-pet-e-chi-kos!"

"Che cosa sono pa-pet-e-chi-kos?" asked Ida in her poor Italian. He lifted his shoulders and shrugged. They heard him laughing as he left, amused by his foreign neighbors.

LM looked up the word in an Italian dictionary and read out loud: "Tiny, invisible, deadly mosquitoes."

"What do you mean *deadly*?"

"I don't know but we have to bring down the swelling right away. I'll get ice."

"Ida, we don't have any ice!"

"Oh right. Well, it's too late to go tonight but I'll go to the pharmacy first thing in the morning. Señor Mario will know what to do."

The following morning she awoke to lit candles on every surface in her bedroom and LM hooking a mosquito net around her bed.

"What are you doing? And why are the candles lit? I'm not dead yet."

"Señor Mario told me to do this." LM held up a bottle. "And he wants me to add this potion to your bath."

"What is it?"

"I don't know. He spoke very quickly and I couldn't understand everything he said."

LM picked up the vase of fresh flowers that she'd given to Katherine for her birthday.

"Where are you taking those?"

"Señor Mario said no flowers in the house. The papetechikos feed on their nectar."

"Don't touch them!"

"But Katie, the Señor was very worried. I think we should do what he says."

"What else did he tell you?"

"Keep your windows closed at night and sprinkle the floor with water. Though I can't understand what help it would be to wet the floor. And, oh yes, as best as I could translate, 'Bear up until after the fruit season.'"

"When is that?"

"A few months from now."

IN EARLY NOVEMBER, a month after arriving at the Casetta, Katherine didn't think she could stay another day without losing her mind. She'd depended on Jack's letters to keep her from giving up, but there were too many days in between and she'd become anxious and depressed. She began to believe he didn't love her and he was never coming back in May to bring her home to the Heron.

The courier would hand-deliver mail in the morning, but when there was no letter from Jack, she'd still hold back her disappointment and wait for LM to check for the evening mail at the post office. Even after she heard Ida bang the front door closed, she'd hold back her disappointment a few minutes, watching the seconds click by on the clock until the strain was unbearable and she'd call out, "Ida, is there any mail from Jack?"

Too often the reply was, "No. Not today."

Sinking into dark moods, she'd write letters to Jack about LM's clumsiness or she'd write letters to her friends about Jack's abandonment. Because LM was with her, she got the worst of it, but even Jack who had previously managed to avoid her sting, was now the targeted victim of venomous letters from Katherine.

Late one afternoon, waiting for LM to return from the post office, she was correcting Kot's translation of a letter Chekhov had written to his wife trying to explain what it was like to be a consumptive:

> *My mind is weakened by illness and I am now like a child: now I pray to God, now I cry, now I am happy.*

How well he speaks of my own symptoms, she thought, tears welling in her eyes. She knew her illness was the cause of her terrible behavior. Her childish tantrums. Her hysterics. Her moments of feverish joy. She felt she had no control over these erratic moods that were inflicted upon her at all hours. If only she could get some sleep, but weeks ago she'd squeezed out the last drops of Dr. Sorapure's laudanum.

At first she was delighted when LM brought her a letter from Jack and miserable after she read it. It was filled with complaints about his cold and no mention of his feelings toward her. No mention of missing her.

She brought out her pen to write back and copied out a sentence from Chekhov's letter to his wife:

> *People love talking of their diseases, although they are the most uninteresting things in their lives.*

She continued in her own words:

> *You see my darling that is why I don't tell you when I'm feeling badly, because it is boring. So please don't bore me with telling me about your illnesses either. We have far more interesting things to consider such as next week's edition of the A. or whether you have yet found the Heron—are you even looking or are you feeling as discouraged as I am today that this house we so wish for is not possible because of that boring thing I choose not to speak of today.*

The doorbell clanged again and again. "Ida!" she shouted. "Get the door."

"I'm coming. I'm coming." Heavy footsteps came down the stairs, like horse hooves clomping down a wooden ramp in her brain.

LM ushered in their landlord, Mr. Vince. "Good afternoon, Mrs. Murry," he said, perspiration dripping from his brow from his walk up the hill from Ospedaletti. "I was in the area and thought I'd come by to see how you two were getting along. Is the water coming through the taps?"

"Yes it finally is. And we are most grateful for our baths." She had no time for the likes of Mr. Vince and said very politely, "Unless there is some other reason for your visit, please stop by the kitchen on your way out and Ida will give you a drink of water."

"Well Mrs. Murry actually there is something else."

"Oh, do you bring news about Augusta? I was worried about her. She seemed happy enough working for us, but she only stayed two days and then abruptly left without notice. Is she ill?"

"I told her to explain to you… but she was too embarrassed and asked me to tell you."

Katherine waited but when he said nothing she said, "Yes?"

"It's your illness again, Mrs. Murry. After the Spanish flu killed so many Italians, they are very sensitive toward sick people. The villagers fear you will infect their village. Augusta's mother told her she couldn't work for you. Augusta was disappointed, but young girls must obey, mustn't they? I am a bit worried about your safety living way out here, just the two of you. I brought you some protection."

He took a revolver from his pocket and placed it on her writing table with a box of bullets.

"For Jesus' sake. What's that for!" said LM, stepping back.

"With the war ending the way it did and the bad feelings here about us English plus the epidemic only last year, and what with Mr. Murry away and you being, well, you know—sick—I think you need to watch out for yourselves."

"Have you had trouble, Mr. Vince?" He had lived in San Remo before the war, and then returned after, but he was still an Englishman, a foreigner, and for four long years the enemy.

"Goodness no, Mrs. Murry, not in San Remo. There are so many of us there. It's a regular old British colony. But here in the countryside, well one never knows what might happen in these isolated parts."

Katherine picked up the revolver, handled it, feeling its weight. She sensed fascination and terror simultaneously and put it back down. "Thank you Mr. Vince for your concern. It is true that the doorbell has been ringing late at night but no one answers when we call out. I haven't paid it much mind."

"You see. Just what I suspected. These Italians don't realize that we're no longer the enemy. Our presence is a strong reminder of their defeat. They also fear we want to occupy their country. Anyway, I'll feel a lot better myself knowing you have this. May I show you how to use it?"

"Please do."

"Katherine!" said LM, shocked.

"Mr. Vince would never have brought us this revolver if he wasn't concerned for our safety." She picked up the gun again. "Is it loaded, Mr. Vince?"

"No. I was going to show you how to put in the bullets and give you a little target practice."

"Excellent. We could both use a little practice, right, Ida?"

"No thank you. My father taught me how to use a gun in Rhodesia when he took me hunting. I think they're repulsive and very dangerous."

In the garden, he loaded the gun for Katherine and brought her arm up, showing her how to pull the trigger. She liked the feeling of power it gave her and the pleasure of knowing it bothered LM. After Mr. Vince left, she put it away in the hallway table drawer, unloaded, but with a box of bullets nearby.

The next morning LM brought Katherine's breakfast tray and then said she was taking a bus to San Remo to visit a few friends. "Are you sure you don't mind being on your own for the day?"

"No, actually, I look forward to it."

WHY CAN'T Ida put anything back after she uses it? Katherine asked herself after almost tripping over a rake in the garden. She sighed and sat down in her wicker chair to enjoy the warm air, like silk against her skin. Seated such a short distance from the crystal blue Mediterranean made it possible to see the arms and legs of swimmers paddling underwater. She wished she could join them.

Sailboats glided past. A reminder of her bedroom in Wellington where she could see the port. In the distance, white slivers of light flashed across the horizon. She thought to describe them metaphorically in a poem or a short story as they were like moments of being. But when would she have the time? Every hour was occupied with the novel-reviews, the Chekhov translations, and the revisions to her short stories for the anthology. And the fatigue from her illness made even picking up her pen an exhausting effort.

She read a new letter from Kot that ended with: *Your indomitable will has kept you alive this year. I am absolutely sure you will get well and grow into your dream of achievement.*

The warm, soft breeze dried her tears. The sun slipped briefly behind a white cloud and came back out again as if had forgotten to light the rose-red geraniums blooming in the garden. How beautiful life is, she thought, breathing in the salty, sea air.

Encouraged by Kot's belief in her and the beauty surrounding her, she put pen to paper and wrote: *Yes, Kot, you are right. I will be healed here in this fairy-tale house in Ospedaletti. In spite of having to share it with Ida, my albatross. And I will start to write again soon.*

She also promised herself that as soon as she could write again she would dedicate her next story to her dear loyal friend Kot who hadn't forsaken her like Jack and the others.

Her renewed belief in the power of her will didn't last long. She awoke in the middle of the night believing she was being eaten alive and screamed for help. LM came running into the room to find Katherine sitting up in her bed pointing at the white cotton headboard.

A large, fat-bellied mosquito was resting after its meal on Katherine's blood, the evidence still dripping from its mouth and staining the headboard like wine.

LM caught the perpetrator in her big hands, opened the window and flung it out.

"You let it go?" yelled Katherine. "After what it did to me, you didn't crush it?"

"I couldn't kill her, Katie," LM said as she shut the window. "The poor thing has no choice. She has to bite her victims so to fertilize her eggs. Certainly, you understand her need to do that."

In a fury, Katherine re-opened the window. "Then let's leave it open so she and the rest of the maternal monsters can come in and feast on me. We certainly don't want to wipe out their population because of my selfishness. What a shame that your blood does not whet their appetites, as I'm certain you would be far more willing to sacrifice yourself for their progeny than I am."

"Now, Katie, you're getting into one of your dark moods again. We don't want a fever coming on. It's true that I would prefer if they attacked me instead of you, but they like you better. Certainly a few tiny bites are no reason to kill a future mother, are they?"

Katherine glared at her. "I see through your pitiful self-sacrifice. I know what you want—you're just like them, you want to eat Me! You think I'm stupid but I know you're seeking revenge. I took your life from you and now you've come to kill me. Admit it. You are my Albatross!"

"Katie. Please stop! Don't say such horrible things. You know you'll be sorry later. You always are."

"Don't you call me Katie. I'm Mrs. Murry to you now. You hear that? Mrs. Murry." Katherine grabbed the drinking glass and threw it. "Get out!"

Katherine hid from the mosquitos under the netting and the bedcovers. When she finally got back to sleep, she dreamed she was standing in the garden aiming Mr. Vince's gun at an olive tree for target practice. A grinning LM in the bulbous body of an albatross walked by her carrying a tea tray. She turned the gun on her and pulled the trigger.

The albatross fell to the ground. Her white feathers stained in blood, her broken wings spread across the pathway.

NOVEMBER, 1919

The Diagnosis

*I am sitting in the dining room. The front door is open,
the cold salt air blows through. I am wrapped up in my
purple dressing gown and Jaeger rug with a hot bottle
and a hot brick. On the round table is a dirty egg-cup
full of ink, my watch (on British time an hour slow) and
a wooden tray holding a manuscript called "Eternity"
which is all spattered over with drops of rain and looks as
though some sad mortal had cried his pretty eyes out over
it. There is also a pair of scissors—abhorrèd shears they
look—and two flies walking up and down are discussing
the ratification of the Peace Treaty and its meaning re our
civil relations with Flyland.*

LETTERS—KM

K ATHERINE PUT DOWN HER PEN, closed her notebook, and walked out onto the veranda to watch what in the last few days had transmogrified from a sun-drenched, turquoise pool into a dark, treacherous sea. Casetta Deerholm was no longer a safe shelter-in-place. The frigid wind now beat against her and the unprotected precipice she stood on. She was under-dressed in a purple dressing gown but she didn't care. The only one who did care, LM, had gone to meet a Dr. Bobone at the bus stop.

Any doctor, Katherine had said to her, any doctor with a stethoscope hanging from his neck will do. Not because Katherine was feeling terribly ill, to the contrary in the last month she was feeling much better, but she needed confirmation that being quarantined with LM, deprived of Jack's companionship, had been worth the cost—that her lungs were healthy. In the past, too often she had thought herself cured only to relapse and be bitterly disappointed.

Medical confirmation that her disease was inactive, even gone, meant there was a future for her and Jack, that her pursuit of a cure wasn't a false optimism, not a denial of the truth that she was dying. And she also needed a prescription of Dr. Sorapure's tincture to keep away the night terrors.

DR. BOBONE pressed his cold stethoscope against her chest.

Before he asked her to unbutton her blouse, she had asked him if he didn't want to review her medical records first

He replied offhandedly, "Not necessary. My ear hears everything." She listened to him listening. Was it the log in the stove or did she hear her lungs crackling? Like all the others, he gave nothing away while he listened.

When his two fingers tapped on her chest it felt like an ox's stomping hoof. "Rest. Sunshine. I warn you. If fever. You die."

"But I thought I was cured. My cough has subsided. I feel much better. I just don't sleep well."

"The apex of your left lung is affected, Fräulein."

She turned away from him and buttoned her blouse. What a waste of my bloody time. He doesn't know anything. I'll have to get another opinion but at least he can give me a tonic.

Putting her jacket on she said, "I'm out of the tonic my English doctor gives me to sleep. Can you mix a bottle for me?"

"If you mean laudanum, no, I cannot," he said, taking an ugly muddy brown bottle from his medical bag. "Once we heal the underlying cause of your illness then you'll be able to sleep. Swallow this, Fräulein, make your lungs strong."

She compressed her lips and shook her head. "I must ask my pulmo-nologist doctor in London before I take anything he hasn't prescribed."

"Not to worry, Fräulein. It won't harm you. Make you feel better or does nothing. I'll leave here. You can take later."

Katherine paid his bill, which she thought was way too much consid-ering his diagnosis was a death threat.

After he left, she escaped out onto the veranda. The tormenting wind whipped at her dressing gown. She gripped the railing, closed her eyes and imagined she was at the helm of a ship heading home to New Zealand. Dr. Bobone only a bad dream.

Katherine climbed upstairs and took to her bed for several days. She wrote Jack asking him to see Dr. Sorapure immediately and to send her the herbs Dr. Bobone denied her. The San Remo pharmacy would mix it for her as they had before. She gave him the name of Bobone's tonic saying she wouldn't take one spoonful without Dr. Sorapure's permission.

The sparse bedroom gave little comfort. The small coal stove hissed and sputtered; barely keeping her warm. The little pink house hanging over the precipice trembled from the thunder. She wrapped the Jaeger rug tighter and dug her feet down into fur hand muffs, but the fierce wind penetrated through the cracks in the Casetta's walls and wrapped her in his freezing arms.

LM came in holding a glass of warm milk on a tray. After the incident with the mosquitos, Katherine had apologized and given her permission to speak.

"This might help you sleep," said LM, putting the tray down on the bed. "Oh my, don't tell me you're still cold, dear Katie. You just have no fat on that thin body of yours. I gave the stove the last of the coal an hour ago. Are you really that cold?"

"Yes, I'm *that* cold," she said, her teeth chattering.

"Let's take your temperature. We can't be too cautious, can we? Remember what Dr. Bobone said about 'No fever. No die.'"

LM giggled at her German accent but stopped when she saw Katherine wasn't amused. "Why your hot-water bottle is frozen too. I'll put it near this nice fire to warm it up, shall I?"

LM slipped the thermometer between Katherine's dry lips and took her pulse while looking at her watch.

In the fading twilight, Katherine stared at her caregiver's foamy, big arms like feathered wings, her eyes like black beady stones, her nose the bulbous curved beak of an albatross. Breadcrumbs wedged into the corner of her orange beak.

Katherine slammed shut her eyes. I'm becoming a fiend, she thought, and I can't control myself. I've lost all sense of reality.

LM removed the thermometer. "Thank goodness. No fever. Now drink your milk while it's still warm."

Katherine was afraid LM had put drops of arsenic into it. She asked her to taste it first saying, "I don't want to burn my tongue."

LM took a sip and handed it back. "It's just right. Now drink it all down, my dearie."

A FORTNIGHT WENT BY before she received Jack's response to her letter. Dr. Sorapure's herbs had arrived that morning in the same packet and LM had taken the herbs and the emerald green medicine bottle to the San Remo pharmacist to make the tincture.

Jack wrote that her last letter had depressed him. She mustn't believe that village quack, Bobone. He advised her to take courage as he had done when obligated to attend yet another dreary party without her. She laughed out loud at what he called 'courage' wishing she too could "suffer" at a dreary party. Poor, poor Jack!

She worked on a review for his precious *Athenaeum* until the clanging doorbell interrupted her. Walking by the side table drawer that held the revolver, she hesitated, reasoned with herself that it was the middle of the afternoon and murderers and thieves only come out at night. Besides the two women had nothing worth stealing.

The door opened on a small, stooped-over man who leaped inside like a bright-eyed cat. Shocked, she pulled back. "Who are you?" she asked hoping to be rid of him quickly.

"Dr. Ansaldi," he said tipping his straw hat. "Here at your request, I believe, but does not appear so."

"Oh yes." She'd forgotten Mr. Vince's offer to send her a specialist in respiratory diseases from San Remo.

Dr. Ansaldi suggested he examine her in the warm kitchen. She watched him bend down and add wood to the kitchen stove. He turned to her, "You must stay warm during this unusual frigid winter on the Italian Riviera. Isn't what you expected, is it? Not the weather promised in the tourist brochure that bring you English here."

He drew a much more sophisticated modern stethoscope than Bobone's and used a percussion hammer instead of a finger. Without being asked, knowing too well what was expected of her, she removed the Jaeger rug and several layers of sweaters and scarves she'd been wearing.

"Excellent. You know to dress warmly," he said, looking at the woolens now piled on the floor. After his examination he read over Dr. Sorapure's medical report, studied the charts, and jotted down notes in a journal similar to the one Dr. Sorapure carried.

Over a cup of tea he gave his opinion.

After he left, she added a log to the already toasty fire and poured herself another cup of tea. She held off writing Jack. She wanted to self-indulge in Ansaldi's news. But realizing she was too excited to wait another minute she picked up her pen and wrote:

> *My bad lung is drying, there's only a small spot left at the apex. The other lung also has a small spot at the apex but it's improved.* She stopped to sip her tea and eat a fig just to stretch out her news a little longer: *Ansaldi says 'It will take two years to cure me but that I shall be a great deal better by April.' Yes, Jack! Dr. Ansaldi said I could be normal.*

That night she stood at the window looking out at the starry night and shivered, not from the cold, but from unadulterated joy. She had the sudden irresistible urge to leap into the air, something she'd been afraid to do for quite some time. What if I fall? What if Dr. Ansaldi hasn't told me the truth? What if my heart stops when I am in midair? She ignored her voice of doubt and walked to the center of the room, stood perfectly still, took a deep breath, closed her eyes and jumped once. And then jumped again much higher.

Her heart beating fast, she stood in front of her mirror to see if she looked any different and saw a very bright, lively face that she hardly recognized as her own. Climbing into bed and propping up her pillows she wrote to Jack:

> *What is the Present when the Future is removed, when life is haunted, not by Death in the fullness of time, but by Death's fast-encroaching shadow? But I now say, 'away with that shadow and come no more.' I will live in the Present and no longer fear the Future. Five months and a fortnight, my dearest, and we will never be separated again.*

LM came in holding Dr. Sorapure's emerald green bottle in her hand and waving a spoon. "Look what I have, Katie."

"You are a wonder," said Katherine who was feeling particularly benevolent toward her loyal caregiver. "I shan't need more than one spoonful. There will be no terrors tonight. We'll both get some sleep."

SHE RECEIVED NEWS from her father that after his long stay in London with her two sisters, before returning to New Zealand, he was to visit his cousin at her winter villa in Menton, France.

Katherine wrote to tell him that Ospedaletti was just on the other side of the border from Menton, a simple day's excursion. Anxious that he might not visit her, afraid of her illness, added: *Please come, Pa, I am much better. I no longer have a cough or fever so you needn't worry about getting infected.*

She was thrilled when he wrote back accepting her invitation. He would bring his older cousin with him, Miss Connie Beauchamp, and her long-time companion Miss Jinnie Fullerton. The two women had managed a nursing home in London but now retired they invited their previous patients to Villa Flora, their winter home in Menton.

The Casetta looks far less rundown in sunlight, she thought, standing on the veranda waiting for her father's arrival. A fancy white open motorcar rolled up the hill driven by a uniformed chauffeur. She rushed to the gate.

"Pa. I'm so glad you're here. Come in. Come in. Hello Connie. Oh! You must be Miss Jinnie. Welcome! Welcome to Casetta Deerholm." Two matronly women, one stout and one tall, in their fifties or, perhaps older, and her robust father, who in his finely tailored Bond Street suit reminded her of King Edward, followed her into the entryway that was hardly suitable for her royal guests.

"Why it's a dollhouse!" exclaimed Jinnie. Seemingly charmed by the sitting room, they looked around for a closet to hang their furs and shopping bags and plopped them in the corner. The only other surface, the writing table, had been set for lunch.

No one but Katherine seemed to notice the too thick onion slices or the burnt potatoes or the overcooked roast. LM glowed when Jinnie thanked her for the delicious meal and complimented her on the lovely table setting. "Why you have such a colorful variety of china," said Connie. LM had used every cracked and chipped dish found in the cupboard.

Her guests had stopped along the route to buy knick-knacks and had been particularly amused by a shop selling reading spectacles. They'd each bought several pairs that they now modeled and passed around for everyone to try on. Katherine felt impoverished with her one pair remaining in her pocket. Connie gave her a pair of horn-rimmed specs, saying they were very special. Katherine was touched by her generosity.

Her father suggested a car ride and she was bundled up in a fur rug and seated next to him. She rested back against the velvet cushions, snuggling up against his fur coat. In her desire to be independent she had run away from his opulence that she found suffocating, but now it seduced her. Let the car drive on forever, the motor purring, and his arms around her, sheltering her from the harsh poverty that consumed her.

He told a story about having his wallet stolen on Bond Street in London. He said the loss of ten pounds was nothing compared to the embarrassment of being made a fool of.

Ten pounds! thought Katherine, wishing she had been the thief. What was 'nothing' to her father she could have lived on for a month. He had no idea how she struggled to keep a budget that excluded multiple spectacles and motorcar rides. And she preferred it that way rather than humbling herself by describing the paucity of her life.

Mr. Beauchamp amused the ladies by speaking into the limousine's horn to the chauffeur in Maori, the native tongue of New Zealand, which he was sure the Italian driver could not understand. The colonies were far away from here and no Maori had ever set foot on Italian soil or so he thought. The driver stopped at the top of the hill so they might admire the cliffs. Connie and Jinnie took a short walk. Pa pulled off his fur-lined leather gloves and slipped then onto Katherine's bare hands. He spoke softly, calling her by her childhood name.

"Kass, I am very worried about you. You look much too pale for someone recovered." Like Jack, he never called her disease by its name. "I hardly recognized you when you greeted us. You're way too thin."

"You needn't worry. I'm better. I told you what Dr. Ansaldi said."

"You also told me that you had to leave London or you wouldn't survive another winter but where you're staying now seems to be as damp and as bitterly cold as London. Your Casetta is completely unprotected from the wind and so are you. Nor are either of you insulated for winter." He didn't give her time to argue.

"I've never understood Jack's lack of duty toward you. But certainly he would never have abandoned you here if he'd seen these harsh living conditions. And such isolation. What would happen if there was an emergency?"

"Oh Pa, you're exaggerating. I'm not entirely alone. Ida is here." She didn't mention the gun Mr. Vince had given her for emergencies. "And Jack did see the Casetta and wholeheartedly approved of it. As far as the isolation, I prefer writing in remote natural settings. And now that I'm feeling better, I have much work to do."

"But why isn't Jack here?"

"He has promised to come for me in May and then we will move into a cottage in Sussex where we will live most comfortably. I just have to continue my rest-cure through the next five months."

"Kass, this is all wrong. A husband shouldn't leave his wife, particularly a wife in your weak condition, in a foreign country where you have neither family nor friends. There is something you are not telling me. I ask you again, why isn't Jack here?"

"He has his career. Certainly you can understand that. It would be unwise for him to leave his new editorial position at *The Athenaeum* and I wouldn't ask him to do it. Why should both of us suffer for my illness? Besides we have no choice. We need his income. My stories are selling, but there are medical expenses."

Her father turned away and looked out at the sea. She hoped that once he considered her expenses, he would offer to increase her allowance without her directly asking him for it.

He turned back to her and said, "If you were my wife I would take you away from here today. Jack is way too self-absorbed. I've always thought so. He takes no responsibility for you as if he thinks you can live on mulberry leaves like a silkworm. Where is that man's sense of duty?"

"He does his best," she said, giving him back the gloves.

He called out to the chauffeur to take them back. Jinnie and Connie, seated behind them, filled the awkward silence with chatter comparing their wonderful Menton to Ospedaletti: "How lovely this view is but wait until you see ours. You must come stay with us, Katherine."

Back at the Casetta, her father's kindness returned. He admired the garden and tied a bouquet of daisies and one orchid with grass and handed it to her. The invitation to Villa Flora was repeated. Ida was invited, too.

Before leaving, her Pa said, "I cannot tell you what to do, Kass, I never could, but I do hope you accept Connie and Jinnie's invitation and leave here very soon. This is a dangerous place for you and the sooner you get away the better. If there is anything I can do, please write me."

"You've done more than enough, Pa," she lied.

He wrapped his arms around her and said, "Get better, you little wonder. You're your mother over again."

Katherine promised the ladies she would visit in the spring and, after waving them all off, she put her father's bouquet next to his gift of five Three Castle cigarettes, which he had left on her writing table to find later.

COME THE LAST DAY OF NOVEMBER, she hurried to get a letter off to Jack before the post office closed. She picked up her pen and wrote:

> *Jack you will find this hard to believe but I have gained five pounds by daily eating bowls of macaroni soaked in butter and fresh vegetables and fruit. I weighed myself on the drugstore scale as I do every few weeks and I have gone from 97 to 102 pounds. Isn't that wonderful? It bodes well for our future at the Heron. Also, the tonic has had a most superb effect. Très potent!* She looked over at Dr. Sorapure's bottle. *Strongly effective. Even on stormy nights.*

Suddenly overcome by sadness and yearning, she added, *I do wish you were here, Jack. I don't know how long I can continue on this journey alone.*

She left Jack's letter on the hall table for LM to post and climbed upstairs reciting the poem she'd written when she and Jack had been happily together in Bandol:

> *We might be fifty, we might be five*
> *So snug so compact, so wise are we!*
> *Under the kitchen table leg*
> *My knee is pressing against his knee.*

DECEMBER 1919

The New Husband

Someone came to me and said
Forget, forget that you've been wed.
Who's your man to leave you be
Ill and cold in a far country?
Who's the husband—who's the stone
Could leave a child like you alone?

THE NEW HUSBAND—KM

AT MIDNIGHT gale-force winds shook the Casetta's foundation. Katherine gripped onto the bedpost in fear of being dragged out into the turbulent sea where not even Dr. Sorapure's tincture would save her from being sucked into the abyss.

By morning, the storm had passed and the grateful sea returned to its calm self. Katherine wrapped herself in her rug and moved her chair to the window to look out on the calm, blue Mediterranean gilded over by a wide, wide pale yellow sky.

If one were not alone here, she thought, then the cold would not matter. Ospedaletti is so simple and unfashionable that no parasitic life can exist as there is nothing for the greedy to feed upon. This is quite the most beautiful place I've ever been, even more beautiful than Bandol but there Jack was with me. If he were here now to see this beauty he would give up London, give up *The Athenaeum,* and return to his own writing. Together, here, we could accomplish so much.

DR. ANSALDI CAME BACK to reexamine Katherine. After he left, she furiously paced the veranda. All lies. Fever and melancholy and rage, how well they feed each other, she thought, bringing her cold hands up to her flushed cheeks, and how well I know the signs. Afraid of a chill, she returned inside hoping by writing to Jack she'd gain control over the dark mood coming over her.

She dipped the dry pen into the inkwell and wrote:

> *Dr. Ansaldi was here today and I will not be cured in two years. In truth, I will never be cured. Do you hear me, Jack? There will be no Heron for us. Never. The truth is that my lungs are in the same or worse condition than before I left London. Nothing has changed for us. The other truth remains the same. You cannot leave the A. to attend to your invalid wife and I would die if I came to London.*

> *Ansaldi is a charlatan. After groping me with his stethoscope and beating me up with his hammer, he told me emphatically that I could not winter in England next year or the year after, that I must have sun and warmth. Can you imagine the polite smile with which I listened?*

> *I asked him if it was consumption that brought on the melancholia that not even Dr. Sorapure's tincture could keep at bay. He said, "Yes, melancholia is part toxin poisoning from your disease, but also because you are alone wiz nobody near to love and 'sherish' you. Where is your husband, Fräulein?"*

She put down the pen. The Terra Cotta stove was steaming but the chill deep within her could not be melted by fever or fire. Where was the shawl that Jack had promised? The shawl he had bought for her to wrap around her shoulders until he could keep her warm himself. He said he'd sent it weeks ago. Where was it? Instead she used the woolen rug.

She wiped the leaking nib across the hog hairs inside the hollow back of her small brass pig penwiper: her father's parting gift when she left Wellington.

She wrote:

> *Why don't I adopt a baby boy? A nurse could care for us both at the same cost,* she wrote. *Would you mind if I did that, Jack? Of course I would be responsible for all the costs.*

*I can't be left on my own like this ever again. I haven't
written any stories since I left London. I have no one to talk
to, no one to hold me. But if there was an adopted child for
me to cherish and play with I could live alone.*

Writing to Jack had not calmed her. The dark mood she'd tried to
hold at bay was pressing in on her, pushing her toward the abyss but
she kept writing.

*It is loneliness that is weakening my heart and crushing my
breath. You only live with me in the future when we will
have our fairy-tale house, The Heron. It's cruel to make
such plans as they will never come to be. It's false of you to
pretend. You must face the truth that I will never be well
enough to live with you in England. We must make other
arrangements. Yes there must be future plans but not built
on fantasies. Truth between us is what is needed now.*

*If I have to spend next winter abroad, I can't spend it alone.
And no, Jack, I don't want you to quit the A, borrow money
from my father and come here to replace Ida to care for your
invalid wife. It's not in your character to be a caregiver. It
would destroy us.*

Goodbye darling, I am ever your own...

She reached for a sheet of blank stationery:

*Someone came to me and said
Forget, forget that you've been wed...*

Her pen began to scratch across the paper as more verses rushed
forward:

*I had received that very day
A letter from the other to say
That in six months—he hoped—no longer
I would be so much better and stronger
That he could close his books and come
With radiant looks to bear me home.*

The only other sound besides the scratching pen was the waves rubbing against the rocks below her window. As she hurriedly wrote more verses, the gurgling in her lungs, the gnawing ache in her hips, and the loud beating of her heart became silent, even her loneliness seemed to hush:

> Ha! Ha! Six months, six weeks, six hours
> Among these glittering palms and flowers...

She stopped and looked up thinking she heard footsteps but no one was there:

> So I became the stranger's bride
> And every moment however fast
> It flies—we live as 'twere our last!

Exhausted, she put down her pen. The verses that had been shifting in her mind ever since her father's visit now put to paper.

She enclosed the poem in Jack's letter, requesting that he put it safely into her deposit box until she had time to review it before publication. After leaving the envelope on the hallway table for LM to post, she went upstairs to bed.

THE FOLLOWING MORNING LM found Katherine trembling uncontrollably under the heavy bedcovers. She rasped, "Find me a doctor! But not those charlatans, Ansaldi and Bobone. A real doctor, not an idiot. Or send me to the Devil."

Just then the doorbell clanged and LM ran downstairs. It was Ellen Turner, one of many wealthy Englishwomen who had taken up residence in San Remo and occasionally dropped in on Katherine out of curiosity to see how a famous writer lived. After LM told her how sick Katherine was, she rushed off, returning with her own physician.

"Your left lung is infected. Your right lung is quiescent," said Dr. Foster, after carefully packing away his tools in Katherine's bedroom. "But there is good news, Mrs. Murry. It's not galloping consumption that gave you a high fever. What you have is a mild case of bronchial pneumonia that can be cured with bed rest."

She whispered hoarsely, "How do you know it isn't active tuberculosis that caused my fever?"

"The stethoscope. Bronchial pneumonia clogs the airways of your lungs. A quite different sound than the crackling of active tuberculosis. Once I knew this, it was simply a matter of tapping your lungs until I found the infection, which was when you cried out. An infected lung is filled with pus and painful. Fortunately only one lung is infected."

"I'm not dying?"

"No, certainly not, though you probably feel like you are." He looked down at his notes. "If you stay in bed, stay warm, drink hot liquids, and eat well you'll get better. I wish there was something I could give you but there is no medicine yet that can kill a lung infection. At least not yet, but we are working on it. We don't want another outbreak of the Spanish flu." He smiled at the pack of Abdullah's on her bed table. "Mrs. Murry, you smoke my favorite brand. I haven't seen those for a while."

He turned to LM hovering by the door, "It would be a good idea to move Mrs. Murry downstairs. She must stay in bed until she's out of danger and this room is too damp." Before departing, he took her hand and while he checked her pulse looked into her eyes. "In a week or so you will feel much better. I promise."

MR. VINCE CAME and with a neighbor's help they put Katherine's writing table in the kitchen to make room for her bed in the sitting room.

Four days later her temperature dropped. Her body had not given up on her; it wasn't her enemy; she would revive; she would have more time to write, to continue her work.

"I was saving these until you felt better," said LM, handing her a packet of letters. "There's a wire from Jack and several letters from your friends. You see, my dear Katie, you are not alone. And you always have me, too." She set the tea tray in Katherine's lap.

"Please let Mr. Vince know that we would like the bed moved upstairs again so I can have my writing room back."

"I don't know if that's wise. Your fever just broke—"

"Ida, do as I ask… please." LM shook her head and went back to the kitchen.

The first envelope she opened contained Jack's wire:

8 DECEMBER 1919: WILL COME FOR WEEK OF XMAS.
STOP. LETTER EXPLAINS. STOP. JACK

"Oh no!" she called out. Now look what I've done. I should never have sent that pitiful letter and that poem. I'm so sorry, Jack.

"Ida!" she shouted. "Why didn't you give this to me earlier? Quickly bring me my pen and writing paper."

She asked him to remember when they lived with D.H. Lawrence and he had one of his tuberculosis "rages" brought on by fever. Like D.H. she'd had a fever when she wrote him and was afraid it was galloping consumption because of Dr. Ansaldi's diagnosis. But it had turned out to be a mild case of pneumonia. Not to worry. LM was taking care of her and soon she'd be well.

She ended with:

> *I've driven you to this. I won't be such a vampire again. We must stick to our plan. In May I shall be better. All will be different. Above all there is no need for you to come now. DON'T COME; DON'T COME.*

Worried he wouldn't get her letter in time she sent a wire:

> 9 DECEMBER, 1919: IMPLORE YOU NOT TO. STOP. WRITTEN. STOP. DISMISS IDEA IMMEDIATELY. STOP. GREATEST POSSIBLE MISTAKE. STOP. BETTER TODAY.

Afraid he wouldn't believe her she wired again:

> 10 DECEMBER 1919: URGE YOU MOST EARNESTLY NOT TO COME. STOP.
>
> UTTERLY UNNECESSARY. STOP. ENTREAT YOU TO WAIT TILL MAY. STOP. LETTER SENT EXPLAINING.

Four days passed before Jack's belated letter arrived. LM brought it upstairs to Katherine. Her bed had been restored to its proper place and she was resting. She tore it open:

> *12 December, 1919*
>
> *My own darling,*
>
> *I got your Thursday letter and the verses called "The New Husband." I've wired you today to say I'm coming out for Christmas. I feel there is not much more I can say.*

*I don't think that at any time I've had a bigger blow than
that letter and these verses—more like a snake with a
terrible sting.*

Her heart was beating so fast she had to put down her pen and rest her head in her folded arms.

She waited until LM brought the tea tray and then read Jack's letter. It was terrible—half was an account of what she had done to him and the other half about his debts. She forced herself to get out of bed and go downstairs to her writing table. A log sputtered in the Terra Cotta. She added another one before sitting down. She decided to respond to one paragraph at a time otherwise it was too exhausting.

After accusing her of being a snake he wrote:

*But it's kind of you to tell me you have those feelings: far
better, for me anyhow, than keeping them from me. You
have too great a burden to bear; you can't carry it. Whether
I can manage mine, I don't know. We'll see when I get out to
you.*

She wrote her response:

*However ill I am, you are more ill. However weak I am you
are weaker—less able to bear things. You make me out so
cruel that… I feel you can't love me in the least—a snake
I am not. Are you fair in punishing me so horribly? I will
not receive your dreadful accusations into my soul for they
would kill me.*

She read through his next paragraph:

*What is certain is this can't go on—something must change.
My faith at present is that my coming out for a little while
will put you right. But I don't see why it should. I feel that
everything depends upon me; that I have to do something
quite definite, very quickly. But I don't know what it is… I
wish to God I were a man. Somehow I seem to have grown
up, gone bald even, without ever becoming a man; and I
find it terribly hard to master a situation.*

She responded:

> *The truth is that until I was ill you were never called upon*
> *'to play the man' to this extent—and it's <u>not</u> your role. When*
> *you once told me that you ought to be kept, you spoke the*
> *truth. I feel it. Ever since my illness this crisis I suppose has*
> *been impending, when suddenly in an agony I should turn*
> *all woman and lean on you. Now it's happened. The crisis is*
> *over—You must feel that. It won't return. It's over for good. I*
> *will not lean on you again.*

She stopped to watch the sputtering fire before picking up his letter
again to continue reading:

> *At present I'm trying to clear up the remains of last year's*
> *debts. Until they are cleared I shall stick to the A. That's*
> *callous, I suppose, but I can't help it. You know my position*
> *as a previous bankrupt. I dare not leave our debts unpaid.*
> *Once we're straight—and if things were to go moderately*
> *well I shall be straight by April—I'll do anything. But I know*
> *that to cut with little money coming in and heavy debts*
> *would mean inevitable disaster.*

I had no idea, she thought, before picking up her pen:

> *Jack, why have you kept me in the dark? Have your creditors*
> *come down on you? What are these terrible debts? I must be*
> *told them. You hint at them and then say I lack sympathy.*
> *You're not a pauper. You have £800 a year and you only*
> *contribute to my keep—not more than £50 a year at most.*
> *You write as though there were me to be provided for,*
> *yourself, and all to be done on something like £300. I know*
> *you have paid my doctor's bills and that my illness has cost*
> *you a great deal. IT WILL COST YOU NO MORE. I cannot*
> *take any more money from you ever and as soon as I am*
> *well I shall work to make a good deal more so that you have*
> *to pay less. But your letter frightens me for you—I think you*
> *have allowed this idea of money to take too great a hold on*
> *your brain.*

And yes I know your previous position as a bankrupt. Need I remind you that we used my allowance to pay those debts.

Reading his next paragraph she felt his anger replaced by resignation:

If I felt certain that my being there would really make things right until May, then nothing would matter. But now I can't pretend to a certainty I don't feel. We just have to leave it and see.

Her tears bled onto the ink of his letter. She brushed her tears aside. Why must he wrench my heart? No, I will not feel sorry for him. Not this time. Angrily, she underlined the *I*'s in his letter and asked herself how anyone could write a letter with fifty-five *I*'s. He'd piled delicate agony after delicate agony as if he was writing a tragedy, documenting himself as the martyred hero that he would publish after she was dead.

She thought about how to end her letter. What did she really want from him? There was no clear answer. But what she did know was that without Jack, she had no one to love. A barren, lonely life was unlivable. She wouldn't be able to bear the emptiness. Faced with this truth she wrote:

Let us bury the past—and go on and recover—We shall. Our only chance now is not to lose Hope but to go on and not give each other up. Your devoted—yours eternally, Your wife.

She wanted to believe what she wrote would make a difference, that their marriage could be saved, but she couldn't shake the fear that something was deeply wrong between them and it might be irreparable no matter how hard she clung to him.

She scribbled onto the envelope of his letter, *You have killed something within me and I no longer fear death.* She enfolded his letter and put it in her drawer to be filed later with the others. Her letter she sent to the post office with LM hoping it would arrive before he left London but maybe it was better if he did come after all.

Jack did not respond to her first telegram but after receiving the second one he sent a short letter:

It's no use you know: I've made up my mind to come.

He went on to say that he bitterly regretted what he had written on December 12, and asked her to:

Forget it, Burn it. It's got nothing to do with me, but only with a me that was harassed and inclined for a moment to throw up the sponge. But once the decision was taken, I've been a changed man. I've thought of nothing but the sheer happiness of being with you.

DECEMBER 1919

Loneliness

Now it is Loneliness who comes at night
Instead of Sleep, to sit beside my bed.
Like a tired child I lie and wait her tread,
I watch her softly blowing out the light.
Motionless sitting, neither left or right
She turns, and weary, weary droops her head.
She, too, is old; she, too, has fought the fight.
So, with the laurel she is garlanded.

LONELINESS—KM

THE CASETTA WAS TOO SMALL for the three of them. LM stayed in San Remo at the house of a new friend she'd met during her shopping excursions. In her absence, a maid was found by Dr. Foster, after he squashed the rumors in the village that the Casetta was a dark, foreboding house of contagion, inhabited by two women, one a giant and the other a consumptive.

One evening a thunderstorm kept LM at the Casetta and she cooked a special dinner from one of Katherine's recipes. Even Katherine thought she did an admirable job and hoped Jack might say something kind. But he had been suffering all day from neuralgia, and couldn't see past the shooting pain in his face and hands.

"Oh, you have no idea how intolerable this is. I am in agony," he cried out. LM rolled her eyes at Katherine as if to say how could he possibly not know that Katherine was an expert on *agony*.

"Let's go sit by the Terra Cotta and play Demon" said Katherine. "That will help you forget our agony and it will be warmer by the fire."

"You have no sympathy, Katherine. Neuralgia is extremely painful and no card game is going to distract me from it." He sank his head into his hands and moaned.

"Bogie, I'm just trying to help you feel better. I know for myself that distractions do relieve pain. Pain only becomes unbearable when one has no escape. C'mon, let's play cards."

LM got up to do the dishes. "No Jones, you too. As I recall you once played Demon with Jack and beat him to his greatest displeasure."

"No," said LM, surprised. "I don't remember it being that bad."

"You don't. He wanted to prove to us that the way to win was by taking several minutes before each move and his indecisiveness cost him the game. You beat him with your spontaneous quick plays and sheer boldness. Let's see if you can take him on again tonight and still be victorious."

"That's unfair of you to ask me to play," said Jack. "Can't you at least pity me for my sufferings."

She and LM exchanged smiles. "Oh come on, Jack, at least try."

Katherine and LM set out the three decks of playing cards and Jack came to the table unwillingly. He lost every game and finally threw in his cards and retired to the tiny spare bedroom that LM had vacated.

LM waited until she heard Jack's snore before coming into Katherine's room and making a bed for herself in the corner. Katherine thought it was better that he didn't know LM often slept there in case Katherine needed her, because it made her look too dependent on her caregiver.

Lying in bed, listening to LM settle down in her bedroll across the room, Katherine considered how much she relied on LM for everything. And how different a caregiver she was from Jack. LM ran to her when she coughed, offering a glass of water or a clean handkerchief; Jack ran from her when she coughed. LM asked about her symptoms every day; Jack never asked about her health or discussed her illness, not even naming it.

The pleasurable hours with Jack were when she pretended to be well. On those days, seated cross-legged on the floor like children, they imagined their future life together. As steam wafted from the Terra Cotta's burning logs, Jack sketched the Heron's floor plan, outlining the library and Katherine's writing room. In this dollhouse of their shared illusions, she drew in the china, furniture and knickknacks they'd both been collecting for their life together—after her rest-cure.

If not playing like children, they'd sit up late into the night discussing Dostoevsky, Chekhov or T.S. Eliot and Aldous Huxley who were contributing writers to Jack's magazine. Or they might discuss their own projects and their goals for the coming year. Jack was writing notes for a book on the style of writing and she planned to write many short stories and work on a novel. She couldn't have this kind of discourse with anyone in Ospedaletti, and their conversations reminded her of how much she missed talking about writing with Virginia Woolf over a cup of chamomile tea.

But only sixteen days into his visit, Jack departed for London and Katherine returned to her bed. She was exhausted from playing the role of a strong, healthy woman to keep him at ease. *Honesty should be prized above everything*, she thought, *but I pretended I was well. Our relationship is now based on a lie and it will not survive.*

On one of her many sleepless nights, the thunder raged, lightning struck, and the wind bit down hard on the roof, carrying off some of the tiles. She locked the windows, drew the heavy curtains against the siege and hid under the eiderdown, but the surf slamming against the rocks made sleep impossible.

Earlier she had been disturbed by someone crying out in pain but when she tried to get out of bed, she couldn't move. Her legs and arms were bound in ropes. Her mouth gagged. When she awoke the next morning she was relieved that she could lift her arms.

Stretching out on her bed bathed in sunlight, she knew it had been a dream, but the physical sensation of being entrapped, unable to save someone calling out for help, haunted her.

The melancholy she had kept at bay while Jack was there now sucked her down into its cave and, too weak to resist, she crawled inside and curled up like a hurt child. She had nothing left in her to fight her demons. Without her daily writing practice and no passion to write her stories, she'd lost the will to continue. She'd lost the will to survive.

The only work she finished was *The Athenaeum* novel-reviews. They didn't require creativity, but they did require countless hours of reading books that she thought should never have been published. She decided that reading books for the vast majority was not a literary passion but a pastime, and writing books, for the majority of authors, was also a pastime and not a passion.

The only reprieve from her melancholy was when Kot sent his translations of Chekhov's personal memoirs for her to edit.

In spite of his consumption, as a doctor, he never stopped tending to the sick, and as a writer he never stopped writing and publishing his work.

There was a quote from the short story writer Alphonse Daudet that Chekhov had jotted down in his journal, which she now jotted down herself, because it explained perfectly why she, too, wrote short stories:

"Why are thy songs so short?" a bird was once asked. *"Is it because thou art short of breath?"*

The bird replied, *"I have very many songs and I should like to sing them all."*

Dr. Chekhov openly discussed his symptoms as a consumptive. If there was no fever or cough and, if one continued to gain weight, the tuberculosis was quiescent. He also said it was not a death warrant if there were bloodstains on your handkerchief. For Katherine this was so freeing. She could now stop checking her handkerchief every time she coughed. And Chekhov said he coughed up blood for years before he died and it never stopped his work. He was determined to go on while he could, to value every living hour regardless of his fate.

She now knew what she had to do, if she was to sing any songs ever again. Stop writing novel-reviews for Jack's magazine. So what if Lytton Strachey said her column was well written or Jack said that the magazine would lose subscribers if she stopped.

Isn't my own work more important, she said to herself, than any of that drivel I review? Is this what I want to be remembered for? A reviewer of cheap inconsequential novels. God, no.

She picked up her pen and wrote in her journal:

> *Can I not make myself felt as a real personal force? I have had experience unknown to others. Surely I do know more than other people. I have suffered more, endured more. I know how they long to be happy and how precious is an atmosphere that is loving, a climate that is not frightening. I must cultivate my garden and do it now. I am the one who needs saving and only I can do it.*

The following morning she walked to the village drugstore without LM and without her cane. Weighing herself on the scale made her joyous. She'd gained another pound. With a lilt in her step, she was heading back to the Casetta when an idea for a new story came to mind and she hurried home to get it down before she forgot.

At her writing table she wrote a quick sketch about a young, single woman who has just found out she's pregnant. Up until she found out for sure, she'd been afraid but now that it was certain she knew what she had to do. It would be difficult but she had the courage and the impulse to see it through. Her only problem was her boyfriend, Roy. He always said he'd marry her if she'd have him, and he would want to do the proper thing by her. So she decided it would be best if she didn't tell him. Her doctor agreed to lie for her and he told Roy that she was just tired and needed a stay at the seaside. When she returned a week later, she could eat caviar sandwiches and drink champagne again—the danger had passed.

Now that she was feeling so much better, she insisted on LM taking a day off to visit her friends in San Remo. Katherine had to push her out the door, saying, "Don't worry. I'll be fine." LM promised to be back by nightfall.

All day Katherine worked on her new story without stopping to eat, and had just written down its title "Last Spring," when she became aware of a loud thumping in her chest. She pressed her hand against her heart to slow it down. Brandy would help but it was upstairs. She got up out of her chair to go get it and had to gasp for air.

She stumbled toward the staircase. Her heart racing ahead. She felt herself falling over into darkness.

When she awoke, a blurry face was hovering over her. She felt the cold, hard floor beneath her but, just like in her dream, she couldn't move. Nor could she speak.

She was scooped off the floor by strong, sturdy arms, carried upstairs and set on the bed. The eiderdown was gently draped over her and she was tucked in. "Mother, is that you?" she whimpered.

"You're going to be all right, my dearest."

The soft cool hand on her brow lifted and she called out, "Please don't go."

"I have to go to the village to telephone Dr. Foster in San Remo," said LM. "I'll be right back."

"Tell me what happened?" she said, trying to raise her head but it was too heavy.

"When I came back this evening, I found you on the floor. You gave me quite a fright. You must've fainted."

"Am I dying?"

"Certainly not, Katie. You've just had a terrible scare. We both have." LM poured her a glass of brandy and held up Katherine's head so she could take a sip.

"My feet are so cold."

"I'll fill your hot-water bag before I go," said LM, putting down the empty glass. Katherine grabbed hold of her hand. "Please don't leave me alone."

"I have to call the doctor. I won't be long."

Katherine awoke to her feet being gently massaged and then set near a heated bag. Normally she resented LM touching her but now she was very grateful.

"Thank you, Jones. You are such a comfort to me. I don't thank you enough, do I? What would have happened if you hadn't come home? I don't know why you stay with someone who treats you so cruelly. I've become a fiend."

"You're not a fiend, Katie. It's the illness that makes you act like that. I never take it personally. And what with these storms every night and not being able to sleep… why you just haven't been yourself."

"Would you pour me another brandy and have one yourself. It must have been a fright for you, too."

"Let me just go downstairs to fire up the Terra Cotta and get some heat up here. The fire must have gone out after you fainted. Then I'll join you for a glass."

Jones only wants the best for me, she thought. Like Coleridge's Albatross who *every day for food or play* loyally followed the Ancient Mariner's ship. And then the ungrateful Mariner shot him down. I will suffer from guilt like the Mariner if I don't change my thoughtless ways. If not for Jones, I'd still be lying on the floor.

LM joined her under the covers like they used to do in school, and after their brandies, Katherine drifted off to sleep.

In the early morning light, she awoke to a warm room. LM must have gotten up earlier to light the fire and brought her a pot of tea as she used to do when they were at Queen's college. Katherine smiled, remembering when she first asked LM to be her friend.

IDA WASN'T HER FIRST CHOICE. She made other school friends and only spoke with Ida when they practiced in the music room. She found her to be a sullen, slow-thinking girl and wondered how she'd ever managed to win the highly competitive President's Scholar award that paid her tuition.

Ida had been born in England, but was raised in Rhodesia, where her father was a doctor. When the family returned to London, she and her sister May attended Queen's College as day students. Their home nearby, the two sisters would walk to school together. Katherine would see May, crippled from polio, lean against Ida for support. Even back then, Ida had found a calling in taking care of others.

She was fourteen when her mother fell suddenly ill with typhoid fever. Ida nursed her through increasing stages of delirium and fever until her tormented death a month later. Immediately after the funeral, her father, Dr. Baker, locked up their house and took May and her brother back to Rhodesia. He said he couldn't bear staying in London where memories of his loving wife were too vivid. He arranged for Ida to move into Queen's College as a boarding student. Inconsolable, she withdrew from her school friends and kept to herself. Then she met Katherine who had just arrived from New Zealand.

One afternoon coming back from class, Katherine found Ida in her room, reading a poem she had left out on her bedside table. Ida jumped when she came in and quickly put down the paper.

"Sorry I came to deliver a letter and—"

"Don't be embarrassed. I like having my poetry read."

"You wrote this?"

"Yes. Do you like it?"

"Very much."

"Are you also a poet?"

"Heavens no. I can't write anything, but I very much appreciate people that do."

After that exchange, Ida would visit Katherine in the evenings. They'd sit together on the floor while Katherine read. Ida an uncritical listener.

But she wasn't always so shy and acquiescent. They were both on the school debating team and Ida was a star at arguing a case, often winning, even against Katherine who didn't take well to losing.

When Queens College girls took chaperoned walks in Regents Park they had to follow the strictly enforced rule of staying in a crocodile line, which meant you were not to break out of line or you'd get in trouble.

One day on their walk, Katherine was surprised to see the usually compliant Ida break out of the line to chase leaves falling from a giant oak, its limbs shaken by a sudden gust of wind. As the gilded autumn leaves fell, Ida reached out for them with her large clumsy hands and without breaking any, gently pressed them against her breast. When she saw Katherine was watching her, she smiled as if offering to share her joy in the fleeting beauty of Nature.

Katherine waved to Ida to join her when the girls stopped to rest on park benches. Ida hesitated. "Come on, silly. I don't bite. Come and sit with me." Ida sat down, still holding the captured leaves.

"Let's be friends," said Katherine.

Ida recoiled and said solemnly, "Friends don't happen just by saying it, Katie. Friendship is a very serious matter. Friends are something you become in time through loyalty and consideration."

The crocodile line was reassembled for the march back to school and Katherine didn't mention her request again, feeling rather slighted by Ida's response. Several students had already rejected her friendship. They found her too bold with her emotions and called her the Little Colonialist from New Zealand. But she had thought Ida would have welcomed her friendship having so few friends herself.

She waited a few weeks before approaching her again. This time during afternoon teatime, she flopped down next to her. "Now that we've taken a walk together and shared a pot of tea, can't we be friends?"

Ida giggled and put her hand up to her mouth. Then she covered her other large hand over Katherine's small hand and said, "Yes, friends. Friends forever!"

HEARING DR. FOSTER CLIMBING the stairs, Katherine sat up and put on a smile.

After his examination, he sat down on the bed and took her wrist in his hand to check her pulse against his pocket watch. "Your heartbeat is still weak."

"I'm not surprised. It's exhausted. I don't ever want to hear it thump like that again. I was sure I was dying."

"People often say heart palpitations feel like that. To us doctors they are dire warnings to our patients to take better care of themselves. Your attack was brought on by acute nervous exhaustion, Mrs. Murry.

"You're too isolated here in Ospedaletti and our winter storms are too harsh on a woman in such poor health. You fought a good fight but you don't have any strength left. You need people around you who care about you. Ida can't do it all. She's worn-out too and could become ill herself."

"But you said I wasn't contagious."

"I still think so. But what if she had an accident? Took a fall. Then what would you do? No one is impervious to bad luck.

"How long has she been in your service?"

Katherine laughed. "She's not in my service. We've been friends since we met at school sixteen years ago. After I was diagnosed a consumptive, she moved in with my husband and me as my companion and housekeeper. That was a year ago. Even before then she took care of me during several of my illnesses, but she was never my servant."

"Then you're quite fortunate to have her. There are very few Griselda's in our modern world who dedicate their lives to serving others without financial reward."

"So you've read Chaucer's "Canterbury Tales."

He smiled. "Yes, but a very long time ago in school."

"Well, it's very perceptive of you. Ida is an enigma like Griselda. I've never been able to figure out why she is so devoted to me."

He wrote down a prescription, put it on her bed table and said, "This will help a bit, but to be honest, Mrs. Murry, you need to seriously consider going where the weather is more moderate and where you can receive excellent medical care."

"Do you mean a nursing home, Doctor?"

"Yes, I do. You must have complete rest until your heart is stronger."

"A tuberculosis clinic?"

"No, that won't be necessary. As I said, I'm not worried about your lungs. It's your heart that's at risk. You might have another attack, if you don't get away, and not be so lucky."

After he left, Katherine wrote a letter to Connie and Jinnie in Menton asking for their help. A few days later she received their response.

L'Hermitage, a nursing home in Menton, had a room available. It wasn't too expensive and it was very near their own home, Villa Flora. And there was a position for Ida in another nursing home nearby that would help defray expenses. Ida could stay with them at Villa Flora and once Katherine was feeling better she could join them.

In the same post was a letter from her sister, Chaddie, with news that upon their father's return to Wellington, he'd married Laura Kate Bright, their mother's best friend. Katherine wasn't surprised at his marrying again though she was disappointed he hadn't confided in her during his visit. Since her mother's death the previous year, he had been miserable living alone. She expected Jack would also find another woman to love him when she died, if he hadn't already. He was too dependent on others to be alone.

She envisioned Laura Bright standing on the Wellington dock as Pa came ashore. She saw him step off the gangplank and could feel the warmth and safety of his arms embracing his future wife.

It gave her an idea for a story that she scribbled down in her notebook. It would take place on a similar dock. But it would be about a wife returning home after a long voyage and the impatient husband waiting on the dock.

"YOUR PULSE IS STILL WEAK," said Dr. Foster holding her wrist at his next visit. "Have you thought more about what I said about leaving Ospedaletti?"

"Yes, I have. My cousin has found me a nursing home in Menton. She and her companion reside in their own villa nearby."

"I'm very pleased to hear that. With Ida and your cousin there to take care of you, and the professional care of a nursing home, I am certain you will fully recover."

"A full recovery, Doctor? My lungs, too?"

He hesitated. "I don't believe in giving my patients false hopes. As you well know, we haven't found a cure yet for tuberculosis. But if your heart regains its strength, a woman with your determination has a fighting chance. But for now you need to rest in bed."

She was cautious in writing Jack about her palpitation attack and her plans to leave Ospedaletti. After what happened the last time she confessed the true state of her health, he had jumped on his white stallion to come rescue her, which did neither of them any good.

> *Now, my precious, please forgive what I am going to say. And do not think you came here all for nothing or anything dreadful like that—It's just my peculiar fate at present which won't leave me—I must tell you, but there is no action for you to take—nothing for you to worry about in the very slightest. I don't ask your help or anything & God forbid I should make you work harder. Just go on as you are and I shall manage what I have to manage.*

She told him about the nursing home in Menton and that LM would be traveling with her. And then she went on to explain briefly what happened after he left:

> *It is not feasible to believe—She was away one day this week—I was alone. It was evening. I had a heart attack in my room & you see there was no one to call... Now don't think that means I regret you are not here now. It does not— All it means is that I must not be alone.*

DECEMBER 1919

Griselda

There is no thing, and so God my soul save,
That you may like displeasing unto me;
I do not wish a single thing to have,
Nor dread a thing to lose, save only ye;
This will is in my heart and aye shall be,
Nor length of time nor death may this deface,
Nor turn my passion to another place.

CANTERBURY TALES—GEOFFREY CHAUCER

THE MONDAY BEFORE THEIR DEPARTURE, at the end of January, a postal strike was announced. Italy was demonstrating its resentment against the Allies for not giving them what they asked for at Versailles—the Adriatic Coastline—and for not treating the Italian Prime Minster with respect during the treaty negotiations. Italians also started to taunt English tourists in the streets.

The morning of the strike LM was sneered at by several Italian men yelling, "You'd better pack up your traps and go. We don't want any more of you English here. We're going to clear you out."

If only they knew how soon and with what delight Katherine accepted their orders to 'pack up your traps and go' and with what great anticipation she planned her exodus. What she couldn't anticipate is how Jack would respond to her leaving Ospedaletti before she completed her rest-cure in May. This is not what they'd planned together.

In bed that night she thought about the letter she'd carefully crafted to Jack about her heart attack and her pending departure. It made her anxious that she'd censored her true feelings so that he might not suffer for her sake. But why should she have to suffer alone? Unable to sleep, she propped her ash-wood writing case on her lap, took a pen from its holder and wrote what she'd held back from saying earlier: *These are the worst days of my whole life.*

She blew out the gaslight and sank into her pillows hoping to sleep. But a glimmer of a story kept her awake. Characters started to speak to her in settings she created.

The moment she heard LM stirring across the room, she called out, "Bring me my morning tea right away," quickly forgetting her resolution to be gracious to her Griselda.

Throughout the day she stayed in bed and wrote, stopping only when LM brought afternoon tea and egg sandwiches and insisted Katherine eat.

By late that night Katherine crossed out *The Exile* on the title sheet and wrote *The Man Without a Temperament*. Finally satisfied, she placed the title sheet on top of a stack of written pages. A story had enfolded about a husband who took a two-year leave of absence from his profession to go into seclusion with his ill wife. He chose a hotel in southern France where she could recuperate. The wife knows she's a burden and tries not to ask him to do things for her, but her illness has made her an invalid and needy of his care. The husband can't accept the pale, emaciated woman she has become and turns away from her to dwell in the past, when she was his beautiful, passionate wife. The other hotel guests find his trance-like state inhuman and his distant eyes reptilian. The children are afraid of him. Only his wife forgives his lack of compassion.

Exhausted from her work, Katherine tried to sleep but the stormy night shook the Casetta and the sea howled. She searched for a match and relit the gaslight to write in her journal notebook:

> *I have made it a rule of my life never to regret and never to look back. Regret is an appalling waste of energy, and no one who intends to become a writer can afford to indulge in it. You can't get it into shape; you can't build on it; it's only good for wallowing in.*

When she closed her eyes again…

She found herself standing in front of the familiar Bavarian pension where she had stayed many years ago, her hand on the doorknob… "Don't open that door!" she heard herself say. Her stomach cramped. Her hands felt sticky. She screamed out, "No!"

LM came running to her bedside and, as she had so often done before, rocked her until she stopped shaking and the night terror slipped away.

Katherine awoke to LM bringing in her morning tray. "I can't bear another day in bed. If it's warm enough outside I want to spend it on the veranda editing my story. Don't look at me like that. Get me my cane."

"Didn't Dr. Foster tell you to stay in bed?"

"I didn't say I was going for a walk. Just outside on the veranda."

She sat in the wicker chair until a brisk wind forced her indoors. Next to the warmth of the crackling Terra Cotta, as tired as she felt, she refilled her pen in the inkpot, dried its nib against the hairs of her little brass pig and wrote to Jack:

> I am sending to Arts and Letters by post registered this day
> a story called "The Man Without a Temperament." The MS I
> send is positively my only copy.

She had decided if A&L didn't want it, she would ask them to send the MS to Jack. If they did want it then they were to send the MS and their proofs to Jack so he could compare them and correct any errors before the story went to print.

She asked Jack to have the original MS professionally copied at her expense as she did not have:

> so much as a shaving or a paring of it wherewith I could
> reconstruct its like. I hope I do not exaggerate. If I do—
> forgive me. You know a parent's feelings—they are terrible at
> this moment. I feel my darling goes among lions. And I think
> there is not a word or comma I would change or that can be
> changed.

LM IN FEAR of the recent altercation between her and the Italian men spitting at her on the street had taken to sleeping in her day clothes. When she heard the doorbell clang repeatedly, she rushed to Katherine's bedroom window, peeked out and reported back to Katherine that there were several men stumbling around their front door. Because the night was well lit by the full moon, she could see their silhouettes. The bell kept clanging over their raucous laughter.

"Why don't they go away?" said Ida, anxiously.

"Because they've nothing to fear," said Katherine. "We have no phone and even if we screamed for help the neighbors are too far away. They have us!" She whispered, "Get the gun."

LM hesitated, shaking her head violently. Katherine whispered again, "Get the gun!" LM tiptoed downstairs and returned holding the gun stiffly away from her like it smelled bad.

At the window Katherine called out a warning, "Go away or we'll shoot." The bell stopped clanging. The men could be heard arguing. Then they started clanging the bell again. LM moved Katherine away from the window and aimed the gun down at the men. A shot rang out followed by shouts and running footsteps fading into the night.

Katherine stared in wonder at LM's large figure standing at the moon-lit window in her day clothes at midnight with her finger still on the trigger. She roared with laughter.

"Katie, this is not funny. What if I've hurt someone and they're injured or dying?"

"Serve them right." She started laughing again. "Oh Jones, I do wish you could have seen yourself pull that trigger. You were fearless."

LM raised her empty hand to her mouth and started to giggle.

"I think we should toast you with a glass of brandy after your brave deed," said Katherine. "Don't you?"

LM set the gun down timidly next to the brandy and poured two generous glasses. She joined Katherine under the eiderdown and both enjoyed a pleasant silence after the jarring noise and commotion.

Katherine broke the silence, saying, "I'm sorry that I've been so cross with you. It must not be easy to help someone who doesn't want to be helped.

"When Dr. Foster referred to you as my servant it made me realize how awful my behavior is toward you. I set him straight, of course, but he was right to think that. I do treat you like a servant. And I'm sorry. I wish you would speak up when I treat you unkindly. I really don't want you to be my Griselda."

"Who is Griselda?"

"She is one of Chaucer's most famous and mysterious characters in the *Canterbury Tales*. Her husband was a king and to prove her love for him she was willing to sacrifice her children if it pleased him. He even tested her love by bringing a woman into his castle and then threw Griselda out, but she never weakened in her resolve to remain faithful to him."

"How wonderful that Dr. Foster sees me as Griselda. She sounds magnificent."

"No. No. You misunderstand me. Chaucer was warning women not to follow the way of Griselda:

> *Nay, follow Echo, that holds no silence,*
> *But answers always like a countervail;*
> *Be not befooled, for all your innocence,*
> *But take the upper hand and you'll prevail."*

Katherine reached over and slipped her hand under LM's much larger one. "You should take the upper hand. Don't let me boss you around. You're not my Griselda. You're not my wife or my servant, but my dear loyal friend, as you promised to be when we were students."

LM pushed her hand away and got out of the bed. "It's you that doesn't understand," she said angrily. "I am honored to be your Griselda. I consider it my art, my profession to take care of those I love. I grew up taking care of my sister and then my mother when she became ill and then when my father needed me. I'll never forgive myself for leaving him on his own in Rhodesia. If I'd stayed with him, he might not have taken his own life."

"Jones, you never told me that was how your father died. I'm so sorry."

LM looked down at her with the same sad eyes that had first drawn Katherine to her at school. "I don't need your pity. This is what I do. If I wasn't taking care of you, I would be taking care of someone else."

LM sat on the edge of the bed and Katherine put the eiderdown around her and gave her a hankie for her sniffles.

"I don't believe anyone should sacrifice their own life for someone else. It isn't right that I ask that of you just so I can be free to do my work. You shouldn't let me take advantage of you."

"But your work is far more important than anything I could possibly do. And Jack isn't ever around and when he is he doesn't take care of you like I do."

For a moment Katherine felt she should defend him but wasn't Ida only speaking the truth. "Sometimes I think you would prefer he and I remain apart."

"Well Jack is JACK! Thoughtless and terribly self-absorbed, now isn't he?" said LM sharply. "He distracts you from your work because he thinks his work is more important."

Katherine smiled. "You're right, Jones, but he is also my husband and I accept his faults as I ask you to accept mine. Someday, when we are all living at the Heron—"

"I thought you didn't want me to come with you to your country house," interrupted LM. "That's why I have never felt comfortable here at the Casetta, never even unpacked my trunk. I know any minute you'd be sending me off."

"Oh dear, Jones. How heartless I've been to your feelings. But consider that to be in the past. I ask you now to share my present minuses in the hope that you'll be able to share my future plusses. After what we've been through here at the Casetta, I can't imagine you not staying with me. Will you join us at the Heron?"

"Yes, Yes. Of course, I will," said LM, without hesitation.

"But you must try to get along with Jack, if only on my behalf." She paused and smiled again. "But feel free to beat him at Demon anytime. It does him good to be knocked around a bit."

SHE PACKED HER NOTEBOOKS, ink and pens into her wooden writing case. Her traveling companions, the grinning nutcracker crocodile with a hinged jaw and the brass pig penwiper, were packed last so they could peek out on the long taxi ride across the Italian border into Menton, France.

She sat down to reread a few of Jack's letters before putting them in the trunk. His fraught tone disturbed her. She opened up her notebook and wrote:

> *I know now that I can only write when I am in the Present*
> *and my writing is what matters, nothing is more important.*
> *I must write. But how to make Jack understand that if he*
> *cannot live in the Present with me then it is best that we*
> *remain separated.*

The last few days spent writing a successful short story had filled her with new hope. It was the absence of work, the meaninglessness of her existence that had brought her to the abyss. Writing was the cure. It always had been. Another idea sprang into her thoughts and she opened her notebook again:

An old woman sits in her living-room window knitting.
She looks up at a funeral march passing her window.
She's surprised and rather frightened when they stop.
A man jumps out of the carriage and walks toward her
door. She drops her knitting in fright thinking there must
be some mistake.

She closed her notebook with a sigh, unsure of where the story would go from here but confident she would continue with it once she was settled in Menton. Oh, Menton, she thought, how can one word sound so wonderful?

She wrote Jack one last letter and posted it before they left, hoping it wouldn't be held up too long by the postal strike.

My dearest Bogey:

Ever since you left here this time—since this last 'illness' of mine—my feelings toward LM are absolutely changed. It is not only that the hatred is gone. Something positive is there which is very like love for her. She has convinced me at last, against all my opposition, that she is trying to do all in her power for me—and that she is devoted to the one idea which is (please forgive my egoism) to see me well again… My hate is quite lifted—quite gone; it is like a curse removed. LM has been through the storm with us. I want her to share in the calm—to act Marie's part for us in our country house. Do you agree? I feel I cannot do without her now. It was only when I refused to acknowledge this—to not acknowledge her importance to me—that I hated her. Now that I do, I can be sincere and trust her and of course she, feeling the difference, is a different person. Her self-respect has all come back.

You must realize that now that we are at peace I am never exasperated and she does not annoy me. I only feel 'free' for work and everything.

After finishing Jack's letter, she wrote to his brother, Richard. He had sent her a bound leather copy of a story she'd written before coming to Italy, *Je ne parle pas français*. Richard had helped design and set the print. It was to be distributed by their own small publishing house, The Heron Press. She thanked him for the beautiful job he had done on the illustrations.

She told him how much she looked forward to leaving the horrible days and nights spent in the unpleasant climate of Ospedaletti behind her.

> *Yet there are moments you know, when after a dark day there comes a sunset—such a glowing gorgeous marvelous sky that one forgets all in the beauty of it—these are the moments when I am really writing—Whatever happens I have had these blissful, perfect moments and they are worth living for. I thought, when I left England, I could not love writing more than I did, but now I feel I've never known what it is to be a writer until I came here.*

JANUARY, 1920

L'Hermitage—Menton, France

A gulf of silence separates us from each other
I stand at one side of the gulf—you at the other
I cannot see you or hear you—yet know that you are there.
Often I call you by your childish name
And pretend that the echo to my crying is your voice.
How can we bridge the gulf—never by speed or touch.
Once I thought we might fill it quite up with our tears
Now I want to shatter it with our laughter.

THE GULF—KM

S HE OPENED HER EYES upon cornflowers, jonquils and rosemary sprigs arranged in a crystal vase on her bedside table. Outside her open window morning birds sang and a soft warm breeze carried the faint fragrances of tangerines with just a touch of nutmeg. Under the cuddly warmth of a lambskin blanket, she ran her hands along the fine linen sheets that had gently held her sore and tired body through the night. I must be dreaming, she thought. There was a soft tapping at the door and she sat up against the fluffy pillows.

"Come in," she said, expecting a fairy godmother to appear. A young girl tiptoed through the doorway. She was wearing a golden yellow uniform with a starched white apron tied around her tiny waist. She curtsied and said, "Bonjour Madame. Bienvenue à L'Hermitage. Je m'appelle Marie. Would you like your breakfast in bed this morning?"

Katherine looked in wonder at this wingless angel and nodded.

Marie set down a white basket tray with a blue china teapot, matching china piled high with toast, a pot of honey, a thick slab of butter, and a bouquet of violets. Katherine thanked her and asked if she could see a British newspaper. Marie curtsied again and said she'd see what she could do.

Katherine's eyes flitted like a butterfly over the huge room, taking flights of fancy from the purple floral couch to the yellow needlepoint chairs to a large writing table with a cut-glass inkstand that she longed to sit at soon.

She squeezed her eyes shut and opened them again to be certain this wasn't a dream. Yesterday, she said to herself, I was an impoverished woman in distress being carried downstream in a raging river and just look at me now. If I can't be cured here, I will never be cured.

The startling juxtaposition from Ospedaletti to Menton brought to mind a camping trip she had taken at the age of nineteen, just before she left Wellington for London and never returned.

She'd camped out on the hard ground and played with the Maori children, asking them many questions and scribbling down their answers in her notebook. The quick sketches of the rough, impoverished lives of North Island's inhabitants were later used in *The Woman at the Store*, the story that had brought her to Jack's attention. The camping trip had been a grand adventure but she'd been relieved to return home to the comforts of Wellington, just as relieved as she was now to find herself surrounded in such finery after roughing it at Casetta Deerholm.

She admired an electric lamp under a gold, silk shade on her bed table. She flicked it off and on with child-like joy. No more lighting gaslights with a match she could never find.

Slipping out of the bed she carried her teacup over to the wide-open windows that let in the warm breeze that had awoken her earlier with the fragrance of tangerines. The first window she stood at looked out upon olive groves, the sea in the distance. She called it "blue view." The other window she christened "green view" as it looked over the mountains forested with high pines. The sky had never been a deeper blue. The marble balcony was inviting but she felt too fragile to step out quite yet. All in good time.

She'd just gotten back into bed to have her breakfast when there was another tap at the door. Two real fairy godmothers made their entrance: Jinnie Fullerton, tall and regal, and Connie Beauchamp, stout and matronly; both elegantly dressed, effervescently charming, and motherly.

"Welcome, dear child. How are you? Do you need anything? No don't get up."

Katherine smiled, reclining on the pillows. "Much better thank you. Ida didn't come with you?"

"She is settling in at the health clinic where she will be employed while you are here. She's very pleased with the arrangements and asked me to tell you that she came by last night but found you asleep."

"We thought you might like something to read," said Connie, placing a few English magazines and two Christian pamphlets with embossed gold crosses on her quilt. The pamphlets didn't surprise Katherine. Her father had forewarned her that they would try to convert her to Catholicism.

"How did you know those are my favorite flowers?" she said, looking over at Jinnie arranging a bouquet of budding yellow jonquils in a vase.

"A little angel told us," they said, giggling.

"We won't stay too long, my dear. You mustn't be anxious or worried about anything for the next several weeks. Let your heart heal. If there is anything you need, tell Marie, and we'll bring it on our next visit."

"Well, there is one thing," she said, and smiled. "Please tell me this is not a dream. You really are standing here with the sunshine streaming behind you. Tell me I will not fall back asleep and wake up with a thunderstorm raging down on the Casetta. Have I truly escaped?"

"Yes, dear child. You're safe with us."

"This is all too wonderful."

After they left she used the bed tray to write Jack the good news. There'd be no more miserable letters written with her pen.

After a week of bed rest, she ventured downstairs to eat with the other nursing home guests. The pretty dining room with all its elegant trimmings could not hide the pain and suffering of the people slumped at the tables. Many had private nurses spoon-feeding their lax mouths with green pudding that slipped down on to their clothes. Other guests sunk down in their wheelchairs seemed to be half alive. The ones with hacking coughs were quarantined in a corner where a seat had been reserved for her and marked with a name card. She wanted to say there was some mistake, she was here to heal her heart not her lungs, but then had an embarrassing coughing spasm.

She stared down at her plate through dinner, unable to bear looking into her companions' sunken eyes, eyes that had the feverish glints of consumption. Do I look as mad? As emaciated? As old? Or is this what the final stage of my disease looks like? she wondered, forcing her hand to pick up a fork and eat.

After two weeks at L'Hermitage she was cheered to return to her room after lunch and find a stack of mail that had been forwarded from Italy and another stack that included letters addressed to Menton. She immediately opened a letter from Jack.

In her first letter to him from Menton she had listed the many expenditures she was forced to make at L'Hermitage. She told him she was even willing to sell her new story collection outright for £20 as long as she would receive the cash immediately. She found it too humiliating to ask for his help directly but hoped he would consider it on his own, though Jack was never quick to open his wallet to anyone. How ironic that the only two men she could appeal to for financial help, Jack and her father, were both renowned misers. Whereas LM, who had far less income than either of them, was always generous.

How abominably selfish, she concluded after reading his letter through a second time, it's all about his walk through Sussex. *A day's sheer happiness—Drunken with the magnificence*—has he no understanding of what life is like here living with the very ill and wondering when I will be one of them? The last line in his letter was the most inexplicable: *How's money—let me know, please.* Didn't he read my letter? How much clearer must I be without humiliating myself?

As the days passed, she became more wretched and bitter toward him. But she held off writing him, hoping a more compassionate, empathetic letter would arrive soon.

One morning as she looked out at the "blue view," she was trying not to be impatient while she waited for the mail. When Marie finally tapped on her door and entered again with empty hands, Katherine grabbed her fountain pen and set to writing Jack the letter she had written in her head several times but hoped never to send:

PLEASE READ THIS ALL THROUGH she scratched in thick ink across the top of the page.

> *My dear Bogey, you have hurt me <u>dreadfully</u>—if you reflect for one moment you will perhaps realize how your 'how's money?' struck me. Did I not tell you the expenses I had coming here—the bills to settle, the hire of the motor, the theft of my overcoat, the more expensive room, the extras such as goûters, frictions and LM to look after. Yes, I have*

told you all these things. I imagined you would immediately wire me £10. <u>I imagined</u> you would have written, 'It's gorgeous to know you're there & getting better. Don't worry. Of course, I shall contribute £10 a month towards your expenses.' But no nothing at all.

In addition I <u>counted</u> on your loving sympathy and understanding, and the fact that you failed me in this is the hardest of all to bear. I really wonder Bogey if you even read my letters.

So now I will be direct... I ask you to contribute £10 a month towards my expenses here...

It is so bitter to have to ask you this—terribly bitter. Nevertheless I am determined to get well. I will <u>not</u> be overcome by anything—not even by the letter you sent me in Italy telling me to remember AS I grew more lonely SO you were loving me more. If you had read that in a novel what would you have thought? Well, I thank God I read it here and not at the Casetta.

I've nothing to say to you, Bogey. I am too hurt. I shall not write again.

Your Wife

The next day she received a second letter from him. Their letters had crossed in the mail and she felt a rush of guilt when a check for £20 dropped out of it. That was until she read his letter and learned the check was not an expression of her husband's generous love. To the contrary, he was offering it, like a book agent would, as an advance on her next short story collection. A check he would get back as soon as he negotiated a publishing deal.

His letter rambled on about another trip to the '*breathtakingly lovely country*' of Sussex and how he would '*beat the country thoroughly*' the next weekend searching for their Heron.

A third letter quickly followed: *Though things are tight, I will send you another cheque for £20 tomorrow, if you will repay me when you get the money for your book.* And then in the evening mail he withdrew his offer, writing that he could only manage ten.

She stood at the window looking out at the boats bobbing back and forth anchored in Menton's port and wondered where he spent his thousand pounds a year salary because he certainly wasn't sharing any of it with her.

She sat down at her writing table and wrote:

> As regards the advance money I would rather wait and receive it for my book than that you should lend it to me. I MUST have it for my overcoat, fare home, etc., and I certainly do not want to borrow it from you. Perhaps I did not make clear that I BOTHER you for the £10 a month—I mean, NOT as a loan.

> If you can agree to allowing me £10 a month for my expenses while I am here I shall look upon this cheque as the first 2 months installment. I would perfectly understand your money is <u>tight</u> had I NOT consumption, a weak heart & chronic neuritis in my lower limbs.

As far as her not writing more often:

> It's no good my writing every day. I can't. I simply feel you don't read the letters—I try and do my own work instead. There's a much better chance that you'll read that one day— though why you should I don't know.

She reminded him that she must now correct the proofs of *The Man Without a Temperament* as he was living at such racing speed, she didn't think he had the time to do a good job himself. Anxious that her story might go to print without her seeing the proofs, she wrote:

> Every word matters. I can't afford mistakes. Another word won't do. I chose every single word. Please answer this request when you next write.

THE CONSTANT NOISE of patients, nurses, and servants clattering back and forth in the hallway made it impossible to write. She complained and was moved to another room but it was just as bad. In three weeks her residence in L'Hermitage had proven to her that she would never get well in a sanatorium because she'd never get any work done. The voices and words and half visions that she couldn't write down were driving her mad.

She was behind in her novel-reviews and the last short story she wanted to include in her short story collection wasn't finished. She had decided to call the collection *Second Helping* and thought it an appropriate title for her second collection. Usually she would ask Jack's opinion, as he was always helpful when it came to her work, but she no longer trusted him. How could she when he had withdrawn so from her? His mind was only on his own financial worries and the magazine and his "torturous walks" through the countryside searching for the Heron that she would never live long enough to see.

After weeks of bed rest, she was still unable to walk beyond the garden at L'Hermitage. On her own she at least took a few short steps into the garden, enjoyed the winter blooms of pale violets, and particularly the lovely palm with large green fans that she often watched from her window. Its friendly fronds seemed to wave to her and she'd wave back.

She returned to her room determined to make the final edit of *Second Helping*. Only that would relieve her melancholy. At the end of the day she had finished and, quite pleased with herself, opened to a blank page in her notebook and wrote:

> *Work will win if only I can stick to it. It will win after all*
> *and through all.*

Jack's next letter gave her some relief as his response clearly showed he had read every word of her last letter. If she would send *Second Helping* he would type it himself and send it off to the publisher. And "without fail" he'd read the proofs for *The Man Without a Temperament* before sending to her, but would not change one word.

As much as she appreciated him finally responding to her requests and also asking her to write to him every day, she needed to speak the truth from her heart, not caring if he would suffer from her honesty. She must tell the truth:

> *My darling, I can't write every day—I love you but*
> *something has gone dead in me—rather—no, I can't explain*
> *it. Explanations are so futile—you NEVER listen to them,*
> *you know—I shrink from trying anymore. Give me time will*
> *you? I'll get over this—I get over everything but it takes time.*

But darling, darling, that doesn't make me love you less—I
love you—that's the whole infernal trouble!

After sending these anguished words, she collapsed into her bed with
a painful, throbbing headache. The doctors insisted she take Veronal but
she no longer trusted their medical advice. They became angry when
she refused, but after withdrawing from its addiction in Bavaria she had
sworn never to take it again.

Several days later she received Jack's response to her letter and sat a
long time looking out on the "green view" before opening it.

As before, she was disappointed. She searched for the passion that
his letters had once evoked, but he now played the part of a book agent,
informing her that her publisher, Constable, had agreed to the £40
advance for the collection.

His coldness tore her heart apart. Has he forgotten why I am in the
south of France and not at home with him? she asked herself. I wasn't
looking for a review from *The Man Without a Temperament*. It doesn't
help us to say it was *amazingly good, no one can write like you-but it's
also extraordinarily beautiful*. I wanted you to read the story and maybe
understand *us* better. Didn't you recognize yourself in the reptilian
husband?

He finished off his "agent" letter asking her to make up her mind as
to which stories were to be included in the second collection.

"Where is my husband?" she asked aloud, looking around her lovely,
lonely room.

The only warmth she could wrap around her chilled shoulders was
his sign off: *Your own, Boge.*

She cried as she wrote in her notebook:

> *It was a question of sympathy of understanding, of being the*
> *least interested, of asking me JUST ONCE how I was.*

She sent a wire with the pretense of requesting to hear a response from
their cat "Wing," as she couldn't bear another formal letter from Jack:

THURSDAY LETTER CAME. STOP. TELL WING WIRE
IMMEDIATELY. STOP. YOUR COLDNESS KILLING ME. STOP.

She used his nickname for her to sign off: "WIG"

"Wing" immediately responded:

WIRE RECEIVED. STOP. ALL WELL. STOP. HE LOVES YOU
DESPERATELY. STOP. HE CAN'T DO MORE. STOP

A few days later Jack wrote again:

*I've waited a minute. Lit a cigarette. I must be calm. For
somehow in spite of myself our destiny has come to tremble
on a razor's edge. Hitherto I have written desperately, and
made the wounds I have inflicted on you worse. I must be
calm.*

*Darling my own heart the very me. I feel tonight at the end
of my tether. Some blind force is crushing the hope out of
me. For I swear to you as my lover and my wife that all I
have done since I came back from Italy has been with a
single thought—love of you. Instead of bringing us nearer it
has driven us apart.*

*There is, Wig, a certain amount of real insensibility in me. I
think that has been proved now. I must just accept it: I hate
it, and try to kill it. But the fact remains that I never realized
how much you were suffering in Ospedaletti, nor how great
would be your anxiety about money in Menton. Both those
things you had a right to expect of me as your lover and,
there's no doubt in my own mind that I failed in them both.*

*You see my darling it's wrong for us to be apart. That is what
it comes to at the last. You can understand my harshness,
blackness, my habit of silence when you are near me, and
make allowances; but when we are so far away that is
impossible yet it is more necessary than ever.*

*The only thing is for you to get well. Get well my darling,
and let's put an end to this time of torture. Your voice is
sweet, but mine is harsh when we call from so far away.*

*Let me hold you in my arms. Let this ghastly nightmare go.
Your own Boge*

Katherine let out a sob. Finally he had heard her. Finally she could feel his arms tighten around her.

Her writing case propped on her knees, she wrote back:

> *Your Saturday evening letter has come with the*
> *'explanation.' Don't say another word about it. Let's after this*
> *put it quite away. Yes, I felt in Ospedaletti that you refused*
> *to understand and I have felt since I have been abroad*
> *this time that you have turned away from me. Withdrawn*
> *yourself utterly from me.*
>
> *Let's get over all this. What has been—has been. Not being an*
> *intellectual I always seem to have to learn things at the risk*
> *of my life—but I do learn. Let's be wise, true, real lovers from*
> *now on.*
>
> *Let's enter the Heron from today—from this very minute*
> *and I shall rejoice in you and if it's not too great an effort—*
> *dear love—try and rejoice in me.*
>
> *It's lunch time. I'm in bed, I must fly up. My nib will not*
> *write—It must write that I love you and you only world*
> *without end amen—*

Villa Flora, Menton

*Today Jinnie arrived with a carriage and fur rugs and silk
cushions. Took me to their villa… a chaise longue in the
garden—a tiny tray with black coffee out of a silver pot,
Grand Marnier, cigarettes, little bunch of violets. Their
villa is a dream—Spanish silk bed coverlets, Italian china,
stillness, maids in tiny muslin aprons flitting over carpets…*

NOTEBOOKS—KM

JINNIE AND CONNIE wrapped her in fur rugs for the first visit to
Villa Flora. LM, who lodged nearby, joined them for tea in the salon.
Katherine was shown a silver bedroom with a splendid balcony view of
the Mediterranean. "I would love to live here."

"It is our wish too. We're sure you'll get well here under our care.
This is what we have wanted since we met in Ospedaletti," said Jinnie,
looking terribly concerned. "But we have to consider our other guest.
When we mentioned it to Mr. Davis, who has been most generous to us,
he was quite concerned, being of weak health himself, that your illness
might be infectious. We wouldn't want him to leave on your account,
now, would we, dear?"

"Certainly not. But if Dr. Rendall gave a favorable diagnosis, could
I come?"

"Nothing would please us more," said Jinnie, warmly hugging Katherine. "We will pray that Dr. Rendall will find you on the mend."

A few days later a letter came from D.H. Lawrence with a packet
of other mail. They'd had their turbulent moments in the past but she
still considered him one of her closest friends and, not having heard
from him for quite some time, she hoped he was writing to renew their
friendship.

She couldn't have been more wrong.

I loathe you. You revolt me stewing in your consumption.
You are a loathsome reptile—I hope you will die.

She cried out, "Lawrence! Why? Why do you turn on me like this?"

After such a shock, she stood on the balcony for several minutes. What have I done that you have such a low opinion of me to want me dead? she asked herself. I can forgive you if you wrote this in the middle of one of your TB rages. That I might be able to understand having said vile things myself during my own high fevers. Yet I've never said anything as vile as this or wanted anyone to die!

She wrote to Jack to tell him what Lawrence had said, including calling Jack a "dirty little worm." She asked him how he could continue to be her man if, after this letter, he could still befriend Lawrence and review his work in *The Athenaeum.*

Be proud! she wrote. She was about to tell him to hit Lawrence the next time he saw him when there was a knock at the door. "Come in!" she shouted angrily, swinging her own clenched fist.

Dr. Rendall walked in carrying his medical satchel. "Hello Mrs. Murry, are we feeling a bit cranky today?" He looked amused.

"Forgive me, Doctor Rendall. I've had some bad news."

"I'm so sorry. Shall I come back later?"

"No. It's just a question of pride." She smiled. "Please come in."

He set down his satchel. "And what can I do for you today?"

"I've been invited to Villa Flora by my aunt, Miss Beauchamp, and her associate, Miss Fullerton, but only if you can tell them that I'm not infectious."

"Let's have a listen, shall we?"

After he finished his exam and put away his stethoscope and hammer, she tried to keep still while he wrote his notes. She was ready to plead with him if she had to, if it would help get her out of L'Hermitage.

It seemed forever before he looked up and said, "You still have a low fever but that's normal for your condition. Your cough is infrequent and dry and your air passages are clear. I'll let Miss Beauchamp know that you are not a threat to their other guests."

Katherine would've hugged him but he was very English, like Jack, and would've been uncomfortable with such an emotional display. Instead she shook his hand and thanked him.

"Thank you for such good news. But why stay in Menton when I can go home to London?"

"I didn't say—"

"You see my husband is buying a house in Sussex to avoid the brutal London winters. We've spent so little time together because I've been so sick. And by living together in Sussex we won't have to be away from each other so often." She wanted so much to convince him to let her go home that she couldn't stop now that she had started.

"He believes a house in Sussex, which is known to have the most moderate temperature in England and the most sunshine, will be a safe haven for me."

"Mrs. Murry, please you're getting overexcited. Sit down, please"

"No. What is it? What's wrong? Why are you frowning?"

"Anywhere in England is out of the question even if your heart is strong. I can't recommend such a move. You would be putting your life in danger."

Katherine walked out on the balcony wishing she had the courage to jump.

"Mrs. Murry, please come back inside before you catch a chill. I'm sorry. I shouldn't have been so abrupt, but I thought you knew."

She sat down in the yellow chair that had once given her such pleasure.

"No, I didn't. I keep believing if I rest…" She wiped back a tear. "Forgive me. It's just that my husband needs to hear that I'm cured and if I tell him what you just said, well I don't know what he would do. You see, Doctor, he will accept nothing less than a cure. His happiness depends upon it and therefore mine."

"Doesn't he know how ill you are?"

"I try not to tell him too much. You see, he's rather delicate himself. He only wants to hear that I'm well and coming home."

"I see. Didn't you say Mr. Murry was also a writer?"

"Yes. Why?"

"Why couldn't he leave London temporarily and work here where the climate is the most beneficial for your health."

"How long is *temporarily*?"

"Probably two years."

"Two years! No. That would never do. He'd be most unhappy here with an invalid wife."

"Mrs. Murry, may I be direct?"

She nodded yes.

"With continual bed rest your heart will get stronger. The problem is your lungs. Right now, the tuberculosis is quiescent in your right lung, but the left lung is permanently damaged. The bacteria lodged in either lung could become active at any time. They're like an alarm clock about to go off. And because you can only breathe out of one lung, it puts a tremendous strain on your heart."

She looked away, embarrassed by her tears. She took a few minutes to compose herself and then said, "Thank you, Dr. Rendall. You've made my situation very clear to me. But for now I think I should keep this from my husband. I don't know what he might do if he found out."

"Perhaps your husband should consider your health more than his own."

THE FOLLOWING MORNING Jinnie arrived unexpectedly. "Sorry to burst in on you like this but we couldn't wait another minute."

"What is it, Jinnie?" Katherine said, worried that something might have happened to LM, who was the only one she could still count on.

"I've come to take you home. Dr. Rendall has just told us the good news. You will be safe with Connie and me and the Good Lord looking after you. Connie would be here with me but she's preparing your room."

Katherine was overcome with gratitude as she looked upon this kind, generous woman whose only thought was her welfare. Jinnie handed her a lilac-perfumed lace handkerchief.

"Thank you but I shouldn't use your hankie."

"Not to mind, darling. It's yours now," she said, raising her eyes to the ceiling and pressing her hands together, "The Lord has delivered you into our hands and please be God's will to cure you." She returned her gaze upon Katherine, "Don't look so sad, Katherine. Everything is going to all right. I'll go ask Marie to help with the packing. We must hurry, the carriage is waiting."

Katherine looked over at the stack of notebooks that she had hardly opened since her arrival at L'Hermitage and said to herself what she would never say in front of her new benefactors: "My work is the only possible cure, not God. He's the last one to help me."

AT VILLA FLORA, Katherine settled comfortably into the luxurious life she had known as a child in New Zealand. Everything was done for her and her heart grew stronger. She was so seduced by their generosity and gentle kindness, the carriage rides in the hills above Menton, the champagne picnics and elegant accommodations that she even thought of converting to Catholicism just to please her benefactors.

Wanting to be a polite guest, she had attended Mass, read sections of the Bible, and listened to Jinnie's persuasive words. To encourage her further, Jinnie gave her *The Imitation of Christ* to read. But when Katherine read "It is a very great thing to be in a state of obedience, to live under a superior, and not to be one's own master" she scribbled *Nonsense* in the margin. Her possible conversion would have to forego any belief in God as the Almighty.

She confessed her religious leanings to LM, but so embarrassed at the idea of becoming a Christian, she told her in a letter and made her promise not to tell anyone because she was only thinking about it.

One evening, returning from an elegant picnic on the hillside and a tour of Monte Carlo, Connie and Jinnie invited her into their drawing room for a glass of champagne before retiring. Joyous from their excursion, she sank into the plush silk sofa and watched the bubbles rise and pop in the offered crystal flute.

"Do you think you would like to speak to our priest?" asked Jinnie. It was the first time she had directly brought up Katherine's possible conversion.

Katherine was surprised by the rising bile in her throat at the suggestion of her speaking to a priest. She put down the bubbly flute on the mahogany table. "You have both been so dear to me. It's because of you that my despair has been lifted and I am filled with new hope. For this reason I do admit that I have been tempted to join the faithful." There she stopped. They looked so hopeful until she said, "But I cannot do so."

"But my dearest," said Jinnie, taking her hand in hers, "With faith you will see the light and not be afraid."

"Yes, you're right, I do need faith. But I can't believe in a personal Deity like yours."

"Not a Deity who loves you very much and waits patiently to hold you in His arms?"

Katherine tried not to laugh as she envisioned herself in God's arms. She'd tell him a thing or two about having her brother Leslie killed at the age of twenty-one in the war and making her a consumptive at the age of thirty. But for now Jinnie and Connie would have to do, even if it meant the end to all these wonderful comforts.

"It's difficult to trust in a God that brings such evil into the world. How can I have faith in such a God that allows so much pain and death. For those of us who suffered through the war, He is now gone."

"Katherine!" said Connie. "I fear for you when you say such things. You must learn to open up your heart to Him so that you might see His Way."

"I'm sorry, Connie, but it's not God that I should open up my heart to. It's humanity."

She sat forward taking them both in with her eyes, wanting them to understand what she had come to realize these past few months that made her Christian conversion impossible.

"I want to live by the spirit of Love. I want to see into things so deeply and truly that I can love all things. Love is to be found in each other. We must feel that we are known, that our hearts are known as God once knew us. If we can love each other for everything and through everything, our love becomes our faith. Faith in humanity. It can't become anything less."

"Oh Katherine," said Jinnie, visibly disappointed. "You are truly a challenge to God. The Virgin Mary, too, has trouble forgiving you."

Katherine was taken aback. Had they not heard anything she just said? She sunk back into the couch, resigned. "What did I do to the Virgin Mary?"

"It's how you described her in that story you wrote. I don't know if all your stories are like that one, but I couldn't really make much sense of it. Why do you write such blasphemy?"

Katherine didn't know that they had read her stories. She picked up her glass and took a sip rather than saying that story had been her battle cry against corruption. A cry that came from a deep sense of hopelessness, of everything doomed. The first draft had been written during the war, when it was never out of her mind and everything was poisoned by it. The story's cynical character expressed that sense of doom. She looked back up at her gracious hostesses and recited from *Je ne parle pas français.*"

> "*One would not have been surprised if the door had opened and the Virgin Mary had come in, riding upon an ass, her meek hands folded over her big belly.*"

Connie shifted uncomfortably and couldn't look directly at Katherine. "I discussed that story with your father, when he visited us. I found it very unpleasant to read and I asked your father if he had read it. He said he didn't think it was clever and chucked it in the fireplace."

Katherine felt her heart quicken and, not wanting Connie to see how hurtful her words were, she kept her gaze on the now disappearing bubbles. She'd given her father all her stories, but he never mentioned reading them.

"I'm feeling rather tired," she said. "I'm sorry if I've disappointed you. I wanted to join your faith but I can't if I don't believe in your God. But you needn't give up on me yet." She pulled herself up from the chair. With as much dignity as she could muster leaning on her mother's cane, she said, "Thank you for the champagne, it was most delicious."

ON APRIL 27, after three weeks at the L'Hermitage and two months at Villa Flora, she and LM left Menton to travel by train to London. Dr. Rendall's diagnosis be damned. Rather than give it any legitimacy she hadn't told her husband what he said.

Jack had finally found the Heron in Sussex. The current tenant wouldn't be vacating for a year but until then she'd stay with Jack at the Elephant through the summer and then return to France for the winter.

Connie and Jinnie were moving to another villa across the bay from Villa Flora, and perhaps not giving up yet on her conversion, had offered her, come October, a long-term lease on a smaller independent villa on the same property. Katherine had fallen in love with Menton and didn't hesitate to say yes. LM had promised to return with her.

Katherine no longer wanted Jack to come unless he did it for himself and not for her. If he came as a man without a temperament, a martyr, sacrificing his own life to take care of his invalid wife, it would be unbearable.

MAY, 1920

The Elephant House—London

*Just wait till I get home, that's all the best. And we shall
be alone & all the house ours and a perfect table & the
new cups and saucers with their flowers & fluting. And
the windows shall be open—you in your old clothes, I'll
be in fair ones. Our cats Wing & Athy there—fruit in our
Italian dish—HAPPINESS, happiness. I'll be able to pick
up your hand—look at it—kiss it—give it back to you. I'll
say BOGE my own; you'll say, yes. We'll look at each other
and laugh—Wing will wink at Athy and pretend to play
the fiddle. Oh I love you. Je t'aime. Wig*

LETTERS—KM

"JACK! JACK! I'M HOME." Katherine called out, opening the front door of 2 Portland Villas and expecting to fall into her husband's arms.

It was their housekeeper Violet who rushed forward to greet her. "Mrs. Murry. Can this truly be you? Why—" Katherine saw the shock in her face but Violet recovered quickly, "why you look—wonderful. Here let me take your coat. You must be so tired from your long journey. Mr. Murry didn't know when to expect you and I was to call him at the office when you arrived. So glad to have you home again. And, you too, Miss Baker!"

"Please don't call him," said Katherine, hiding her disappointment. "I'd like to rest before I see him."

"The weather couldn't be pleasanter for your return, ma'am. I think you'll be most pleased with the garden." Katherine noted the marigolds set on the entryway table along with a stack of mail. "Nothing there for you ma'am," Violet said. "I put your mail up in your bedroom just like I used to."

"Thank you, Violet. Did Mr. Murry cut these flowers for me?"

"Oh no, Ma'am, he never has time for anything but the magazine. I've been tending the garden."

"I'd like to plant some vegetables this summer. Perhaps you'll help me."

"Yes, ma'am. I'd like to do that."

The familiar light gray wallpaper she'd chosen for the stairwell made her feel at home and encouraged, she started the climb upstairs. "I'll be all right," she said, shrugging off LM's offered arm.

"I don't remember this hallway being so dark," she said, pausing in front of her bedroom door.

"Shall I bring tea?" asked LM.

"Not yet. Let's wait until Jack comes home."

"Are you sure you don't want me to help you unpack your—"

"Ida! I'm not a child! Let me be."

She turned the knob and stepped inside, relieved to see her writing table was as she left it. Just a few letters had fallen on the floor when Violet had aired the room and left the window open. She stooped down to pick them up, noting the addresses: Kot, Lady Ottoline, and Virginia, her loyal correspondents that followed her from place to place.

She brushed her gloved hand across the bright yellow writing table where she had written her will eight months ago, now safely locked away in her bank deposit box with instructions not to be opened by Jack until ... Don't be afraid to say it, she said to herself, until my death. She placed her notebooks on the table, making a promise to write a few lines every day.

AFTER A MONTH AT HOME, it became painfully apparent to Katherine that the adventures they'd planned for "come May," and the plans for a holiday in Sussex to show her the Heron, weren't going to happen.

May had come and gone, and tonight, like every night, she waited for Jack's footsteps to come up the stairs. She lay back on her pillows, very still, but her mind raged.

Yes, the deadlines for a weekly magazine demanded his full attention during the day, but the evenings, too? And what about his other distractions? While she was gone, he'd taken up tennis with their mutual friend Dorothy Brett. Obviously a sport she could not play. And because she was too tired to go out at night, Brett had made herself available.

Brett had written to Katherine in Menton about the "orgies" she and Jack frequented. Offended by the unsavory details, Katherine had written to Jack and warned him about drinking too much wine. He'd replied that Brett had exaggerated. They weren't "orgies," just insufferable parties that he was required to attend as *Athenaeum*'s editor. He dragged Brett along to keep him company.

When she heard his footsteps, she flipped on the reading light and reached for the nearest book so he wouldn't think she'd been waiting for him.

"Are you still up?" he asked cheerfully.

How handsome and healthy he looks, she thought, which only added to her irritation. "Why are you so late?"

"Sorry. Didn't I tell you? I had to stay at the office to finish an article before tomorrow's deadline. What did you do today?"

"Nothing."

"Well, that's a shame. Listen, I had an idea on my way home tonight," he said, sitting down on the edge of the bed. "I'd like you to start writing a monthly fiction column for *The Athenaeum*."

"But your magazine doesn't publish fiction."

"Not yet, but as its editor I can change that. There weren't any novel-reviews either until you started writing them. And look how successful they've been. It will have to be limited, of course, to one column but I think our subscribers will be very pleased to have you onboard. It will probably increase our subscriptions, but more important, it will give you a home for your stories."

She felt the warmth of his hand gently covering hers and her anger melted along with her fear of being a jilted wife. "All right. I'll start on a sketch tomorrow."

"Good." He bent down and brushed his lips against her cheek. "Good night, my love."

"Where are going? Aren't you coming to bed?"

"No. I mean yes. Actually, to tell you the truth, I've been meaning to say something about our sleeping arrangements. I think we'll both have a better rest if I sleep over there." He pointed to the alcove sofa. "I'll still be right here if you have one of those terrifying dreams. That was certainly a bad one last night. I couldn't get back to sleep."

She didn't like him sleeping in the alcove but why should he lose sleep because of her night terrors though come to think of it LM hadn't minded so much.

She woke up the next morning with her loyal caregiver standing over her with the breakfast tray. "Where's Jack?" she asked, looking over at the folded sheets on the sofa.

"Brett came by earlier and they went off to play tennis. Didn't he tell you?"

"No, it must've slipped his mind. He's been so busy lately."

After her breakfast, she sat down at her writing table to write down a sketch developing in her mind. To her satisfaction she had completed *Revelations* by late afternoon, in time for *Athenaeum's* mid-June issue. How right Jack was to suggest this, she thought. And having deadlines will help me get back to work and I won't miss him so much."

A week later, out of the blue, Jack invited her to visit his office. "You're such a strong influence on the decisions I make at the magazine, I want everyone to meet you. And wouldn't it be nice to get out of the house for some fresh air? You're looking way to pale, my dear. I don't want anyone to ever think I'm not taking good care of you."

She hesitated. It was true she needed to get out and it would be nice to ride in a carriage with Jack. Just this morning she'd looked out of her bedroom window at the brilliant violets in her garden and thought it was a beautiful day for a ride.

"All right, Jack, let me get my hat and coat."

"She looks worse than I expected" was written on everyone's face when she walked into the *Athenaeum* office. They tried to recover saying "Mrs. Murry, how good to see you. My you are looking well," but she knew what H.G. Wells and the others were really thinking: "Poor Jack. What a saint he is putting up with a dying wife."

After her visit to Jack's office, she only went out to sit in her private garden. Her friends came to the Elephant if they wanted to see her.

Revelations was an immediate success and she wrote another story for the July issue. Because of the cramping in her rheumatic fingers, Jack loaned her his portable Corona typewriter. Tapping on the round keys made the words flow easier and she was able to write her short stories and novel-reviews for the magazine.

Besides her time in the garden, the only other time she left her room was to go downstairs to see occasional visitors. When Virginia came by they shared their frustrations and excitement when writing in the modern form of stream of consciousness. She was relieved that Virginia never mentioned the negative review she'd given her novel, *Night and Day*.

She gave a dinner party for T.S. Eliot, whom she'd wanted to meet, and his wife Vivienne. Her least successful party. She didn't think Eliot liked her and she certainly didn't like Vivienne.

She had hoped that she and Brett, who lived nearby, would renew the friendship that had developed through their correspondence, but Brett seemed quite occupied and uncomfortable in Katherine's presence.

Brett had been introduced to her and Jack at Garsington, Lady Ottoline's 1500 acre estate outside London. Ottoline, though not an artist herself, supported the arts and invited artists to reside in various cottages on her property. It was an oasis from bombed-out London. She enjoyed having parties that mixed the "underground" artists like Katherine, Jack, and D.H. Lawrence, with the Bloomsbury group, wealthy middle-class intellectuals who didn't have to make a living by their art alone.

Hon. Dorothy Brett, who called herself Brett, was a Bloomsbury member with the proper credentials; her father a barrister and legal advisor to the Queen of England. But she, like Lady Ottoline, leaned toward the more bohemian life style of the "underground" and like Katherine and Ottoline, Brett had a special friendship with D. H. Lawrence. Later, she would follow him to his artist colony in New Mexico.

What Katherine and Brett had most in common was their passion for impressionist art. Katherine felt her stories, like these paintings, were fragments, sketches and small forms. Brett, schooled in the art of impressionism, painted still-lives and portraits that pleased Katherine's eye.

Brett, five years older than Katherine, had been deaf most of her life. She was known to carry an ornate brass ear trumpet named Tobey wherever she went. Katherine would have to shout her ideas, interrupted by coughing spasms, into Brett's trumpet and Brett would respond by shouting back, "What?" "What?" It was not pleasant.

One afternoon, Brett arrived for teatime just as Katherine was finishing *Escape*, her story for the July edition. The writing had gone well and she was excited to talk about it. Losing patience while waiting for Brett to unpack her trumpet, she shouted, "When you paint apples don't you feel that your breasts and your knees become apples, too?"

Brett's face flushed so Katherine was sure she had heard her and went on. "You think I'm speaking great nonsense, don't you?"

Before Brett could reply, Jack arrived, apologizing for being late for their scheduled teatime.

Brett and Jack sat across from her. She poured the tea. Jack mentioned their last tennis game and Brett put down her trumpet and launched into an enthusiastic description of how they'd beaten their opponents. Katherine felt excluded, and relegated to the role of observer. She noted Brett's blush when Jack leaned close to her ear to make sure she heard him when he said, "It was your strong serve that won the match."

Several days later Katherine happened upon an open letter sitting on Jack's desk. Recognizing Brett's handwriting she read it just as she might have read any of the letters Jack carelessly left around the house. They had always been quite open about each other's correspondence.

Why Brett has come unbalanced! What on earth is she talking about? *Rush into the cornfield… he must smack her hand*—threatens to cry over him until he's all wet and tell him that he's *awakened her.* Poor pathetic wretch!

She avoided speaking to Jack about the letter, certain the passion was one-sided. She hoped Jack would soon put an end to Brett's foolish crush on him as she had no intention to play the role of the jealous wife and tell him to break it off. Jack was always hungry for affection. But with Brett? That seemed utterly ridiculous.

COME SEPTEMBER her return to Menton drew nearer and her wanting to go. Her health, as Dr. Rendall had predicted, was being badly affected by the damp London air and she feared for her lungs with the coming autumn chill.

Connie and Jinnie had kept in touch and told her about the splendid small villa that awaited her. Jack would stay in London and keep the magazine running. Hopefully he'd find time to visit in the summer.

A few days before her departure, she and Jack were having their last discussion about the submissions for *Athenaeum*'s next edition. Since their days as young editors at his magazine *Rhythm*, they had made editorial decisions together. Satisfied with their work, they sat back to sip their tea.

"I can't believe you're leaving so soon," said Jack. "What will I do without you?"

"It won't be any different for you than last time. We'll correspond over the submissions and I'll send you the novel-reviews and the sketches for my fiction column."

"Yes, of course, but it's not the same as having you here with me. You don't realize how large and empty this house is without you, and what a huge responsibility. The truth is I don't think I can bear another winter here alone." He stopped to light his pipe. "I was thinking of renting it out."

"But where would you live?"

"Brett has come up with a practical solution."

"Oh really. How wonderful. I'm sure she has come up with something very clever. Do tell." Her sarcasm was missed by Jack.

"She's invited me to come and stay with her."

Katherine's estimation of Brett's attraction toward Jack being one-sided had obviously been wrong. "Am I to understand this is nothing more than *l'amitié pure*?"

"C'mon Katherine, don't be silly. I have no deep feelings for Brett if that is what you're asking. I'll be staying in her spare bedroom. My relationship with her is merely a convenience. If I take her up on her generous invitation, I could lease the Elephant and relieve myself of its financial burden."

"I'm not sure why you are discussing this with me since you've already decided," she said, putting down her teacup and gathering her papers.

"Brett asked me to."

"Brett? Did she? How thoughtful of her." She swallowed the bitter taste in her mouth.

"Don't be snide Katherine, it doesn't become you. She wants you to be comfortable about our arrangement. You're a close friend and she wouldn't want you to think badly of her for coming to my rescue."

"Oh I see. She's on a rescue mission. How heroic. And my feelings don't enter into it?"

"Why of course. But for now, what's important is Brett's feelings. It's important to her that you continue to be nice to her."

Katherine pushed herself up from the chair, held onto its arm, and willed her legs to cross the room gracefully. At the door she turned back and said, "Tell her *the arrangement* is fine with me."

Alone in her bedroom, she broke into tears. "Nice to her! He's asking me to be nice to her."

She scribbled angrily in her journal:

> *I suppose one thinks the latest shock is the worst shock. This is quite unlike any other I've ever suffered. The lack of sensitiveness as far as I am concerned—the <u>selfishness</u> of this staggers me. This is what I must remember when I am away. He thinks no more of me than of anybody else... I must remember he's one of my friends—no more. Who could count on such a man! To plan all this at such a time and then ask me to be nice to Brett. How disgustingly indecent! I am simply <u>disgusted</u> to my very soul.*

KATHERINE INVITED Jack's brother Richard to see the Russian Ballet at the Royal Opera in Covent Garden. During her absence, they had become close correspondents. He was only eighteen but they shared a passion for art and nature. He arrived in a carriage and escorted her to the theater doing everything he could to make sure she was comfortable.

They returned to a dark, cold house that seemed very dreary after the bright cheery lights of the concert hall and the inspiring music they had enjoyed so much.

"Where's Jack?" he asked.

"Probably at the office." The truth was he was with Brett, but saying it made it too painfully real.

Richard lit the logs and joined her on the couch, watching the fire build. The crackling flames warmed Katherine's feet but she still felt a chill from being out in the night air. Richard saw her shivering and asked her where her shawl was.

"It's up in my bedroom, but you needn't get it."

He ran up the stairs and returned, gently wrapping the shawl around her shoulders. He added another log to the fire.

"How different you are from your brother," she said. "He never notices when I'm cold." She laughed. "But then again, maybe that's because I'm always cold."

"Katherine it shames me to see how unfairly my brother treats you. When you cough, he hides his face with his fingers because he's afraid of getting ill. There's just something missing when it comes to him being sensitive to anyone other than himself. He's always been like this, but I find it embarrassing how he mopes around with that dour look on his face as if he's the one who's sick and not you."

"It's not that he's without feelings—he's just not in touch with them," said Katherine, wanting to defend him though she wasn't sure why.

"That's just his excuse. He's self-absorbed, Katherine. He never bucks you up at all. I don't know why you put up with it."

"Please, Richard, don't talk to me about your brother that way. I had such a wonderful evening with you, let's not spoil it." She got up. "I'm quite tired. Will you show yourself out?"

He stood up. "May I help you upstairs?"

"No, I can make it on my own. Would you leave a light on for Jack? He doesn't like it to be dark when he comes home."

SHALL ONE EVER BE AT PEACE with oneself, ever quiet and uninterrupted—without pain—with the one whom one loves under the same roof? It's all I've ever wanted with Jack. A home for the two of us. I can't expect Richard to understand that Jack is everything to me and I can't let our love die. But the only way I can keep it alive is by being cured. She looked into the mirror at her pale, haggard face that makeup could not hide. An old woman at the age of thirty-one. He cannot love me the way I am now. He cannot love a consumptive.

Elizabeth von Armin

There are always these moments in life when the limits of
suffering are reached and we become heroes and heroines.

REVELATIONS—KM

"**W**ELL, THAT'S A SURPRISE!**"** Katherine said looking up from a letter at LM. "Elizabeth has accepted my invitation to tea."
"That's nice, dear. Shall we get those special scones for the occasion? A little expensive but if you have a very special guest coming... Who is Elizabeth? I can't remember."

"My father's cousin. I wonder why she accepted my invitation? I only invited her because Pa asked me to. She's had a rather miserable time of it, he says, since her divorce from Earl Russell. Pa thinks she was mistreated and needs someone in the Beauchamp family to lend her support. Or perhaps my recent short story reviews have been printed in the New Zealand papers and he's read that widowed, divorced and disenfranchised women are consoled by them."

"Well I don't know about being consoled but I've certainly felt an affinity for the women in your stories. I consider them now to be my friends. Katie, do you not want that piece of bread and butter?" She shook her head and continued reading a letter. "Then I'll take it, if you don't mind," said LM, reaching out for it and continued chattering. "Earl Russell? Isn't that Bertrand Russell's brother? Oh yes, I met Bertrand when I came to fetch you from those Bloomsbury gatherings at Virginia's. He used to come around to that flat you shared with several other bohemian artists in Bloomsbury... during the war, wasn't it? You'd shoo me away so you could be alone with him. What was that flat called?"

Katherine dropped a sugar in her tea. "The Ark, Ida, the Ark. And you needn't mention Bertrand or his brother when Elizabeth comes for tea."

"Of course not. You know how well I keep your secrets. It must be a long time since you last saw her because I've never met her and I thought by now I'd met all your family. When did you last see her?"

"Ten years ago at a tea given at my uncle's house to introduce George and announce our engagement."

"She met George Bowden? How unfortunate for her."

"George wasn't so terrible. It was my fault marrying him."

Katherine felt LM's eyes on her when she poured another cup of tea. Stare all you want, she thought, just don't start up again about George or Jack for that matter.

Katherine's thoughts turned to the famous Elizabeth. She'd grown up listening to her father talk about how extraordinary she was, a cut above all other women. Not only had Elizabeth become an extremely popular author in her early thirties when she published *Elizabeth and Her German Garden*, reprinted twenty-one times in the first year, and translated into several languages, but she'd also married a wealthy German count and given birth to five children. Katherine had fallen short of Elizabeth's achievements. Jack was certainly not a count and though they still spoke of having children, she was childless. And she was not rich from what she considered her meager body of work.

Elizabeth's taxi pulled up at #2 Portland Villas, ten minutes late to Katherine's masked irritation. Katherine found the famous writer's light gray wool skirt and jacket and matching grey plumed hat enviable. Wishing she had taken more time with her own dress, she quickly covered its drabness with her multi-colored, embroidered Spanish shawl and stood up tall to greet her.

As she pulled back from Elizabeth's kiss on her cheek, she saw the familiar shocked look on her face. The look that was on all the faces of those who'd heard she was ill but didn't know *how* ill until they saw her. But in Elizabeth's face she also saw authentic concern and felt moved by it. "I was surprised to hear back from you," said Katherine, offering a chair and then sitting herself. She preferred the sofa but didn't want to limp across the room in front of Elizabeth.

"I've been planning to visit but, as you well know, being a writer yourself, there is never enough time to write, and when one does find the time everyone and everything is forgotten."

They looked at each other for a long moment before Elizabeth said, "Your Pa has kept me informed about your illness and tells me how hard you've fought against it. He's very worried. I told him I would help anyway I could. All you need to do is ask me." Katherine heard no pity in her voice just an honest appeal to be friends and she liked her for it.

LM brought in a tea tray laden with scones. Katherine poured the tea and was relieved that her hand didn't embarrass her and cramp.

"I wish my stay in London was longer so I could visit you more often," said Elizabeth, "but I'm leaving next week for my chalet in Randogne, Switzerland. Perhaps someday you will visit me there. Many Londoners come to the Alps to take open-air cures."

"Yes, an open-air cure has been suggested to me but I have a terrible fear of the cold. That's why I go south to the Riviera, but perhaps someday I'll change directions."

"Your father tells me that you're an ardent admirer of gardens. If you visit next summer you will have an opportunity to admire mine as I have had the privilege to admire your novel-reviews in *The Athenaeum*."

Katherine looked down at her teacup rather than show her blush.

"Your husband was very clever to add your review column. Or was that your idea? I find them well thought out and often quite amusing. I have read several books based on your reviews and skipped several others for the same reason."

Katherine looked up at her cousin. "Thank you, Elizabeth, you're most generous with your compliments."

"Your husband, too, has gained much respect in the literary world as a brilliant young editor with modernist views. But perhaps you are the one to be congratulated. Am I right in thinking you instrumental in his decisions?" She continued without waiting for Katherine to answer. "From what I've read of your work, I can tell that you are a modern woman with very strong opinions. But why haven't I been able to find any of your new stories? Are you not publishing?"

"There is my new fiction column in *The Athenaeum*."

"Ah yes, I read *Revelations*. I couldn't get my heart around that one like I did with that brilliant masterpiece *Prelude*."

"Thank you. I'm planning to write several new stories this winter that take place in New Zealand as *Prelude* did. But I have so little time to work here. I'm most anxious to return to France for this reason and am leaving in a few weeks myself."

"Yes, one must write mustn't one? How else can we writers enjoy life?" she said, and smiled.

Katherine's eyes lingered on Elizabeth's. They were the same deep brown as the cup of tea she lifted to her lips and as unreadable.

"Please tell me about yourself, Katherine. I want to get to know you."

"I don't have much to tell. My stories tell much more about me than I ever could."

"Yes. I can see that. Your stories about women are quite believable. Your characters unforgettable, I might say, even haunting. You are a far more serious writer than I am. Your stories go beneath the surface. Mine are far more superficial."

"Yes, but you have achieved great popularity. Pa admires you. It influenced his decision to let me come to London on my own. He thought I might follow in your successful footsteps. So far I've disappointed him. Brief sketches compared to your novels."

"Oh but you could write a wonderful novel. Have you ever considered it?"

"Yes… often. Started several times. Notebooks filled with scenes and character sketches. I even have a title for it, *Karori*—my childhood home. The story takes place there and in London." For a moment she submerged herself in the landscape of *Karori*. She awoke to Elizabeth's curious stare. It had only been a brief second but she felt in that moment that her cousin had shared a foreigner's landscape that separated them from ever being authentic Englishwomen. A separation they were both proud of.

"You must accept my invitation to Chalet de Soleil in Randogne. I've written my best novels there. It's remote… quiet… There's solitude. The pure alpine air will revive you as it does me. Listen to me," she laughed. "I sound like an advertisement in the *Times* for open-air clinics. Sorry, but know that my enthusiasm is authentic and so is my invitation. If you come in the spring or summer, we can spend time together working in the garden."

"I think I might just do that, Elizabeth. Thank you for asking me."

They spoke further about the books they were reading: Katherine—Shakespeare, Elizabeth—more current work. Some Katherine liked, others she didn't. She spoke of her concern after reading so many after-the-war novels that ignored how the war had changed the way they lived. How writers wanted to continue telling stories as if the war had never happened. New ways must be found, particularly for female writers to not tell us how the world had changed for them but show us and in showing us reveal the truth. Yes, show the beautiful leaf but do not ignore the worm underneath it. That was Katherine's challenge and should be every writer's challenge who cared passionately about their art. Elizabeth spoke of the novel she was now working on that she hoped Katherine would someday review. All of Elizabeth's books were protests against female weakness in a man's world.

They then spoke of their linked family, the Beauchamps, and when the clock on the mantelpiece chimed five times both were surprised how late it was.

"Oh dear, I always forget the time. I must leave. I have a train to catch. You needn't get up, my dear, I can find my way out."

"Thank you for coming Elizabeth. Unfortunately, very few members of my family find their way to Portland Villas at Hampstead Heath and it has been a special treat having you here. Perhaps because we are both not truly English, that I feel an affinity with you that I don't feel with my English friends."

"Do you ever think of going back home for a visit?" asked Elizabeth.

"Oh my yes. But with Jack's position as *Athenaeum's* editor he hasn't the time to go with me and I'm not well enough to go alone. But as soon as I'm better."

Elizabeth stood up to leave, put on her plumed hat, and adjusted it in the mirror over the mantel. "Please tell your husband I was sorry he wasn't here for us to meet, but I did enjoy our time alone. Men too often interrupt honest conversations between women with their need to express their importance on all matters. I look forward to longer chats in Randogne. I believe we have much in common."

After she left, Katherine felt dreary. Elizabeth's cheerful affirmation of life had been so brilliant that the parlor sagged without her. Perhaps an open-air cure in the Alps is a good plan, she thought.

THE MORNING she and LM left for the train station, Jack was under a deadline at the paper and couldn't see her off. They had both avoided discussing his move to Brett's, and kept their conversations about the paper. As long as she didn't know anything about it, Katherine had decided she didn't care about his ridiculous affair with Brett.

I don't love Jack less, she thought, just differently. My love for him has become a cannonball tied to my feet, when I am already trying not to drown. If he could only, for a minute, serve me, help me, give HIMSELF up! I never could get well with him. I must go it alone. It's the writing that will see me through. That's where I must focus all my attention.

After her trunk had been taken downstairs to the waiting taxi, she turned back at the bedroom door to say good-bye. Stripped of its props, the room became an empty stage. Its main actress, the heroine, was traveling on to another play, another story that would be far more joyous.

And I can't write it here, she thought, putting a new notebook in her traveling case to use on the train. Until I'm cured, it's better for both of us that we live separate lives.

She closed the curtains on the windows that looked out on the park, switched off the gaslight, and firmly closed the door behind her.

WHEN SHE AND LM stepped off the train in Menton she felt she'd come home. The familiar sweet air touching her face, the brilliant sunlight, the small quaint station with only a few people, the silence. A porter found them a carriage that transported them and their luggage to her new home that Connie and Jinnie had prepared for her—Villa Isola Bella.

"Can this truly be the place?" whispered LM, when they pulled up on a leafy lane thickly overhung with lush green plants. "Look. There's Connie's maid, Annette, waving at us."

Katherine was too tired to enjoy the garden. She requested that Annette bring her immediately to her bedroom. Before retiring she stood on the balcony and listened to the cicadas, the frogs and someone playing notes on a flute. She felt tears of joy blur her eyes and whispered, "Let the new play begin."

The next day before allowing Annette to bring her breakfast she sat up in bed and guiltily wrote the novel-review that she promised to send from Paris. She'd been too tired on the train. After sending LM to the post office, she finally allowed herself to breathe deeply under the shade of a giant date palm. Her eyes took in a vast budding magnolia and a tangerine tree covered in green balls. Her thoughts turned to Jack and how happy he would be here. She went inside to write him her first impressions while fresh in her mind:

A real little salon with velvet covered furniture and an immense dead clock and a gilt mirror; and two very handsome crimson vases which remind me of fountains filled with blood. It has 2 windows. One looks over the garden gate, the other opens onto the terrace and looks over the sea. The dining room is equally charming in its way & has French windows, too. Upstairs are four bedrooms with balconies overlooking the sea and are carpeted all over & sumptuous in a doll's house way.

I do not know <u>what</u> it is about this place. But it is enough just to be here for everything to change—I think already of the poetry you would write if you lived such a life. I wish you were not tied. I have always at the bottom of my deep cup of happiness that dark spot, which is that you are not living as you would wish to live.

OCTOBER 14, 1920

32nd Birthday

*When I first saw her, October 15, 1920, Patient had been
suffering from lung troubles for three years, and at the time
was complaining of bad attacks of coughing, especially
morning and evening, of much stiffness and pain in the
right hip joint and muscles round and also in the spine,
and of palpitations in the heart on the least provocation.*

*History: After an attack of peritonitis in 1910 at age 21
(very likely from gonococcal origin previous four months
of white discharge), left Fallopian tube was removed.
Has been more or less troubled ever since, suffering from
rheumatism, in various muscles of the body, hip joints and
small joints in feet.*

DR. BOUCHAGE—MENTON, FRANCE

KATHERINE DIDN'T SEND Dr. Bouchage's medical report to Jack.
Not because of the "origin" of an earlier illness first explained to
her by Dr. Sorapure and then to Jack, but the description of a chronically
ill wife would frighten him. And it was very limited in its scope.

What was not described in Dr. Bouchage's report was the happiness
she'd found on her walks in Isola Bella's verdant garden, her reflections
as she watched the gilded sunset on the sea's edge, the appetizing food
prepared by her new cook and housekeeper, Marie, and the pleasures
found in her dollhouse villa where she could write freely without interruption. In the one month since she'd arrived at Isola Bella she'd managed
to keep up with the weekly novel-reviews, written what she called her
hallucinatory story, *The Young Girl*, and managed to start a new story
for the next issue.

"I'm not dead—at least not yet," she said aloud. She walked without
limping over to her travel chest that she brought from one rest-cure

to the next. It stored her letters from family and friends, comforting knowledge that there were others who also considered her still alive.

The letters in her travel chest also represented stability in her impermanent life. She felt the same way about all her possessions that she'd placed around the rooms in her Menton villa. Each vase, bowl, even the medicine bottles, created a balance, a flow. Like each comma in her stories, their placements were not arbitrary decisions but well thought out. She didn't want Jack or any other editor removing her commas and she didn't want Ida or Marie moving her ornamental placements. With her personal belongings rooted around her, she was no longer an aimless weed. She'd transformed herself into a seed planted in rich soil—not random—but useful, purposeful, fertile as she grew and bloomed.

Outside her bedroom was a very small balcony that she'd named *le balcon de Juliet et Romeo*. Standing on it, she heard LM call up to her from the terrace below. "Katie, come down. I've brought you a stack of letters from the post office."

She briefly looked in the mirror, pleased that her recent gain in weight had filled out her face and her cheeks were pink from daily sunshine. She passed by her mother's now unnecessary cane and descended the spiral stairs on her own. In the black and white marble entry, she stopped to smell the fresh bouquet of jonquils.

Out on the terrace was a tray arranged with fresh bread and jam and several letters. She settled back into her wicker chair and chose Jack's letter to read first. She almost knocked over the cup of tea LM had just poured. "Oh no!" she exclaimed.

"What's wrong now?" asked LM, accustomed to Katherine's outbursts when reading Jack's letters.

"Floryan is back in London. Why can't he leave me alone?"

"Who?"

"How can you not remember? He's the man who took care of me in Bavaria after I left George. He's the one who gave me gono… "

Her cough stopped her rant. Though she was feeling much better, her damaged lungs were taking the most time to heal.

LM handed her a glass of water saying, "Of course I remember, but you asked me to never mention his name so I don't. In all honesty I remember him quite well. I didn't like him. An insidious pest who shows up whenever things are going well for you like right now."

Years ago, Katherine and Jack had moved to a humble flat in Runcton after *Rhythm's* owner had run off with the magazine's assets and left Jack bankrupt. The owner's creditors insisted that Jack pay the overdue printing costs and Katherine gave him Pa's allowance. It was just before the war when Floryan showed up at their doorstep expecting Katherine to give him a place to stay as he had once done for her in Bavaria.

Ida added, "Need I remind you that I was the one who forced him to leave your flat in Runcton where he had comfortably settled down to live off you.

"What does the beggar want now?"

"Blackmail. He wants forty pounds for the letters I wrote to him when I was too young to know better."

"Forty pounds!"

"He tried the same thing with Bernard Shaw but Shaw told him the letters had no value and he went away."

"Well perhaps you should follow his example. Why pay forty pounds for some foolish love letters sent by a lonely young girl who had lost—" LM was stopped by Katherine's glare and asked instead, "Must you agree to it?"

"What if he gave them to the press to publish? I don't want that foolish period in my life revealed to anyone. Jack writes that Floryan must have found out about the advance Constable offered for my story collection as he asked for the same amount.

"But I won't get paid until the stories are published and Floryan demands payment now. I don't want to ask my father for an advance on my allowance and asking Jack would be worse. You know what misers they both are and I'm certain Jack would try to negotiate and that would only make Floryan angry."

LM put down Katherine's bed jacket. She was sewing on new buttons now that Katherine had put on weight and it was too tight to wear. "Let me help you, Katie."

"I can't ask you to do that, Jones. You've helped me out enough."

"I won't have you upset over this. Your health is far more important to me than forty pounds. Please, I insist. It'll be your birthday present."

Katherine sighed. How could she ask LM to give up her savings that she'd need when Katherine moved back in with Jack and no longer needed her as companion and nurse. But she had no one else to turn to. "I'll agree to your generous offer," she said, "but only on one condition. It's a loan and I will pay you back when I get paid by Constable."

Ida tried to convince her that she didn't need to do that but finally accepted her gift as a loan.

Katherine wrote to Jack asking him to settle with Floryan, telling him that LM would be sending him the money.

> *Please take Floryan to a solicitor and get his sworn statement that he will never threaten me again. Don't trust him Jack. Recover those letters before you pay him. Once you have them, destroy them.*

A week later she received a telegram from Jack:

LETTERS IN MY POSSESSION. STOP. FLORYAN SIGNED DECLARATION. STOP. POSTING THEM TO YOU IMMEDIATELY. STOP. YOU MUST BE THE ONE TO DESTROY THEM IF THAT IS YOUR WISH. STOP. LOVE, JACK

A week went by and the letters didn't arrive. Katherine found it impossible to work. She wrote to Jack and he responded by telegram:

SORRY. STOP. FORGOT. STOP. SENT THE PACKET TODAY. STOP. JACK

How could he forget something so important to me as those letters? Doesn't he know I will be in turmoil and unable to work until they're gone.

When the packet finally arrived, she carried it up to her bedroom, but did not open the envelopes. These letters were written during what she called her wild "Oscar Wilde" stage, when she risked all for the experience and made the biggest mistakes of her life. She didn't need to revisit those mistakes.

"Annihilate the past," she said, holding up the packet. She made sure a letter in her penmanship was enclosed in each envelope, lit it with a match and tossed it into her coal heater.

One by one, words to ashes—a ceremonial cremation of her sordid past.

ON HER 32ND BIRTHDAY, Katherine polished the silver spoon Jack had sent to Ospedaletti on her last birthday. This time he sent neither a card or a gift. A painful reminder of how estranged they'd become and how thoughtless he really was. Her only birthday present was Dr. Bouchage's weekly iodine injection to relieve her rheumatism. She told him this was the last time she'd take his experimental injection. The only effect from the iodine were mood swings, fever, and headaches.

The candles lit, she sat down and sipped cream of mushroom soup from Jack's delicate spoon. A fairy spoon she'd been saving to place in the Heron's cupboard, but since their dream cottage in Sussex was a thing of the past and they never discussed it why not make use of it?

A few days later too weak to get out of bed, probably brought on by the iodine injection, she propped up her bed pillows and opened Jack's most recent letter. Inside she was surprised to also find a letter from Brett addressed to Jack. After reading both letters, she wrote in her notebook: *Jack wishes me dead.*

"Why else would he send me her obscene letter?" she asked her lasciviously grinning crocodile watching her from the bedside table. His hinged nutcracker jaw ready to crack open her heart if Jack didn't do it first.

Brett's letter was written in green ink on willowy stationery and stunk of cheap perfume. She reread the lovesick woman's paragraph about wanting to peep under Jack's shirt and her lascivious threat to be severe with him if he didn't comply.

In his letter he asked Katherine to rescue him from an hysterical woman. That her wanton behavior was not his fault. That he hadn't encouraged her at all.

No Jack, it is all your fault, said Katherine to herself. It's your vanity and self-absorption that delivers you into the arms of weak, lonely women and when they become inconvenient by making demands on you, that's when you ask me, your wife, to step in and get rid of them because you don't have the courage to do it yourself.

You ask me if I resent Brett's letter?

She picked up her pen and answered:

I do resent it most deeply. I feel violently physically sick.

RETREATING TO HER BATH, after reading Jack's letter, she considered buying Isola Bella and making it her home. If that was not possible, she hoped Jinnie and Connie would accept her offer to lease it for another year. She knew she had disappointed them by not converting to Catholicism but hopefully they wouldn't let that influence their Christian generosity.

Submerged under the warm water, her arms at her sides, her legs straight out, she thought, this is how they will arrange me in my coffin. She pressed her wet toes against the end of the bath. They look so gay, so unconscious of their fate. They are smiling all in a row—the little toe so tiny.

"No, not yet," she said aloud, throwing her sponge at a spectral row of distinguished white-uniformed doctors leaning over her, stethoscopes swinging from their necks, hammers in their hands.

"Fooled you, didn't I?" she shouted at them. "All of you said two to three years if I checked myself into a sanatorium and stopped writing. Ha!" Her raucous laughter sent them scattering.

She climbed out of the tub, put on her dressing gown and stepped out onto the moonlit balcony. The sea's white caps glistened under the full moon. The mimosa's fern-like leaves whispered gently to her, "Don't worry. You're going to be all right without Jack."

A new idea for a story started to form itself in her mind and she returned inside.

At her table she wrote a quick sketch about a seductress who jilted one man for a younger lover and was now about to jilt him for someone else. The seductress felt no remorse because promiscuous love affairs lack true emotions. The title for the story came quickly and she scribbled down: *Poison*.

LM found her still at her writing desk when she brought in the morning tea.

ONE OF THE MANY PLEASANT AFTERNOONS she and LM shared at Isola Bella found them seated on the cobblestone terrace sipping chamomile tea under a giant umbrella that half-shaded them from the bright sun. The late autumn breeze was brisk but while the sun shone they were warm.

An ancient brick wall protected them from the eyes of curious passersby and allowed only a breeze from the Mediterranean to pass over the wall onto the terrace. The drifting puffy white clouds provided a pretty landscape to complement Katherine's tranquil mood. She closed her eyes and felt the breeze brush against her face. On days like this she never wanted to return to London or the literary salons that she once found so seductive.

Stretched out on a cane longue, she picked up one of her older notebook from 1903 that she kept in her travel chest. It was the year she and LM had first met at Queen's College in London.

She was amused by how little LM had changed since they were students. *A giant body with a little voice. So much wanting to please others that she had made it her life's ambition. So afraid to give her own opinion that she didn't have one. So shy that when she expressed herself, she looked down and mumbled incoherently. Incapable of making the slightest decision without approval.*

"Do you remember Queen's College fondly?" Katherine looked up and asked.

"Why do you ask such a silly question. We wouldn't have become such good friends if we hadn't met there. Nor would I be so pleasantly sitting here with you now. So yes, I remember it fondly."

"There's something that I have always wanted to know, Jones. Why didn't you ever boast about your prestigious scholarship prize? I only knew about it from the other girls. If it had been me, I would have shouted the news from the courtyard."

"Oh, it wasn't that important!"

"Not important. You got the highest marks in our class. You could have succeeded in so many ways. Musician? Scholar? Instead you gave it all up for me. I still don't understand why?"

"It's what I do best. And by the way you are much easier to take care of than my father was. After my mother died, his grief was really inconsolable. He looked at me with such disapproval and scorn as if he held me responsible for her death. The smallest task I accomplished displeased him. I tried to take charge of the household but he argued against all my decisions down to the smallest detail. If I bought one pound of flour I should have bought two or if I bought two I should have bought one. And always the cost. I had to budget every penny but he still thought I was extravagant."

Katherine laughed. "He sounds like me!"

LM blushed. "Well, yes, you do have similarities, but he was far more of a tyrant than you could ever be. And you're not cruel."

Oh yes I am, thought Katherine.

"At the end of each month he would call me into his dark, clammy study to go over the accounts. Even with the fire blazing there was a chill. He'd thump his cane on the stone floor." LM's usual canary voice turned loud and gruff as she humped over and imitating her father said, "I told you not to make any purchases without my permission." She hit her fist on the table, rattling the teacups. "Do you hear me, young lady!"

Katherine laughed at LM's mime.

"I swear there were times when I walked by and he stuck out that horrid cane to trip me intentionally. My mother's sudden death had cut out his heart. I was terribly afraid of him and afraid for him at the same time."

Katherine poured them both another cup of tea, and thought back to the winter before in Italy. "You weren't afraid when you shot at those prowlers with the revolver."

"I had to. They might have hurt you."

"That night I realized how much you cared for me and I've felt very safe ever since. Truthfully, Jones, I don't think I'd be as happy here without you. Here at Isola Bella I've had the best working conditions I've ever known and you have a lot to do with that. You leave me alone and keep others from bothering me."

She looked closely at LM's blushing face, a face that could pass for a grinning pumpkin but there was still no laughter in the eyes. The eyes were dark holes, without any light illuminating from inside. "You were so sad at school and so quiet," said Katherine. "Even Professor Lester, the kindest of our teachers, couldn't get you to speak above a whisper in his writing class. He was the one who encouraged me to become a writer."

"He encouraged me, too," said LM, so unexpectedly defensive that Katherine sat up.

"You were interested in writing? Wait. I do remember one night when you came to my room gripping sheets of paper you wanted to read to me. You were so excited. The most excited I've ever seen you. I had just put down my pen after writing a story for Lester's class. I read first. I remember you were quite moved by it. I think you cried. I don't remember what the writing assignment was. Do you?"

"I'll never forget it," said LM. "We were to write a story about some-one in our lives that had profoundly influenced us and share it with the class. I wrote about my mother."

"But why didn't you read it?"

"Not after you read yours. Your story was so much better than mine, Katie. You wrote about your mother, too, but she came alive when you described her coming to your room at night to tuck you into bed and how you felt safe knowing she was there. She smoothed things over, kept all your lives in order. You see, you were also describing my mother, but doing a much better job of it. I stopped writing after that."

The setting sun cast shadows across Katherine's longue. She would have gone inside sooner but it was so seldom LM talked about herself. "I'm so sorry I didn't hear your story that night," she said. "I'm sure it was very good."

Katherine enjoyed a few long drags from her cigarette and said, "You were such a mystery to me and the other students. You hardly ever said a word but then in debating class you came alive. You were a very power-ful debater. I was often jealous when the girls voted for your argument over mine."

"That was only because you were full of original ideas that we English girls found shocking. You were foreign to us, even exotic. Spoke differ-ently. Dressed differently. We were unaccustomed to seeing such boldness in a fourteen-year-old schoolgirl. Even the way you walked expressed a confidence we didn't have. That's why we called you the Little Colonial."

LM stood up. "Shall we go in or shall I get you the eiderdown?"

"The eiderdown. I'd like to watch the sunset."

Katherine opened her current notebook for writing down ideas. She thought to write a story about two sisters. She'd call one sister Constan-tia, as constant as LM was.

The story would open with the Colonel, their father, dead a few days. The two daughters suddenly liberated from his tyranny didn't know how to behave. Never given the opportunity to mature, to develop their own ideas, they'd sacrificed their youth serving their father.

The story captured her full attention for several days. She was late on the novel-reviews, but she dedicated her every hour to *The Daughters of the Late Colonel*, her longest story since *Prelude*.

DECEMBER, 1920

Villa Isola Bella

And now I'll be personal, darling. Look here you ought to have sent me your Corona! You really ought to have. Can't you possibly imagine what all this writing out has been to a person as weak as I damnably am? You can't or a stone would have sent it. You knew what a help it was to me in London.

But oh dear I don't mean to accuse you—because I can't bear, as you know, to make you feel unhappy. But what you could have saved me—I can't say! Isn't it awful that I have not dared to add to your burdens by reminding you before?

I must remind myself that the hole I might so easily trip into is far bigger—far blacker than your troubles.

LETTERS—KM

D R. BOUCHAGE PRESSED THE STETHOSCOPE to her chest and up close she saw what she had missed before—his feverish eyes. All consumptives have that same inextinguishable fire burning deep within.

"Your right lung is still inflamed but quiescent," he said after his examination." She thought how tedious it had become hearing doctors diagnose her symptoms, drug her, offer no cure, and then ask her to be their guinea pig so they could test their experiments. As Dr. Sorapure had explained, she was only a cog in the wheel in helping science to discover a cure. A cure that she feared would not be found until after she was dead and would do her no good but, she hoped, would help cure other consumptives.

"It's your inactive left lung that is pressing against your heart," said Dr. Bouchage. "That's why it's painful and belaboring to breathe, even on short walks or climbing a few steps. Your heart is exhausted from the strain of keeping you alive. It needs complete rest. Your life will be shortened if you don't cut back on your work."

"I can't do that! It's my writing that keeps me alive, not my heart! I might as well be dead if I don't write."

"Please calm down, Mrs. Murry," he said squeezing her shaking hand. "You must listen to me. Your life is in danger. If you can't stop writing than at least limit it to a few hours a day."

She looked again into his enflamed eyes. "Am I right in believing that you have a personal understanding of what it's like to be a consumptive? Can you stop your work?"

"You are an astute diagnostician, Mrs. Murry. Yes, I am a consumptive and, like you, I continue my work, but I'm careful."

"I'm sorry you're one of us, but because you are perhaps you can help me understand why there are times when I feel very alive and full of promise and the next moment I'm suddenly drowning in despair. Is it me or the illness?"

"It's most likely the fever brought on by your illness. Melancholia is not unusual for us and, in your case, even hysteria. When one has suffered as long as you have, one has a different sense of reality, a heightened sense. The world can appear awful at one moment and quite beautiful the next."

"You make it sound like I'm going mad."

"No, you just experience life differently from those who are unconscious of death's approach." He put his stethoscope in his bag and pulled out an amber colored tincture and a needle.

Katherine pulled away. "No more of those iodine injections. They make me too tired and bring on headaches."

"But isn't there less pain in your hips, less cramping in your hands?"

"No, not really." She smiled. "I need a typewriter more than I need iodine."

"Is that so hard to find?"

She laughed. "It shouldn't be. I've asked my husband to send me his and I'm waiting for his response."

"Certainly he'll say yes."

She smiled again. "I hope so."

He started to leave and then changed his mind. "Mrs. Murry do you believe in God? Or do you have some other spiritual faith?"

"If you mean, do I get down on my knees and pray to a merciless god, no, I don't. What I do believe is that if I could accept Death, submit to the inevitable rather than fight it, my days would be far more bearable, even peaceful.

"When I sleep, Death comes to me in my dreams. He's a toady looking dwarf. In one recurring dream he rows me away from shore in a boat. We approach a black gulf and I cry out—'take me home.' But it's a futile cry and I wake up screaming."

She thought to stop, but he seemed really interested in what she had to say and she continued.

"At times I plead with my husband to come before his Christmas visit, but that's only when I'm feeling despair and loneliness. Then there are other times when I'm writing and I don't want to be disturbed by anyone. Then I cling to my solitude and search within for Truth in the comforting silence. These are the brief moments when I glimpse reality but then a veil covers my view and I can't see clearly anymore."

She realized she was gazing out at the sea and turned her gaze back on him. "Doctor, do you understand what I'm talking about or does all this sound ridiculous? Jack tells me I'm going mad."

"No, Mrs. Murry. What you're experiencing is quite understandable. Thirty-two is way too young to have to come to terms with the pain and fatigue that two incurable diseases are forcing your body to bear every day. Such heavy suffering is untreatable with anything I have here." He patted the satchel sitting in his lap having put away the iodine.

"You know there are moments when I believe my suffering is a rare privilege and just like in my dream I should stop resisting it."

He pulled out his pocket watch. "Oh dear, look at the time." He snapped his satchel shut and stood up to leave. "I must hurry. Other patients are waiting for me. I'll be back in a few days to check on you."

His abrupt departure was a disappointment. She had hoped because they were both consumptives that he would tell her how he dealt with his own personal suffering and maybe, being an older man, he could offer her advice on how to keep Death away. Or, she thought with a shudder, was Death even closer than I realized and seeing it in my eyes made Dr. Bouchage run away. Well, if that's true, then I have much to do.

She sat down at her writing table and wrote Jack:

It is with the most extreme reluctance that I am writing to
tell you that Katherine can't go on. She will review the last
two books you sent and can do no more.

She looked out her window at the arc of the rising new moon and
added:

I am not dying. If I were I would have you come
immediately. It's a question of shortening my life if I keep
writing the reviews and I can't do that. I do not want to die
because I have done nothing to justify having lived yet. I
must keep alive until there is a modest shelf of books with
K.M. backs.

A WEEK LATER, she received Jack's reply and before opening the envelope she anticipated a sympathetic, loving response. But instead it was
his confession—*Thinking about my lies this evening, I discovered that*
if I had told you the whole truth from the beginning, I should not have
been corrupt...

In one week, he'd considered sleeping with a tart but took her to
dinner instead, impulsively kissed their close friend Anne, took Brett in
his arms, caressed her and, revolted, pushed her away. A few days later
he'd shared a car with Princess Bibesco and impulsively kissed her on
the cheek. He was afraid that these women would think from his sudden
intimacy that he wanted to make love to them, but he didn't. What he
really wanted was to be held gently and comforted and though he didn't
come right out and say it she knew he felt it was her fault because she
was ill and unavailable to him.

Too angry to write back she sent him a wire:

STOP TORMENTING ME WITH THESE FALSE DEPRESSING
LETTERS. STOP. AT ONCE BE A MAN OR DON'T WRITE ME.

Later, after calming down she wrote him a letter:

I told you to be free—because I meant it. What happens in
your personal life does not affect me. I have of you what I
want—a relationship which is unique, but it is not what the
world understands by marriage.

She hesitated. Was that really the truth? Did she want him to be free?

That is to say, I do not in any way depend on you, neither can you shake me. Nobody can. I do not know how it is, but I live withdrawn from my personal life. (This is hard to say.) I am a writer first. In the past, it is true, when I worked less, my writing self was merged in my personal self. I felt conscious of you—to the exclusion of almost everything, at times.

But now I do not. You are dearer than anyone in the world to me—but more than anything else—more even than talking or laughing or being happy I want to write. This sounds so ugly, I wish I didn't have to say it. But your letter makes me feel you would be relieved if it were said...

She quickly sealed the letter and asked LM to take it to the post office before she changed her mind.

Two days later the misery she felt from cutting Jack off was far worse than anything he had done to hurt her and now she feared he wouldn't come for the Christmas holidays. She shuddered thinking of the cold, colorless, and friendless life she would have without someone to love. No, she must find a way to forgive him, even share the blame for his infidelities.

She sent him a telegram:

PAY NO HEED MY LETTER. STOP. ILLNESS EXASPERATED
ME. STOP. ARE YOU ARRIVING TUESDAY. STOP. IF SO
WON'T WRITE AGAIN. STOP. FONDEST LOVE. STOP. REPLY.

SHE PUSHED AWAY HER WRITING CASE and got up from her bed, laughing and shouting, "It's finished! It's finished!"

"Katie! What's wrong?" shouted LM, awoken from her sleeping corner.

"Why must you always think the worse has happened when I call out? Look at how happy I am," she said, grinning like a madwoman. "I'm inviting you to celebrate my happiness with a bottle of champagne."

"But, Katie, it's three in the morning."

"What better time now that my story is finished." She waved a thick stack of pages. "It came very quickly, with hardly a break or correction." She stopped to catch her breath. "*The Daughters of the Late Colonel* is my best story ever and it all came together in a few days. Champagne Jones! We must have champagne."

LM returned with a bottle in an iced bucket and two crystal flutes. They sat cross-legged on Katherine's bed and took tiny sips, letting the bubbles tickle their lips.

Katherine said, "Did you know that I've always had a longing to heal people and make them whole, enrich them? Not just in my writing, I want to do it in life, too. You're like me, that way. Why I bet if you were free of me, you would be saving the entire world."

LM swung out her large hands and caught a mosquito that she then carried to the window and flung out.

Katherine sighed. "Oh, LM, I know you don't like to talk about this but you could be doing so much more than saving me from mosquito bites." Katherine joined her at the window and put her hand on her caregiver's shoulder. "If not saving me, you could be settled down by now with a husband and children."

LM closed the window, turned to her and firmly said, "I have no desire to marry. And the stories you write are like my children. Or at least I'm their godmother. I have all the happiness I need right here with you."

They both looked out at the moonlit sea.

Katherine said quietly, "I won't always be here to give you happiness."

"Katie, please don't talk like that. For me you'll always be alive."

Katherine grabbed her arm and swung her around. "Listen to me, you silly woman. I'm trying to warn you. Know that someday I'll be gone and when that happens, please don't waste a minute believing I'm still alive in the next room." LM backed away, frightened.

Katherine changed her tone and said playfully, "To be sure you don't, I'll send you a small matchbox with a coffin's worm in it to remind you where I've gone."

An unamused LM stuck the neck of the empty bottle of champagne in the bucket of ice, tossed in the empty flutes, and without saying good night, left the room.

Katherine was still too excited from finishing her new story to hurry after Ida and apologize though she knew she should. Instead, she put the writing case on her knees and wrote in her notebook:

> *I simply can't afford to die with one very half-and-half little book and one bad one and a few stories to my name. In spite of everything, in spite of all I know and have felt—I have this longing to praise Life—to sing my minute song of praise, and it doesn't matter whether it's listened to or not.*

She jotted down a sketch about a maid who chooses to remain with her mistress after being sorely tempted to leave with a man who has asked her to be his wife.

ON THE APPOINTED DAY, December 20th, Jack arrived at Villa Isola Bella. LM showed him upstairs explaining that Katherine was too tired to greet him downstairs. He was very pleased with all he saw in the villa and told Ida if he had known how beautiful it was, he would have come sooner. A loyal caregiver to his wife, she wasn't amused by his bantering.

"Oh Boge, is it really you?" Katherine called out hoarsely from her bed. "I thought I'd frightened you away."

"You will never frighten me away," he said, putting his Felti on the table and leaning over to kiss her lips. Something he hadn't done in a long time and it took her by surprise. He sat on the edge of the bed and for a while they watched the crackling logs spark and sputter in the stove.

"I know I've hurt you, Katherine, and I am very sorry. Will you forgive me?"

"I've been lying here, waiting for you," she said quietly, not answering his question. "And now that you're here, I can tell you that I strongly believe suffering can be tolerated. I don't mean physical suffering. It's child's play compared to emotional suffering.

"Emotional suffering is boundless. It's unavoidable. And I mustn't fight it any longer. It's better to accept it fully—make it a part of Life by transforming it into Love. I must give to Life what I once gave only to you. I must pass from personal love, which has failed me, to greater love."

"Katherine, your wrong. Our love has not failed."

"Yes it has. Accept the truth, Jack. The fearful pain I felt from your last letter—I will now gain strength from it. I will learn the lesson it teaches. This present agony will pass. As in the physical world so in the spiritual world—pain does not last forever."

"Oh, Wig!" Jack cried out, reaching for her hand. "Don't say that. This is all my fault. You will suffer no more on my account, I promise."

She pushed him away. "Don't move and don't say a word. This is difficult enough to confess without your interruptions. I must finish and you must listen." She raised herself up straight so her eyes could look deeply into his.

"It's hard to make a good death. And your claim not to suffer anymore on my behalf was hurtful. It was base in its selfishness."

"I know that, Wig. That's why I had to come. When I'm separated from you, I feel completely desperate and terribly lonely and I do foolish things but I never stop loving you. None of those women meant anything to me. It was only a distraction—a selfish way to escape from my own suffering. I don't desire any woman but you."

Jack looked at her so plaintively that she couldn't resist pulling him toward her. He was essential to her. For all their differences, they were two sides of the same medal. She had wanted to become independent of him but now that he was there, she didn't have the strength to let him go.

His head on her breast, her hands combing his hair, she whispered tenderly, "I still love you Jack. I will always love you." And in that moment she found the compassion to forgive him and the courage to risk everything, if only to be with him again.

ON CHRISTMAS DAY he surprised her with his Corona typewriter and her doll Rib that she had left behind in London to keep him company.

In the weeks that followed, Katherine's weakened condition improved and she was certain it was because Jack was with her. She could come downstairs again and take short walks with him in the garden.

LM moved into a nearby pension so they could have their intimacy. Marie, now in charge, enjoyed setting the table for candlelight dinners and serving lavish 3-course meals to such an appreciative, loving couple. She enjoyed being near their happiness so much that they had to find excuses to send her away so they could make love. After, they drank champagne late into the night and made plans to travel the world, chasing the sun forever.

They decided Jack would resign from *The Athenaeum* in April. After all his Herculean efforts the paper's circulation hadn't reached his expectations and was losing money. Even increasing its circulation by merging with another magazine, *The Nation*, hadn't improved the situation. For income, because he was a well-respected literary critic, he would write articles for *The Athenaeum/Nation* and other intellectual publications. And an admirer, Sir Walter Raleigh, had commissioned him to give six literary lectures at Oxford on *The Problem of Style*.

For Katherine and Jack, they were as happy as they'd been at Villa Pauline in Bandol five years ago. Sharing books. Sharing ideas. Sharing the writing table. Sharing the fire. Sharing the bed.

Reluctantly, Jack returned to London in January to complete his obligations with the magazine. He'd only been gone ten days when Katherine took a turn for the worse and he had to come rushing back. He stayed with her until she recovered from a high fever.

He returned to London again to resign from *The Athenaeum* two months earlier than he had planned and give a farewell party for the staff and his friends. He wanted Katherine to come with him but Dr. Bouchage said it would endanger her recovery.

At the end of February, he took up permanent residence at Isola Bella with Katherine, both acknowledging that the England where they had worked together to build their literary reputations was no longer a desirable shelter for their marriage.

Plotting Another Escape

I am not in despair about my health. But I must make
every effort to get it better soon, very soon... I was not
born an invalid and I want to get well... I feel every day
must be the last day of such a life. I must escape.

NOTEBOOKS—KM

S HE PUSHED HERSELF OUT OF BED when she heard Jack calling,
"Katherine!" She wanted to be on the terrace when he returned
from his afternoon walk but she'd fallen asleep. The scarf hanging on
her bedpost and Jack calling out her name reminded her of what she
dreaded doing that day and the reason why. At the mirror, she wrapped
the scarf around her swollen neck with a scarf and lowered her cloche
down over her dark-circled eyes.

If only I could've put off this surgery until LM returned from London,
she said to her reflection. LM was in London to sort through, store, and
give or throw away most of her and Jack's possessions that remained
at the Elephant. Katherine would have preferred waiting until she
came back, but the pain in her neck was interrupting her work and
Dr. Bouchage said the only way to give her relief was to puncture the
infected gland pressing against her artery. She would just have to trust
Jack to care for her in LM's absence, which was worrying.

"We're going to be late. Did you order a car?" she called out from
the stairs. Jack was standing in the entry hall watching her walk stiffly
toward him.

"A car? Wouldn't the walk do you good?"

"How can I walk there when I can hardly make it down the stairs?"

"Right. Silly of me," he said half smiling.

After the surgery Katherine felt faint and leaned on Jack while climbing into the hired car. She reached for her purse to pay the cabbie but

Jack told her not to worry he'd take care of it. "That's nice of you," she said, and leaned her head on his sturdy shoulder.

After he helped her upstairs, she didn't see him again until that evening when she woke up to the sound of a scraping pen coming from her writing table.

"Water please. My throat is parched," she said hoarsely.

"Are you feeling better?" he asked, pouring her a glass from the pitcher.

"Yes. Only tired and a little sore." He had returned to the writing table before she could finish telling how she felt. "What are you doing, Jack?"

"I'm going over our budget, trying to put things in order. I have a few questions for you."

"Right now?"

"It'll only take a few minutes."

Her heavy eyelids shut as he listed their expenditures since he joined her in Menton. She drifted in and out until she heard "your share of today's cab fare" and pulled herself awake. "You want me to pay for half the fare?"

"Look here, no need to get upset, you don't have to pay me right now. Tomorrow will be fine."

"Take it from my purse on the armoire. Take it all!"

"God, Katherine, there's just never a good time to discuss our money affairs."

She watched him count the money from her coin purse, slip several coins into his pocket, and walk out the door.

How can I possibly rest now? she thought. She stacked the papers he'd carelessly left behind on her writing table and took a sheet of stationery from its drawer.

LM had sent detailed, irritating questions about what to do with several items left at the Elephant. After Katherine answered her questions, she went on to tell her about the meanness of Jack over the taxi fare and how much his stinginess with money reminded her of her father. She also told LM how she missed her thoughtful care. Jack was inept at taking care of the villa and her writing had fallen off.

She finished off the letter by asking LM to return soon.

KATHERINE WAS READING THE MORNING MAIL on the sunny terrace when she suddenly shouted, "Ida! Where's Jack?" LM rushed out, dishtowel in hand.

"He went for a walk."

"That was hours ago. Did he see the post before he left?" Katherine demanded angrily.

"No, I think he'd already left. What's wrong, Katie?"

LM had only been back a week but in that week had put the villa back to order, which allowed Jack more time to go off on long walks and Katherine to return to her story writing.

Katherine waved an envelope in her face.

"Hold still," said LM. "I can't read it. Bi-bes-co? Who is that?"

"Madame la *Princesse* Bibesco. Listen to how she scolds me about *her* Jack."

"*Her* Jack?" Katherine got up and paced the terrace as she read the letter like a jilted wife in a play:

20 March 1921

Dear Mrs. Murry. I cannot let Jack suffer any more because of your selfishness. How dare you keep a hold on him when you are incapable of performing as his wife? You can't make him happy when you are living in France and you have told him you won't come back to London. Even after he made a home for you there, you left.

Katherine started coughing and handed the letter to LM, who continued to read it out loud but not as dramatically:

I regret that you are ill. But this is not Jack's fault though he feels it is. I can't believe it is your intention to use your illness to keep a hold on to him. No one could be that cruel. You must realize, the observant writer that you are, how the man suffers from loneliness and lack of affection.

He wants to be free of you but every time he tries to tell you this he says you faint or have one of your coughing spells. Not wanting to be the cause of your condition worsening, he sacrifices his own happiness.

He has told me that you are a wonderful, sensitive woman but I find that hard to believe by your actions. Understand that Jack can't go on like this. Your hold on him is killing him. He needs to be loved and caressed. I can give him what he needs. He knows that but his guilt keeps him from me. I beg you to let him loose. Please Katherine, I beseech you.

Sincerely, Princess Bibesco

"Oh my," said LM. "Who is this woman?"

"Another one of his floozies." Katherine laughed harshly. "This is not the first I've heard of the Princess but he promised to put an end to it."

She was folding up the letter when Jack walked in. "I've just read a letter from your Princess Bibesco."

LM said she had work to do and backed off the terrace.

"Shouldn't you have left it for me to read?" he said defensively.

"It wasn't addressed to you."

"Why would she write to you?"

"That was what I was going to ask you."

"I have no idea. I've only met her and her husband a few times socially and there was that time I impulsively kissed her in the carriage. But I told you about that." He sat down across from Katherine and poured himself a cup of tea.

"Then why does she tell me…

He wants to be free of you but every time he tries to tell you this he says you faint or have one of your coughing spells.

"Silly schoolgirl," said Jack.

"Why didn't you tell me you arranged personally to have one of her short stories published in *The Athenaeum*?"

"She's lying. Let me have a look." He snatched the letter from Katherine's hand.

While he read, Katherine watched, hoping for signs of guilt or culpability or at least embarrassment, but he remained emotionless.

He folded it up into small pieces all the while shaking his head in mock disbelief. Katherine grabbed it back before it disappeared inside his jacket pocket.

"What are you going to do about this?"

"Why do anything? It's bollocks. Ignore it. She won't write again."

"Are you so sure of that? I'm not. She sounds extremely confident about your affections and seems to think she's better suited to take care of you than I am. Perhaps she's right." She unfolded the letter. "How did she so politely put it? Oh yes here it is:

> I can't believe it is your intention to use your illness to keep a hold on to him. No one could be that cruel. You must realize, the observant writer that you are, how the man suffers from loneliness and lack of affection.

"I promise you there is not a bit of truth to what she's saying. Why I hardly know her."

"Really, Jack? I think she knows you quite well. But she doesn't know me."

"What are you going to do?"

"First tell me what *you* are going to do. Don't you think this letter requires some formal declaration on your part to rid us of this woman?"

"Yes… I could write something I suppose."

"Never mind. I'll do it myself. I'll tell her never to write to my husband again as long as we are living together under the same roof. I will also scold her for considering a liaison with a married man when she was already married herself, and suggest she turn to her husband for a lesson in etiquette."

Jack laughed. "Yes that should do it. Good idea. And she's more apt to believe it coming from you. You know what a pushover I am."

Katherine never heard from Princess Bibesco again. But she confided to LM that she doubted it would be the end of Jack's affairs with other women. She predicted Jack would marry Brett after she was gone. "Brett gives him exactly what he needs from a wife; flattery, reverence and adoration."

DURING A FREEZING MARCH, the splendid view of sea and garden from her bedroom balcony was off limits and her writing had also reached an impasse.

Dr. Bouchage's iodine experiment had been a failure and continually piercing her swollen neck glands was no picnic for either of them. She recognized the symptoms of a doctor giving up on his patient, she'd seen it happen before. He became unavailable or late to appointments and gave quick examinations without offering any sympathy or promising what he could not deliver. A cure.

There were other doctors she could see, but now that Connie and Jinnie had reneged on another year's lease on Isola Bella, Katherine wanted to leave Menton. But where would they go? And how convince Jack it was time to leave the Riviera when he was producing good work? He'd finished writing the six lectures for Oxford, and was thinking about writing a book of poetry or finishing the novel he had started in Bandol now that he was no longer obligated to *The Athenaeum*. The deciding moment was after she coughed up blood and Dr. Bouchage telling her that the hot, humid summer would not be good for her rheumatism or her lungs.

She remembered her conversation at the Elephant in London with her cousin Elizabeth who had recommended Katherine go to a sanatorium in the Alps for a tuberculosis cure. At the time, Katherine balked but not now.

She started her research in a British magazine "Tubercle." There were many advertisements for treatments or cures or miracles. She'd hide the magazine from Jack who didn't believe in miracles or anything else lacking scientific proof.

A full-page advertisement for a tuberculosis clinic in Switzerland caught her attention. It was the same clinic Elizabeth had mentioned and it was near her mountain chalet.

But her excitement grew when she turned the page and read an article on Dr. Spahlinger, a Swiss microbiologist, who claimed he had discovered an anti-tuberculosis serum—a serum produced from horses infected with tuberculosis. There had been a hundred or more miracle serums or other fake cures for tuberculosis, but the British government was financially backing this one.

She calculated the travel and living expenses in Switzerland and wondered how she could afford it. She had the income from *Bliss & Other Stories,* which was selling way beyond expectations after excellent reviews, but it would be several months before she was paid royalties. Maybe with her allowance it would be enough. If she had to, she could ask her many friends for a loan. She never thought to ask Jack and she'd heard through Connie that her father resented giving her an allowance when she had a husband to provide for her.

Once her mind was set on going to Switzerland, she invited LM into the drawing room to join her for a special afternoon tea while Jack was on his walk. She'd asked her earlier to purchase a selection of chocolate éclairs, macarons and mille feuilles at the local patisserie.

When LM brought in the tray of pastries, she seemed to know something was up. Katherine was seldom so generous with pastries. They both stared at the delicious plate of morsels while the tea brewed.

Once the tea was poured and LM had eaten a few pastries, Katherine thanked her again for moving them out of the Elephant and told her how much she appreciated all her work. She couldn't resist adding, "But you did ask too many questions while you were away. I didn't expect you to ask my approval on every item in the house."

"But what if I'd thrown out something you really cared about?"

"You needn't have worried. Everything I need is right here—my pen and writing materials and a few souvenirs. What ever fits in my travel chest. The rest is superfluous. What need have I of gowns when I have no interest in returning to London?"

"Oh Katie, you say such silly things. You'd never give up the art galleries or the Ballet Russe or the concerts at Queen's Hall and what about all your London friends. You're having one of your dark moods, aren't you?"

"No, Ida, I'm not having one of my *dark moods*," she said losing patience. This conversation was not going the way she had planned. She changed her tone, "Shall I pour you another cup of tea?"

Ida insisted on pouring herself and Katherine got up to close the door, peeking out in the entryway first. She sat back down and said, "I wish to speak to you before Jack returns. I've decided to leave Menton. There is a Dr. Spahlinger in Geneva I need to see as soon as possible."

"Leave the villa? Spahlinger? Geneva? What on earth are you talking about," said LM, dropping powdered sugar from the feuille on her skirt and smearing it when trying to brush it off.

Katherine handed her a napkin. "Yes, leave the villa, leave Menton." LM took another bite from her feuille. "Please put that down, Jones, and I'll explain everything. But we must hurry. Jack will be back any minute and I don't want him to know my plans, at least not yet."

"But doesn't he need to know. Isn't he coming with us?"

"No he isn't. And he'd like to stop me from going. Dr. Spahlinger is not officially a medical doctor and Jack doesn't want me getting my hopes up. I had to beg him to ask his associate, Sullivan, who knows Spahlinger personally, to get me an appointment as there are hundreds of other wandering consumptives seeking cures from this doctor."

Katherine gave LM the article about Dr. Spahlinger from her tuberculosis-labeled folder and told her to read it later.

"I must say you have shocked me. I thought you'd finally found the perfect place to get better."

"Better? Do you think I'm better, Ida? We've been here since October and I've already had several relapses. You're not listening. Spahlinger is offering a cure for TB patients. I must find out for myself if he's legitimate or just another quack."

Katherine watched LM's vague, inexpressive face and hesitated before making another effort to rally her to her cause. "Jones, don't you see, we must pin all our flags on Switzerland."

LM came out of her stupor. "Yes! Of course, my dear. Certainly. It's just a lot for me to take in. Horse serum… cures… leaving Menton… It all seems so abrupt. But yes I'll do whatever I can to make your journey comfortable. And of course I'll go with you."

Katherine reached out and gripped LM's hand in hers. "Thank you, my dear loyal friend. Now this is what you must do right away." Katherine knew she was getting overexcited but now that they were actually going she wanted to move fast.

"First, go to the train station and see about tickets… and find out about Swiss accommodations. We might be there for a considerable time. Perhaps stay in Montreux instead of Geneva. It's less convenient but Geneva would be very expensive and we must consider the costs."

Katherine thought she heard Jack's footsteps and lowered her voice,

"And there's something else we need to discuss. Hear me out, Jones, and don't interrupt before I'm finished. From now on I want you to look on me *not* as a friend who needs looking after but just as a friend. I mean that in all its implications. Do you understand?"

"No, I don't understand. What implications? Katie, speak in plain English."

"What I'm trying to say is that I don't want you to *hover* over me as if I'm a wounded bird that can't fly without your assistance. You've been my nurse for too long. Instead, I want you to be my companion. In other words, be independent from each other, each pursuing our own interests."

"But you are my only interest," interjected LM, wiping the éclair cream off her hands.

"That's the problem. I can't have you offering yourself to me like a sacrificial lamb. If you can't agree to my terms, I'll have to make other arrangements."

"No. Don't do that. I'm going with you, but don't expect me to move into my new position too quickly. You know it takes time for me to adjust to new ways of doing things."

A MONTH LATER, Katherine was seated at her table writing letters to her sisters in New Zealand and anyone else who would want to know her plans to move to Switzerland. She still couldn't bear to write to her father after what he'd said about resenting her allowance when she had a husband to depend on.

Jack had left that morning for London. He'd finally come around to understanding her need to see Dr. Spahlinger. If he turned out to be a charlatan, which Jack thought he was, she'd try an open-air cure in a Swiss sanatorium. After his Oxford lecture tour Jack would come there and together they'd find a chalet for just the two of them with a house-keeper living nearby—but not LM.

This was Jack's idea. He thought Katherine was too dependent upon her caregiver and it was a wedge between their own relationship. She knew it was unfair not to tell LM that their new arrangement was only temporary, but she needed her until Jack arrived.

And she hoped by having Ida behave as her companion instead of as her nurse that she could slowly train her to become independent. That way when they parted it would not be so painful for LM. And when she had a family of her own she would thank Katherine for forcing her to leave.

MAY, 1921

Sierre, Switzerland

*I see a small white chalet with a garden near the pine
forests. I see it all very simple, with big white china stoves
and a very pleasant woman with a tanned face and
sun-bleached hair bringing in the coffee. I see winter—
snow and a load of wood arriving at our door. I see us
going off in a little sleigh with huge fur gloves on, and
having a picnic in the forest and eating ham and fur
sandwiches. There is a lamp—très important—there are
our books. It's very still. The frost is on the pane. You are in
your room writing. I in mine. Outside the Stars are shining
and pine trees are dark like velvet.*

NOTEBOOKS—KM

ARRIVING AT the Clarens-Montreux train station, Katherine
booked a room at the Hotel Beau Site and LM checked into a
more economical hotel in nearby Blonay.

After unpacking her notebooks and setting up a writing table, Katherine opened wide the French doors onto her fourth floor balcony. She tested her lungs and breathed deeply without pain or cough. The crisp alpine air felt pleasantly cool as it passed down through her inflamed lungs. She was right to have left Menton.

A tap on the door and a large muscular Swiss maid in a starched white apron entered carrying a tray laden with a silver coffee service, fresh-baked croissants, strawberry jam and an assortment of Swiss cheeses. Katherine asked her to put the tray out on the sunbaked balcony.

After breakfast, she dressed quickly. She didn't want to be late for her appointment with Dr. Spahlinger that had finally been confirmed. LM offered to go with her but Katherine wanted to meet Dr. Spahlinger on her own.

As she was taken by carriage to her appointment, she reread the article that had brought her here:

The British government has definitely decided to acquire the rights for making the anti-tuberculosis serum which Henry Spahlinger has discovered after research and experiments lasting more than ten years. His father's mansion has been converted into experimental rooms, while the grounds are largely used for stabling and keeping horses, cows, donkeys, goats and other animals needed for his experiments of extracting serum... Hitherto Spahlinger has never received remuneration, direct or indirect, from his patients.

When she arrived, Spahlinger's agreeable assistant was there to help her out of the carriage. She was then given a tour of the converted-barn laboratory that housed the farm animals. In the laboratory, the assistant pointed out several tubes of growing bacilli cultures. Katherine protectively covered her lungs with her hands feeling her infected bacteria salivating as if hungry for what was in the tubes.

"The culture specimens are injected into farm animals and then, after they build up immunity to the bacteria, their serum is injected into our tuberculosis patients." She turned to smile at Katherine, "Like you, Mrs. Murry."

The scientific process these animals underwent was fascinating but creepy. Katherine was revolted by the idea of a horse's blood mixed with hers and, though Dr. Sorapure would have appreciated this evolving science of microbiology, she wondered if he would have encouraged her to offer herself as a guinea pig.

Spahlinger's assistant told her they must hurry. Dr. Spahlinger had squeezed Katherine into an already overbooked day. She was ushered into his examination room where the doctor was working at his desk.

She'd expected a far more mature scientist than the youthful, robust man looking up at her entrance. His Swiss mountain-climber ruddy complexion didn't look like someone who had dedicated his life to growing bacteria cultures in a lab. He might even be younger than herself.

The examination of her lungs was very brief. Moments later she was seated across from his desk anxiously waiting while he reviewed her medical dossier. It was a lot of material and she was irritated that he hadn't already read it in preparation of their meeting. She began to feel she'd made a terrible mistake coming here.

He looked up at her and spoke with a heavy boarding-school English accent, "Mrs. Murry, I am pleased to tell you that you are curable—that is, if you are patient with us. Our methods take a very long time to produce results. It's necessary to find the right combination of cultures that can destroy your particular tubercular bacteria." He spread his hands in the air, "And of course there are no guarantees."

She cleared her throat. "The word 'patient' has a double meaning, don't you think, Doctor? I find it ironic that I am already a patient but when it comes to being cured you say I need to be *patient*. Perhaps you don't realize it, but you are offering hope to hundreds of terminal patients like myself who've been without hope, so you can hardly expect any of us to be patient when every day Death draws nearer."

The phone rang and after a long-winded conversation in German, he said, "Now where was I?"

"We were talking about *patience*, Doctor," she said, finding his rudeness and lack of professionalism disturbing when they were talking about a life or death situation.

"Sorry about that. I'm terribly in demand and we're understaffed. What I was going to say is that the treatment for your particular tuberculosis requires that you live here in Geneva where your progress can be monitored closely after each inoculation period."

"How long would that take?"

"Oh," he shrugged, "give or take a year or two. Once we find the right serum, then the restoration period can be quite short, for some of our patients only a few months and they go home cured."

"I see. May I ask what your treatment would cost?"

He looked insulted. "Cost? I don't expect a fee from you, Mrs. Murry. My remuneration is adding you to the list of patients I've cured."

She was suspicious of a doctor that didn't charge a fee. The truth was that the British government was considering a large investment in Dr. Spahlinger's vaccine, but not before there was confirmed statistical evidence that his patients had been cured. And once Britain invested, many other countries would also invest tremendous amounts of money. The doctor would not only become famous but very rich. She quickly decided that he needed her as much as she needed him, if not more.

He looked back down at her file and scribbled a few notes. She sensed he was calculating her chances of being one of the lucky ones added to his statistical evidence.

He was frowning when he looked up. "It's unfortunate that you were diagnosed with tuberculosis in 1918. That makes your cure less probable than my newer patients. I see you also have a weakened heart from the strain of breathing through your damaged lungs. And rheumatism. Your case would be a challenge."

Katherine put away her notepad and stood up to leave.

"Mrs. Murry, I said a *challenge*, I didn't say impossible. You are very ill but you are also very young so a cure is possible. But only if you're willing to live in Geneva. I assure you my staff will find you comfortable accommodations.

She had remained standing. "I'm sorry but that is impossible. I'm a writer and it's very important for me to continue my work while I'm being treated. I couldn't do that in Geneva. I need a more natural landscape."

She thought she saw relief in the young doctor's face. "Then let me make another suggestion. There is a famous tuberculosis sanatorium a few hours from here up in Crans-Montana run by Dr. Théodore Stephani. I highly recommend his open-air cure. He's had excellent results with TB patients. If you like, I'll send him your dossier."

"Yes, please do that." She put on her gloves. "I won't take up anymore of your valuable time, Doctor."

Sad bovine eyes looked up from their grassy meals as Katherine hurried past them. She shuddered at the thought of horse blood coursing through her veins or any other blood but her own. She turned her eyes upward to the pure white alpine mountains.

WITHOUT CONSULTING LM, or writing Jack, she called Dr. Stephani. When she was given an appointment, she smiled up at the Matterhorn that filled her balcony view.

In two days time, they were to meet in Sierre, a village below Dr. Stephani's clinic. Without thought of cost, she impulsively hired a motorcar to drive her up the mountain.

The brisk pure air was magic to her lungs and she arrived refreshed at Hôtel Château Bellevue where Dr. Stephani was waiting for her in a private salon. He was wearing a hiking outfit and on the table was a camera and her medical dossier. He said in broken English that when he wasn't visiting his patients he was taking photographs on the mountain slopes. The gold-framed round spectacles on the end of his nose magnified his intelligent blue eyes that took her in without judgment. Older than Dr. Spahlinger, he had a much kinder bedside manner when he asked her to lie down so he could hear her lungs.

From the lofty, gilded ceiling of the salon hung teardrop crystal chandeliers that tingled like bells when touched by the breeze. Katherine was hypnotized by their illuminated beauty until she felt the familiar icy stethoscope pressed against her chest.

He examined her far more thoroughly than Dr. Spahlinger, took more time writing his notes and seemed quite knowledgeable about her condition, having read her files beforehand.

She dressed and sat across from him on the divan but was again distracted, this time by a pair of bees spinning over her head as if dancing in the lucent sunlight. Today is divine, she thought, and that was all that mattered.

She had learned a lesson with Dr. Spahlinger and was determined to live only in the moment without false expectations.

In the distance, she heard Dr. Stephani's gentle voice and she came to attention, embarrassed as if she'd been caught sleeping in a classroom.

"Mrs. Murry?"

"I'm sorry, there must be something in this high altitude that makes me wander off. What did you say, Doctor?"

He began discussing her lungs, repeating what other doctors had said.

She felt like saying, "Yes all that's true, but do let's listen and watch the bees instead. And do you see that exotic, lush plant outside the window? It reminds me of pictures I've seen of Africa."

But then she remembered why she was there and turned her attention away from the beauty surrounding her and onto Dr. Stephani whose clear blue eyes were looking at her with such sincere concern.

"You're a young woman with great courage to come here on your own considering your poor health. Many consumptives give up early on, not only physically but also emotionally and spiritually."

"The hope of a miracle gave me the strength, Doctor Stephani."

"Then I must tell you that I don't believe in miracles but I do believe in science's ability to give our sanatorium patients several more years."

"Do you think I could be one of those patients?" He hesitated. "Please don't lie to me, doctor. Tell me the truth. Is it too late for me?"

He looked down at his notes for what felt like hours as she was holding her breath.

"Yes, Mrs. Murry, I do. I have known patients with lungs as compromised as yours who have fully recovered. I can't tell you how long you will live, but our open-air cure can increase your survival if your body is strong enough to tolerate the frigid air."

Katherine could've hugged him but hugged herself instead. "You've made me very happy, Doctor Stephani. I will make arrangements to move to Sierre and start your program immediately."

"My dear young lady, don't you want to think this over. This is too serious a commitment to make in a second. Why not discuss it with your husband?"

"Not necessary. You and your clinic have an excellent reputation. And I already feel restored just by breathing in this pure air and looking at these immense gorgeous mountains."

"All right. I will arrange with my associate Dr. Hudson to supervise your case. He's an Englishman, like yourself, and a very qualified pulmonary specialist. We work as a team and he will report back to me on your progress."

Katherine thought to tell him she was actually a New Zealander but decided that didn't matter here in the Alps where patients came from all over the world.

"Our sanatorium is at the Palace Hotel in Montana, a short trip from here on the funicular but fifteen hundred meters higher in elevation. Until a room becomes available, you can start your open-air treatment immediately at any local Sierre hotel with a full service restaurant that offers the same menu as our clinic and a balcony large enough to accommodate a chaise longue.

"Don't all balconies in Switzerland accommodate chaise longues?" said Katherine feeling delightfully lightheaded.

She was pleased when he laughed at her joke. The only doctors she trusted were capable of a good laugh.

For her return trip, Katherine settled down comfortably in the velvet cushions of the hired car. She had the driver stop on the side of an avenue lined with poplars. In this bright green corridor dabbled with sunlight she watched wooden carts pass by crowded with laughing families. The market square ahead was hung with garlands and the villagers were dancing to a band of musicians. Most of the women carried huge bunches of crimson peonies, flashing like bright lights. Villagers were buying and selling farm animals in the marketplace. The cafés were crowded with merrymakers shaded under pink and white blooming chestnut trees. At the windows of the houses there were pots of white narcissi on the window sills and girls with orange and cherry bandanas wrapped around their heads peered out. She was tempted to join the festivities but it was getting dark and the driver wanted to get home to his own family.

That evening back in her hotel room she wrote in her journal:

> *It's an infernal nuisance to love life as I do. I seem to love it more as time goes on rather than less. It never becomes a habit to me—it's always a marvel. I do hope I'll be able to keep in it long enough to do some really good work.*

She looked up joyfully at the full moon gleaming on the snow-capped Bernese mountains and started making plans to return there as soon as possible.

The following morning at breakfast she rushed through her news with LM. Told her about her depressing meeting with Dr. Spahlinger and then what a joy it was to go up the mountain and meet Dr. Stephanie, who was wonderful.

She laughed at LM's shocked face. "See, I told you I could do things on my own if you just leave me on my own."

She had seen a lovely hotel called Hôtel Château Bellevue in Sierre and asked LM to find out if rooms were available and the rates. "Geneva is so ugly compared to the villages I passed coming down the mountain yesterday. And the air, LM, the air was so refreshing when I breathed it into my lungs."

Wanting to start right away, Katherine spent the afternoon stretched out on her balcony's chaise longue reading the pamphlet Dr. Stephani had given her about his open-air treatment program. She felt rather foolish buried up to her neck in every blanket she could find in her room but the slow long breaths of air she took into her bruised lungs made her feel better already.

A FEW DAYS LATER, SHE and LM moved into Hôtel Château Bellevue. Jack was sent her new address, soon to be theirs after he finished the Oxford lectures. LM seemed to flourish in the high altitude. The Alps suited her own bulky shape and she happily took daily mountain climbs leaving Katherine to her "treatments" on the balcony.

In Montreux, Katherine had received a packet in the mail from her father but had not opened it. Knowing that her father thought it was Jack that should be giving her an allowance and not him, she'd been afraid he was going to cut it off.

Without her allowance, she would not be able to continue Dr. Stephani's open-air cure. Each time she thought to open it, she panicked and put it back down.

She decided that Jack should open it first and tell her what was inside. *Jack,* she wrote, *I feel certain this letter from Father contains that Blow I am always expecting. Will you open it & read it & wire me what result?*

The packet was returned with a letter from Jack. It was only her bank deposit book. Mr. Kay from the bank had accidentally sent it to her father and he was returning it to her. Jack told her she'd been foolish to ever think her father would stop her allowance?

Relieved, she picked up her pen to finally write to her father with the news of her move to Switzerland and about Dr. Stephani's open-air cure. She put her pen back down. Too much time had transpired since their mutual silence. On her side, she still felt terribly hurt knowing he chucked her stories into Connie's fireplace and said it was rubbish.

She'd write later when her recovery was imminent and she could surprise him with her plans to visit her family in Wellington. A trip long overdue.

JUNE-NOVEMBER, 1921

Chalet des Sapins

There was a tremendous fall of snow on Sunday night.
Monday was the first real perfect day of the winter. It
seemed that the happiness of Bogey and of me reached
its zenith that day. We could not have been happier; that
was the feeling. Sitting one moment on the balcony of the
bedroom for instance, or driving in the sleigh through the
masses of heaped snow. He looked so beautiful, too, hatless,
strolling about, his hand in his pocket... Then I came away
after a quick but not hurried kiss.

NOTEBOOKS—KM

J ACK AND KATHERINE WROTE passionate love letters during their separation. From Oxford he wrote:

Trust me as though I were part of your own heart. I am
part of your heart. And now I have you in my arms my
wonderful wife. You will be there always till I come in July.

She replied:

I have never loved you more than I love you now. This must
be our Indian summer, I think.

His arrival in Montana was a joyful bright moment in an otherwise dull routine. She had moved into Dr. Stephani's sanatorium, the Palace Hotel to take the open-air cure. The hotel had been converted into a clinic for tuberculosis patients.

She was restless at the sanatorium after one week. Montana was too taken up with pomp and circumstance for her rustic taste. It was a resort where well-to-do consumptives, transformed by disease into desperate patients either hobbled on crutches or were pushed around in wheelchairs, a too-visceral vision of her own dreaded, unspeakable future.

And there were too many rules. Dr. Stephani insisted that stress encouraged tubercular bacillus growth and therefore complete rest was necessary to benefit from his regime. Rest made Katherine nervous. No good would come of her lying around idle. The pure, elevated air had improved her breathing and appeased her cough so, yes, she accepted reclining all day on a chaise longue five thousand feet above the sea but she needed a notebook on her writing case and a table nearby with paper and ink.

When Jack arrived, she saw no reason why they shouldn't immediately rent a chalet where they could continue working together as at Chez Pauline in Bandol and Isola Bella in Menton.

Dr. Hudson, assigned to her by Dr. Stephani, saw nothing wrong with that idea and suggested they lease his mother's remote chalet, which hung on the edge of a precipice over Montana.

Chalet des Sapins was very isolated but for Katherine's needs, perfectly situated. It was only a thirty-minute alpine walk down to cousin Elizabeth's Chalet du Soleil in Randogne and, in the other direction, a short carriage ride to Montana where she could continue her check-ups at Dr. Stephani's clinic.

LM was taken aback by Jack's arrival but took it with her customary resilience. Katherine's "independent" training had paid off and she felt better knowing she had more time for herself. She was happy living in the Alps and found a nursing job at one of the tuberculosis clinics in Montana where she also had a room. Jack and Katherine could call upon her when needed to run errands for them in the village.

Katherine hired a local woman, Ernestine, to do the cleaning and cooking. In the small chalet, there were three levels, plenty of room for Jack and her to have their own studios. The ground floor had a sitting room with a fireplace so massive that Katherine shivered just thinking of the snowbound chill that would make such a fireplace necessary. The weather was so moderate in the summer it was hard to imagine the approaching harsh winter.

A routine was soon established—they would work on their own in the morning, meet in the afternoon for a picnic or a walk, more work in the late afternoon. After supper they read to each other from what they'd written that day and from other books they were reading and played chess and card games.

Katherine thrived that summer in her magical chalet on top of the world. She still walked with a limp, but her heart was stronger and she could take walks in the woods with Jack. On mild days she could even walk to Elizabeth's chalet for afternoon chats. They saw no one else except LM when she brought requested items from the village and stayed for teatime.

Katherine's mild cough didn't keep Jack awake and they slept together in the bedroom on the middle floor, which had the largest bed and a heating stove.

One such evening they were seated cross-legged on their bed drawing designs for the chalet they had decided to build nearby. They lifted their champagne glasses and toasted their decision to never return to England. Their own Heron chalet would be built right here. Why not? Where else could they be happier? And, cut-off from the world below, it felt like they had unlimited time to accomplish their work.

Elizabeth had warned them that it was natural for newcomers to the Alps to become invigorated by the pure air and the high elevation, the magnificent mountains and the beautiful weather. It could go to their heads. The air was intoxicating. It aroused passions. Their response to her warning was, "Let it happen!"

Jack had started his second novel, titled *The Things We Are*. Katherine was writing new stories every day. Stories that figuratively flew out her balcony window to various publishers in London. None were rejected and from her friends' correspondence she learned that she was well spoken of at the salons. To pay for their bliss on the mountain-top, she had picked up a lucrative contract to write a bi-monthly story for the British newspaper, *The Sphere*. And Jack, now one of London's most popular critics, contributed with payments from his essays and reviews.

On their bed that night they imagined their Heron—the pine forest at their back door, the Bernese-Ober blocking the icy wind blowing from the north, and, like Chalet des Sapins, two wide balconies facing out on the massive Mont Blanc and the Matterhorn, with the green Valais valley stretched out below. The vision made them both giddy and they fell on the bed laughing. He took her into his arms and made love to her.

"Let's call it Chalet Content," said Jack afterward, his voice muffled in the feather pillow.

She looked around their bedroom and smiled. Earlier, Jack had taken her riding in a horse-drawn cart and they'd been thrown back and forth on the rough road until they found a picnic location on a grassy knoll overlooking the snow-capped Weisshorn. They'd brought back souvenirs to add to their growing collection. On every surface she'd arranged bouquets of alpine flora and other discoveries Jack had made on his mountain hikes. Many flowers were pressed between the pages of books filling the shelves and stacked on the floor against the walls. Enough books to keep them busy for the many joyous years to come.

She closed her eyes to hold in her happiness. Jack mumbled, "Certainly not more than two floors and a large open fireplace." He put out his arms and she snuggled up to him. Cuddled together they gazed out at the quarter moon in the center of a multitude of glittering stars.

She whispered in his ear, "What about bees?"

"Most certainly bees, and I aspire to raising a goat." She laughed. She couldn't imagine her lazy, intellectual husband waking early to milk a goat.

"Thinking about goats and bees makes me hungry," he said, sitting up. "You too?"

"Oh, yes, famished."

"I'll go downstairs for a plate of Ernestine's lemon cake and you warm the milk here on the stove."

Wingley, curled at their feet, awoke and applauded their plans with purrs and smacking lips. LM had brought him back from London on the train in a basket after Katherine had mentioned how much she missed her cat.

11 SEPTEMBER 1921—*Snow still lingered like linen hung out to dry on the rocks and on the tips of pine trees*, she wrote in her notebook. She'd been contemplating the high ridge in the distance. Covered in blankets and lying on her chaise longue on the balcony, she watched the sun peek over the ridge. She had worked at her writing table through the night in a nine-hour pulse to finish one of her longest stories, *At the Bay*, and it felt good to stretch her legs and feel the rapture that came after a story's completion. She was particularly pleased with this story as it fulfilled

the promise she'd made to write about family love and her childhood, a memorial to her twenty-one-year-old brother who had died in the war.

She thought to wake Jack but he was not one to appreciate the early morning hours, particularly with a chattering wife. I must talk to someone, she thought, and lifted her pen to start a letter to Brett, who as a painter understood the rapture after finishing one's work. The breach between their friendship during Brett's misguided affair with Jack had been mended and they'd kept up a steady correspondence since Katherine's move to Switzerland.

> *The pleasure of all reading is doubled when one lives with another who shares the same books. But I would be lying not to say there is one thing one does miss here, and that is seeing people. One doesn't ask for many, but there come moments when I long to see and hear and listen—listen most of all.*

The only listening to be heard this morning was Jack's deep breathing in the bedroom below.

She tapped the pen against the paper, blotted the ink stain and continued:

> *I've just finished my new story. I've been at it all night. It's about sixty pages. I've wandered about all sorts of places—in and out—I hope it is good. It is as good as I can do. All my heart and soul is in it— every single bit. Oh God, I hope it gives pleasure to someone. I must tell you that it is so strange to bring the dead to life again. I felt I was saying to them, 'You are not dead, my darlings. All is remembered... you may live again through me in your richness and beauty.'*

She thrilled in bringing life to her own people. She compared it to strokes across the canvas that draw forth an image, a memory of something once felt, something once seen, until those remembered thoughts became figures on the canvas.

Wingley interrupted her letter, leaping off the windowsill onto the balcony to stretch out his long, plump body on the first patch of morning sunlight.

The last edge of the night sky had made way for a new day. Is there really an unseen stage manager running the show who just now lit the stage, she wondered? Seated on her balcony, she could almost believe in such a God when witnessing Nature waking all around her to a new day.

No, we certainly won't be back in England for years, she wrote Brett. *You will have to visit us here.* A mist filled the valley shrouding the sun's burst of light. She shivered and brought the eiderdown closer to her. *But you must dress warmly.*

Finally admitting to herself how exhausted and chilled she was, she went downstairs and slipped under the covers next to Jack.

IT WASN'T UNTIL after she and Jack celebrated her 33rd birthday that dark clouds completely blocked out the sun and the days got shorter, a harbinger of winter's approach. The exhilaration from the pure air and elevation stopped working its magic in a chalet that was never quite warm enough despite the big fireplace on the ground floor and heated pipes hissing through the rooms.

Katherine had been initially pleased with her two stories *At the Bay* and *The Garden Party*. Now she felt they could have been much better. Jack disagreed telling her it was her best work. But she felt something lacking. She didn't know what it was, but knew the answer was there if she kept up her writing. She started another story, *The Doll's House*, which also took place at her childhood home in New Zealand.

After the first winter blizzard, her hacking cough returned and she moved up to her writing studio on the third floor so Jack could sleep. More frequently, he escaped into the woods where she couldn't follow, climbing craggy peaks in pursuit of never-before-seen plant specimens or skiing down slopes with Elizabeth and her friends.

Katherine told him she was happy to be on her own, but became anxious when she'd hear the front door slam followed by a heavy silence and not know who it was. And she began to worry about having another heart attack like she did in Italy, but this time no one would be there to rescue her, because Ernestine only came upstairs if Katherine called.

And then there was the gross lack of housekeeping. Jack was sloppy with his things and dropped them wherever he happened to be. His clothes draped on every chair. He assumed that Katherine would order the food, plan the menus, and take care of the accounts.

What with her daily chores, she was too exhausted to keep up her writing schedule or to take the daily open-air cure out on her balcony. Some changes needed to be made and she invited LM to tea.

Her companion, who enjoyed living alone in the village, had made new friends and was very satisfied with her work at the sanatorium taking care of the sick. Katherine wasn't sure how she would respond to her request to return as a paid aide and companion.

"What about Jack? Can't he help?" asked LM when she was told.

"Oh you know Jack. He has a way of disappearing for hours, and when he's home he's distracted or working in his study. I would only ask that you bring me lunch and serve us at teatime and tidy up things a bit and keep me company when he's away."

They both looked around the sitting room that was quite out of sorts. LM didn't answer right away and Katherine said,. "Do you want a few days to think about it?"

"No-no," said LM. "Of course I'll come if you need me. But before I ask to change my hours at the sanatorium, have you told Jack?"

"You needn't worry about that," said Katherine.

"Then I'll be back tomorrow." LM picked up a sweater Jack had tossed on a chair and hung it in the closet on her way out with the tea tray.

AFTER COMPLETING *The Doll's House*, Katherine wrote in her notebook:

> *Words cannot describe how cold I feel, and it's not even*
> *winter yet. We have central heating that never goes out, but*
> *I must remain outdoors at least six hours of the day and*
> *even buried in blankets my fingers turn to icicles.*

At night, she and Jack huddled by the fire in the downstairs sitting room where they read to each other Jane Austen's novels. They had finished *Emma* and were now on *Mansfield Park*.

Near Christmas time a packet arrived from Katherine's previous editor and former close friend, Alfred R. Orage. She wondered why the packet was addressed to Jack. Orage and Jack had never really been friends. At one time they had both competed for Katherine's stories to be published in their magazines.

She watched Jack open the packet addressed to him. He frowned at the enclosed book "Cosmic Anatomy."

"Why on earth would he send me a book with such a hocus-pocus title?" He read the enclosed letter and looked up at Katherine, "Orage has asked me to write its review. Is he trying to be funny? He knows I have no interest in theosophy or mysticism or, as the author Dr. Wallace says here, the 'will to believe.'"

He flipped through the pages shaking his head, slammed it shut and left it on the table. When they got up to go to bed, Katherine picked it up.

"What are you going to do with that?" Jack asked, sneering at the book in her hand. "Certainly your mind will be better nourished reading Chaucer or Shakespeare than that fluff."

"Why are you having such a violent reaction to a book you only glanced at? Orage wouldn't waste your time with a book that didn't have value."

"Well, I would rather you didn't read it."

"Why Jack?"

"I don't know. Something suspicious about Orage sending this to me. He's always been jealous of me taking you away from him. There is some alternative reason. Stay away from it. It could be dangerous."

A FEW NIGHTS LATER, she reached for "Cosmic Anatomy" on her bed table and opened to the first page. An hour later she was still reading. Wallace's philosophy was difficult to understand and she was left with many questions and was curious about Wallace's belief that the reactions to certain causes and effects have been the same throughout time.

Jack came in to say good night and sat on the edge of her bed. "So you're reading that book after I told you not to."

"Why Jack, I think you're the one that's jealous. You've always resented my relationship with Orage, but I've never known you to censor my reading material. Dr. Wallace is obviously an educated theologian and quite knowledgeable on what you look down on as 'occult doctrines.' They're really religious principles. Alternative approaches to experience could make for an interesting discussion between you and I. It might do us both some good to see things from a less lofty intellectual plane."

"My integrity as a skeptic would never allow me to consider theological thought as having any value," said Jack, sharply. "That's why I won't review his damn book. I came in just now because I thought I heard you mumbling something in voodoo that was rather frightening."

She laughed. "Oh, Jack, that wasn't voodoo. It's a Upanishad verse. *Om, krato smara, klibe smara, kritam smara.*"

"What does it mean?"

"I don't know yet."

He frowned.

"Can you please show some tolerance for ideas that are different than yours," said Katherine. "It's most unbecoming on your handsome face when you look so cross. Look, it's not the only book I'm reading." On her bed table lay Shakespeare's *Antony and Cleopatra* and the *Bible*."

"Interesting collection, my dear." He kissed her on the forehead. "Don't read all night. I'll wake you with tea in the morning before I go skiing with Elizabeth."

After he left, Katherine picked up her notebook: *I feel there is much love between us. Tender love. Let it not change.*

But laying in the dark, her thoughts turned to Orage and she went to her traveling trunk to find the original draft of a letter she'd sent him last year from Menton:

> *This letter has been on the tip of my pen for many months.*
>
> *I want to tell you how sensible I am of your wonderful unfailing kindness to me in the "old days." And to thank you for all you let me learn from you. I am still—more shame to me—very low down in the school. But you taught me to write, you taught me to think; you showed me what there was to be done and what not to do.*
>
> *My dear Orage, I cannot tell you how often I call to mind your conversation or how often in writing, I remember my master. Does that sound impertinent? Forgive me if it does.*
>
> *But let me thank you, Orage—Thank you for everything. If only one day I might write a book of stories good enough to "offer" you… If I don't succeed in keeping the coffin from the door you will know this was my ambition.*

When she first met Orage she had argued against his theological beliefs. And when she had stopped writing for the *New Age* she became even more critical about theological books. She'd even claimed in Jack's *Rhythm* magazine that mysticism was a passionate admiration for that which has no reality at all and leads to the annihilation of any true artistic effort.

She didn't know if she believed that anymore. It sounded more like something Jack would say.

Now lying in her bed looking out at the snow-capped mountains reflecting in the moonlight, she wondered if she'd been wrong all this time to rely on doctors to heal her. What if she could annihilate her physical disease on her own, without the help of science or medicine, which was failing her once again. Recently, she'd begun to recognize the symptoms of bad bacteria invading her lungs. And though she hadn't started coughing up blood, she knew it was only a question of time before she'd be bedridden again.

"Cosmic Anatomy's" author believed that the mind could control, transcend, and even survive the body. Could she do that? If she mentioned that idea to Jack, he would have sneered at her or worse snarled. But Orage would take her spiritual questions seriously being a true believer himself.

She closed her eyes and saw him standing over her in his tilted felt hat as if it had just been yesterday and not twelve years ago.

IN FEBRUARY 1910, he'd published *The Child-Who-Was-Tired,* the short story that had launched her career. His intellectual literary paper *New Age* was about literature and the arts, politics, spiritualism, and he was a supporter of women's suffrage. Jack's magazines were similar in content, with the exception of women's rights and spiritualism.

Before the war, *The New Age* became a haven for modern writers. At twenty-one, Katherine was the youngest on his roster. It gave her immediate respect and instant notoriety to have her stories published along with the likes of Ezra Pound, George Bernard Shaw, H.G. Wells and G.K. Chesterton.

She remembered back to the first day she climbed the stone steps to his office. What a very attractive man, she thought, when she first saw him. As they shook hands he looked directly into her eyes, challenging her, and she in turn gazed into his hazel eyes without flinching though she had to tilt her neck back because he was so tall.

She thought he would just ask her to leave her three stories, like the other publishers did, but instead Orage asked her to sit down and wait while he read.

She looked around the scruffy, dim room. There was only space enough for the two chairs they sat in, their knees almost touching. She noticed his boots were more worn than hers and wondered how he afforded to pay his writers.

As his long graceful fingers flipped each page, he crossed and re-crossed his long legs several times, bumping into hers. His lips moved silently as he read. His expressions indecipherable. Uncomfortable, she wanted to look away but stood her ground, focusing her eyes on his flame-colored tie. Orage had a reputation for wearing vivid ties and was easily spotted at salon gatherings amongst all the men wearing somber, funereal ties.

He startled her when he slammed two of her stories down on his desk and held up the last one in his hand. "This is just what I've been looking for," he said, "drama arising from bad sociological conditions. What's the title?" Without waiting for her response, he looked at the cover page: "*The Child-Who-Was-Tired.* Perfect. I like it. Bring me more stories like this and I'll publish them, too. I'll even give you your own column—we'll call it, *Bavarian Babies.*"

She wished he'd chosen a different story. *The Child-Who-Was-Tired* had been written in Bavaria after Floryan had introduced her to Anton Chekhov's short stories. She had written it more as an exercise in learning Chekhov's style of writing and had borrowed his ideas for her own story. She could be accused of plagiarism, but she'd have to risk that.

Orage was writing down some notes and didn't notice her worried look. "Do you have a nom de plume, young lady?"

"Katherine Mansfield."

She corrected him when he misspelled her first name.

"Bring me more satirical stories like this one and I'll make you famous."

She didn't have any more stories like that one. She'd been writing sentimental stories, even mawkish stories, thinking they'd be popular with women readers and she'd be paid well.

New Age had a reputation for not paying much. The magazine had over thirty thousand subscribers but it barely turned a profit.

"May I ask how much you pay your writers?"

He tossed back his head and burst out laughing, while reaching up with his large hand to toss back a long tuft of brown hair that had fallen over his forehead, a gesture she remembered now with fondness.

Orage had said, "I'll pay you ten shillings for this story right now and the same for each additional one I accept."

It was more than she'd expected and that he paid her right then had made her stomach gurgle, she was so hungry for a tart or scone.

Orage did more than publish her stories. He took her under his editorial protection for two years and encouraged her to write serious pieces and avoid being overly sentimental. With his encouragement and excellent editorial talents, she gained confidence.

And with a passion for technique, she created a unique style of condensed sentences full of meaning and truth. With a "special prose" that was neither poetry nor prose but stream of consciousness, she entered the minds and souls of her characters. Her unique style of writing would come to have a strong influence on the writings of Virginia Woolf, T. S. Eliot and other modern writers.

Orage was furious when she started to write for Jack's magazine. He considered it a betrayal after all he'd done for her and he gave her an ultimatum: "You write for *New Age* or you write for *Rhythm*." When it came to her work, she hated being told what to do by Orage or anyone else. She swore never to work with him again, telling Jack, *"Orage is too ugly!"*

Though estranged for these many years, she'd never forgotten her indebtedness to him. And now he was the person she needed to turn to about the theosophy of "Cosmic Anatomy" and other spiritual matters that now filled her mind.

DECEMBER, 1921

Dr Manoukhin's Cure

Congestion is quite simple. The lung becomes full of blood,
and that means the heart beats too fast and that means
one has fever and pain and one puts oneself to bed.

LETTERS—KM

IN EARLY DECEMBER, Katherine coughed and blood sprayed into
her handkerchief. She remembered Chekhov saying he had coughed
blood for years without dying, but she was still horrified.

When Jack came into her bedroom carrying her morning tea, she hid
the blood stained evidence that she knew would scare him, too.

"How are we today?" he asked, looking down at her with his lopsided
smile that she still found endearing. "You look a bit tired. I hope you
didn't stay up all night working."

"No." She stopped from saying bitterly that she'd spent it coughing.
Instead she chose to pretend cheerfulness, no reason for them both to
be miserable. "Do you have plans for today?"

"As a matter of fact, I do. After that blizzard last night there are several
feet of fresh snow so I thought I'd walk over to Elizabeth's. She offered
to give me a few skiing lessons on some of the easier slopes. That is, if
you don't mind?"

"No. Not at all. Go ahead. LM will be here later. Please send Elizabeth
my love."

After he left, the vision of Jack and Elizabeth, twenty years older than
Katherine, skiing down the slopes together made her jealous. Not jealous
of a possible romance between them, but that she wasn't skiing herself.

The truth was she hated Jack leaving her on her own. His absence
hadn't mattered when she was occupied with her writing, but now that
she was ill again she needed him there with her. But if she told him
the truth, he would get depressed and make her feel even worse. She'd
learned by now that it was better when he was oblivious to her sufferings.

She picked up the English newspaper he'd brought in on the tray. There was an interview with the Russian author Maxim Gorky who was also a tuberculosis patient. Her interest peaked when Gorky stated that a fellow Russian, Dr. Manoukhin, had "at last discovered the remedy" for his disease. He was the same doctor Kot had suggested she contact a month ago.

Gorky went on to say that Dr. Manoukhin had seen miraculous results from irradiating the spleens of Russian tuberculosis patients and he had moved his patented X-ray machine to Paris where he was receiving patients.

Either Jack hadn't read the article or he thought it was another witch doctor and not worthy of discussion. He'd put his faith in the open-air cure and believed Dr. Hudson who said it could take a year or maybe two before her lungs were cleared of the bacilli. Now that she was coughing blood again, she no longer believed in Dr. Stephani's cure.

Jack would never understand what it felt like to urgently write a story in fear of never finishing it. Unaware of Death knocking at her door, he leisurely wandered the mountains and spent his afternoons visiting Elizabeth and her guests at Chalet du Soleil. Why not? He had all the time in the world. In the evenings, when he returned home radiating good health, she had to turn away to not show her jealousy. How she hungered to get outside and run in the wind.

She asked Kot for Dr. Manoukhin's address and then wrote to him. Two weeks later an answer arrived in the mail. She hid the letter from Jack and waited until she was alone. Wingley sat up on his haunches and watched her tear open the envelope.

"Yes, I think I can help you, Miss Mansfield. Come to Paris as soon as possible. After I examine you, I'll know if you are strong enough to tolerate radiation treatments."

Wingley's attention was taken up with unfurling a ball of yarn and didn't hear her read it again. She was too excited by his response to stay in bed and wrapped herself in a blanket to stand by the window. She imagined herself outside building a snowman. He would look like Jack with a pipe between his lips and a carrot for a nose.

But now I've come to hate snow, she thought, particularly snow like this that never ceases piling up layer after layer of white upon white.

How delightful it would be to walk among the floral shops in Paris and talk to people. Sit at a café and watch the world walk by.

> *Thank you for giving me hope. I will have my assistant call your office to set an appointment.*
>
> *Warmly, KM*

DOCTOR HUDSON came to see her after she sent an urgent note. "You must eat more, rest more, and work less to bring down this fever," he said firmly, waving the thermometer in her face.

She buttoned up her bed jacket, sat up against the pillows and said, "Doctor, I actually asked you here to speak to you about something else. Would you mind closing the door?"

He did as she asked, returned to his seat and waited while she drank a glass of water to clear her throat.

"There is a Dr. Manoukhin who claims to have found a remedy for tuberculosis. Have you heard of him?"

"No, I haven't." He laughed. "I wouldn't have time for my patients if I tried to keep up with every new remedy that came along for tuberculosis. As you know, there are many doctors and clinics who deceive patients like yourself with false hope. I've heard there are even experiments to cure tuberculosis with elephant serum. You did the right thing coming to us. No one will be able to extend your life as much as the open-air cure we practice here."

"There is no serum involved. Dr. Manoukhin thinks that radiating the spleen triggers the immune system to build up antibodies that kill the tubercular bacteria."

"Wait a minute. I have read about Dr. Manoukhin's remarkable X-ray machine invention. I must admit that the anecdotal reports have been, shall we say, promising. I can't advise you one way or the other, Mrs. Murry. But I can tell you that radiation is very hard on the body and could be quite dangerous for someone in your condition."

"He won't radiate if I'm too weak. You know as well as I do, that Dr. Manoukhin might be my last chance.

"No I don't think that's true," he said defensively, his pudgy hand still wrapped around his stethoscope. "I have just listened to your right lung and it's practically healed. And the left has improved."

"Then why are my lungs on fire? Why do I have to force myself to get out of bed? Why am I losing weight? Why do I have a constant fever? Why is my heart always beating like I just ran up a mountain. Why am I spitting blood?

"Not to be vulgar but these creatures that you call bacilli are gobbling me up and I can't stop them and I'm no longer sure you can."

"It's not the bacilli that makes your heart beat so fast. It's your diaphragm that can't expand because your lungs are damaged."

"But you just said they're better."

"They 'sound' better but they're permanently damaged." He folded away the stethoscope in his bag and snapped it shut. "I do think a lower elevation might be kinder on your heart. And if the remaining tubercular bacilli *can* be destroyed by radiating your spleen, at least one of your lungs could do a better job of expanding your diaphragm."

"You're confusing me, Doctor. Are you now advising me to go to Paris and be treated by Dr. Manoukhin's machine?"

"How long would you have to be away?"

"Long enough to meet with him and," she covered her mouth self consciously, "see a dentist about my rotting teeth. I would return to Paris again in May for the first round of radiation."

"It's the trip to Paris that worries me. Do you think we could use Dr. Manoukhin's method here at our clinic? We are very well equipped with the latest in X-ray machines. And if he was to instruct us on what to do…"

"I will write and ask him."

"Splendid." He got up to leave.

"Wait." She reached out for his hand. "I have another favor to ask before you go. Will you sit with me for a moment longer?"

"What is it, Mrs. Murry?" he said, crossing his hands over his portly stomach.

"I would prefer if you did not discuss this with Mr. Murry." She smiled. "I'm afraid he doesn't believe in miracles. And no reason to upset him when we don't know for sure what I am going to do."

They both watched him twirl his thumbs. He looked up. "This is an unusual request. It is customary to keep the husband informed, but I'll make an exception, if you promise to tell your husband as soon as you hear back from Dr. Manoukhin."

"I will, Doctor. I promise.

DR. MANOUKHIN DID NOT RESPOND favorably to Dr. Hudson's offer to collaborate. His patented X-ray machine was specifically made to his calculations and he didn't have the time to personally train anyone else to operate it.

A few days later Katherine's fever lifted and she asked LM to make their travel arrangements. Now the difficult part. Telling Jack.

That evening after dinner, they settled down in their reading chairs next to the fire to read the end of Jane Austen's *Mansfield Park*. Before he started, she said, "Jack, we need to talk."

He looked up over his lit pipe. So handsome and still so young, she thought, feeling how old she'd become. "Must we now, my dearest? I've been waiting all day to know the ending!"

"This is far more important. I don't think you saw it, but I read an interview with Maxim Gorky in the *Times*. He mentioned a Russian doctor who is having excellent responses with his tuberculosis patients. Many claim to have been cured by his new scientific methods, including Gorky."

"Ah yes," smoke rings from his pipe floated above him. "I read that interview. I was surprised to find out he was a consumptive. I sometimes wonder why all the great authors and poets have tuberculosis?"

Katherine was stunned. "You read that article and didn't say anything to me?"

"I didn't think it was that important."

"Jack! It wasn't just about Gorky. Didn't it interest you, weren't you curious in the least that his doctor claims to cure tuberculosis. Didn't you think for one moment that you should mention it to me?"

"Sorry, Wig. But it sounds god awful. Fry the spleen with radiation? Why would anyone do that. You didn't take it seriously, my girl, did you?"

She sighed. Jack was Jack and there was no point in getting heated up about it. "Yes I did. I took it very seriously. So seriously that I've made arrangements to see Dr. Manoukhin in Paris."

"Oh no, Katherine, not again. I thought you were happy here. Dr. Hudson says you're making marvelous progress. Are you going to give that up for yet another witch doctor?" She watched his face redden. "Why is it whenever we settle down somewhere nice you want to move? This time I really can't let you go. And if you do, I won't be here when you get back."

She knelt down in front of him. "Jack, look at me. Really look at me and then tell me I'm getting better. And then look here at my handkerchief stained in blood and tell me again how well I'm doing. I'm scared, Jack. I'm scared for us. This might be my last chance. I have to go."

He stood up and tapped his pipe against the mantel, putting it out. He looked down at her.

"If you believe Dr. Manoukhin can save you, then you're right, you have to go. But what upsets me is that you didn't talk to me about it. Didn't ask my opinion? Don't I have a say about what my wife does?"

"I'm sorry. I should have told you. It's just our happiness these last months has been so wonderful. Our Indian summer. I didn't want anything to destroy that happiness."

He pulled her up off the floor and warmed her hands between his. "My dearest. Nothing will destroy our happiness. I'll go with you. Stand by you through the radiation treatments."

"Not this time. You should stay here and work. I'm only going to meet with him. I can do that on my own. If Manoukhin agrees to take me on as a patient then you and I can talk it over. We will decide together what I should do. If we think it's a good idea, then I'll schedule the treatments in May and you can come then. But you should know that the radiation treatments are very expensive and I need to make some money before I can do it."

"I'll help you. I'll have several more articles published by then and maybe I can get an advance on my next novel."

"Thank you Jack, but let's talk about that after my meeting with Dr. Manoukhin."

"I don't like the idea of you going to Paris alone."

She smiled and tilted her head. "Jack, sometimes I don't think you see very well. How did you ever become The Critic of London when you miss what's right in front of you. Do you really think I'd travel on my own in my condition? I'd never make it to the train. Ida has offered to come with me."

Later that night he came upstairs. "Katherine, I'm sorry you couldn't talk to me about your illness. I've been caught up in my own work and I've neglected you, haven't I? I'm so sorry. I didn't want you to go to sleep without knowing that I love you very much and if you need me to come with you to Paris I will."

"Don't worry. I'll be all right." She didn't mention that she also had an appointment to see the dentist about capping several rotten teeth. He might find it too high an expense on their budget but she saw it as a necessity.

LM was able to book passage on Monday. It would take a few hours to get from Montana to the Geneva train station and then the train to Paris would be much quicker.

Katherine spent the weekend straightening out her affairs. She called it making a clean sweep of her camp, leaving no mess behind. She wrote a few letters telling her family and friends her plan to see a new doctor and then finally worked up the courage to write her father.

She pressed the pen down onto the paper and asked his forgiveness for having been an extraordinarily unsatisfactory and disappointing child. She ended with:

> *Father don't turn away from me, darling. If you cannot take me back into you heart believe me when I say I am your devoted deeply sorrowing child Kass.*

Before going to bed, she wrote in her journal:

> *Whenever I prepare for a journey I prepare as though for Death. Should I never return all is in order.*

Last Chance

The great thing to remember is we can do whatever we wish to do provided our wish is strong enough. But the tremendous effort needed one doesn't always want to make it, does one? And all that cutting down the jungle and bush clearing even after one has landed anywhere it's tiring. Yes, I agree. But what else can be done? What's the alternative? What do you want most to do? That's what I have to keep asking myself, in the face of difficulties.

NOTEBOOKS—KM

MONDAY MORNING SHE AWOKE CHOKING for air and pulled herself up on her pillows. "I can't breathe any better than a fish in an empty tank!" she rasped, waking Wingley who leaped off the bed, fleeing out the open door.

In her mind she covered the deep snow beyond the window with new spring grass and set herself down on a bed of yellow and white Alpine flowers.

This Last Chance is the miracle I've been seeking—the Last Chance for Jack and me, she thought. My days of a wandering consumptive will soon be over. No more medicine bottles. No more sleepless nights. No more nightmares. No more breakfast trays.

As if on cue LM walked in with the morning tray and Katherine laughed. One last tray.

Jack saw them off at the funicular, which brought them down to Sierre. From there they took a local train to the Geneva station. LM checked in the baggage and joined Katherine in their cabin. The train whistled and they pulled out of the train station.

LM frowned and gripped her travel chest. Katherine teased her but LM spoke harshly, "This reminds me too much of our trip from Bandol to Paris in 1918. We barely arrived still intact. I'll have no stolen luggage this time."

"C'mon, Jones. The journey we took from Bandol was held up first in Marseille and then in Paris because the German's were dropping bombs on us. Look outside. Do you see any marching soldiers?"

They both turned to look at the peaceful white landscape covered over with a deep blue, cloudless sky.

"You should've waited until after the war to marry Jack," said LM. "You were safe in Bandol."

"You know my aversion to safety. Just think, if we'd remained in Bandol, we wouldn't have had those thrilling moments down in the hotel basement while the Germans bombed Paris."

"Thank you very much but I could do without such thrilling moments. And you were always angry back then. Blamed me for not finding us passage to London. As if it was my fault there was a war."

Katherine laughed. "Oh dear Jones, you're so right. I do drag you into terrible situations. But isn't that part of the fun of being my traveling companion, not knowing what might happen?"

"Not really. The *fun* as you call it is knowing I can protect you from danger, and right now I'm not having any *fun*."

Towering over the attendant, LM paid for the tea service. Katherine noted the generous tip with her money and stopped herself from saying anything. She had promised not to criticize LM for her generosity to either mosquitoes or humans. This was to be an enjoyable train ride and LM was so sensitive that a few misplaced words could have her pouting all the way to Paris.

When LM sat back down and poured the tea, Katherine said, "Please don't be cross with me."

"I'm not cross with you, I'm cross with myself for bringing you. This is risky business going to see another doctor who's filled your head with miracles. Too many times I've brought you home and seen the disappointment on your face when these "cures" didn't work. You're jeopardizing what health you have on a fool's journey and I don't like it."

THE VICTORIA PALACE HOTEL that her painter friend Anne Drey had recommended was more than satisfactory. She set up a table for writing in front of a window that looked out on a narrow tree-lined street. Across the street a woman could be seen feeding her caged canaries on a sunlit balcony.

The following afternoon, Katherine and LM left the hotel for Dr. Manoukhin's office. Though a chilly winter's day, she convinced LM that a walk through the streets of Paris was not only economical but a needed exercise after the many cramped hours spent on yesterday's train.

"This must be it," said LM with confidence. They turned into a narrow street but it ended at a brick wall.

"I thought you knew where his office was?" said Katherine, losing patience. Having slept poorly and woken with a headache, she didn't need to be lost and late to her appointment.

"I never said that. You rushed out of the hotel and I followed you. You know very well that I have no sense of direction. You're the one who knows Paris."

"Don't get haughty with me, Miss Ida. As you're of no help to me like this, you should return to the hotel. I'll find my own way."

"You can't possibly get there on your own. Look at you. You can hardly breathe. You left so quickly you even forgot your cane. Here, lean on me."

"No. I won't lean on you." Katherine straightened herself up as best she could and walked off. She felt LM's eyes drilling through her back even after turning the corner, but she didn't look back and was a bit disappointed LM didn't chase after her. So be it. I will find my own way.

She hobbled down one street and then the next. She found the street, but not having the number, it took knocking on several doors before she arrive at the right one. Entering Dr. Manoukhin's reception area, she collapsed in a chair.

"Êtes-vous bien?"

Katherine looked up at a tiny prim girl in a nurse's uniform looking down on her with great concern.

Katherine answered her in French. "It was a long walk from my hotel and I got lost. I have an appointment with Dr. Manoukhin. He and I have corresponded."

"Voila! You must be Madame Murry. We were expecting you. I'm Sonja, his assistant and translator. It's wonderful that you speak French as my English is not very good."

Katherine coughed.

Sonja brought her a glass of water and told her she was next.

Through the open door Katherine saw a few men speaking over each other in Russian while drinking coffee. There was one distinctive countertenor rising above the others. She hoped it was Dr. Manoukhin.

She wished she'd learned Russia so that she could read Dostoevsky, Tolstoy, Turgenyev, Pushkin and the other Russian writers she loved so much instead of the translations. But now that I have a future, she thought, I can start now. And I will have a child, too, and name him Anton.

Her thoughts turned to Chekhov. He and so many other Russian writers had expressed such an outpouring of passion for their country, their culture, and their people. It was à propos that she should find her miracle among the Russians whose literature she so admired.

Sonja ushered her into Dr. Manoukhin's plain office. His bulky size startled her. She had expected someone taller, thinner, with a more sensitive face like Dr. Anton Chekhov. Without introducing himself, he pointed to a chair in front of his desk and she sat down. His brusque manner was disappointing but she wasn't here to make a friend.

"Remove your jacket and blouse, Madame Murry." Sonja translated his Russian into French. Katherine looked around and seeing no gown or curtain to disrobe behind, she did as she was told.

She was so close to him when he bent down to listen to her lungs that she could smell dark roasted coffee beans on his breath and could see new hairs sprouting under his goatee. His eyes were black and unreadable. She closed her own and breathed in and out while he listened with a cold stethoscope.

After the exam, he gestured with his short, thick arm for her to dress. He sat behind an enormous desk. Sonja stood next to him and translated.

"You are a sick woman, Madame Murry. You have tuberculosis in the second degree—the right apex very lightly engaged but the left apex is full of rales." Sonja's guttural French r-r-r-ales made vivid the death rattle he must have heard, her left lung full of crackling tubercular bacilli. "But your condition is better than third or fourth degree when both lungs are full of rales. Your time in the Alps has helped."

He explained through Sonja that his radiation equipment was explicitly built to his specifications. "No other X-ray machine like it. Doctors from around the world have come to observe it and they leave very impressed."

Sonja's Russian-French accent was difficult to comprehend and Katherine tired from her journey and getting lost in the streets of Paris was having trouble understanding. If only Jack was here, she thought, holding back her tears. She looked down at her worn boots, feeling tired and discouraged. *I never should have come here alone.*

Dr. Manoukhin finally stopped promoting himself and his wonder machine and said in a gentler voice, "You are strong enough for my machine. We can cure you, Mrs. Murry."

She repeated his Russian word for cure, "лечение." She'd learned its meaning from Chekhov's letters.

She sat up and looked at Sonja. "Is he certain?"

"Oui," said Sonja and continued translating. "It will take fifteen séances—once a week—perhaps more often depending on your body's toleration of radiation, then a period of repose preferably in the mountains for two, three, perhaps four months. Then you should return to Paris for ten more séances. After the first series you should feel perfectly well. The last ten are to prevent any chance of relapse."

Katherine hadn't expected it to be so soon. "I was planning to wait until May when my husband can join me."

He pulled again at his goatee and studied her. "Madame Murry, your answer surprises me. Why wait? Wouldn't it be better for you to start now. Your condition is favorable. But, of course, it's your decision."

Before she could respond, he spoke curtly to Sonja and got up and left. Katherine got up, too, believing her interview was over and had gone badly.

"Attendez," said Sonja. "He had to make an urgent call. He's coming right back."

When he returned, he leaned against his desk in front of her and seemed in a far better mood after his call as he said quite pleasantly through Sonja, "Please do not misunderstand me, Madame Murry. I do not insist on your beginning now. I do not say you will be greatly harmed by waiting. The great advantage in starting now is that you are here, that's all. If you wait to start in May it would mean being in Paris for the summer. The humid weather not good for you. Better to heal in the mountains."

Outside in the reception, Sonja and Katherine sat together on the couch. Sonja went on and on enthusiastically about the miracles she'd witnessed while working for Dr. Manoukhin. She'd also traveled with him from Kiev where he had treated thousands of soldiers at the Red Cross Hospital.

While Sonja answered a phone call, Katherine argued with herself. Yes, why wait? Now when I'm so close to being cured, why hesitate?

Sonja got off the phone and opened her thick calendar book. "Why don't you start tomorrow?"

"Tomorrow?" said Katherine, "but doesn't he have other patients?"

"Bon chance. There's been a cancellation."

"I'm sorry but I'm finding this all so abrupt. I thought I'd have more time to prepare. I don't even know what the radiation treatments cost?"

Sonja explained the fees and that she didn't have to pay all at once.

Katherine added up the fifty pounds in her savings. How many stories must she write to earn an additional fifty pounds?

She told Sonja she'd think it over and call back in the morning. Sonja reminded her of what an opportunity this was that she could start now because of the cancellation and not to wait too long to call.

Katherine took a taxi back to the hotel. Her head pounding. Her thoughts split in two.

Back in her hotel room, she sat down and wrote to tell Jack her *desire was not to stay. Why? Because of our life. I feel I cannot break it. I fear for it.* She asked him to make the decision for her or if that was too hard to at least advise her. *But don't forget that above all I love you.*

When she awoke the following morning, her first thought was that she must meet with Dr. Manoukhin again. And not at his offices. She wanted to see the famous X-Ray machine that was going to cure her and then she'd decide what to do.

She added to Jack's letter, *I feel this morning perhaps we forget a little what a difference it's bound to make to us both if I was well. And to wait for that longer than we have waited is perhaps foolish.*

She sent a note to Dr. Manoukhin's office by courier asking for a second meeting. She received his response by the same courier: "Come to our clinic at five."

Dr. Manoukhin and his French partner, Dr. Donat, greeted her at the door. The clinic was much larger than Manoukhin's office and Katherine was impressed by the sophisticated, shiny new medical instruments and appliances though not knowing what they did.

In contrast to Manoukhin's short, rotund appearance, Dr. Donat, was a handsome elderly gentleman with kind, trustworthy eyes and dressed in a doctor's white coat and skullcap like Dr. Chekhov might have worn.

They showed her the radiation room and where she would lie down under the huge X-Ray machine for two hours at each séance. She asked Dr. Donat to explain the process thoroughly so that she might understand the risks and the benefits.

"Dr. Manoukhin's radiation acts like immensely concentrated sunlight. What the sun does in a dissipated way this machine does more quickly. There is no risk," he raised his index finger, "but there is a cure. He recently healed an Englishman in the third degree. After twelve séances he had no more bacillus in his sputum. We can do the same for you, Mrs. Murry."

She stared at the daunting apparatus. Could this hovering iron monster cure her if she lay under it and let it penetrate her body?

"You've been ill for a long time," said Dr. Donat. "One has not an endless supply of force, but you're young. I assure you the air of Paris and Dr. Manoukhin's machine will cure you. Of that I am confident. But I don't want you to think this will be easy. The X-Rays are concentrated onto your spleen. The first five weeks of séances will be most uncomfortable and exhausting. It will take time for you to recover."

"I am well versed in discomfort, Doctor."

Returning to her hotel, she wrote Jack:

> *I have just returned from meeting with Dr. Manoukhin and Dr. Donat to find out more about their X-ray treatments. After my meeting I am confident that the radiation of my spleen is without risk. Dr. Manoukhin has discovered that the spleen is the spot where the blood changes and if the spleen is fed with X-rays the blood is likewise fed. He has experimented on so many animals and so on and found such and such results. It is the latest thing in science. I felt at their clinic that I was in the presence of real scientists—not doctors. I imagine Pasteur's Institute would be of similar quality and professionalism.*

Thursday morning Jack's telegram arrived:

YOU MUST DO WHAT M. SAYS. STOP. BEGIN THE TREATMENT NOW. STOP. CRIMINAL FOR YOU TO COME BACK. STOP. YOUR LOVING BOGE

She was relieved. Jack had decided for them both. She called Dr. Manoukhin's clinic, and the following day at two o'clock, Katherine arrived at the clinic. LM had offered to come with her but she wanted to go alone.

She was reading in the reception while waiting her turn in the radiation room when she looked up to see Dr. Manoukhin walking quickly toward her with a wide grin. He gripped her hand and surprisingly in French said, "Vous avez decidé de commencer avec le traitement. C'est très bien!" He then rushed past her out of the room turning back to say, "Bonne santé! Tout de suite."

I'll never forget his act of kindness, Katherine would later write Kot, *the act of someone very good.*

Exhausted after her first treatment, and knowing there were fourteen more and she'd be in Paris for four months, she felt deflated and missing Jack she sat up in her hotel bed and with her writing case propped against her knees wrote him:

> *Even though I had a great confidence in Manoukhin—very
> great and yet... I am absolutely divided. You know how,
> to do anything well, even to make a little jump, one must
> gather oneself together. Well, I am not gathered together. A
> dark secret unbelief holds me back.*

She hoped he would come to Paris, if only for a few days, but didn't ask him directly because she wanted him to decide on his own.

He wrote back:

> *I hope, darling, you won't think this very cold and
> calculating. But I feel that if I don't work now, I never shall;
> and that if I don't break the back of my year's work, it will
> drag on and on. I am deep into writing my book. If I leave
> now, I'll never get it done. But I'm not so much in love with
> my own idea that I can't believe in a better one. I mean, if
> you would rather I stayed in Paris now, say so straight out.*

His letter kept her awake all night. He was relieved to have her gone. No mention of coming, even for a few days. He spoke of "fetching" her in May.

Katherine didn't write back. She felt quite weak and needed to conserve her strength for the next séance. Corresponding any further with Jack or even thinking about him made her agitated.

He wrote to her again. He wasn't sure he had made the right decision and asked her to tell him what she wanted him to do. When she didn't respond, he sent a wire asking her if he should come.

> *Please do not come here to me,* she replied. *It's no good. I now know that I must grow a shell away from you. I want—I 'ask' for my independence. At any moment in the future you may suddenly leave me in the lurch if it pleases you. It is a part of your nature. Finish your book. What does it matter that this is one of the most important moments of my life. Come in May and hopefully I'll still be alive to welcome you.*

But there will be no *fetching,* she said to herself angrily.

He wrote again now insisting on coming.

I would rather stay here alone, she wrote back.

> *I have seen the worst of it by myself i.e. going alone to Manoukhin, having no one to talk it over and so on. I want now intensely to be alone until May. Then IF I am better, we can talk things over and if I am not I shall make some other arrangement. Let us be independent of each other till then— shall we?*

Jack had disappointed her for the last time. She must not depend on him.

I must heal my Self before I will be well, she wrote in her notebook.

> *Yes that is the important thing. This must be done alone and at once. I have given up the idea of true marriage. (By the way what an example is this of the nonsense of time. One week ago we never were nearer.)*

> *It's true I cannot bear to think about the things I love in him… little things. But if one gives them up they will fade. I am not complete as I must be. It is at the root of my not getting better. My mind is not <u>controlled</u>. I idle, I give way, I sink into despair.*

To be sure he wouldn't come, she sent a wire:

DO NOT COME HERE. STOP. SENDING LM. STOP. SHE WILL
"FETCH" WHAT I NEED AND RETURN.

He wrote back that she was *an upsetting soul.*

*I want to make quite clear that I have, of my own free will
and in my right mind, calm as ever I hope to be, decided
to come to Paris till your fifteen séances are over. I suppose
you beg me not to come because you imagine that I am
doing something that I don't want to do myself, for your
sake. Well, I'm not. I have realized that I shall be intensely
miserable here by myself so far from you, that I shan't
be able to work, and as I explained that my first burst of
feeling that I could be a hermit doing eight hours a day was
simply due to the fact that I hadn't yet realized that you
were gone. Boge. There's not much love in this letter, but
there's plenty in my heart.*

S P R I N G ,   1 9 2 2

Paris Séances

JOB-in-the-ashes. Manoukhin says in eight days now the worst will be over. It's such a queer feeling. One burns with heat in one's hands & feet and bones, then suddenly you are racked with neuritis, but such neuritis that you can't lift your arm. Then one's head begins to pound. It's the moment when if I were a proper martyr I should begin to have that awful smile that martyrs in the flames put on when they begin to sizzle! But no matter it will pass...

NOTEBOOKS—KM

J ACK ARRIVED AT THE PALACE HOTEL and stood in front of her room with a suitcase in one hand and a letter in the other. He asked her to read it before they spoke:

> *When I knew you were going to stay in Paris, I shirked it. The day after I told you I wouldn't come I knew it was impossible for us to be apart. I began to be anxious every hour of the day: I had lost my mate.*
>
> *I wasn't claiming any freedom; I don't want, never have for a year now even dreamed of wanting 'freedom'. I was just shirking, shrinking from being uprooted. The last four years have taken away what little courage I had—and I never had any. That is a ghastly confession to make for a man who is well, to his wife who is ill. I am utterly ashamed. But what can I do? I fight against it. But when the moment comes I'm just petrified with fear. I can't move. And I forsake you.*

Her heart ached for him as she read his words and when she looked up and saw the fear in his eyes, a reflection of her own fear, she realized that she could not give him up. Not while there was new hope for a cure and an end to their suffering.

His lopsided mouth, which had drawn her to him when they first met, melted what resistance she had left and she opened up her arms to him.

They decided LM should go back to Montana and move into their chalet. If she could rent the other vacant rooms that would cover her expenses and also pay the chalet's rent. If LM felt disappointed with these new arrangements she didn't show it and quietly left the following morning. Katherine's nights of insomnia and coughing spells were too fitful to share and Jack moved into LM's vacated room.

IN HER CORRESPONDENCE with Elizabeth and Brett, Katherine told them how happy she and Jack were to be together again in Paris; how supportive he had been, taking her to the clinic each week and bringing her home afterward. He did the shopping, brought home bread from Ferguson's, petits fours from Conte, and the most wonderful teas that they'd share in their quaint room above the crowded, noisy streets of Paris. In the evenings, they played chess or acted out roles in Shakespeare plays.

She let her family and friends know that Dr. Manoukhin was pleased with the early results of the radiation and that she and Jack were floating together on a new optimism. If only that was the truth, thought Katherine, after sending off another false letter.

The reality was that the side effects of radiation were brutal and she suffered from headaches, stomach pain, and fatigue. In spite of her physical sufferings, she had to write "spasms" of stories. The income from these stories published in *Sphere* paid for the expensive séances. Jack could offer no income while he was working on his novel, *The Things We Are*, and Katherine had foregone having her teeth capped.

Several of her stories written at the chalet were now published. *The Garden Party* had been serialized for three weeks in the *Westminster Gazette* and the reviews from her short story collection under the same title were excellent. The Pinker Agency, famous for only representing the most popular authors, was now her agency and through them she published with other magazines.

Come late March, as promised by Manoukhin, the worst effects of the séances were over. Her appetite returned, her heart quieted down, and she could take short walks with Jack in the nearby Luxembourg Gardens. She had to move slowly and if she became dizzy Jack was there to lean on.

Timidly at first, but with mounting evidence that she was better, she and Jack began making plans for the months ahead, even projecting into the years ahead.

She came up with an arrangement that she thought would be satisfactory to Jack and LM. She would live the warmer months with Jack in England and the other six, October to March, she and LM would return to the south of France or Italy.

> *You know by that, I mean they will be my working months*
> *but apart from work—walks, tea in the forest, cold chicken*
> *on a rock by the sea and so on we could share.*

In the same letter, she promised to cover her companion's expenses during the six months they were together, but was worried what LM would do for income the rest of the year? Katherine suggested she manage a teahouse somewhere in England. She'd be very good at that.

She reread her letter to LM. Had she said all that there was to say? "Tell the truth," she heard the yellow canaries chirp from across the courtyard:

> *We three can never live together again. That is impossible. For*
> *we must be happy. No failures. No makeshifts. Blissful happiness.*

Katherine knew this would depress LM and suggested a book by the French psychotherapist, Dr. Emil Coué. She was practicing his methods of auto-suggestive psychotherapy, popularly known as Couéism. Coué prescribed a mantra to his followers that was to be repeated as fast as possible, from morning to night, so to keep bad thoughts out of their minds. Katherine wrote the mantra down for her: *Day by day, in every way, I am growing better and better.*

KATHERINE WAS ALSO STUDYING Dr. Wallace's "Cosmic Anatomy" for help in becoming one with mind and spirit, in becoming a whole person. She would try and discuss with Jack her spiritual quest to heal her "divided" self, but conversations on what he considered the "occult" always ended in arguments. His mind was closed to any ideas that couldn't be proven medically or scientifically.

He withdrew from any discussions on free will or on taking responsibility for one's actions or the idea that what we cause to happen will ultimately have an effect. When she said her mind had expanded by studying "Cosmic Anatomy," he would look down at the chessboard and make his move.

What he wasn't silent about was his antagonistic feelings toward her mentor, Orage. Jack never stopped cursing him for sending "Cosmic Anatomy," which he felt was the cause of the growing breach between him and Katherine. She decided it was time to write Orage, the only one who would understand her need to heal her divided self and offer help.

One afternoon when she was in the middle of practicing a Coué mantra, "I am hap-py, I am hap-py" over and over, Jack rushed into her room, all white in the face. "I've lost my wallet!" Before she could ask him where he lost it, he rushed back out and made a terrific banging noise in his room.

She walked in on him dumping out the wastepaper basket on the floor. He pushed past her back to her room and shuffled through her papers, banged doors, pulled the bed apart and shook everything but her. He finally gave up and slumped down on the bed.

It was at times like this that she really wished she could manage on her own. Jack's outbursts exhausted her. She tidied up the mess he'd made on her worktable and tried to return to work, but after several minutes of him sitting in utter despair, she went to look for his wallet in his room.

"No, it's no use," he shouted. "It's gone. I've looked everywhere. It's hopeless."

Minutes later, Katherine returned, waving his wallet in the air. "I found it." Now could she get back to work.

IN MAY, Katherine had a setback. She was writing one of her "spasms" for *The Sphere* when she felt her heart suddenly pound against her chest. She gripped the table afraid she was going to pass out and called out for Jack to call Dr. Donat.

After listening to her heart, Donat told her they would have to postpone her last séance for two weeks. He assured her the palpitations were not caused by the séances but rather by the last remnants of the tubercular bacilli remaining in her lungs.

Frightened by her attack, Katherine and Jack put away the brochures advertising destinations in Italy and cruise ship voyages on the Pacific. It would be safer to go back to the Alps to wait for the second series of séances in the fall. They chose Randogne, not as elevated as Chalet des Sapins and nearer Elizabeth, whom they had both grown quite fond of during their stay in Switzerland.

Katherine hurriedly wrote LM to find them lodgings. No longer required at the chalet because they weren't coming back, LM decided to return to England and open a tearoom in Brighton. She'd wait there to hear from Katherine about their trip South in the winter.

Katherine and Jack were still in Paris at the Palace Hotel when Ida stopped to see them on her way home.

"So you're going to go ahead with the tearoom?" Katherine asked, after they were comfortably sipping their tea.

"Yes," said LM, biting into an éclair that Katherine had especially bought for her visit. "Yes, that's my plan for now, or at least I think so unless you—"

"I think a chocolate shop *and* a tearoom would be best. There's an awful lot to be made out of a good tearoom at the seaside, with morning buns after bathing and so on. But I'd make it very original, very simple, with a real style of its own. The great point is to be 'noted' for certain specialties and to make them as divine as possible."

"My new partner Ms. Suchard would surely agree with you. She's most enthusiastic about specialties. She's found a seaside tearoom in Brighton and is waiting for me to sign the lease so we can get started. I hesitate to do that without talking to you."

"Why talk to me?"

"I don't know if Ms. Suchard will find it acceptable if I only manage the tearoom for six months because I will be your companion during the other six."

Katherine had forgotten the promise she'd made. Across the courtyard, she could hear the caged canaries chirping as they often did now that she was improving her moral self with studies in spirituality. "Tell the truth. Tell the truth," they chirped.

She offered LM another pastry before saying, "I've been meaning to write you, but better that you are here. I must first tell you that I had a peculiarly odious dream about 'us,' and though that didn't change my feelings, au fond, it made me feel that perhaps I'd been premature in speaking so definitely about the future... Perhaps you felt that too?" LM's pumpkin cheeks drained of color and Katherine hurried on.

"I am simply unworthy of friendship, as I am. I take advantage of you, demand perfection of you, crush you."

LM took out her handkerchief from her purse. Her bottom lip trembled.

"Jones, please don't cry. I'm not saying we are to live apart for all our lives. I just think it's best to leave the earth alone for a bit."

LM looked at her oddly.

"Do you know what I mean by that?"

No, LM didn't understand at all.

"What I mean to say is let it rest as it is and leave what's there to either grow or die down or be scattered or flourish. By the earth I mean... the basis... the foundation of our relationship... the stable thing that it is." Even Katherine was getting confused. "Oh, let it rest!"

She looked over at LM's muddled face and realized she would have to be far more direct.

"In the host of indefinite things there is one that is definite. There is nothing to be done for me at present. And Jack can help out when needed. Not that he can take care of me as well as you do. And he can be a real pain, as you well know."

LM smirked.

"What I'm trying to say, Jones, without being too harsh, is I'd far rather take care of myself than have it done by you. You see, it's a false position between us. You deserve to have a life of your own.

"You would have been married by now if you hadn't taken care of me these past five years. I want this for you. It's only fair. What about taking up with that young man you introduced us to?"

LM giggled. "Katie, that was five years ago."

"No, is that possible? Well, you'll meet someone else once you're free from your obligations to me."

"I don't want to be free, Katie."

"I know that. You are truly my Griselda." She offered another pastry. LM didn't want it.

Katherine continued, "Now that I'm being well paid for my work I want to offer you an income to help you start your new business. Do you know to this day I still don't know how you manage, what you live on. I can't afford very much but I was thinking maybe five pounds a week?"

"I don't want your money, Katherine. I've been more than paid for my services to you."

Katherine reached across the table and put her hand on LM's. She wanted to offer something so she wouldn't feel so damn guilty giving Ida the boot after promising otherwise.

She tried again, "I don't see my way at present, I confess, but perhaps in the future I could pay the travel expenses for a visit to Rhodesia to see your sister."

"You needn't do that." LM looked down at her watch, pushing away Katherine's hand. "I must go now or I'll miss my train."

Katherine handed her an envelope of money she had prepared earlier. "Please take this."

LM shook her head.

"Jones, please. Think of it as a token of our endearing friendship. I'll be most upset if you don't take it."

LM stuffed the envelope in her coat pocket. Katherine kneeled down to say good-bye to Wingley who LM had brought along with her in his traveling cage. He was to live with her in Brighton. For one moment Katherine thought to keep him but no that would never do. She had to break all ties to those she loved until she was well.

Katherine called out to Ida as she stood waiting at the lift. "I know your tearoom will be a great success. Write me. Let me know how you're getting along."

"I will, Katie."

"And please depend on me. I'm just the same whatever is happening even when I don't write."

The lift door opened and LM stepped inside. She didn't return Katherine's wave.

IT WAS A STRAIN to keep writing moneymaking "spasms" for the commercial *Sphere* magazine. She felt no loyalty toward them, only distaste. But she had ten more séances to pay for in the fall. And her readers liked the *Sphere* stories even if she didn't. It was her uppity literary circle who looked down on these stories from their intellectual perches who didn't have to make an income from their writing. Even Virginia, had turned on her, saying she expected more from her.

Katherine slammed her pen down on the table and got up, restlessly walking over to the window to watch the canaries flit from one perch to the other in their limited space.

After her final séance in Paris, Dr. Manoukhin advised her to be patient. Her heart would grow stronger during the break between séances. Until then he warned her not to walk more than ten minutes a day. He was confident that the radiation to her spleen had put a stop to the bacilli growth in her lungs and that the séances in the fall would kill off the remnants. If not me, she thought ruefully.

She looked forward to leaving Paris and returning to the healing powers of Nature. The more she saw of life in Paris the more certain she felt that the people who live remote from cities are the people who inherit the earth. She imagined the early summer flowers on the sloping grass hills of the Valais valley.

She repeated, *Day by day, in every way, I am growing better and better* twenty times. In the mirror reflection. she blew out her cheeks and pinched them until they had a healthy bloom.

A fake smile spread across her face when she heard Jack open the door and shout, "I'm home. Where's that girl of mine?"

JUNE, 1922

Montana-sur-Sierre

Timidly timidly she lifts her head from her wing.
In the sky there are two stars
Floating, shining...
O waters do not cover me
I would look long and long at those beautiful stars!
Oh my wings—lift me—lift me!
I am not so dreadfully hurt.

THE WOUNDED BIRD—KM

PACKING WAS CHAOTIC AND HECTIC. Jack kept forgetting where he put things and had to repack. Then he forgot to hire a cab and Katherine feared they would miss their train to Geneva. Somehow they found a porter at the train station who hurried them on just before the whistle blew. The money she had given Jack to manage the travel expenses was lost when he overpaid the porter and gave him fifty francs instead of five.

The train was overcrowded with travelers heading for a summer event in Lausanne. There were no available seats left. Fortunately, a gentleman must have noticed how pale Katherine was and offered her a seat. Jack commented after the trip that he was surprised the passengers treated Katherine as if she were an old woman or a wounded bird. Yes Jack, she thought to say, they see me for who I really am. Why can't you?

The next afternoon they arrived intact at the Hotel d'Angleterre in Randogne. Well, not entirely intact. Jack had managed to lose his only fountain pen as well as Katherine's traveling clock, a clock she'd coveted through all her journeys.

Her first impression of Hotel d'Angleterre was not favorable compared to the elegant Palace Hotel in Paris. But within the first week she came to appreciate the Swiss simplicity of the sparse furniture and the raw beauty of the bare wood floors. She and Jack were their only guests. The season was over and the sanatoriums and hotels were mostly vacant.

In spite of her joy in returning to the Alps, her health immediately took a turn for the worse. She left Paris with the beginnings of a cold and then caught a chill on the train when Jack couldn't find any blankets. She ended up with pleurisy, which kept her in bed with a fever and a cough. D'Angleterre's proprietors, an elderly woman and her sister, did everything they could to make her comfortable, bringing her tea and soups.

After a week of bed rest she felt able to sit on her balcony and listen to the herd of cows shaking their cowbells as they headed down the mountain pass after a day of happy munching and sunshine. She breathed in the pure air and stunning view of the Valais valley and vowed to never be a city dweller again.

The cows stopped under her balcony and looked up at her. What did they want, she wondered. In her mind they started to dance, prance and play together for her entertainment, their symphony of cowbells ricocheting against the mountains.

Still weak, it took an hour to dress. In the mirror, the jacket and skirt she had filled out eating in Paris cafés now drooped on her. The weight she'd gained, a manifestation of Dr. Manoukhin's healing powers, was being shed daily in spite of the kind efforts of her landladies endless supply of fresh bread, milk, cheese and butter.

She'd decided all the doctors she'd seen in the past four years in pursuit of a cure were charlatans, except dear Dr. Sorapure, but he never offered her a cure. How could she have foolishly wasted all that time as a wandering consumptive when all along the real cure was inside her.

She sat at her writing table but the pen was too heavy to lift. Though behind in the "spasm" stories promised to *Sphere* magazine, she felt no enthusiasm for writing. Not even her more literary work. She was just too tired.

Not Jack. When he wasn't working on his novel, he escaped outdoors, hiking, fishing, collecting flowers and butterflies, and visiting Elizabeth at her nearby chalet.

In her notebook she wrote:

> *Why, just because I am bedridden, should he not be able to enjoy the vibrant Life surrounding us? But I will never get any work done if things continue the way they are.*

The truth was she needed LM to come back. She couldn't depend on Jack to take care of her and she was too weak to take care of herself. She hesitated, then lifted her pen and wrote two letters to her companion.

She tried to explain to LM that the séances had made her more ill and she couldn't write and take care of the daily chores. The second letter was subterfuge. She wanted LM to copy on her own stationery what Katherine wrote, then sign and mail it back. It was the only way she would get Jack to agree to LM's return. In the fake letter, LM pleaded to return in the capacity of Katherine's companion-secretary, explaining that things hadn't worked out with the tearoom and she was desperate for a position at six pounds a month.

LM wrote back immediately and Katherine showed the letter to Jack. He agreed that they should help poor LM after all she'd done for them. Katherine sent money for a train ticket and warm wool socks. The following week LM arrived and moved into D'Angleterre on the same floor but down the hall so they could still have their privacy.

With LM taking on all the responsibilities, Katherine was able to start *The Dove's Nest,* a story she hoped to develop into a novel.

One evening Jack returned from dinner at Elizabeth's and surprised Katherine who was in the middle of chanting Dr. Coué's mantra. She knew Jack disapproved and she only chanted when he was away.

"Katherine, darling, you're not starting up with that again, are you?"

It angered her that he'd interrupted her but worse he was scolding her. "And why not?"

"Because I find it quite shocking that a woman of your vast intelligence would consider such hogwash. There is no scientific or medical proof that you can use your Will to heal yourself. The only person who can cure you now is Dr. Manoukhin, an acknowledged medical expert. Why would you consider anything other than his proven methods?"

"Jack, look at me."

"Oh there you go again. Don't be silly. I look at you all the time. You are my lovely wife."

She cupped his hands on her face. "Take a long look at the real me, Jack. Not how you see me in the future or in the past, but now. Feel my scarecrow hands, see my burning eyes, touch my alabaster skin and move your hand down my hollow cheeks. And then tell me what you see." He turned away. "No. Look at me," she ordered. "Stop denying the truth. You must do this for *us*." He did as he was asked. "Now, Jack, tell me if you truly believe those body-burning treatments I suffered through in Paris have cured me like Dr. Manoukhin said?"

"Well… certainly not cured but you are better. He said it would take time. Let me take you out in the carriage tomorrow. Get some sun on your face. We'll have a picnic just like we used to do. Wouldn't you like that?"

"Jack, what are you talking about? I can hardly walk across a room let alone go outside."

"Then I'll carry you. We can—"

She cut in, "Orage has written me—"

"Orage! Did you write to him?"

She nodded yes. "I asked him to help me find peace within myself."

"Peace? Don't you think that's a misuse of a larger concept that has to do with after a war?"

"Not at all. The war is within myself."

"Stop this silly prattle. This is his influence. You never used to talk like this. He speaks of things he knows nothing about and fills your head with them. Don't follow him, Katherine. It will only bring you harm. That theologian is a witch doctor."

"Isn't that rather extreme?"

"A doctor of theosophy is not going to cure you."

"I disagree. This book that you find so detestable, though you've never read it, has helped me to come to terms with my illness. I want to discuss what I've discovered with you."

"Discuss what? Free Will? You really think you can focus your conscious mind on your illness and make it go away?"

She looked up at him. Perhaps he had read it.

He knew what she was thinking. "No I haven't wasted my time with that foolery and you shouldn't either. And Orage? The devil himself. Have you forgotten the horrible things he and that awful woman Beatrice used to say about us?"

"It was me who judged him unfairly. It's a bad habit of mine."

"So now I'm the one you're going to judge unfairly. Perhaps you should ask Orage to come here and oust me?"

"Jack stop sounding like a spoiled child. Orage helping me with my spiritual faith doesn't preclude my relationship with you."

KATHERINE'S HEART PALPITATIONS and difficulty breathing did not improve as Dr. Manoukhin had promised and her arguments with Jack were becoming unbearable. She decided to move down the mountain to Sierre, a lower elevation of fifteen hundred meters.

She'd been lying to herself and to Jack. She told him she was writing everyday but in truth she hadn't written since they left Paris. She only pretended she was working when he came in her room, which was seldom. She hoped to feel stronger at the lower elevation so that she could resume her work.

Her cousin Elizabeth offered Jack a guestroom at her chalet. Jack was very pleased with the new arrangement and promised to visit Katherine on the weekends.

Before she left D'Angleterre, her cousin came to visit her.

"I wish we'd become good friends earlier," said Katherine after they had settled back on the divan with their cups of tea. "Do you remember when I first met you at your father's house in London? Probably not. I was so in awe of my cousin, the famous author, that I was afraid of say anything that might make me appear stupid. Pa called you his brilliant star. I thought by becoming famous, he would think of me as his brilliant star, too."

"And doesn't he? He must appreciate how well you've done in such a short time."

Katherine half smiled. "It doesn't matter to him. I've heard through my family that he doesn't ever read the stories I send him. In his letters he tells me how proud he is of my sisters and their children."

"Your father is a fool if he doesn't recognize your valuable contribution to modern literature. Your work is on a much higher level than mine, and you're over twenty years younger! I've always envied the originality of your stream of consciousness style. I'm afraid I'm just a simple storyteller."

"But a very good storyteller. Both Jack and I couldn't put *Vera* down until we finished it. And what an ending! It's far more popular than anything I've written."

"What are you saying my silly cousin? Look how many printings your short story collections have had. Look at the reviews praising your genius. You're in great demand. Why I don't know anyone who hasn't read your stories in the *Sphere*."

"Ah yes, the *Sphere* stories. I write those two-thousand-word 'spasms,' often in one day, to pay for my radiation treatments. That's not literature. It's sheer entertainment. I was hoping to get my father to increase my allowance so I could turn to more challenging work."

"Ask him to pay for Dr. Manoukhin's next séances? He's a banker and can certainly afford it."

She gazed into Elizabeth's eyes searching for understanding. "He'll never offer to raise my allowance as long as I'm married to Jack. With my father it's propriety. Yes he's enormously rich but he doesn't want my allowance to make life easier for Jack."

"Do you agree with your father? Should Jack be your provider?"

Katherine laughed. "Heavens no. He's just as miserly as my father. With Jack I understand it better. He grew up with very little and holds on tightly to what he earns. If I were to depend on him, I'd be wearing rags. Yes, he gives me money occasionally but he expects me to pay him back. He even demanded that I pay my share of a taxi ride when we were coming back from a clinic just after my neck gland was lanced!"

Katherine laughed at Elizabeth's shock. "How do you put up with him?"

"I'm not as good as you at being independent of men."

Elizabeth blushed. "Now wait a moment, that isn't fair. My first husband died. It was only my second husband that I divorced."

"Don't get me wrong, dear cousin. I still love Jack very much in spite of his miserliness, self-absorption, and indifference." Katherine had meant it as a joke but it rang too true.

"Then I'm right?" said Elizabeth, leaning toward Katherine. "*The Man without a Temperament* is Jack. You, too, turn to autobiography for your material. I certainly did in *Vera*. Fictionalizing my husband's dark side helped me through a miserable divorce."

"Jack read it as a tribute to his great love for me. He'll always delude himself into believing he sacrificed his life and career to care for his dying wife and he is a shining prince because of it."

Elizabeth put her hand over Katherine's. "You've had to make so many compromises for your husband, haven't you? Women do, you know." Elizabeth released her hand. "Are you no longer willing to do so?"

Katherine put down her teacup. She hadn't been able to form her new position into words, but her cousin had, and Katherine didn't need to answer, her eyes spoke for her.

"Oh my dearest Katherine, I wish there was more I could do to make life easier for you. It has not been fair to you."

"You have by taking Jack in. It's much easier leaving him knowing he's safe with you."

"I don't know if I'd want him as a husband, but he's a pleasurable guest. Never dull. His intelligence challenges my own in a way I don't often find in society. That's why I've become such a recluse. Society bores me."

"Jack is great for intellectual conversation but he needs to be reminded to smell the roses along the way."

"Yes, I've noticed that," said Elizabeth. They both laughed.

"But let's not talk of Jack anymore," said Katherine. "Tell me about your new man. Are you happy? You certainly look happy when you're together."

"Oh yes, very. But sometimes I worry he's becoming bored with me. He's so much younger than me."

"I wouldn't worry about that, Elizabeth. I've enviously watched the way he looks at you. I doubt you sleep in separate rooms."

Elizabeth laughed. "Separate rooms? Certainly not. Do you and Jack?"

"We have to when I'm sick, which is more often than when I'm well."

Embarrassed by their confidences, they both studied the tea leaves in their empty cups. Elizabeth looked up and said, "I'm curious about something. Do you think you would have become a writer if you hadn't been a *femme malade*?"

"I've reached the conclusion that I'm a writer in spite of my illness but my suffering has given me the opportunity to see clearly what others might miss. My illness has expanded my vision. I'm searching now for a more honest way to express what I've learned so I can help others to see." She hesitated and then said, "If only I had the time to fulfill my purpose."

Katherine was touched when Elizabeth's eyes filled with tears that she didn't try to hide. Elizabeth had seen in her pale, weary face what Jack would never acknowledge. She was dying.

She watched her cousin climb the trail toward her chalet. Her heart cramped knowing she would never see her again.

JULY, 1922

_____

Château Bellevue

I must confess that there does seem to me something sad in life. It is hard to say what it is. I don't mean the sorrow that we all know, like illness and poverty and death. No, it is something different. It is there, deep down, deep down, part of one, like one's breathing.

THE CANARY—KM

KATHERINE ENTERED THE MASSIVE GLASS DOORS of the Château Bellevue in Sierre. Coming in from the bright sunlight it was as dim and chilly as an empty church. She'd stayed there at the beginning of Dr. Stephani's open-air cure, hard to believe that was only a year ago. Pierre, the hospitable bellboy, remembered her and set her at ease with his welcoming smile.

"Hello Madame Murry and, ah, yes, Madame Baker isn't it? Come in. Come in. We were expecting you." He took their baggage and led them up the hotel's spiral stone staircase, illuminated like a rainbow by the sun streaming through the stained-glass windows.

At the top of the first landing they stopped so she could catch her breath before climbing to the next floor.

At a heavy, dark mahogany door marked #12, Pierre said, "This is your room, Madame Murry. I hope you find it to your taste." He unlocked it with a large brass key, put her baggage on a wooden chest and slipped away, leaving Ida a key to her room down the hall.

The emerald-green wallpaper seemed to brighten with Katherine's arrival. The polished wooden floors designed like tortoise shells were miraculously matched on the ceiling. Brass hooks held back the floral-brocaded drapes so she could look out their windows onto the sun-gilded grassy fields with the ever-present Alps above.

She felt the soft, sweet alpine air drift through the opened windows and whirl around her, as if whispering 'come dance with me.' It was all so splendid that it made her dizzy and she had to hold onto a bedpost until the room straightened again.

At a table adorned with a vase of saffron yellow and orange zinnias, she sat down. I could get a lot of work accomplished here, she thought. If only my frightened heart would stop thumping so violently, I'd be ever so happy.

LM started bustling around the room unpacking her clothes.

"Please not now, Jones," she said, looking over at the low wooden bed draped in quilted green satin that was waiting to soothe her sore body. "I need to rest. Get settled in your own room and we'll meet for dinner."

"Are you sure you'll be all right?"

"Here in this room, how could I be anything else but all right?"

After LM left, she curled up on the bed and fell asleep chanting, *Day by day, in every way, I am growing better and better.*

The following morning her heart had quieted and, anxious to start on a new story simmering in her mind, she set Jack's Corona typewriter on the table. The story had been conceived while hearing the caged canaries sing on the balcony across from her Paris hotel room, but she hadn't had the strength to give the story life.

I need to get inside that birdcage, she thought, her hands resting on the typewriter keys; know his feelings, his dreams, the life he led before he was imprisoned or the lives his ancestors lived in either a South American forest or on the coast of its immense perfumed sea... how can words express the beauty of that canary's song that I heard so often from my bed when I was too ill from the radiation treatments to rise.

After a few days of intense writing, Katherine finished *The Canary* and, keeping the promise she'd made to Brett, she dedicated it to her.

She took out a sheet of stationery:

> *Dear father, I have just finished a story with a canary for the hero, and almost feel I have lived in a cage and pecked a piece of chickweed myself. I hope you will like it.*

Having finished the story, Katherine felt a celebration was in order. A walk outdoors would do and she timidly came downstairs and approached the hotel's pretty garden. After resting on a bench for a moment, she ventured past the hotel walls.

Deep in her thoughts, she didn't realize how far she had strayed until she looked back and saw the hotel was barely visible. She'd need to rest before returning and found a soft bed of grass to stretch out on. Above her, the tree branches were patches of azure sky. At that exact moment she found the peace she'd been searching for.

This is the greatest happiness I shall ever know, she thought, I want to feel like this the rest of my life.

Later, leaning up against the tree's trunk, she wrote in her notebook:

> There's nothing to prevent you living like this but it is incompatible with Jack. You are the most stupid woman I have ever met. You never will see that it all rests with you. If you do not take the initiative nothing will be done.
>
> I should be concentrating on the things that count—like the sight of this tree with its purple cones against the blue and wonder how am I to put it that there is gum, on the cones— gemmed? No beaded? No they are like crystals.
>
> There is something I should be learning. What is it? I must find out and start fresh with a new style. Something is missing in my stories. What is it?

A sudden drop in the temperature made her aware of the time. She got up and wrapped her shawl tightly around her shoulders. The hotel was now lit up and glimmering through the evening dusk. How beautiful it is, she thought, I must write a story about it. In the distance she heard LM anxiously calling her.

SHE HAD LOOKED FORWARD to Brett's visit but now she only wanted solitude to consider her next step. She told both LM and Brett that if they saw her walking in the garden they should not interrupt her. She told them her writing would keep her occupied until mid-afternoon and then she'd joined them for tea in the garden. Brett had not come to Sierre only to see her but to paint landscapes and was content to roam by herself with her sketch box in hand. LM went off on hikes.

In the evenings, Brett would visit Katherine in her room. She was inclined to carry on way too long talking about their mutual friends without noticing Katherine was falling asleep. To stop these tedious visits, Katherine asked LM to scoot Brett away after fifteen minutes, saying she needed to rest.

Though she told LM and Brett she was writing, it wasn't true. Her pen hardly touched paper and the punching of the keys on the Corona had ceased. In her letters, she also lied to her friends and family saying she was much better and was busy writing again. To her father, she said her tuberculosis was quiescent. But she didn't tell him that her heart, at any hour, could suddenly become a booming, terrorizing drum.

As promised, Jack came down from Radogne on the weekends. He'd take walks with Brett or play billiards with Katherine in the hotel lounge. When he'd ask how the writing was coming along, she told him she was merging two previous stories, *Prelude* and *At the Bay,* into a novel. The novel would move back and forth between England and New Zealand. It wasn't a complete lie. She was working on it, but only in her head.

As the days passed, staring at a blank page made her anxious, and she started to write brief sketches in her journal. Whatever came to mind.

One afternoon, Brett came out of her room to find Katherine pacing the hallway looking at door numbers.

"What is it? Have you forgotten your room number?"

"I'm working on a story but I've changed it around so often I'm muddled. I need to find the room where the idea originated, but because they are vacated, I've been able to visit all of them. I'm looking for a huge stove. Come along and help me find it."

Brett followed her down the long dim hall as Katherine slipped in and out of the rooms. "Here it is!" she shouted. "Here's what I was looking for." She pointed to an ancient milky white and blue stove in the corner of one room.

She sat down on the bed and took out her notebook. "Could you read the figures engraved on it."

Brett walked over to the stove and read out, "Sixteen hundred and twenty three."

"Yes, now I remember," Katherine mumbled to herself, scribbling it down. "Too perfectly historical for words, don't you think?"

"What?"

"Never mind," she said. "It's just something Emma says to her sister about the stove. If you want, come back to my room and I'll read it to you. The story takes place in this hotel, where Emma and Emily are staying with their father."

Back in her room, she opened to the pages she'd been working on and stood upright in front of Brett, pretending she was giving a reading at a salon gathering, something she had loved doing before she got ill:

"For a long time now—for how long?—for countless ages— Father and the girls had been on the wing. Nice, Montreux, Biarritz, Naples, Menton, Lake Maggiore, they had seen them all and many, many more. And still they beat on, beat on, flying as if unwearied, never stopping anywhere for long. But the truth was—Oh, better not enquire what the truth was. Better not ask what it was that kept them going. Or why the only word that daunted Father was the word—home...

Home! To sit around, doing nothing, listening to the clock, counting up the years, thinking back... thinking! To stay fixed in one place as if waiting for something or somebody. NO! No! Better far to be blown over the earth like the husk, like the withered pod that the wind carries and drops and bears off again."

She broke off, "Well? You like it?"

"Is that it?"

"No, it's just a start."

"Then I think it's very intriguing. I want to know why they are always traveling. And you lend so much to the story with your performance. You know, Katherine, you should've been actress. "

"Now that you mention it, my cousin Elizabeth and I are planning a tour in the States. My books are selling well there and there've been requests."

"That would be smashing! Can I come?"

"I don't see why not." Katherine looked down at her notebook. "But you must leave me now—I have work to do. Tomorrow, let's have dinner together."

"That's what you said yesterday."

"I'm sorry. I've neglected you, haven't I? Then I'll come downstairs tonight. I promise."

"I certainly hope so. I'm leaving for London tomorrow."

"So soon? Have you been here a fortnight already?"

After Brett left, Katherine sat down to pick up her pen but, too tired, she slipped between the silk sheets and fell asleep.

That evening, she asked LM to help her get dressed for her last dinner with Brett.

The hotel's salle à manger was the size of a ballroom. Because it was off-season and bereft of guests, Brett was easy to spot in one of the few inhabited chairs. Before going to her, Katherine quickly wrote in her notebook:

> *All gay, all glittering, the long French windows open onto the green and gold garden, the salle à manger stretched before them. And the fifty little tables with the fifty pots of dahlias looked as if they might begin dancing with…*

Whom? Katherine asked herself, having no idea where the sketch might lead to or if she would ever complete it—so many incomplete sketches in her notebooks. She smiled over at Brett and approached her.

She performed gaily for Brett all evening, miming their friends and telling funny stories. She gave such a brilliant performance she was certain Brett would return to London and tell their friends how well she was.

AFTER BRETT HAD GONE back to London, one evening she and LM were having tea in her room. Katherine was sitting up in her bed writing a few lines of poetry:

> *In the wide bed under the green embroidered quilt*
> *with flowers and leaves always in soft motion*
> *she is like a bird resting on a pool.*

She dropped her pen and called out, "Jones! Jones!"

LM rushed over. "What is it, Katie!"

"My heart is killing me. Please, make it stop."

When Katherine had palpitations, Dr. Donat had instructed LM to sit with her. Keep her calm. Don't leave her alone. Don't let her panic.

It took a few minutes for her heart to slow down enough that LM felt she could leave her to get a glass of water.

"I can't go on like this," said Katherine taking the full glass. "It comes in spasms like my cough used to, but it's so much more frightening. I need to see Dr. Sorapure. He's the only one who will tell me if I'm in danger of dying soon. We must leave for London right away."

LM didn't argue with her and said she'd make the arrangements. She too was frightened by Katherine's recurring attacks and her tendency to sleep all day, never wanting to go out even when Brett was there.

Katherine felt her heavy eyes closing and said sleepily, "Jack is coming down on Sunday. I must speak to him first. He's very content in Randogne... perhaps he'd rather stay and finish his book... you know he's taken up golf... I knew he would someday."

Before she fell asleep she listed in her mind the friends she wanted to see in London:

Pa (childhood/love)
Orage (soul)
Kot (friendship)
Sorapure (heart)

THE FOLLOWING DAY, she wrote to her father, apologizing for the change in her plans, but she would like to meet him in London instead of Paris:

> *To come straight to the horses, my heart has been playing up*
> *so badly this last week that I realize it is imperative for me to*
> *see Dr. Sorapure before I go on with my Paris treatments.*

Jack came down from Randogne and wasn't pleased about her sudden decision to go to London. He assured her or himself that she was only having a minor setback and the radiation treatments scheduled in Paris would fix her right back up again. Wanting to leave him on good terms, and knowing how much it upset him to lose, she let him win their billiard game.

Between hitting balls in the pockets, he offered to come with her. There was only the sitting room at Brett's, so he would have to find somewhere else to stay as would LM.

He stayed in her room for the night and the following morning he kissed her tenderly before returning to Elizabeth's to pack.

After he left and LM brought her breakfast tray, Katherine said, "Jones, I want you to witness my will."

"Katie, sometimes I think you say things just to shock me. It's just your heart that has you worried. I'm certain Dr. Sorapure will set you right again. And hasn't Dr. Manoukhin promised that the next séances will finally cure you?"

"Please don't be like Jack. If I can't prepare for the inevitable with him, I would like to know I can with you."

Feeling Jack's tender morning kiss still fresh on her lips, she said, "If something should happen to me, I want to leave clear instructions for Jack. Otherwise he won't know what to do with my possessions."

LM looked at her sadly and said, "Katie, I'm here to help you anyway I can."

"Thank you. Now please bring me my notebook so we can get started."

The Will that she had written back at the Elephant three years ago when she thought she wouldn't survive the winter in Italy wouldn't do. The Will she wanted to write now would be more specific.

Together she and LM went over a list of her possessions.

"The larger pearl ring to Jack's brother Richard to have for when he marries; Spanish shawl; fur coat; favorite books to various friends; mother's walking stick to S. Koteliansky; writing cases to my sisters; and to my Pa, the brass pig that has been my loyal traveling companion."

She held up the small gold watch and chain she kept on the mantel. "Jones, would you like to have this?"

"If that's what you want to give me," she said in her tiniest of voices.

"It seems the right gift. It represents our long friendship. Now what about my Bible? Would you like that too?"

That was all Ida could bear. "Katie! Please no more. It's cruel of you to go on like this. It's morbid to talk about you as if you're almost dead."

Katherine ignored her outburst and said calmly, "All right. I'll give the Bible to my father."

"Can't we do this some other time?"

"Just a few more things and we're done."

Later, the list completed, LM had never been so relieved to leave her companion.

Katherine picked up her pen to write to Jack:

I have been on the point of writing this letter for days. My heart has been behaving in such a curious fashion that I can't imagine it means nothing. So, as I would hate to leave you unprepared, I'll just try and jot down what comes into my mind. All my manuscripts I leave entirely to you to do what you like with. Go through them one day, dear love, and destroy all you do not use. Please destroy all letters you do not wish to keep and all papers. You know my love of tidiness. Have a clean sweep, Bogey, and leave all fair— will you?

Books are yours, of course… monies, of course, are all yours. In fact, my dearest dear, I leave everything to you—to the secret you whose lips I kissed this morning. In spite of everything—how happy we have been! I feel no other lovers have walked the earth more joyfully—in spite of all."

She looked down at the small daisy-shaped pearl ring that Frieda Lawrence had kindly taken off her own finger when Jack forgot to bring a ring to their wedding. Iridescent under the gaslight. She decided not to leave it behind on her last, grim journey. It would remain on her finger for eternity.

Return to London

*Why hath the rose faded and fallen, yet these eyes have
not seen?*

*Why hath the bird sung shrill in the tree—and this mind
deaf and cold?*

*Why hath the rains of summer veiled her flowers with
their sheen?*

And this black heart untold?

AWAKE—WILLIAM DE LA MARE

L ONDON WELCOMED HER like a loving parent whose wayward
child had returned home. She settled into Brett's sitting room in
Hampstead and LM went to nearby Chiswick to stay with her sister's
family. Jack rented the top floor flat in the house next door to Brett's.
Too many stairs for Katherine to climb, he'd visit her at Brett's for teatime
and meals.

Without LM there to shoo people away, Katherine hung a *Do Not
Disturb* sign on her door. She never could understand why people
thought writers had nothing to do but entertain people who "came by
just to say hello."

Brett was the worse offender. She came to talk at all hours, but Katherine couldn't begrudge her hostess.

When she arrived at Dr. Sorapure's office he greeted her with, "You
look better than the last time I saw you in London. How long ago was
that?"

When people told her how well she looked, she was surprised because
she certainly didn't feel well. Were they just being polite or did they not
realize she was only thirty-three and moved like an old woman?

"It's been three years since you diagnosed my tuberculosis, among
other things," she said.

"Is that possible? Well then the open-air cure has done you good, or perhaps it's Dr. Manoukhin's radiation treatments? Why come to see me?"

"Quite simply because you're the only doctor I trust to tell me the truth."

"That's a compliment coming from someone who's seen as many doctors as you have. If you want my opinion, I'd say whatever you're doing is better than anything I could offer you."

"I'm afraid my appearance is deceiving. I still have debilitating fatigue, my hips are on fire, my cough has returned, and I'm often out of breath. But I'm used to that. I came to see you today because my heart thuds in my ears and bangs twice as fast as it should."

"Does Dr. Manoukhin think it's a side effect from his treatments?"

"Yes, but he said the palpitations would stop after I finished the first fifteen séances, but I finished three months ago and my palpitations are progressively louder and more frequent."

"Then let's have a listen to that pounding heart of yours." The cold metal chest piece pressing against her heart made her flinch.

"Why aren't you using your anti-chill device?"

"The rubber disc? I'm sorry, I forgot to put it on. Not all my patients are as sensitive as you when I listen to their chest." He slipped it on. "Would you like to listen?" he asked.

"God no. I don't need a stethoscope to hear their complaints. They're loud enough without it."

After his examination, he said, "Here's the good news. This might surprise you, but you have the heart of a young woman. It's just that it has to pump very hard to keep you alive. Let me try to explain it with a drawing." He drew a simple child's drawing of an inflated balloon and then a deflated one, side by side. He explained, "Here's a normal lung and here's one like yours."

He drew a wide canal around the deflated white balloon and filled it in with a pencil. "The tubercular lesions have leaked air into the canal between your lungs and your chest wall. This expanded canal is what's pressing against your heart. Your heart must pump much harder to circulate your oxygen-filled blood. If we knew a way to remove the air from this enlarged pleural space, your lung would inflate again and you wouldn't be having these palpitations."

She studied the scribbled pencil drawing and traced her hand across her sad, deflated lung that she felt an affinity with. Other doctors had told her similar things about the condition of her lungs but as always Dr. Sorapure made it so much clearer. She looked up and asked, "How do you know this without seeing it?"

He held up his stethoscope. "There are no sounds of breathing over the affected left lung because it has collapsed. Only your right lung is working."

"Can't you punch it with a scalpel?" she asked, pushing her finger into her chest.

He laughed. "Unfortunately, not. As I've told you before, it's a long process before we discover how to cure our patients, even if we know what's wrong. We've yet to discover a way to let the air out of the pleural canal."

"So there's nothing that can be done to stop my heart's violent bangs?"

"Exercise the lungs. Not excessively, that could be dangerous, but slow ten minute walks. Deep, slow breathing in fresh air will help expand the deflated lung. Just don't run up any stairs."

"So I came all this way to be told if I continue having my spleen fried and take daily walks in the park, I'll get well?"

He smiled. "Not exactly. I wouldn't want to be quoted as saying I recommend radiating your spleen to kill tubercular bacilli. There isn't any scientific or medical data to back up Manoukhin's theories. Right now it's all talk and he's a very good self-promoter.

"For now we only have his word and the testimonials of his satisfied patients—the ones that are alive, that is."

Katherine looked down at the drawing of her pathetic left lung. She'd known herself that the radiation might not work but to hear it from Dr. Sorapure was very disappointing.

"I'm sorry not to give you better news," he said, "after you came all this way to see me."

"But you have, Doctor. Now I know not to panic when my heart slams into my chest. And I thank you for that." She got up to leave. "May I take this drawing?"

"Please do. And let me know the outcome of your radiation treatments. If it works, I will want to try it on my patients."

Katherine, following his advice after leaving his office. took a slow walk in Hyde Park. She sat down on a sunny bench and considered what to do now that she knew her heart was not in immediate danger.

Since arriving in London, she'd felt a sentimental longing to stay for the summer rather than return to Switzerland to wait for the ten radiation treatments scheduled in October. And perhaps she could resume the treatments here in London instead of Paris so to be near Dr. Sorapure and her family and friends.

And Brett had mentioned an available upstairs flat...

She stood up and started walking with purpose. Yes, why not, stay here? she asked herself. And by Christmas I'll be completely cured as Dr. Manoukhin has promised, then... well, that was too far away to consider now. It's important that I stay in the present and not fret about the future.

With an immediate plan in mind, she was ready to knock off two things on her London to do list:

Pa (childhood/love)

A few days after seeing Dr. Sorapure, she took a train to her sister Chaddie's house outside London. Her father was visiting from Wellington and her sister Jeanne was visiting from Canada with her husband and children. She'd feared they would be restrained in their feelings toward her after such a long separation, but it was a spectacular family reunion. No regrets. Lots of embraces and joyous tears. And laughter from her nephews and nieces when they opened the box of puppets their aunt had brought them. Her father seemed sincerely moved by her visit and when she left with feelings of overflowing gratitude because she was once again Pa's loved child.

Orage (soul)

After reading "Cosmic Anatomy" and other books on mysticism and spiritual quests, Katherine had many questions that she thought Orage could answer. Even when she was a young writer of twenty-one, he'd encouraged her to find her own center where the mind and soul worked together to create art. He had also been wary of her promiscuity. Because of her unabated drive to experience life to its fullest, she'd had relationships with several men that Orage considered irresponsible and a bad influence on her young developing mind.

"The young artist who is virtuous will live for his art," he told her. If only she had listened to him back then, and taken her art more seriously.

SHE WOKE UP, two weeks after arriving in London, with great expectations. Today she was having lunch with Orage. As she dressed, her heart quickened but she was certain it was stomping for joy knowing she was going to see her old friend Orage after a three-year separation.

As excited as she was, she took time to dress carefully, checked herself in the mirror, pinched her cheeks, and left Brett's to hail a taxi.

She recognized Orage immediately in the far corner of the Indian restaurant by the same unfashionable felt hat he was wearing when they first met twelve years ago.

When she was within reach, he jumped up and wrapped his long arms around her in a heartfelt hug. She didn't want him to ever let her go again. After he released her, he smiled and said, "Katherine you are so—"

"No compliments, please. I know what I look like and I've always respected your honesty so don't disappoint me."

"What I was going to say is you are so famous. I've kept up with your published work and what you've accomplished is most impressive. You have become one of the finest modern story writers in England and I'm very proud to have been the first to publish your stories."

She blushed. "That's a change. You used to tell me I was 'an empty husk, as promiscuous as a rabbit, as responsible as a bubble, and as deceitful as a cat.'" She put up her hand and clawed the air, purring, "Me-ow."

It was Orage's turn to redden. "Oh dear, I'd forgotten that. Could I have ever been that cruel?"

"It was true. I just wasn't up to someone being so candid."

They ordered lunch and started their conversation with small remembrances in the past.

By the time the waiter brought the port snifters, accompanied by cheddar cheese and figs, the old friends were reclining in their chairs and sharing confidences. "Orage, there's something I'm most curious about. Why did you ask Jack to review "Cosmic Anatomy" for your magazine? You had to know his intellectual integrity would be doubted if he ever accepted mysticism as a valid philosophy. Did you really believe he'd review it?"

Orage burst out laughing. "Dr. Wallace's book was actually meant for you. Not that I wouldn't have liked Jack to read and review it, but I didn't really expect it. Just the title would've made him cringe and then dump it in the trash bin."

Katherine smiled, "It did. But my opinion was entirely different. Wallace set me on a spiritual quest that has brought me to you and I want to thank you for that. His ideas have changed my life, perhaps even saved it."

Orage took her hand in his. "I'm so glad to hear that, Katherine. It's what I was so hoping you would say. "Cosmic Anatomy" had a similar effect on me. Tell me what you've learned."

"Dr. Wallace seemed to understand my dissatisfaction with the idea that Life must be something less than what we are capable of 'imagining' it to be. His teachings have made me aware that I have been living a false life with only brief moments, instants, gleams, when I've felt something much more real.

"I was hoping you could introduce me to people, like yourself, that can help me to develop my conscious awareness."

"And I know just the person you should meet. He has the wisdom you are searching for. Have you heard of the controversy over G. I. Gurdjieff?"

She shook her head no.

"He came here after he escaped from Bolshevik persecution in Russia. His lectures were so popular that the Home Office became overly concerned that there might be unpleasant repercussions and they cancelled his visa."

"Can I meet him?"

"Unfortunately not. Forbidden by law to lecture here, he left for France a few weeks ago. The French are far more receptive to his belief that without self-knowledge man cannot be free, he cannot govern himself, and he will always remain a slave.

"I'm sorry you won't be able to meet him."

"Where is he in France?"

"He's found a new location in Fontainebleau just south of Paris. But there is someone else you can meet. His disciple P.D. Ouspensky will be lecturing on Gurdjieff's teachings. Would you like to come with me to his lecture?"

"Yes, Orage, I have nowhere else to turn." She raised the port to her lips and drank it. "I don't know what will happen to me if—"

Orage took both her hands in his. "What is it, Katherine? What's wrong?"

"I confess this to you, Orage, and you alone. I've stopped writing. I pretend that I am. I even hang a sign on my door that says "Do not Disturb," but behind that door I sit at my writing table and stare at a blank page. Worse, I've reread many of the stories I've written and I don't like any of them. There's something lacking. I'm on to something new, but I just don't have any control over my thoughts. I'll go mad if I continue like this."

"My dear, dear Katherine." He took out his handkerchief and dabbed the tears running down her cheeks. "We'll find a way for you to meet Gurdjieff. Trust me. I know he can help you."

"Has he helped you?"

"Immeasurably. It sounds terribly banal and Jack would laugh, but Gurdjieff has changed my life. For a long time I was asking myself: Who am I? Why am I here? What is the purpose of my life, and of human life in particular? And then I met Gurdjieff who had found those answers."

He hesitated and then said, "Now that we're sharing secrets, here's mine. I'm resigning from *New Age* to join Gurdjieff's new Institute at Fontainebleau."

"You're leaving your magazine?"

"Yes. Gurdjieff has shown me that by practicing self-observation one realizes the necessity of self-change. It's a means of awakening. In order to continue this task of self-observation, I must put it first in my life. I can't afford to squander my time on trifles."

"Dearest old friend, I'm so thankful to have found you again. I know you will guide me toward my own awakening."

THE SMALL DINGY MEDICAL OFFICE of Dr. Manoukhin's protégé, the radiologist Dr. Webster, was quite a step down from the sophisticated clinic in Paris. Katherine found his examination too brief and he was clumsy with the stethoscope, timidly exploring her chest as if he was afraid of setting off a land mine. Worst of all, after trying several times to listen to her heart, he impatiently unhooked the stethoscope from his flappy ears and pressed his sweaty head against her breast.

He then told her without any discussion that she wasn't strong enough to tolerate the radiation. She argued that Dr. Sorapure had found her heart young and strong, just overworked.

"It might be a young heart," he said, "but for now it's old and tired. Rest up for another week and we'll have another listen, shall we?"

Dr. Webster's fee was half Manoukhin's but she still felt cheated. He didn't even have a nurse and though he didn't admit it, she was sure he had never used Manoukhin's X-ray machine on anyone before her.

THE DAYS TURNED GLOOMY. Even the flat she'd moved into above Brett's flat, with its cheerful orange-flowered curtains and her familiar Buddha on the mantelpiece began to feel like a suicide room. And time went ever so slowly. After having three appointments with Dr. Webster, he still held off giving her radiation, saying her heart wasn't up to it.

Meanwhile, Jack had moved to Sussex to stay with friends. After all their plans to live there, Katherine found excuses not to join him. They were having a depressing effect on each other. Jack blamed it on her new "occult passion." She blamed it on his disbelief in her spiritual quest.

As promised, Orage took her to Ouspensky's lecture. The room was packed and airless, but not a person left. Gurdjieff's Russian disciple had everyone mesmerized when he spoke of the loss of the essence that humans are born with, which then causes a lack of harmony. They only develop the other half of their being, the personality, which is a machine that their will has no control over.

He amused his audience by suggesting that on their way home they should try to walk differently than they were accustomed to, even walk backwards to see if by changing their mechanical, automatic behavior they could wake up their conscious mind.

Katherine and Orage were sitting in the first row and she felt Ouspensky was speaking directly to her when he said, "If you practice Gurdjieff's methods, you can become the master of your life and you might become the master of your death."

After the meeting, Orage introduced her to Ouspensky. She was so impressed with what he had said that she immediately asked if she could join Gurdjieff's Institute. Ouspensky said he might be able to arrange it, but first she'd have to meet with him and explain why it meant so much to her. His schedule was very full and she'd have to wait two weeks.

Several days after Ouspensky's lecture, Orage invited Katherine to lunch at the home of science fiction writer J.D. Beresford along with John Sullivan, Jack's previous assistant editor at *The Athenaeum*.

Orage spoke of the new Institute in Fontainebleau where one could develop harmony through self-observation. The teachings at the Institute were presented in three forms: writings, music, and movements, which corresponded to his students' intellect, emotions, and physical body.

Katherine sat next to him in Beresford's living room and listened attentively. She felt a sense of frustration in the room, even an undertone of deep regret, and wondered if it was just her that was feeling it. She spoke up and confessed, "I feel that I'm missing something within myself. That I've given up. This is not what I want. If this is all, then Life is not worth living. But I know it's not all."

She took comfort in finding other people in the room who were also seeking change, even old acquaintances of hers and Jack's—and they didn't laugh at her like Jack did.

Back at her flat, she recalled a dinner at the Elephant with her and Jack's friend, W.J. Dunning. They'd discussed Eastern religion and the practice of yoga. Afterward, she and Jack sat up late talking excitedly about approaches to understanding one's consciousness other than the Western intellectual approach. That night she'd felt a change within Jack, a flicker of inner light. What had caused that light to go out?

She picked up her pen:

> *I wish you found life as wonderful as it seems to me. Even*
> *the least idea—the fringe of the idea—of 'waking up'*
> *discovers a new world. And the mystery is that 'all' of us*
> *in our unlikeness and individual ways do seem to me to be*
> *moving toward the very same goal.*

ON WEDNESDAY, SEPTEMBER 27, she went to her second radiation under the monstrous X-ray machine. When she complained to Dr. Webster about her recurring symptoms, he concluded that they were minor complaints that had nothing to do with the success of her treatments. He scheduled a third treatment for the following week, but she left his office knowing she'd never come back.

That night she wrote Jack in Sussex and told him she'd changed her mind about staying in London. *Dr. Webster doesn't know what he's doing. I will not let him practice on me.* She would be leaving for Paris the next Monday to continue with Dr. Manoukhin. She did not ask him to join her. He did not offer.

She felt their relationship had shifted to brother and sister rather than man and wife.

OCTOBER 14, 1922

34th Birthday

"Do you know what individuality is?" Ouspensky asked.

"I thought I did," Katherine replied. "I'm no longer sure."

"Consciousness of will. Conscious that you have a will and can act. Does this interest you?" he asked.

"Yes, very much so."

FROM KM MEETING WITH OUSPENSKY

WHEN SHE ENTERED HER LONDON FLAT, LM was waiting for her. "What's wrong, Katie. You look feverish?"

"I finally met with Ouspensky," she said quickly, stopping to catch her breath. "I must sit down." She collapsed onto the divan and after taking a sip of the offered glass of water, said excitedly, "There's a chance I will meet Gurdjieff at Fontainebleau in a fortnight."

"Gurdjieff? Ouspensky? Who are they? They sound so foreign."

"Only to those who are small-minded. Two weeks ago I attended Ouspensky's lecture on the teachings of Gurdjieff and today I met with him alone."

"But how can you go to Fontainebleau when you're having radiation treatments here with Dr. Webster?"

"He's inexperienced and not to be trusted. He's a radiologist not a diagnostician like Sorapure, and he couldn't care less about the side effects I'm having. I could burn up on his X-ray table and he wouldn't even notice."

"Would it help if I go with you the next time?"

"You're not listening to me, Jones. There isn't going to be a next time. You and I are leaving for Paris on Monday."

"Monday! That's in two days!"

"That way Manoukhin can give me the third séance on Wednesday so I won't miss any of my weekly treatments.

"Jones, why are you staring at me like I'm—like I'm crazy. I thought you believed in Manoukhin, too? Don't you want to come with me?"

"Yes. Of course I do. It's just so sudden." She looked around the pleasant sitting room. "You've moved in your furniture… it took weeks to get it the way you wanted and now it all looks so comfy. Even your Buddha has settled in on the mantelpiece. Does Brett know?"

"Not yet. I'm going to ask her to sublet the flat with my furnishings. That way I can hold on to it… but please no more questions. I'm so tired. Just do as I ask."

"I'll go to the station first thing tomorrow. Shall I get a ticket for Jack?"

"No. He's staying in Sussex. It's better that way."

Ida brewed a pot of tea and Katherine waited for her to pour before saying, "There is something I want to tell you, but you must first promise me to keep it a secret."

"You know you can trust me, Katie. What is it?"

"I have every intention of continuing Dr. Manoukhin's séances, but if I become terribly sick again as I did before, I'll stop."

"But Katie—"

"I'm fed up with being bedridden and unable to write, while these doctors experiment on me and hold out the false promise that I'll be cured. My God, I'm not an experimental cow. Manoukhin is the last doctor I will give myself over to. If he fails, I will go elsewhere to be healed."

"Where will that take us? The Ivory Coast to see a medicine man?"

Katherine ignored her joke and said solemnly, "The Institute for the Harmonious Development of Man."

"The institute of… what?"

"Gurdjieff's Institute in Fontainebleau. He believes it is possible for an individual to transform illness with the consciousness of one's will, to be one's own master in spite of the circumstances. If he is willing to have me, and Manoukhin fails me, I will go there to study his teachings."

LM put down her teacup, leaned toward Katherine and said, "I don't understand what you're talking about, but I will stand by you regardless."

"Thank you, Jones. I hoped you would say that. Remember this is our secret. I'm only telling you so that you will be prepared. I owe you that."

THE CALAIS TRAIN STATION was sizzling under a blank, merciless sky. An old woman sold luscious pears from her basket that moistened Katherine's parched throat. LM protected her from being crushed by other travelers as they boarded the connecting train to Paris.

Settled inside, she opened her purse and took out Dr. Young's address in Paris that Ouspensky had given her. Because of her poor health, he insisted that she have a physical examination before meeting with Gurdjieff at the Institute.

Dr. Young, both a surgeon and a psychotherapist, was also a disciple of Gurdjieff's. Would he be probing my mind, my emotions or my body, or all three? she wondered. The passing French countryside framed her window like an Impressionist painting and she sat back to enjoy it.

It was dusk when they pulled into the Paris station. The gas lamps were a warm yellow—not like the harsh white lights recently installed in London. "We've come home, Jones," said Katherine.

They went looking for accommodations at the Victoria Palace where Katherine had last stayed with Jack. Seated in its elegant red velvet lobby she thought how estranged they had become when only a few months ago they were inseparable at this hotel.

She now found its opulence distasteful and was not disappointed when LM told her there were no rooms.

After several other hotels turned them away, they checked into a damp room in a boarding house. Katherine's sleep was disturbed by the ghost-like sounds of water sobbing, gurgling and sighing its way through the rusty pipes.

LM slept soundly as usual and Katherine had to shake her awake the next morning. They dressed quickly and escaped to a nearby café to seek warmth. While Katherine sipped her espresso, she had the feeling they'd been there before. She frowned at a small modest hotel across the street.

"Why, Jones, isn't that our old hotel?" she said, reading the familiar marquis out loud: "Select Hotel. I was always amused by that name, as it wasn't a hotel one would naturally select, but at the time we were without options, like now. Do you remember?"

"Certainly I remember. The Germans were bombing Paris. But certainly you don't want to stay there now? That wasn't a pleasant time for either of us."

"I've forgotten all that. What I do remember was its simplicity and the wonderful view of Parisian chimneys from our garret. We could see the Sorbonne decorated with those distinguished gentlemen carved in marble bath gowns. Those rickety stairs we had to climb. The short walk to the Luxembourg Gardens. And it was inexpensive."

"Since when did you want simplicity? You loved your stay at the Palace."

"I'm no longer that person. She's dying, don't feed her."

Katherine laughed at the impression she'd made on LM. "I'm only speaking figuratively, Jones."

In a few hours they were settled in the same garret on the sixth floor that looked out on the Sorbonne. Katherine telephoned Dr. Manoukhin to confirm their appointment for the following day and was delighted when he, Dr. Donat and Sonja, all got on the receiver to welcome her back in English, Russian and French.

BOTH DOCTORS AND SONJA were waiting at the door to greet her with many hugs and kisses as if they were her dearest friends. The dark X-ray room, the clock timer, the frosty metal table were just as she had left them in May. The only noticeable change was Dr. Donat's new beard that tickled when he listened to her heart.

She gave them Dr. Sorapure's diagnosis and showed them his drawing. Dr. Donat translated for Dr. Manoukhin who assured her that when she completed the second series of séances the remaining bacilli would be killed off and her left lung would inflate again and take the pressure off her struggling heart. "My X-ray machine will not fail you."

For the first séance, Dr. Manoukhin lowered the power of the rays and shortened the duration to one hour instead of two. He advised her to rest for the next few days as she would probably have a mild reaction.

They gave her a stack of recently printed pamphlets: *Le traitement de la tuberculose par la leucocytose consecutive a la l'radiation de la rate.* Dr. Donat claimed an extremely high success rate for Manoukhin's patented machine and said it brought about "de véritables resurrections" even with the worst cases. She was asked to distribute the pamphlets in England.

Oui, je suis une resurrection, she thought, reading over the pamphlet back in the garret. She enclosed the pamphlets in a letter to Jack and asked him to pass them on to anyone he thought might help promote Dr. Manoukhin's miraculous cure.

SHE EXPECTED TO WRITE STORIES and a table was ordered for her room. On it, she wrote to Jack of her intention to send him a new story, but the only work she accomplished was correcting Kot's English translations of a few of Dostoevsky's *Letters*.

A week later, after her second séance, she was unable to hold down any food except the soup LM brought her from a local café. Too weak to get out of bed, she postponed the third séance writing to Jack that she could hardly raise her hand, let alone walk.

After finishing her letter, she sent LM out to post it and took out the folded sheet of paper she'd been keeping in her writing case. She telephoned Dr. Young.

Learning she wasn't well, he graciously offered to examine her at the hotel. They set a date for the following week. On the appointed day, she received a letter from Jack. A pressed rose fell out. Only then did she remember it was her birthday.

Dr. Young sat with her for a couple of hours discussing how Gurdjieff's teachings were practiced at the Institute. All residents had to spend time working as laborers in the kitchen, in the garden, or in construction of a new building. She told him she was inexperienced in the kitchen but an avid gardener.

He listened to her heart and lungs and discussed her heart palpitations and fatigue. As she was way too thin, her diet at the Institute would include milk and cheese produced by their own farm animals.

He couldn't make any promises but he would do his best to convince Gurdjieff to invite her to the Institute. But first he needed to receive Dr. Manoukhin's full medical report on her condition.

Orage was in Paris and when she told him it was her birthday, he invited her to dinner.

On their walk to a nearby restaurant they were drenched by a thunderous rain cloud that came out of nowhere. They hurried into the restaurant and took off their wet coats.

"That was so unexpected and vivid," said Katherine, exhilarated by the sudden storm. Seated at a small candle-lit table near a kindling fireplace, she added, "Running in the rain is quite wonderful. It's a sensation that stays with you long after the sun has come out again."

The waiter, dressed in a red vest, white apron and a little gray cloth cap, returned with their orders—big bowls of piping hot beef stew, bread, and a carafe of red wine. She was surprised by her appetite and thanked Orage for taking her out on her birthday.

After a second cognac, they stretched their feet in front of the fireplace and she recounted a dream she'd been having. "I am walking down a cellar staircase and I see a pathetic little girl in rags shivering in a dark corner. I want to bring her up into the sunlight but she shakes her head no and turns away from me. If I am invited to the Institute and have an opportunity to practice Gurdjieff's teachings, I am hoping she will come up from the cellar and join me in the sunlight where she and I both can be healed. Is that too much to ask?"

"Not at all. I believe Gurdjieff can give you the tools to heal yourself. Like you, I've been disconnected from my inner self for some time, but didn't know there was any other way to live that would be more satisfying, more joyous. He gave me the inspiration and courage to transform my life through his teachings."

"Jack says that giving up Manoukhin for Gurdjieff's 'spiritual quackery' would be criminal. 'Wrong, utterly wrong,'"

"Will he try and stop you?"

"No." She smiled. "He was never one to take action with what he feels passionate about. He'll anguish over my decision but he won't try to stop me."

Orage walked her back to the hotel. After reassuring her that he was certain she would be joining him at the Institute, he helped her up the stairs to her room and left.

WHILE WAITING FOR DR. YOUNG'S CALL, Katherine distracted herself with walks in Luxembourg Gardens. She'd wander along their pebbled paths bordered with blooming rainbows of flowers. Or, short of breath, she'd often just sit on a bench near the park entrance. Wanting to be alone, LM watched over her from the café across the street.

When Katherine postponed the third séance, a concerned Dr. Donat rushed to her hotel room to tell her she must be patient. The unpleasant side effects would stop when the radiation séances were completed. He frightened her with notions of what might happen if she suddenly quit and repeated several times that only Dr. Manoukhin could save her.

The following day, with LM's help, she hobbled over to the park and, once she was comfortably seated on what had become her favorite bench, LM took up watch across the street.

She found solace in the vibrancy around her, the children playing on the grass, the sunlit leaves somersaulting one by one from trees shaken by a soft breeze. But she couldn't shut out the turbulent dark ocean that invaded her spirit. Frightened, she gripped the wooden bench as if it was a raft. Violent waves crashed against her, sucking her down.

"Miss… Miss… Are you all right?"

Her face wet with tears, she looked up into the eyes of a kind old man who had heard her cry out.

"Yes… I mean, no." Katherine dried the salty tears with her handkerchief. "I'll recover," she said, embarrassed. "One must, you know. Thank you for your kindness."

She reached for her cane.

"Are you sure I can't help you?" he said, putting out his hand.

"No. I must do this on my own."

LM came rushing over, thanked the old man, and gave Katherine her arm to hold her steady.

The phone was ringing when they reached her room.

"I have good news," said Dr. Young at the other end of the receiver. "Gurdjieff has invited you to the Institute. He only hesitated because of Dr. Manoukhin's report. He said you were too ill to travel and it was in your best interest to stay in Paris under his care. Gurdjieff decided he should meet you and judge for himself."

"Miss Mansfield? Are you there?"

"Yes. Sorry. I just walked in and was a bit out of breath and then to receive such wonderful news. I'll make arrangement to come to Fontainebleau right away."

Her heart still pounding from climbing the stairs and the added excitement of the invitation, she lay down on the bed to rest. Sunlight streamed through the garret window and spread its warmth over her. A thimble of joy passed through her.

If I was not so tired, she thought, I would leap off this bed and dance. She fell asleep with a smile on her lips.

LM was against buying train tickets to Fontainebleau when Katherine told her. Like Jack, she still believed in Dr. Manoukhin's cure. "We're only going to the Institute for a few days," said Katherine, trying to appease her.

And it wasn't far from the truth, thought Katherine. There was no guarantee that Gurdjieff would let her stay.

"Fontainebleau is only a short train ride and I'm told it has a beautiful park. Remember our walks at Queens College and how you used to catch the autumn leaves and bring them to me? We can do that at Fontainebleau."

The following morning, before leaving the hotel, she wrote to Jack:

> *I'm going to meet Gurdjieff. Back in a few days.*

It sounded like a telegram and certainly didn't express her true feelings, so she added:

> *It's not sunny today. What a terrible difference its absence makes. It ought not to. One ought to have a little core of inner warmth that keeps burning and is only embellished by the sun. One has, I believe, if one looks for it.*

NOVEMBER, 1922

Institute for the Harmonious Development of Man

The wise grieve neither for the living nor the dead
Never at any time was I not, nor thou,
Nor these princes of men, nor shall we ever cease to be.
The unreal has no being,
The real never ceases to be.

BHAGAVAD-GITA

K ATHERINE LEANED HER HEAD outside the taxi window and took in the long avenue of trees scantily dressed in autumn's last clinging leaves. The bulk of their discarded garments strewn across the expansive lawn, pooling in piles of gold, red and orange.

As the taxi drew nearer to the immense white château, she looked up at the windows gleaming in the late afternoon light and wondered which floor her room would be on, which view would be hers? Time seemed to stand still at Gurdjieff's Institute for the Harmonious Development of Man.

Dr. Young was waiting for her at the front door and took her small bag from LM. They walked through a white marble entry hall and up a spiral staircase.

It was difficult for her to climb the stairs and she had to lean against the bannister, but she felt revived when the bedroom was the one she had wished for from the taxi.

"How wonderful!" she said, breathlessly.

Her accommodations were way beyond what she had imagined. The wood-paneled walls, antique furniture, ornate Empire mirrors, and the expansive view over the Versailles-style garden with its formal beds of red geraniums, dark blue lobelias, lemon drop calceolarias and pink mesembryanthemum.

Katherine met Gurdjieff that same afternoon at an informal lunch. He was occupied with his other guests and their introduction was brief. Later that evening, after an elegant four-course dinner, the commune students and guests gathered in front of the salon's giant roaring fire. Gurdjieff sat down next to Katherine and spoke to her with the aid of a Russian interpreter. When he stood up and said it was time for everyone to retire, she noticed that LM had already gone upstairs.

"JONES, WAKE UP. WAKE UP!" Katherine called out, bending over the mattress on the wooden floor, shaking her. "I have wonderful news. Please wake up."

Groggily, LM rubbed her eyes and squinted into the flickering candle Katherine was holding.

"What's wrong, Katie? Is it your heart?"

"I'm fine. I want you to come sit by the fire and hear my exciting news." Once LM was seated on the floor across from her, Katherine said, "I spoke to Gurdjieff and he has agreed to keep me under observation for a fortnight to see if I fit in."

"But why would you want to fit in? I certainly don't. Who are these strange people? Where do they come from? I can't understand a word they're saying and they dress funny. There must have been thirty of them all shouting across the table. I thought I was in a mental asylum. And all that drinking of vodka. You don't want to fit in here, do you?"

"Oh but I do. I'll have to work like everyone else, but Gurdjieff says he'll make my chores easier until I'm stronger. There's no staff here. Everyone has chores—even Gurdjieff. I love the chores he's given me. Work in the garden with my hands and on rainy days help in the kitchen preparing meals. And imagine this, the great publisher Orage has been digging a trench for water pipes."

LM forced a smile. "What are my chores?"

"Tomorrow I need you to go to Paris and pack my clothes. Only a few things. I'll give you a list in the morning."

WHEN LM RETURNED FROM PARIS two days later, Katherine thanked her for bringing what she had asked for and suggested they go sit by the garden fountain.

Katherine felt the cold cement penetrate through her skirt when she sat down and shivered. LM automatically got up to get her shawl, but Katherine pulled her back down. "Jones, you're not my servant. I don't want you to ever fetch my shawl again."

She saw the hurt surprise in LM's eyes and though she'd practiced what she was going to say, now face to face, she wasn't sure she could do it. If only she had let her go long ago and not asked her back again and again.

"I've been unfair to you," she said. "I've used you all these years because I feared being on my own without your care. And now you have no one to call your own, not even yourself. And I'm to blame."

LM shook her head. "That's not true, Katie. I chose to take care of you. You mean everything to me."

"That's why we have to separate. You must have your own Life. A Life that I have kept you from by asking you to be my legs. Your devotion has robbed you of your own Life and, to my shame, I've allowed it."

"There's nothing I would rather do than be in your service," said Ida in her tiniest voice and with such humility it was difficult for Katherine to continue but there was no going back. The truth must be told.

"You only think this because I'm all you have. But no more. It's time to break the chain. Let's start with you telling me what you would do if I set you free. Would you like to travel? You've often talked about visiting Russia. Where do you want to go? What do you want to do?"

"Take care of you."

"That's no longer possible, Jones. The Katherine that depended on you has gone away. This Katherine who sits here with you now wants to give you back your Life. Will you let me do that?"

"No. My heart cannot imagine Life without you."

LM looked around the courtyard as if expecting someone to arrive with Katherine's Spanish shawl. "Why are you doing this? Have you found someone better than me to take care of you?"

"No one is better than you, Jones. It's just that nobody at the Institute has a caregiver. Dr. Young has arranged for one of the students to look after me, but only when I can't do something for myself. You see, part of the practice is learning to take care of oneself, to be independent. I'll never do that as long as I depend on you."

LM stuck her hand into the fountain and tread a path through the wet, fallen leaves. She reached for a floating crimson rose and set it in Katherine's lap.

"In time you'll be much happier without me," said Katherine tenderly. "And it's not like I'll never see you again. Just not as my nurse. I want you to leave knowing that when we meet again we will be as equals. Companions."

LM turned her moist eyes toward Katherine. "I'll leave because you're asking me to, but only to return to Paris where I'll wait until I hear from you. That way, if you change your mind, as you always do, I won't have to travel a long distance to come get you."

"That won't happen, Jones, but you will always be near me in spirit. I want you to think of us as continuing to travel together on the River of Life, just not sharing the same boat. Each of us in our own boat, sailing together but independently."

She looked down at LM's folded hands as red from treading the icy water as the wilted rose.

"I'm going to leave you now, Jones," she said. "But let's not say goodbye. I'll just walk away and you wait here until I'm out of sight." She lay her hand on LM's bent head. "Write to me from time to time, won't you?"

Leaning against her cane, she limped back to the château. About to go inside, she thought she heard LM cry out, or was it just the wind shaking loose the last of the fall leaves still clinging to their branches.

KATHERINE SPENT HER PROBATIONARY FORTNIGHT occupied with light chores, which included walks in the garden to pick flowers for the entry hall vases. Otherwise she ate and slept.

One afternoon, relieved to take a break from digging the trench for pipes that would supply water to the new Turkish bath being built, Orage gave her a tour of the grounds. When he showed her where the pipes were being laid, she was shocked to see Gurdjieff down in the trench digging along with his disciples.

Orage told her that if she stayed on she too would work with her hands doing carpentry and farm work. He looked forward to getting out of the trenches, yet it surprised him that he still woke up each morning looking forward to his day of labor—a feeling that he had stopped having in London when he had to get up and go to his office at *New Age*.

She jokingly complained that the hardest chore Gurdjieff had given her so far was to eat three meals a day. She'd never seen so much food served at every meal. The courses were delicious but never-ending and she would certainly gain weight on a rich diet of milk, cheese and butter.

After Orage left her to go back to work, she stretched out on a patch of sunlight in the tall green grass. This is all a wonderful dream, she said to herself. How impoverished my life was before I came here. I'm already back in touch with Life and I've only been here a week.

The dream continued. She'd wake up early each morning, restless to continue her exploration of the château grounds and to meet more of the Russians and other foreigners who were there to study Gurdjieff's teachings.

One afternoon she was seated on what had become her favorite bench under a massive quince tree, like the quinces back home in New Zealand. From where she sat she could see the students digging the trench and wished she could join them. Instead she watched the late autumn colors fade with the descending sun.

She'd had the best of news that day. Gurdjieff said that she could remain at the château as long as she wanted. But as a member of the commune, no longer a guest, she'd have to take on more responsibility by working in the kitchen and tending the farm animals.

She wrote a list in her head of what she'd need for her extended stay and new chores: a wool jacket for sitting in the salon after dinner to watch the dancers and listen to the music; one or two bed jackets for sitting by the fire in her room with her new friends; wool skirt for walks in the garden; galoshes for milking the farm animals.

Back in her room she copied her list to LM who as promised had stayed in Paris in the hopes Katherine would want her back. Katherine let her know she was staying at the Institute indefinitely, but would LM mind shopping for her before she returned to London and enclosed her list. Then, remembering she had taken up the cello again and had promised to teach several of Gurdjieff's students she added:

Would you also please send me a book of instruction for beginning cellists.

She felt guilty asking LM to do errands for her after breaking all ties, but she needed to be practical. The weather had turned cold and she needed warmer clothes. She swore not to ask anything of her again.

LM wrote back that the requested items had been mailed and she was going to London to visit her sister, but just for a few weeks. She planned to see Jack and asked Katherine if she had a message for him as to when she'd be returning to London.

Katherine suggested that maybe Jack should buy a small farm in Sussex and LM could be his housekeeper.

In a letter to Jack she recommended he get outside and work with his hands in the ground; to learn something not taught in books. He was only escaping life with his constant reading and chess playing. She also suggested he attend an Ouspensky lecture and learn about Gurdjieff's philosophy.

Jack wrote back and asked if she was keeping up with her writing and remaining true to her talent. He didn't mention Gurdjieff.

She responded:

> *At the end of my source for now. When I write again—and*
> *write I will—I'll write far more steadily, but not until my*
> *Life flows, as it has been clogged—distant from the source.*

Her new supply of clothes arrived just as the evening temperature dropped below fifty degrees. It was also the same day that she was moved to another wing in the château: the servants' wing. She didn't know why but didn't think it was a punishment. Gurdjieff was known to move his students to different rooms without any explanation. But it was unfortunate that her new small, sparse room lacked a view of the park, but she was too happy with her life at the Institute to complain.

It was only after all her underclothes disappeared from the laundry room, that she first became depressed. Not having the strength to take a taxi on her own to Fontainebleau to shop, she had to write to LM for help again, enclosing a detailed list.

Her room was not the only change for her at the Institute. Gurdjieff had built a small loft overhanging the cow stalls in the stable specifically for her. He wanted her to spend time there breathing in the cows' breath, a cure for tuberculosis practiced by Russian peasants.

Three cows welcomed her with their moos and soft bovine eyes when she arrived at the stable. A resident student had painted the ceiling in gay patterns of trees and flowers, animals and birds and caricatured some of the people of the Institute in the faces of the animals and birds. The walls of her loft space were covered in oriental rugs. Katherine sank into the purple velvet pillows piled on the divan feeling like she was a princess in her harem.

She fell asleep breathing in the sweet fragrance of the cows' breath, but soon awoke to the sound of teats being massaged and pumped and milk slapping against the sides of a tin bucket. She came down the short ladder to find a wholesome young girl with long thick black pigtails sitting on a stool and milking the cows.

"Hello, Mrs. Murry," the girl said with a sweet smile. "I'm Adele Kafian. Mr. Gurdjieff told me to tell you that these are your cows—Mrs. Murry's cows, he said. And when you're stronger you will be in charge of milking them."

Katherine asked her if she could try now, but her arms were too weak and she gave up after a few tries.

"Mr. Gurdjieff told me to keep an eye out for you in the stable," said Adele. "If there's anything you need just let me know." She then scooped up a glass of goat's milk from the bucket and told Katherine she was to drink four glasses a day.

The fresh, warm milk tasted better than she'd expected. She asked Adele how she came to live at the Institute.

Three years ago, she and some of Gurdjieff's other devotees left their homes in the Caucasus Mountains of Russia to establish schools in the West where his teachings could be spread and practiced.

Katherine was surprised a girl of such a young age could have become Gurdjieff's disciple three years ago and felt a bit jealous to not have met him when she was Adele's age. How different her life might've been.

The girl pointed to the loft ceiling and said proudly that she had helped paint the monkeys hanging from the trees.

Katherine wondered if Gurdjieff would let her move into the stable amongst the warm bodies and heated breaths of the cows and the painted animals on the ceiling. If not, she'd at least read and write or just rest in her private harem.

When she returned to her small sparse room in the château, the only furniture a small bed, she wrote to Jack on her writing case. He had complained in his last letter that she didn't write often enough and when she did she told him nothing about the Institute or her health.

Our happiness does not depend on letters, she wrote.

*I don't know how to explain yet what it is like for me here. I
don't want to falsify my position as I am only on the fringe
of what is going on here and can't yet write about it. What I
can tell you is that I am very happy and that every moment
of the day seems full of Life. I have escaped my illness, which
is what I had hoped for by coming here, but I am in a state
of transition and it is difficult to talk about it. What I can
say is that I can never go back to the old life and can't yet
deal with the new one.*

*As far as "us" I feel we have no present relationship but I
know down deep that there is a possibility of one.*

His response came five days later. He told her she had hurt him to
the core. What did she mean they had no relationship? He worried that
she was being too influenced by that quack Gurdjieff and it was causing
radical changes to her personality.

Her intention in writing truthfully had not been to hurt him and she
immediately wrote back:

*I have come here for a cure. I could never have regained my
health from any other treatment. At last I am understood by
someone who wants to treat the whole of me—mentally and
physically. My old friends and my doctors only saw a frail
half-creature—saw only my illness and not the condition of
my withered soul that is now being healed.*

*Someday when I am fully well you and I will live so happily,
so splendidly, just not now. But know we are together. I
love you. You are my man. I want to build and live in that
reality. I believe it's possible. Your loving, Wig.*

DECEMBER, 1922

Confessions at the Ritz

There do exist enquiring minds, which long for the truth of the heart, seek it, strive to solve the problems set by life, try to penetrate to the essence of things and phenomena and to penetrate into themselves. If a man reasons and thinks soundly, no matter which path he follows in solving these problems, he must inevitably arrive back at himself, and begin with the solution of the problem of what he is himself and what his place is in the world around him.

G.I. GURDJIEFF

THROUGH NOVEMBER AND INTO DECEMBER, Katherine was woken by a brilliant light streaming through her window. It gave her the encouragement to dress and go downstairs to do her chores before breakfast.

She clipped the early winter carnations in the gardens and arranged their multi-colored bouquets in crystal vases, and then she helped in the kitchen, peeling and chopping vegetables for the midday meal. After lunch she rested in the stable loft, and, if not too tired, she'd write letters to friends and family, and scribble sketches in her notebook for the stories she would soon write.

Too weak to participate as a laborer, she was instructed by Gurdjieff to observe every detail of the work being done on the commune. She watched his students plant bulbs and seeds before the first frost, watched other students build the Study House brick by brick. She was always attentive of the work being done with their hands as if they were her own. Gurdjieff's other instructions were to memorize a list of Russian words, as well as several math calculations taught to her by him—it was all a practice in mindfulness, he said.

The students became accustomed to her visits and set up a chaise longue for her when she tired of standing. And, if at the end of the day she'd fallen asleep, one of them would gently wake her and walk her back to the château making sure she was comfortable in her room before leaving her alone.

On one chilly afternoon in the stable loft, it was so cold that her fingers were stiff, but she still wrote a long overdue letter:

> *Dearest Pa:*
>
> *After two applications with Dr. M. my heart couldn't take it. I was extremely ill and disappointed. I am now living in Fontainebleau outside Paris under the care of Mr. G.I. Gurdjieff. He has given me gentle exercises and movements. For now I will concentrate on strengthening my heart and then revisit the wings/lungs. I am confident that the lean years in the past will be followed by fat ones.*
>
> *I wish you could see me now in the stable lying comfortably above the cow stalls breathing in cow's breath. It is part of my treatment—good for the damaged lungs. The château is most beautiful under winter light. The rooms most lovely with central heating and hot and cold running water. It is mostly run by Russians (they seem to haunt me). Though I speak French and German fluently, I am fascinated by languages and I hope to learn Russian and then later Italian when I go south after I finish here with my cure.*
>
> *I am determined to regain my health though disappointed that it might take longer than I hoped but know I am feeling better already. I will not give up. I will not accept life as an invalid.*
>
> *I have let LM go as I can now take care of myself. She might work for Jack on a farm he is thinking about buying.*
>
> *Your devoted daughter,*
>
> *Katherine*

Yes it was true, there was central heating but what she didn't say was that Gurdjieff believed it should only be turned on during freezing temperatures. Every decision he made had to do with the practice—the work of healing through constant awareness of the physical, emotional and intellectual self.

She accepted the austerity, but the damp chill in her bedroom without a fire to warm her was endangering what good health she had regained. She lived in her fur coat and, even though there were ten to twenty pots cooking on the stoves in the kitchen, she still shivered when peeling carrots.

After finishing Pa's letter, she bundled under the rugs in the stable loft and considered asking Gurdjieff if she could be moved out of the servants' quarters to a warmer room, maybe one with a fireplace. She was anxious that if her cough became noticeable or she became flushed with fever, he would send her away.

As if she'd summoned him, he suddenly appeared in front of her holding a glass of fresh goat's milk. Though a large robust man, she hadn't heard him climb up the stairs. It was as if he'd leaped up like an exotic dancer.

She sipped the milk, while feeling his eyes studying her before he sat down cross-legged in front of her on one of the pillows. "How are you doing, Mrs. Murry?" he asked, handing her his own handkerchief to wipe the milk from her lips.

"I feel better than I have in years." She was amazed to hear herself say that, but it was true. She actually spent entire days without napping. Up at seven in the morning and not back in her room until late at night.

He asked her what she'd learned living in the servants' quarters and she impulsively replied, "I've learned I can rough it, stand any amount of noise, and put up with untidiness, disorder and queer smells without losing my head."

His wide apart black eyes twinkled and his belly shook with a laughter that was so contagious she had to laugh along with him though she was embarrassed by her outburst.

"Today, Mrs. Murry, you pack your suitcase."

Please no, she cried to herself, feeling her heart cramp. This is where I belong. This is where I've found happiness. This is where I'll be cured.

"Pack my suitcase?" she asked, almost spilling the milk.

He misunderstood the distress in her face and said, "Don't you want to move back into your old room? I'm told you were very happy there."

"Oh yes. Thank you very much. What a relief. I was afraid you were going to send me back to Paris."

"Why would I do that? I'm pleased you are here with us. I only want to make sure you're comfortable." When he smiled his thick waxed moustache smiled too. "You've learned all that is possible in your present accommodations. Adele will help you pack."

He pulled himself up gracefully and, reminding her again of an agile dancer, very quietly stepped over the loft and down the ladder.

She was so relieved he wasn't sending her away it made her giddy and she'd forgotten to give him back his handkerchief. She called out to him.

He peeked his shiny bald head back up in the loft, "That's a gift for all you have accomplished here at the Institute in such a short time."

SACRED DANCES OR MOVEMENTS, as Gurdjieff referred to them, were rehearsed in the salon every evening after dinner—a mixture of Assyrian, Arabian and Dervish dances, which he had witnessed growing up and later throughout his travels to the East. He considered the Movements an integral part of his teachings and he designed and taught the complicated steps personally with great care and attention.

Katherine would lounge in her favorite chair next to the roaring fire and watch the students practice under Gurdjieff's direction. Another devotee, Thomas de Hartmann, accompanied the dancers on piano, playing compositions he and Gurdjieff had composed. Other students would join in, playing Eastern instruments, their sounds exotic and thrilling to Katherine's ear.

The dance Movements were mechanical, like the interior workings of a clock, but they were exciting in their precision and control. Only through practice, memorization and deep concentration were the dancers able to synchronize each movement, creating a harmonious, flowing piece of work that mesmerized Katherine. She so wished she could join them.

She wrote to Jack after watching her favorite dance, "The Initiation of the Priestess":

> *I have never really cared for dancing before, but this—seems to be the key to the new world within me. There is one that takes about 7 minutes and it contains the whole life of*

woman—but everything! Nothing is left out. It taught me,
it gave me more of woman's life than any book or poem.
There was even room for Flaubert's "Coeur Simple" in it, or
Tolstoy's Princess Marya. Mysterious.

One night after dance practice, she invited her new dancer friend, Olgivanna, to share a bottle of wine with her at the Ritz, the name she had affectionately given her bedroom.

Olgivanna, a tall, dark-haired young girl from Montenegro, often came to visit her at the Ritz and also brought her meals when she was too tired to eat in the dining room.

Though only twenty-four, ten years younger than Katherine, Olgivanna was a world traveler, having accompanied Gurdjieff on his pilgrimages around the world.

Katherine reclined comfortably on a divan and her young friend uncorked and poured wine in their glasses. Having changed into her warm, fur-collared dressing gown, Katherine was amazed that Olgivanna could sit there in her flimsy white dance tunic and not shiver. She asked the girl to put another log on the fire. Then struggling in Russian, said, "I'd like to speak Russian with you."

"Why Russian? Don't you like my English?"

"Yes, but I want to learn your language. Doesn't Gurdjieff tell us how important it is for the mind to practice memorization, to help keep one conscious? What better way than learning a new language?"

"I've memorized a few words I looked up in a Russian dictionary. Here, I'll show you."

Olgivanna read through Katherine's copied word list and covered her mouth to stop laughing.

"What's so funny? Did I misspell them?"

"No, not at all. They're perfect. But this reads like a sad poem of your experience here at the Institute. "*I am cold—bring paper to light a fire—cinders—wood—matches—strong—because no more fire—white paper—what is the time—it is late—it is still early—is there a glass of wine?*

"If you're cold all the time why don't you tell Gurdjieff to turn on the central heating?"

"I don't want him to think I'm complaining, when I've never been happier. This place is like a dream—or a miracle." She filled Olgivanna's glass and her own with more wine. "I'd like you to help me add words to my list, words that express my joy. Someday strangers will read my notebooks and I wouldn't want them to get the wrong impression about Gurdjieff's Institute."

"Why do you want strangers to read your notebooks? Aren't they private?"

"Yes, but only while I'm alive. I like to think people might be inspired to overcome their own difficulties after knowing about mine. Seek their own happiness like I'm doing. Find their true self."

"You're my hero, you know," said Olgivanna. "I hope that I can be like you if ever I'm faced with such a terrible, long illness. Do you find Gurdjieff's teaching very helpful?"

"Yes, I do. He's a remarkable teacher. I only wish we'd met when I was your age." Katherine hadn't meant to sound so regretful. She'd made it a rule of her life to never regret, never to look back, and here she was doing just that.

Olgivanna sat on a footstool from where she could add logs to the fire and asked Katherine about her other teachers

"When I was a young girl still living in New Zealand, I read Marie Bashkirtseff's *Journal of a Young Artist*. She started her journal at the age of twelve and she believed, like Gurdjieff, that you have to be true to yourself. Her words encouraged me to follow my own individual path regardless of what others thought I should do."

"What became of her?"

"In 1884, she died of tuberculosis at the age of twenty-four. While she was dying, she worried that her parents would find her journal and destroy it. "*Then nothing would be left of me, nothing, nothing, nothing. To live, to have so much ambition, to suffer, to weep, to struggle, and in the end to be forgotten; as if I had never existed.*"

Olgivanna put another log on the fire, giving Katherine a moment to recover from a coughing fit brought on after her reading.

"Marie was partially right," continued Katherine after clearing her throat. "Her mother did publish her journals, but only after she stripped it of its humanity. Fortunately, the original manuscript was later found and published as Marie would have wanted—uncensored."

"Who else influenced you at my age?" asked her curious young friend.

"Oscar Wilde."

"Oscar Wilde?"

"An English writer who said: '*A man who is master of himself can end a sorrow as easily as he can invent a pleasure. I don't want to be at the mercy of my emotions. I want to use them, to enjoy them, and to dominate them.*'

"I became his disciple without considering where his wild passion for life on his terms would lead me."

She felt the familiar dark spirits hover over her wanting to drag her down into their shared past. A log fell, sparks flew.

Olgivanna moved onto the divan to be closer to Katherine to hear her story because she was speaking so softly, almost a whisper: "Shortly after my fiancé abandoned me, my mother took me to the healing baths in Bavaria that were advertised as a cure for hysterical women. She didn't know my real condition and took the next ship back to Wellington. Miserable in the hotel, I moved into a pension. I was writing… taking long barefoot walks in the woods… all part of the water cure. I was content." She spread her hand over her stomach and held it there feeling a flutter, then a ripple.

"One morning I was reaching up to get my travel chest down from the top of the wardrobe closet when I curled over with stomach cramps. I must have passed out because my landlady found me on the floor. She called a doctor, but it was too late. I'd lost my baby."

Katherine felt herself falling backward all over again. Someone grabbed her hand and yanked her up. She looked into Olgivanna's frightened face.

"That was quite a scare you gave me," said the girl, still gripping Katherine's hand.

"What happened?"

"I don't know. You were telling me about that tragic accident you had in Bavaria and then you fainted."

Katherine looked into the fireplace and willed the dark spirits that had haunted her all these years to go up the chimney in smoke. Poof, she thought, that wasn't so hard was it? She felt so much lighter when she turned away from the fire to face Olgivanna. "Where did I stop? Did I tell you about Floryan?"

"No, you didn't. But I don't want you to tell me if you're going to faint again."

"Don't worry. I'm feeling so much better," she said, and kissed the girl on the cheek, thanking her for her concern. "And it helps me to talk about things I've kept hidden too long. Do you mind?"

"No." Olgivanna poured more wine and settled down next to Katherine.

"I met Floryan in Bavaria after my accident. He translated English and Russian literature into Polish. He read to me and sang songs—a beautiful soothing voice when I woke from my night terrors. He was very gentle and when he wanted to make love, I didn't resist. He offered me safety and I curled up in his kindness.

"It was only later, after I left him, that I found out he'd given me a curse that made me very ill, even before I became infected with tuberculosis."

"I didn't know curses could make you sick. What kind of curse was it?"

Katherine felt just saying the word conjured up black magic and instead she wrote it down for Olgivanna to see: gonorrhea.

Olgivanna grew pale and buried her head in Katherine's neck. "How could he do such a horrible thing to you? Shame on him. Shame on all men like him. You must hate him. I would."

"No, I don't. At least not since coming here."

Katherine suddenly felt a chill and lay down on the rug to get closer to the burning logs. Olgivanna put a blanket over her, placed a pillow under her head, and laid down next to her.

"Don't pity me, Olgivanna," said Katherine, seeing a tear fall down the girl's cheek. "It wasn't all bad. Floryan did introduce me to the writings of Anton Chekhov. After I read his short stories about the Russian people, it gave me the idea to write about Bavarians. Orage published those first stories, calling them *Bavarian Babies*, and that was the beginning of my writing career."

"You mean that grumpy old man who digs all day in the trench and never stops moaning about how sore his body is and how old he feels?"

They both laughed. "Yes the very same. I was a bit younger than you when we met."

"I love your storytelling. I often listen when you make up stories for the children at bedtime. Have you ever written a novel?"

Katherine thought about all the notebooks filled with starts and stops and sighed. "No, not yet. My writing now comes in spurts. A novel would require too much energy. But now that I will be cured, maybe I'll start writing one in the barn loft."

Olgivanna turned away but not before Katherine saw fear or was it grief in her wide, innocent eyes. Am I the only one, she thought, who believes I will be cured.

She sat up and held the glass to her lips like a chalice and drank the elixir that would prolong her life indefinitely so she could write all the stories in her head and many more.

AFTER MENTIONING TO OLGIVANNA that she might write a novel and thinking about it all through the night, come daylight she put on her fur coat and went out on the grounds to find Orage. He had helped her in the beginning of her career and she was confident he could help her now.

She laughed when she came upon him in his mud-splattered overalls, so different from the stylish gentleman she'd known in London. They returned to the château together. He helped her take off her fur coat and brought her over to the roaring fireplace in the salon.

"Look at you," she said. "No one would recognize you on Fleet Street. You look as young as the day I met you and even more handsome."

"Well, for that matter, if we are going to exchange compliments, I wouldn't recognize you either in that plain cotton dress which, may I say, is quite charming on you."

Katherine spun around slowly in her dark blue dress as if it was one of her fashionable silk gowns that she no longer wore.

"And you've changed your hair style. I like you without bangs. Better to see those dark expressive eyes of yours."

He reached for her hand. "Come sit down and tell me how you are doing. Do you sometimes wish I'd never introduced you to Gurdjieff?"

"No. To the contrary. I did have a hard time at first following his instructions to just sit and watch, not being used to being inactive, but now I'm quite enjoying myself and his teachings are having a very beneficial effect on me. I feel... I don't know exactly how to say it, but I feel lighter. The burdens I've carried so long have been shedded."

She closed her eyes so she could feel the overflowing gratitude that was so present in her now. She felt Orage looking at her and opened her eyes so he could see her happiness.

"I remember so vividly the first day you came to me with your manuscripts," he said. "Now here we are, can it be twelve years later, comrades again. And it's good to see you happy, Katherine, after all you've been through. Life hasn't been fair to you. But to look at you now I better be careful or I might fall in love with your ravishing beauty."

"Stop flattering me, Orage, or you'll have me blushing like a young school girl and I might lean over and kiss you."

"But it's true. You're radiant."

"Thank you. If only Jack and Ida could see me maybe they'd stop worrying so much. Jack thinks I've been hypnotized by Gurdjieff and Ida grieves for me as if I'm already dead. In her imagination, I'm wasting away and then she sends me clothes that are way too small on me."

They both laughed.

"I don't know how to explain to them the joy I've found through Gurdjieff's teachings."

"You're the writer. You'll find a way."

She leaned toward him, "That's actually what I wanted to talk to you about. I seem to have lost my creativity or perhaps it's just I need to find another way to express my creations.

"Reading my previous stories, I see that I've been a camera in my writing—a selective camera. My point of view has been partial and misleading and a little malicious. I don't want to write like that anymore. I don't have all my ideas worked out yet, but each day I'm getting a little closer.

She held her right hand up, disturbing the shaft of dust motes. "Soon this hand will write about heroes and heroines measured by the quantity and quality of the effort they put forth and not by their successes." She dropped her hand in her lap.

He looked puzzled.

"I know that doesn't make much sense and I've only been able to write one sketch that expresses what I'm talking about."

"What's it about?"

"There is a young couple who consider loving each other as an art. Both are struggling to have meaningful lives, to forget the past and not worry about the future, as Gurdjieff would say, to live in the present. They live each day fully conscious of life's fleeting joy, bravely accepting their circumstances, be it poverty or illness, and turning them into an opportunity to deeply feel their love for each other.

"The reader's sympathy is maintained by the continuity and variety of the effort of one or both of the characters. They sulk after their first failures, but we admire their endurance or sympathize with their suffering or laugh at their ineptitude.

"When I'm ready, and I'm not ready yet, I want to show that their commonplace virtues are as attractive as the vices expressed in current novels. I want to present the good as the witty, the adventurous, the romantic, the gay, the alluring; and the evil as the platitudinous, the greedy, the solemn, and the conventional.

She raised her hand to her mouth. "Oh, listen to me. I'm so excited about this new attitude I have toward life that I'm exploding. I wanted to ask for your advice and here I am running away with my own thoughts. Do I sound insane?"

"Not at all," said Orage, drawing her hand to his lips to kiss. "I look very forward to reading the many stories that this small, delicate, powerful hand will write."

Initiation of the Priestess

*I want to be all that I am capable of becoming so that I
may be... a child of the sun.*

NOTEBOOKS—KM

T HE CHRISTMAS CELEBRATION ended with nine wide-eyed
children gathered around Katherine in the salon as she told them
stories using different voices and dialects to hold their attention as few
understood English.

It's my facial mimes they enjoy the most, she thought, slowly climbing the stairs to her room. She stopped to catch her breath and looked
down at the green holiday laurels adorning the staircase.

She couldn't believe that Jack's Christmas could have been as wonderful as hers. Even though mostly Easterners lived at the château, Gurdjieff
had organized a traditional Christmas feast to honor his British guests.
Sixty students and guests sat at the table eating soup, spiced meats, fish,
vegetables of all kinds, delectable salads, dishes of oriental tidbits, exotic
fruit, fragrant herbs and puddings and pies.

From halfway up the stairs, the frosted windows looked down on
barren trees. It seemed like it was years not just two months ago, she said
to herself, when the leaves still clung to the trees. Soon spring will be
here, my favorite season. I look so forward to seeing the flowers bloom
below my bedroom window.

"Oh la la!" she gasped, surprised and delighted to find a small Christmas tree in her room illuminated by three flickering candles.

"Do you like it?" asked Adele, surprising her from behind the door.

"Ah oui!" exclaimed Katherine, collapsing onto the couch. "Why are
there three candles?"

"One for you, Mrs. Murry. Another for myself." She hesitated.

"And the other?"

"It's for the one you wish to come here." She blushed.

"You mean Mr. Murry? How odd you should mention him. Just tonight, Gurdjieff told me I could invite him to the opening night of Sacred Dances at the new Study House. I had planned to not see him until the spring. Do you think I should see him, before I'm cured?"

The girl nodded her head up and down enthusiastically.

Katherine turned her attention to the little tree. "What a lovely gift. Did you carry it all the way from the forest? The pines smell so fresh."

Adele said yes and Katherine invited her to join her on the divan so she could plait her long, thick strands of hair.

"You know," said Adele, "my mother used to sit with me by the fire like this, just like I'm doing now with you and plait my hair."

Katherine watched the candles flicker and breathed in the sweet smell of the pine cones hanging from the tree. She thought of her Christmases at home with her family when they were all together and her mother and brother were still alive.

After a while, Adele sat up and asked, "Do you find life here very difficult?"

"No, but I don't work as hard as you do. What I do find difficult is not being able to participate in the Movements. When I hear the music and watch you and the others dance, I want so much to join you."

"Have you asked Mr. Gurdjieff if you could?"

"He says not yet. It's too strenuous. For now I watch and memorize the steps so I'll be ready to join in when I'm stronger."

One candle sputtered and went out. "Is that me?" gasped Katherine.

Adelle jumped up and snuffed out the other two with her fingers. "Now they're all out and who's to say which was yours or mine?" She picked up her basket of unused pine cones and stood by the door. "Perhaps when your husband comes to visit, you can dance for him in the 'Initiation of the Priestess.' Your favorite dance."

After Adele left, Katherine took up her pen:

> *Darling Bogey, Would you care to come here on January 8 or 9 to stay until 14–15? Mr. Gurdjieff approves of my plan and says you will come as his guest. On the 13th our new theatre is to be opened. It will be a wonderful experience.*

She went on to explain which train to take to Paris and where to get the cab to Fontainebleau and then told him specifically what she wanted him to wear. She wanted to show him off to all her new friends.

*I hope you will decide to come my dearest... We can sit and
drink kiftir in the cowshed. Your ever loving, Wig*

TWO WEEKS LATER, the morning of Jack's arrival, she dressed quickly
as she wanted to have her chores done before he arrived. She looked
around and, pleased with how lovely the Ritz looked, she imagined them
sitting in the Victorian needlepoint chairs in front of the fire, sipping
tea. Maybe she should invite Adele and Olgivanna to join them.

No, she thought, I don't want to share Jack with anyone. Certainly
not on his first day. She smiled at her mirrored reflection and feeling so
excited about Jack coming she forgot her cane.

Downstairs in the kitchen the preparations for the gala were in full
swing and she immediately felt her part in the festivities. Two months
ago, she'd only been only an observer when she described the kitchen
crew to Jack in a letter:

> *It's a large kitchen with six helpers. Madame Ostrovsky, the
> head, Gurdjieff's wife, walks about like a queen exactly. She
> is extremely beautiful. She wears an old raincoat. Nina, a big
> girl in a black apron—lovely, too—pounds things in mortars.
> The second cook chops at the table, bangs the saucepans,
> sings; another runs in and out with plates and pots, a man
> in the scullery cleans pots... and it's so full of life and humor
> and ease that one wouldn't want to be anywhere else.*

She walked across the kitchen to her corner worktable where a
stack of carrots awaited her. Shoving up the sleeves of her fur coat, she
started slicing, looking up occasionally to say hello to someone rushing
by. After the carrots were done, she cut bread, making a mountain of
breadcrumbs.

After finishing her kitchen chores, she went outside to cut the Christmas roses and put them in the vases she had lined up in a row on the
banquet table between bottles of wine and candleholders. This took her
the rest of the morning. Tired, she climbed the stairs to her room, stopping along the way to take slow deep breaths to calm her racing heart.

She fell asleep planning what she would wear when she greeted Jack.

Yes, that's it, the purple dress, she thought, rising an hour later
refreshed. She frowned at her face in the mirror and then took out a

hairbrush to retrain her bangs to fall over her forehead. Jack didn't like sudden changes; her new hair style would only worry him and give him proof that she'd been hypnotized by Gurdjieff.

She'd just finished putting on the matching purple jacket when she heard a honking cab and holding onto the bannister rushed downstairs to open the gate.

"Oh, Katherine is this really you," he exclaimed. He threw his arms around her and held her tight.

When they finally broke apart, she said, "Come, I want to show you the stable," and reached for his hand.

He laughed. "Wait a minute. Won't you show me your room first so I can leave my valise there?"

"Of course, how silly of me." She changed directions and brought him to the entry hall.

"But why not leave your things here in the downstairs closet? I don't want to show you my bedroom quite yet. I'm saving that for teatime."

"Then take me to your wonderful stable so we can drink... what did you call it in your letter... kif-tir." He hung his hat and coat in the closet and put his valise on the closet floor.

Outside they met up with Adele, who shyly shook Jack's hand and walked with them to the stable and then left. Up in the loft, they drank kiftir. They lay down under the painted trees and flowers and Katherine pointed out "who was who" drawn in the monkeys' faces.

Then she introduced him to the farm animals and the vegetable greenhouse. "We eat the food grown here," she said and plucked a tomato for him to eat. At the Study House, the final construction was going on with great urgency.

Several students were using see-thru paint to color the windows like stained glass. After introductions, Jack was handed a paintbrush and he added a few strokes to the vivid green, red, blue and yellow patterns, which shone through in the late afternoon sun.

By the time they got up to leave, thunderclouds had darkened the sky and it started to rain. Jack said, "Shouldn't we wait till it clears?"

Olgivanna offered her umbrella but Katherine said, "I love the rain. I want to feel it on my face. C'mon Jack. It won't hurt you."

Back at the château, they dried off in front of the salon fire. Katherine then took her time before taking Jack upstairs. She wanted him to notice everything and she pointed out the Christmas roses she'd arranged in the banquet room for the dinner, the Christmas tree Gurdjieff had cut down in the forest, and the decorations everyone had made that now hung from its branches. They peeked into the kitchen and she pointed to the table where she worked.

At last she brought him upstairs to her bedroom. The moment she walked in she knew Adele had been there. The fire was lit and there was a tea tray set on her writing table.

"What a gorgeous room," said Jack, quite taken aback. "No wonder you're so happy here. You live like a Princess."

"Not exactly," she said, smiling, "but there is a King who lives next door."

"The king?"

"Mr. Gurdjieff lives next door with his wife Madame Ostrovsky, though I hardly ever see him and she's always working in the kitchen. He gets up before everyone and is always the last to bed, and he often makes trips to Paris."

"Come sit down Jack. Let's drink the tea while it's still hot."

Jack watched her pour, impressed that her hand no longer shook. "You seem to manage quite well on your own without LM at your beck and call."

"My friends helps me a bit. It's Adele who brought us the tea tray and then slipped out before we came in. She'd do more for me if I let her. She's adopted me as her mother and I love her as the daughter I never had."

He smiled sheepishly. "I thought from your letters that you'd been hypnotized by Gurdjieff and that this château was filled with devout theologians who would grab me when I arrived and force me to join their cult."

Katherine laughed. "Don't let Gurdjieff hear you say that. He'd throw you out. He hates anyone accusing him of being a theologian."

"What does he consider himself to be?"

"A teacher of dance."

"Really?"

"You'll see him dance tonight. There'll be a dress rehearsal of the Sacred Dances for next week's performance in the Study Hall."

"You mean that giant hangar where I helped paint the glass windows? That will be finished by next week?"

"Yes. If Gurdjieff says so, it will happen. Even if he does it all himself."

"Now off with you," said Katherine. "Go take a walk around the grounds while I dress for dinner."

"Am I all right like this?"

"Yes you look very handsome. Even more handsome than that drawing you sent me that I've shown everyone. Meet me downstairs at six in the salon. We gather there before moving into the banquet hall for dinner."

She took particular care dressing. Over a black chiffon gown, she draped her black Spanish shawl embroidered in crimson roses.

The way Jack looked at her when she came down the stairs made time slip away and she was that young girl he had fallen in love with twelve years ago.

At dinner she listened to Jack and Orage's conversation, their past differences put aside. And Jack seemed quite comfortable talking to the other guests. Perhaps he will stay awhile, she thought, now that he knows how wonderful it is to be here.

After dinner, everyone moved into the salon to watch *the Sacred Dances* rehearsal. Jack was as impressed as Katherine by the dancers syncopated precision. She had memorized the "Initiation of the Priestess," the dance that *gave her more of woman's life than any book or poem* and in her mind she danced.

At ten o'clock, Gurdjieff and the dancers left for the Study House to rehearse again on the new stage.

Katherine was inspired by the dances and taking Jack's hand pulled him toward the spiral staircase. She had hoped to dance for him tonight as the Princess, but seeing that was impossible, then at least she could show off her new energy.

At the bottom of the steps, she let go of his hand and said, "Watch me!"

She leaped up the stairs like a dancer, but she didn't get very far. Overcome by a coughing spasm, she clamped her hand against her mouth and tried to stop the flow of spurting blood that oozed between her fingers. She collapsed before Jack could reach her.

Epilogue

On the evening of January 9th, 1923, Katherine Mansfield, at age thirty-four, suffered a pulmonary hemorrhage. She died thirty minutes later. On January 12th, her remains were buried in the nearby Avon cemetery. Her burial was attended by her husband, John Middleton Murry, Richard Murry, Ida Baker, Katherine's sisters Chaddie and Jeanne, Hon. Dorothy Brett, G.I. Gurdjieff, A.R. Orage, Dr. James Young, and many residents from The Institute for the Harmonious Development of Man. The epitaph on her grave from Shakespeare's *Henry IV* reads:

> *But I tell you, my lord fool,*
> *out of this nettle, danger,*
> *we pluck this flower, safety.*

Perhaps a more significant and meaningful epitaph than John Murry's Shakespearean quote was Virginia Woolf's:

> *"A certain melancholy has been brooding over me this fortnight.*
> *I date it from Katherine's death.*
> *The feeling comes to me so often now—*
> *Yes. Go on writing of course: but into emptiness.*
> *There's no competitor."*

Acknowledgements

This novel wouldn't exist without the encouragement and unwavering faith of my husband, Jim Payne, whose own heroic story of survival compelled me to recreate Katherine's. He had endless patience in joining me in my pursuit up into the hills of Menton to find Katherine's villa Isola Bella and then to Fontainebleau to visit G.I. Gurdjieff's former Institute and then to the Avon graveyard where Gurdjieff and Katherine are buried near each other.

And special thanks to my children, Amie and Sam, who never fail to inspire me with their willingness to climb mountains in pursuit of their own dreams and who encourage me to do the same.

Amie accompanied me on my trip to Bandol, France, to find Chez Pauline and Isola Bella and, between our tears, she read Katherine and Jack's love letters driving back to our summer home in Teyssières. Sam, who often tells me to "keep going," gave me permission to use his acrylic painting for the book's cover.

To my dear friends in and around Teyssières: Brisou, Pierre, Henri, Eddie, Philippe, Carole, and Virginia, who leave me alone to work but always know when I need a break from my writing and invite me for wine tastings or a meal; to Ina who gave me the keys to her Floridian retreat so that I might write in isolation; and to sister Kate who knew to be silent when I was writing in her desert home.

To my editors, Steve Lewis and Jim Payne; I would never have finished this book without your support and advice. To the Duckdog writers' group that sat through the late hours hearing my fledgling attempts at imagining Katherine's story. Go Avatar!

And to Katherine Mansfield who taught me how to hang in there as a writer in spite of it all.

A Note on Sources

While Katherine Mansfield, John Middleton Murry, Ida Baker and other historical figures appear in this book as fictional characters, I have tried to render as accurately as possible the particulars of their lives.

I am deeply indebted to Margaret Scott and Vincent O'Sullivan for collecting and editing Mansfield's notebooks and letters into the five volumes of *The Collected Letters of Katherine Mansfield*. And to C.A. Hankin for *The Letters of John Middleton Murry to Katherine Mansfield*.

I researched a number of other sources, most prominently the insightful biographies of *The Life of Katherine Mansfield* by the late Anthony Alpers; *Katherine Mansfield: A Secret Life* by Claire Tomlin; and *The Life of Katherine Mansfield* by Ruth Elvish Mantz and J. M. Murry. Ida Baker would never have been so fully rendered without the honesty and courage with which she wrote her own book, *Katherine Mansfield: The Memories of L.M.* John Middleton Murry's autobiography *Between Two Worlds* and F.A. Lea's biography, *John Middleton Murry*, allowed me to enter into the life of "Jack." I also learned about Katherine's volatile friendship with Virginia Woolf by reading Hermione Lee's chapter, "Katherine," in her marvelously definitive Virginia Woolf biography.

And a very special thank you to Gerri Kimber and the Katherine Mansfield Society who keep the memory of Katherine Mansfield alive through their symposiums, quarterly magazines, and online presence.

LADRÔMEPRESS.COM

CPSIA information can be obtained
at www.ICGtesting.com
Printed in the USA
LVHW040956261020
669802LV00004B/569